my LITTLE PONY

FIENDship is Magic

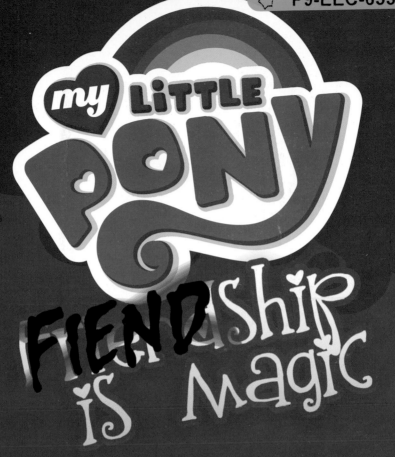

SOMBRA

WRITTEN BY
JEREMY
WHITLEY

ART BY
BRENDA
HICKEY

TIREK

WRITTEN BY
CHRISTINA
RICE

ART BY
TONY
FLEECS

Special thanks to Erin Comella, Robert Fewkes, Joe Furfaro, Heather Hopkins, Pat Jarret, Ed Lane, Brian Lenard, Marissa Mansolillo, Donna Tobin, Michael Vogel, and Michael Kelly for their invaluable assistance.

ISBN: 978-1-63140-339-2

18 17 16 15   1 2 3 4

IDW ® Licensed By: Hasbro

www.IDWPUBLISHING.com
IDW founded by Ted Adams, Alex Garner, Kris Oprisko, and Robbie Robbins

Ted Adams, CEO & Publisher
Greg Goldstein, President & COO
Robbie Robbins, EVP/Sr. Graphic Artist
Chris Ryall, Chief Creative Officer/Editor-in-Chief
Matthew Ruzicka, CPA, Chief Financial Officer
Alan Payne, VP of Sales
Dirk Wood, VP of Marketing
Lorelei Bunjes, VP of Digital Services
Jeff Webber, VP of Digital Publishing & Business Development

Facebook: **facebook.com/idwpublishing**
Twitter: **@idwpublishing**
YouTube: **youtube.com/idwpublishing**
Instagram: **instagram.com/idwpublishing**
deviantART: **idwpublishing.deviantart.com**
Pinterest: **pinterest.com/idwpublishing/idw-staff-faves**

MY LITTLE PONY: FIENDSHIP IS MAGIC. JUNE 2015. FIRST PRINTING. HASBRO and its logo, MY LITTLE PONY, and all related characters are trademarks of Hasbro and are used with permission. © 2015 Hasbro. The IDW logo is registered in the U.S. Patent and Trademark Office. IDW Publishing, a division of Idea and Design Works, LLC. Editorial offices: 5080 Santa Fe St., San Diego, CA 92109. Any similarities to persons living or dead are purely coincidental. With the exception of artwork used for review purposes, none of the contents of this publication may be reprinted without the permission of Idea and Design Works, LLC. Printed in Korea.
IDW Publishing does not read or accept unsolicited submissions of ideas, stories, or artwork.

Originally published as MY LITTLE PONY: FIENDSHIP IS MAGIC issues #1-5.

SIRENS

WRITTEN BY
TED ANDERSON

ART AND COLORS BY
AGNES GARBOWSKA

COLOR ASSIST BY
LAUREN PERRY

NIGHTMARE MOON

WRITTEN BY
HEATHER NUHFER

ART BY
TONY FLEECS

QUEEN CHRYSALIS

WRITTEN BY
KATIE COOK

ART BY
ANDY PRICE

COLORS BY HEATHER BRECKEL
LETTERS BY NEIL UYETAKE
SERIES EDITS BY BOBBY CURNOW

COVER BY AMY MEBBERSON
COLLECTION EDITS BY JUSTIN EISINGER
AND ALONZO SIMON
COLLECTION DESIGN BY THOM ZAHLER

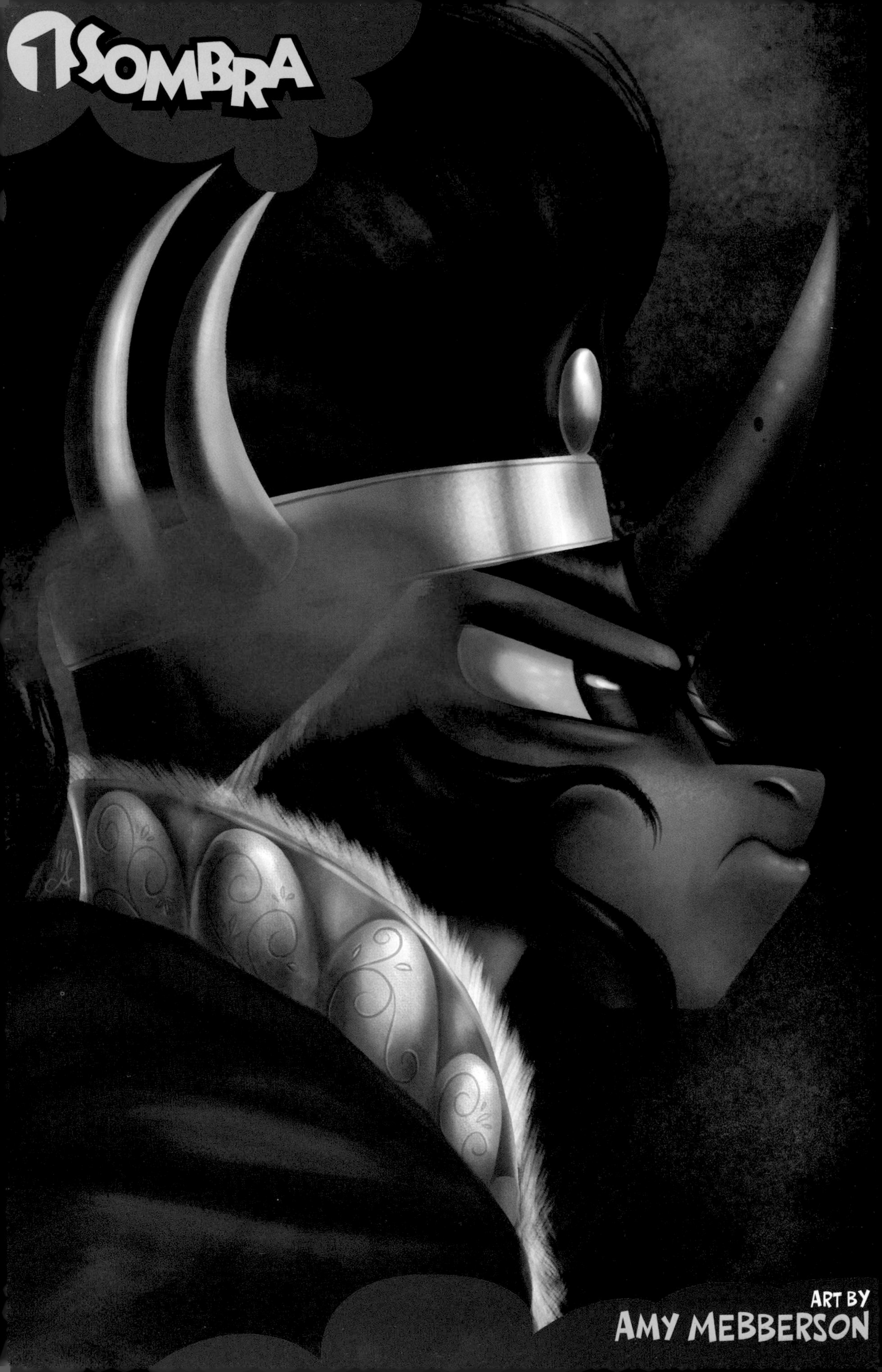
1 SOMBRA
ART BY
AMY MEBBERSON

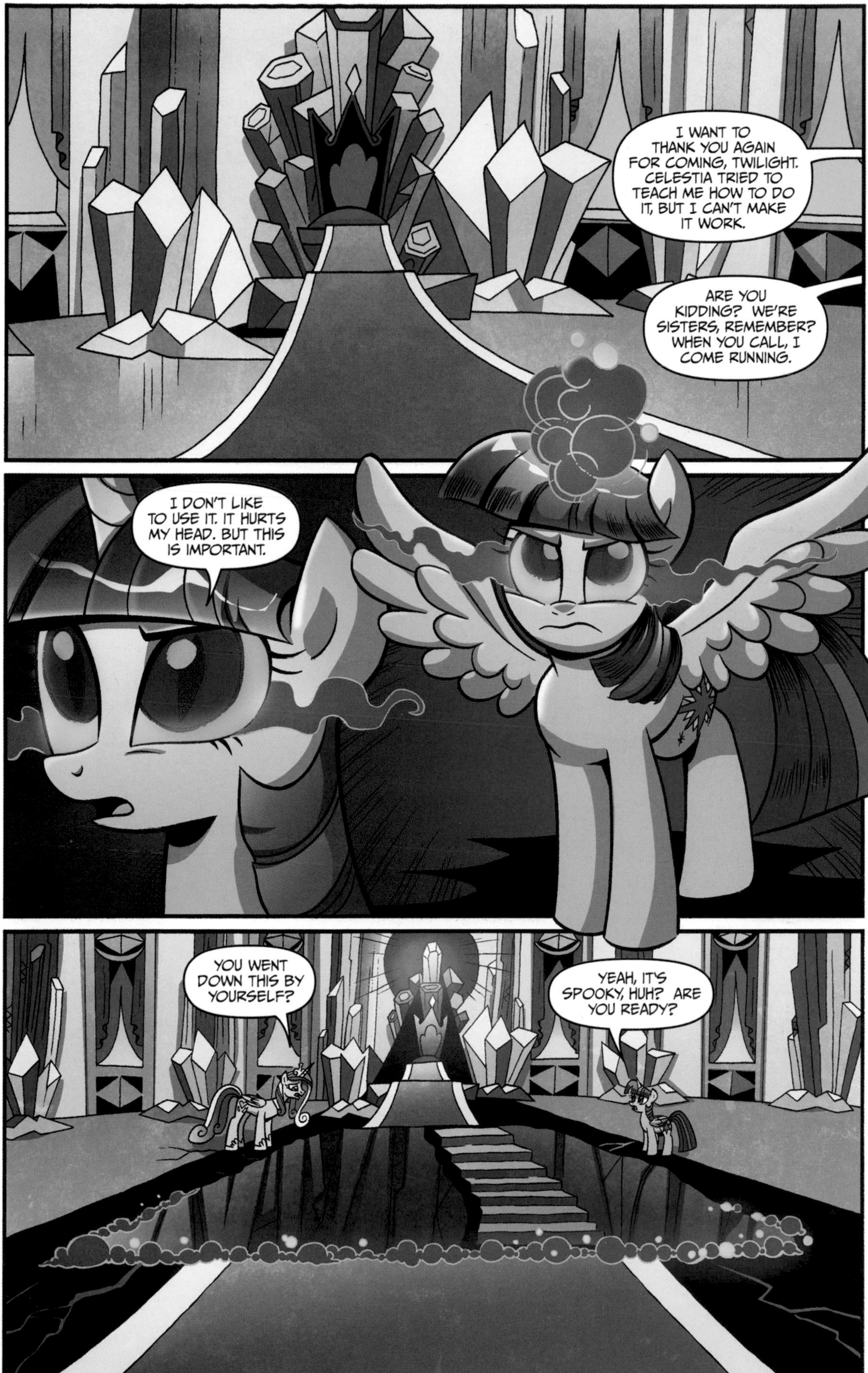
I WANT TO THANK YOU AGAIN FOR COMING, TWILIGHT. CELESTIA TRIED TO TEACH ME HOW TO DO IT, BUT I CAN'T MAKE IT WORK.
ARE YOU KIDDING? WE'RE SISTERS, REMEMBER? WHEN YOU CALL, I COME RUNNING.
I DON'T LIKE TO USE IT. IT HURTS MY HEAD. BUT THIS IS IMPORTANT.
YOU WENT DOWN THIS BY YOURSELF?
YEAH, IT'S SPOOKY, HUH? ARE YOU READY?

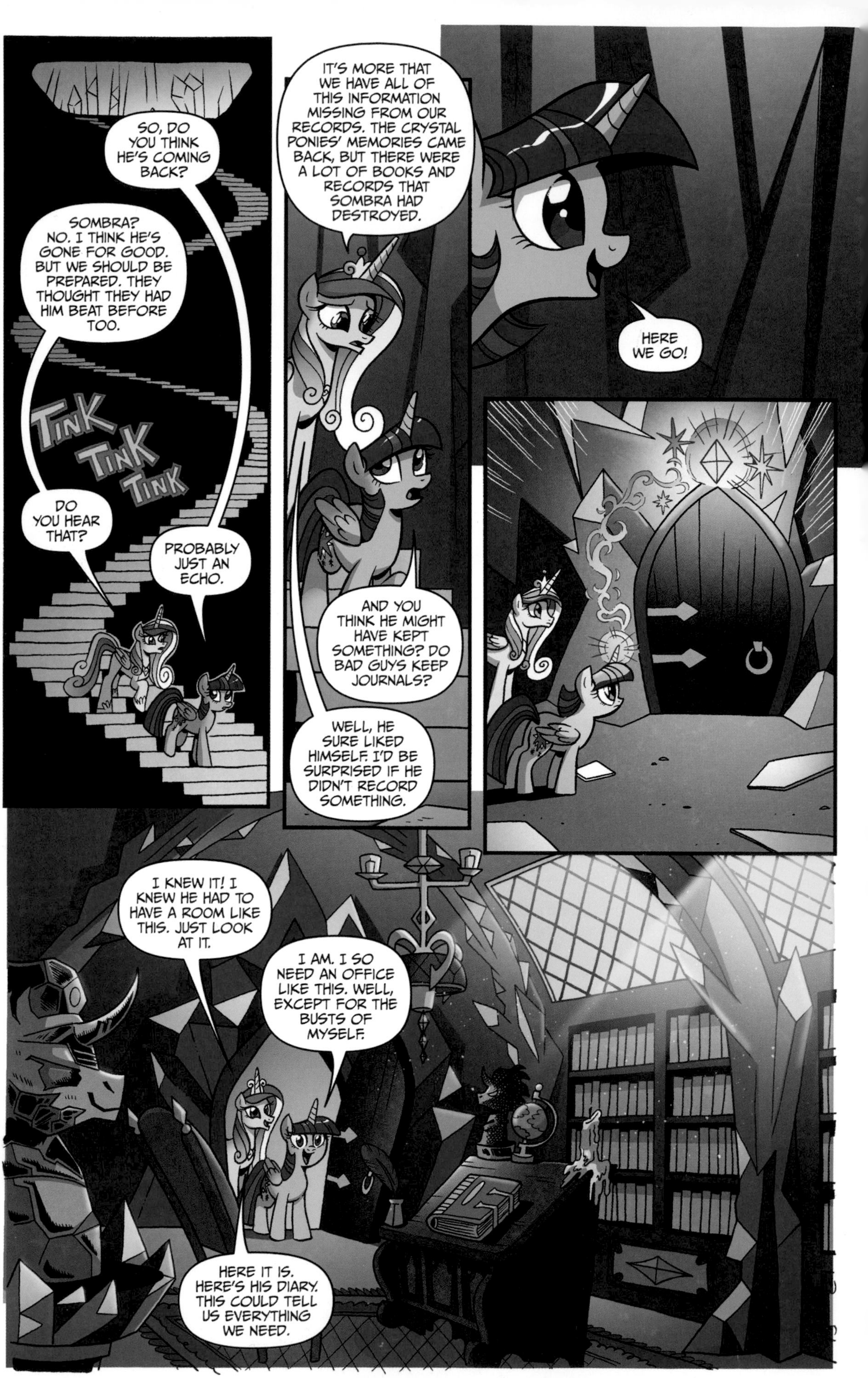

SO, DO YOU THINK HE'S COMING BACK?
SOMBRA? NO. I THINK HE'S GONE FOR GOOD. BUT WE SHOULD BE PREPARED. THEY THOUGHT THEY HAD HIM BEAT BEFORE TOO.
TINK TINK TINK
DO YOU HEAR THAT?
PROBABLY JUST AN ECHO.
IT'S MORE THAT WE HAVE ALL OF THIS INFORMATION MISSING FROM OUR RECORDS. THE CRYSTAL PONIES' MEMORIES CAME BACK, BUT THERE WERE A LOT OF BOOKS AND RECORDS THAT SOMBRA HAD DESTROYED.
AND YOU THINK HE MIGHT HAVE KEPT SOMETHING? DO BAD GUYS KEEP JOURNALS?
WELL, HE SURE LIKED HIMSELF. I'D BE SURPRISED IF HE DIDN'T RECORD SOMETHING.
HERE WE GO!
I KNEW IT! I KNEW HE HAD TO HAVE A ROOM LIKE THIS. JUST LOOK AT IT.
I AM. I SO NEED AN OFFICE LIKE THIS. WELL, EXCEPT FOR THE BUSTS OF MYSELF.
HERE IT IS. HERE'S HIS DIARY. THIS COULD TELL US EVERYTHING WE NEED.

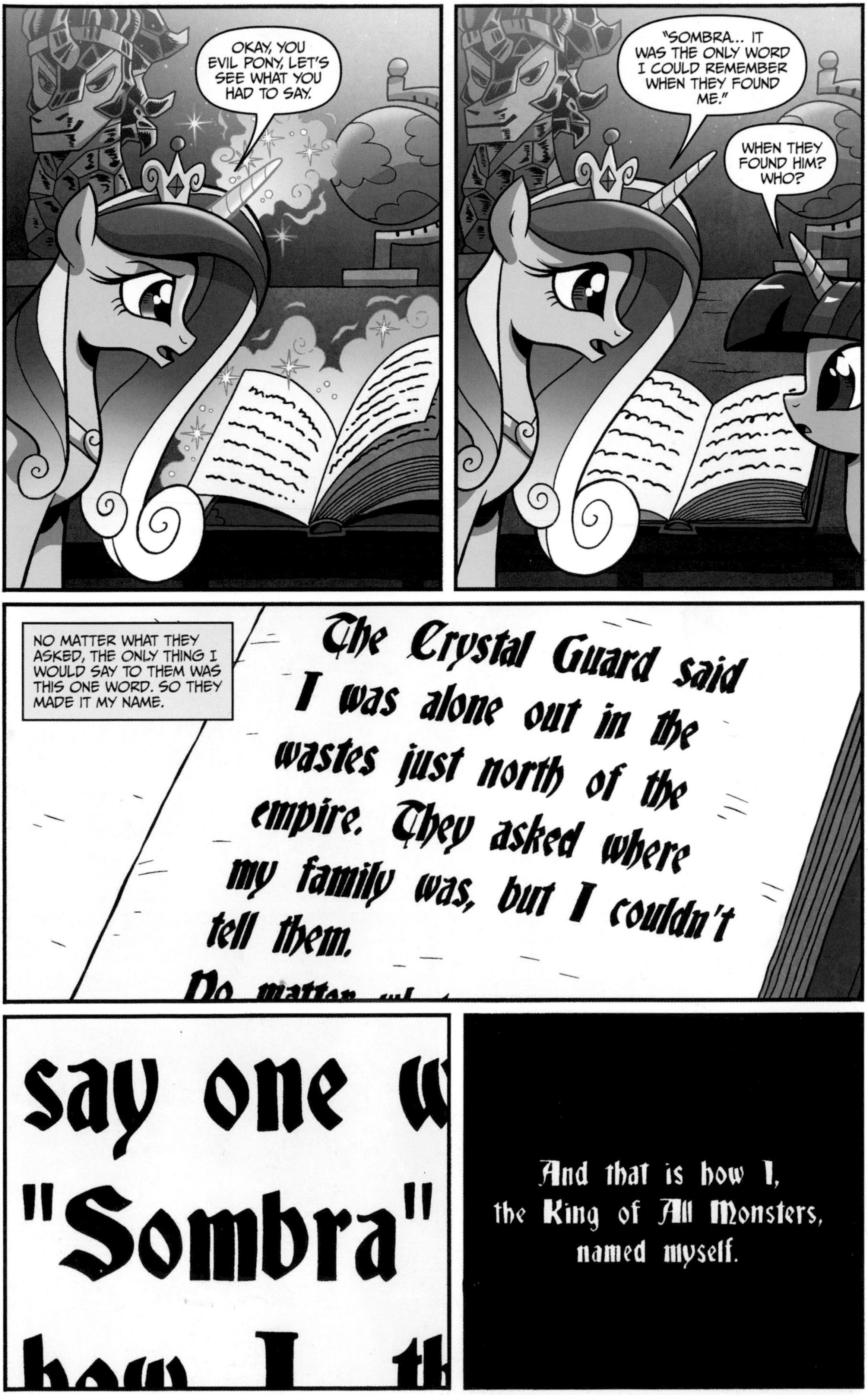
OKAY, YOU EVIL PONY, LET'S SEE WHAT YOU HAD TO SAY.
"SOMBRA... IT WAS THE ONLY WORD I COULD REMEMBER WHEN THEY FOUND ME."
WHEN THEY FOUND HIM? WHO?
NO MATTER WHAT THEY ASKED, THE ONLY THING I WOULD SAY TO THEM WAS THIS ONE WORD. SO THEY MADE IT MY NAME.
The Crystal Guard said I was alone out in the wastes just north of the empire. They asked where my family was, but I couldn't tell them.
say one
"Sombra"
how I
And that is how I, the King of All Monsters, named myself.

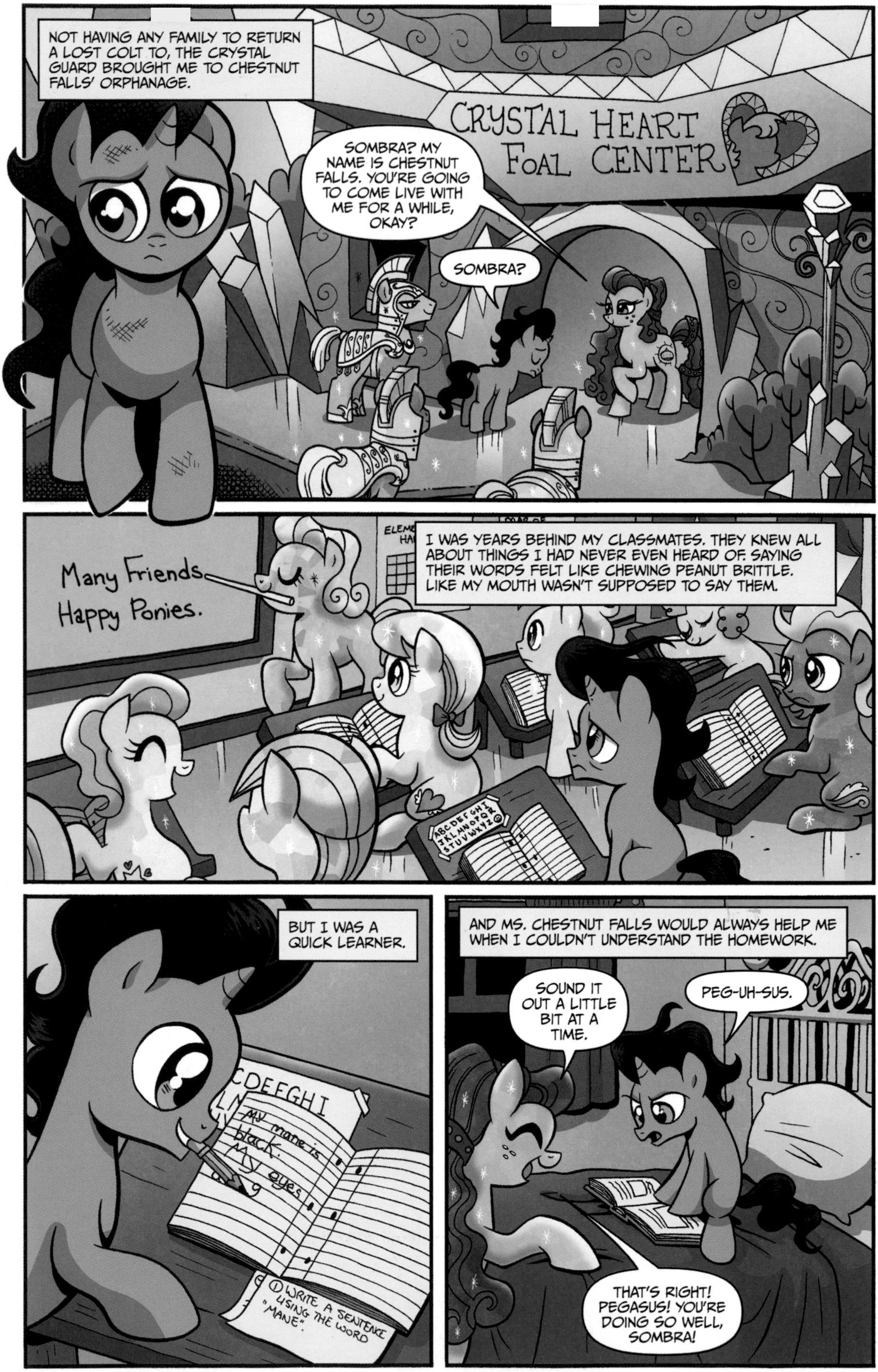

NOT HAVING ANY FAMILY TO RETURN A LOST COLT TO, THE CRYSTAL GUARD BROUGHT ME TO CHESTNUT FALLS' ORPHANAGE.
CRYSTAL HEART FOAL CENTER
SOMBRA? MY NAME IS CHESTNUT FALLS. YOU'RE GOING TO COME LIVE WITH ME FOR A WHILE, OKAY?
SOMBRA?
I WAS YEARS BEHIND MY CLASSMATES. THEY KNEW ALL ABOUT THINGS I HAD NEVER EVEN HEARD OF. SAYING THEIR WORDS FELT LIKE CHEWING PEANUT BRITTLE. LIKE MY MOUTH WASN'T SUPPOSED TO SAY THEM.
Many Friends
Happy Ponies.
BUT I WAS A QUICK LEARNER.
CDEFGHI
My mane is black.
My eyes
① WRITE A SENTENCE USING THE WORD "MANE".
AND MS. CHESTNUT FALLS WOULD ALWAYS HELP ME WHEN I COULDN'T UNDERSTAND THE HOMEWORK.
SOUND IT OUT A LITTLE BIT AT A TIME.
PEG-UH-SUS.
THAT'S RIGHT! PEGASUS! YOU'RE DOING SO WELL, SOMBRA!

SADLY, THE SAME COULD NOT BE SAID FOR OTHERS.

GREETINGS, FRIENDS. CAN SOMBRA PLAY TOO?

WHY DOES HE TALK LIKE THAT? I DON'T KNOW WHY THEY KEEP HIM HERE, HE'S NOT EVEN A CRYSTAL PONY.

I DON'T KNOW WHAT HE IS. HE DOESN'T EVEN HAVE HIS CUTIE MARK.

GET AWAY, SOMBRERO. WE DON'T WANT ANYPONY TO SEE US WITH THE WEIRD PONY.

THEY MIGHT THINK WE'RE WEIRD LIKE YOU.

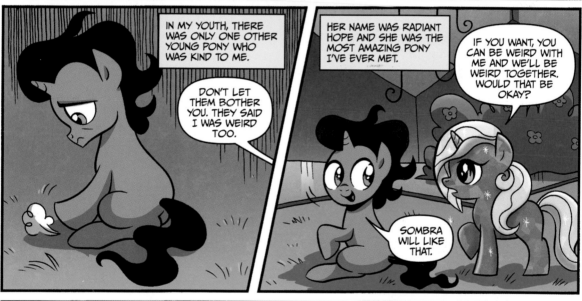

IN MY YOUTH, THERE WAS ONLY ONE OTHER YOUNG PONY WHO WAS KIND TO ME.

DON'T LET THEM BOTHER YOU. THEY SAID I WAS WEIRD TOO.

HER NAME WAS RADIANT HOPE AND SHE WAS THE MOST AMAZING PONY I'VE EVER MET.

IF YOU WANT, YOU CAN BE WEIRD WITH ME AND WE'LL BE WEIRD TOGETHER. WOULD THAT BE OKAY?

SOMBRA WILL LIKE THAT.

GOOD, JUST DON'T TALK TOO LOUD, MY FAIRY FRIENDS DON'T LIKE IT WHEN YOU DO THAT.

OH... FAIRY FRIENDS?

YES, THEY'RE ALL AROUND. BE CAREFUL NOT TO STEP ON THEM. THEY GET GRUMPY.

OH... OKAY.

SHE WAS A BIT WEIRD, BUT I ENJOYED IT. SHE HAD THE GREATEST IMAGINATION.

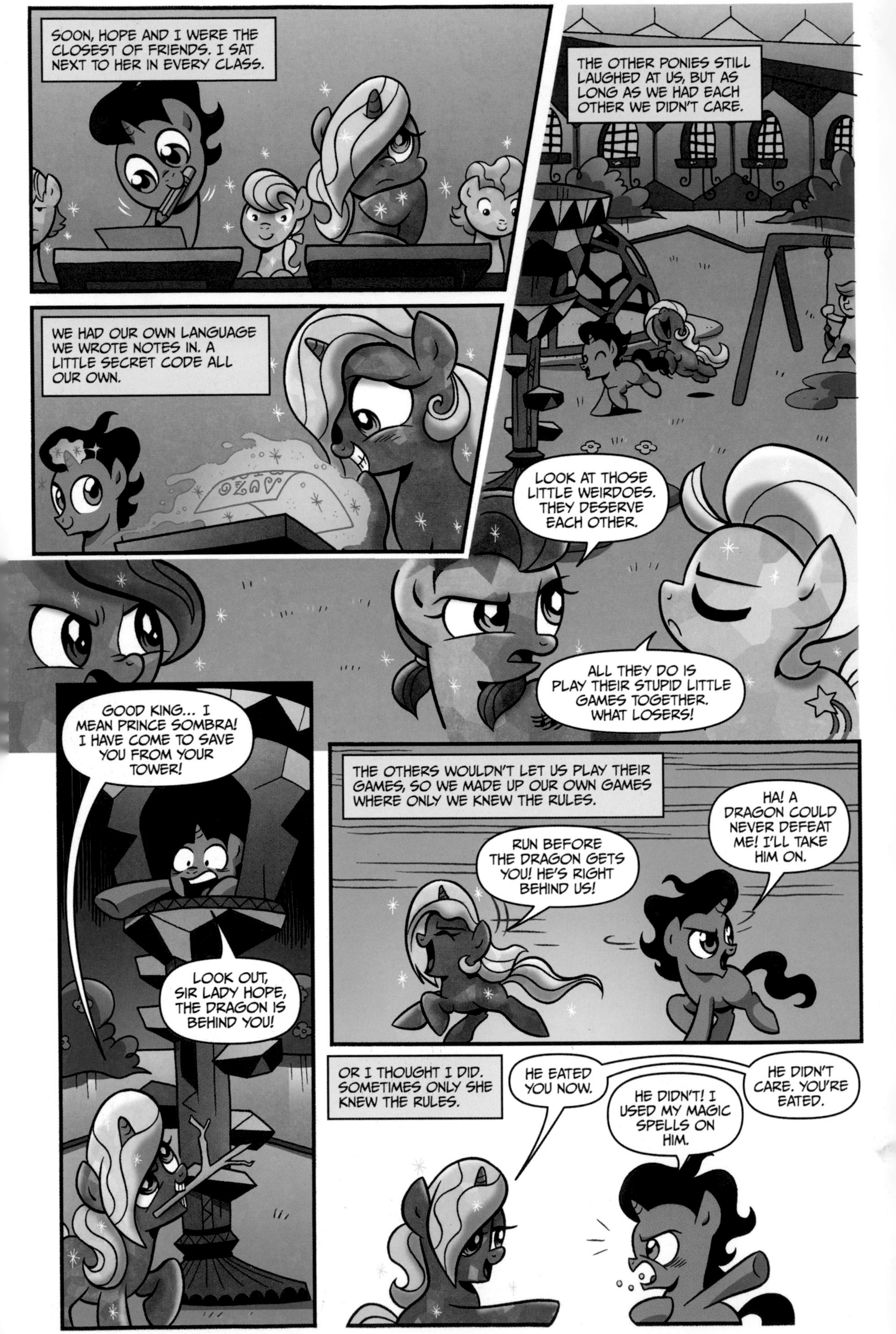
SOON, HOPE AND I WERE THE CLOSEST OF FRIENDS. I SAT NEXT TO HER IN EVERY CLASS.
WE HAD OUR OWN LANGUAGE WE WROTE NOTES IN. A LITTLE SECRET CODE ALL OUR OWN.
THE OTHER PONIES STILL LAUGHED AT US, BUT AS LONG AS WE HAD EACH OTHER WE DIDN'T CARE.
LOOK AT THOSE LITTLE WEIRDOES. THEY DESERVE EACH OTHER.
ALL THEY DO IS PLAY THEIR STUPID LITTLE GAMES TOGETHER. WHAT LOSERS!
GOOD KING... I MEAN PRINCE SOMBRA! I HAVE COME TO SAVE YOU FROM YOUR TOWER!
LOOK OUT, SIR LADY HOPE, THE DRAGON IS BEHIND YOU!
THE OTHERS WOULDN'T LET US PLAY THEIR GAMES, SO WE MADE UP OUR OWN GAMES WHERE ONLY WE KNEW THE RULES.
RUN BEFORE THE DRAGON GETS YOU! HE'S RIGHT BEHIND US!
HA! A DRAGON COULD NEVER DEFEAT ME! I'LL TAKE HIM ON.
OR I THOUGHT I DID. SOMETIMES ONLY SHE KNEW THE RULES.
HE EATED YOU NOW.
HE DIDN'T! I USED MY MAGIC SPELLS ON HIM.
HE DIDN'T CARE. YOU'RE EATED.

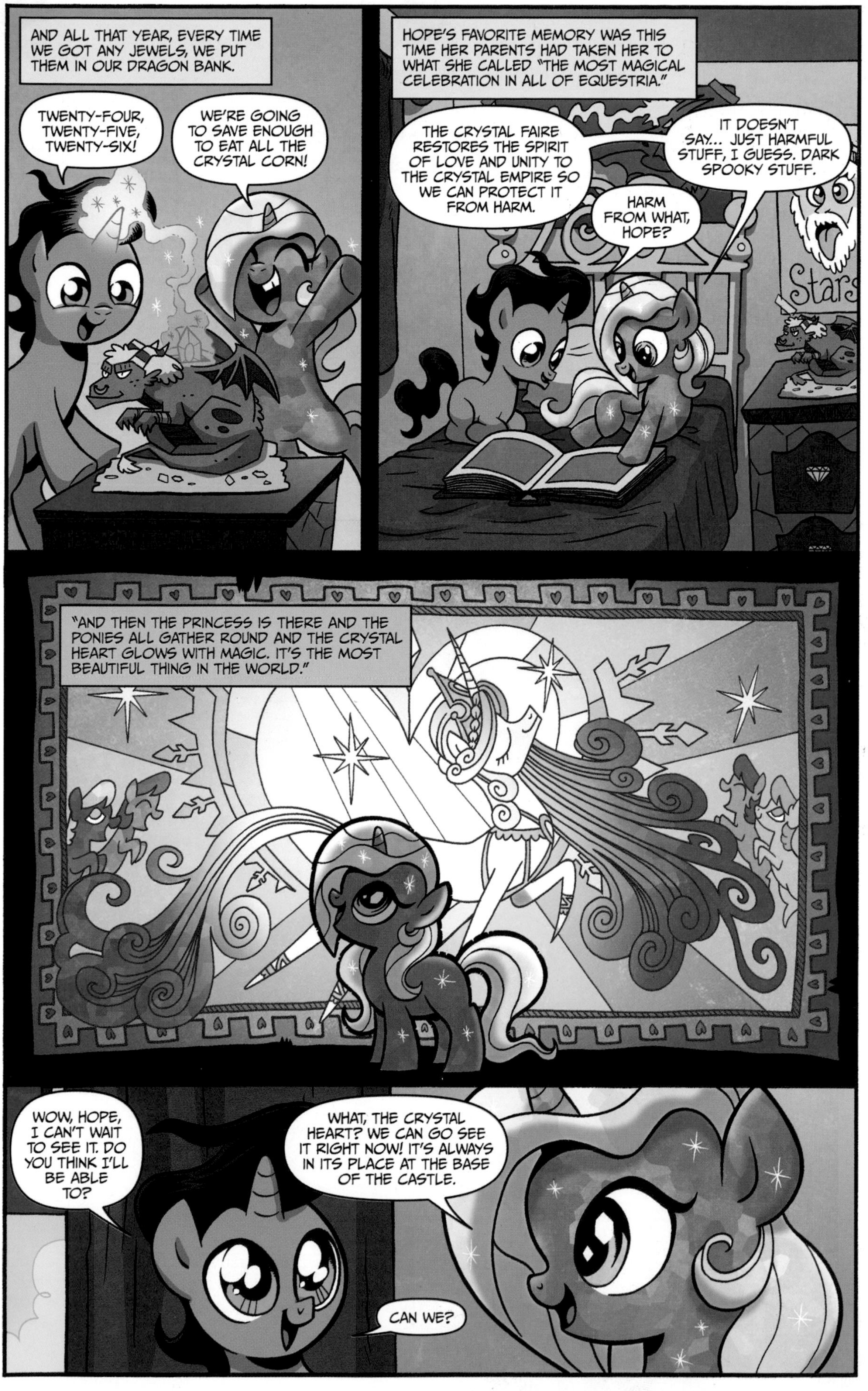
AND ALL THAT YEAR, EVERY TIME WE GOT ANY JEWELS, WE PUT THEM IN OUR DRAGON BANK.
TWENTY-FOUR, TWENTY-FIVE, TWENTY-SIX!
WE'RE GOING TO SAVE ENOUGH TO EAT ALL THE CRYSTAL CORN!
HOPE'S FAVORITE MEMORY WAS THIS TIME HER PARENTS HAD TAKEN HER TO WHAT SHE CALLED "THE MOST MAGICAL CELEBRATION IN ALL OF EQUESTRIA."
THE CRYSTAL FAIRE RESTORES THE SPIRIT OF LOVE AND UNITY TO THE CRYSTAL EMPIRE SO WE CAN PROTECT IT FROM HARM.
HARM FROM WHAT, HOPE?
IT DOESN'T SAY... JUST HARMFUL STUFF, I GUESS. DARK SPOOKY STUFF.
Stars
"AND THEN THE PRINCESS IS THERE AND THE PONIES ALL GATHER ROUND AND THE CRYSTAL HEART GLOWS WITH MAGIC. IT'S THE MOST BEAUTIFUL THING IN THE WORLD."
WOW, HOPE, I CAN'T WAIT TO SEE IT. DO YOU THINK I'LL BE ABLE TO?
WHAT, THE CRYSTAL HEART? WE CAN GO SEE IT RIGHT NOW! IT'S ALWAYS IN ITS PLACE AT THE BASE OF THE CASTLE.
CAN WE?

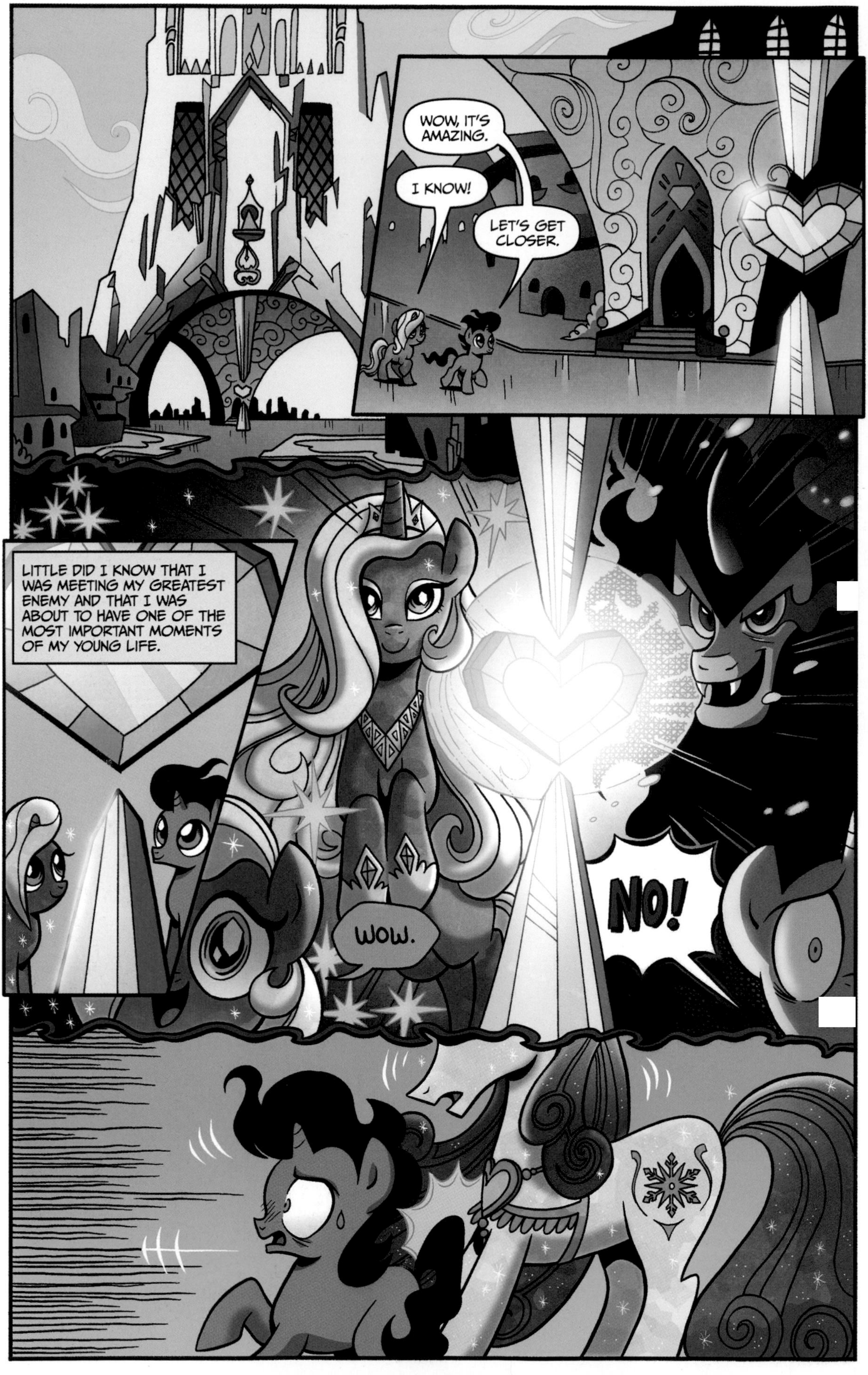
WOW, IT'S AMAZING.
I KNOW!
LET'S GET CLOSER.
LITTLE DID I KNOW THAT I WAS MEETING MY GREATEST ENEMY AND THAT I WAS ABOUT TO HAVE ONE OF THE MOST IMPORTANT MOMENTS OF MY YOUNG LIFE.
WOW.
NO!

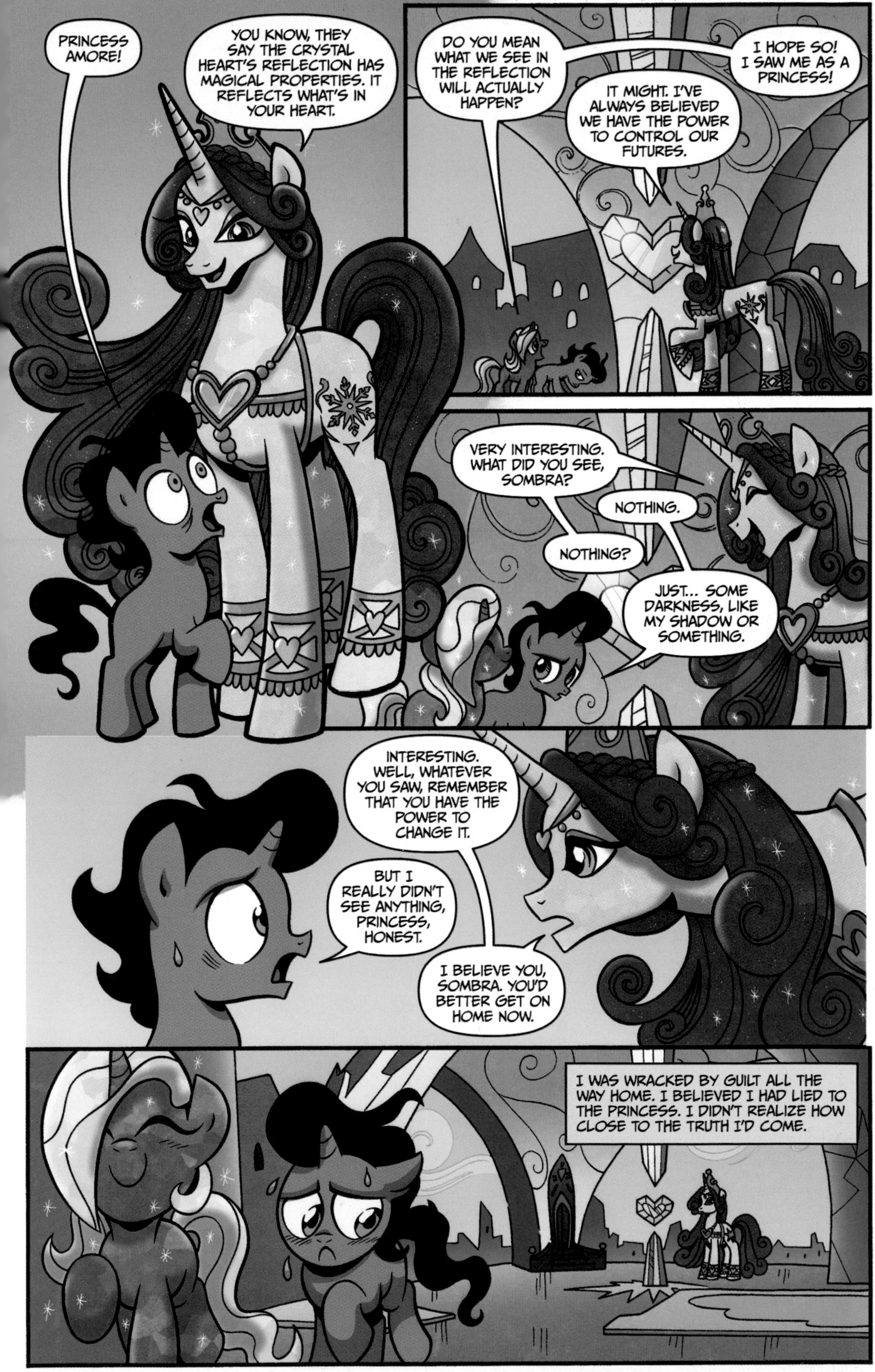

PRINCESS AMORE!
YOU KNOW, THEY SAY THE CRYSTAL HEART'S REFLECTION HAS MAGICAL PROPERTIES. IT REFLECTS WHAT'S IN YOUR HEART.
DO YOU MEAN WHAT WE SEE IN THE REFLECTION WILL ACTUALLY HAPPEN?
I HOPE SO! I SAW ME AS A PRINCESS!
IT MIGHT. I'VE ALWAYS BELIEVED WE HAVE THE POWER TO CONTROL OUR FUTURES.
VERY INTERESTING. WHAT DID YOU SEE, SOMBRA?
NOTHING.
NOTHING?
JUST... SOME DARKNESS, LIKE MY SHADOW OR SOMETHING.
INTERESTING. WELL, WHATEVER YOU SAW, REMEMBER THAT YOU HAVE THE POWER TO CHANGE IT.
BUT I REALLY DIDN'T SEE ANYTHING, PRINCESS, HONEST.
I BELIEVE YOU, SOMBRA. YOU'D BETTER GET ON HOME NOW.
I WAS WRACKED BY GUILT ALL THE WAY HOME. I BELIEVED I HAD LIED TO THE PRINCESS. I DIDN'T REALIZE HOW CLOSE TO THE TRUTH I'D COME.

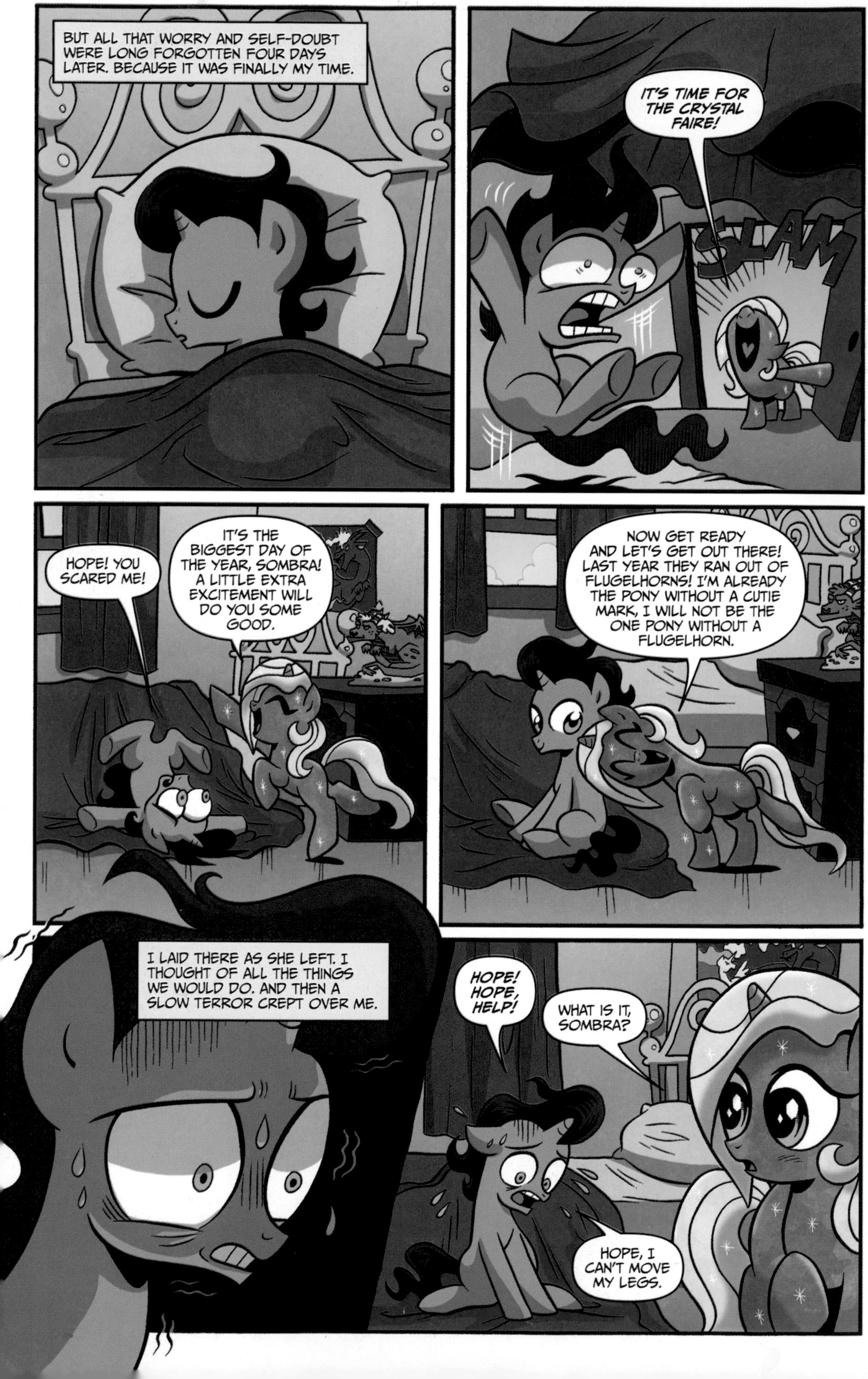
BUT ALL THAT WORRY AND SELF-DOUBT WERE LONG FORGOTTEN FOUR DAYS LATER. BECAUSE IT WAS FINALLY MY TIME.
IT'S TIME FOR THE CRYSTAL FAIRE!
SLAM
HOPE! YOU SCARED ME!
IT'S THE BIGGEST DAY OF THE YEAR, SOMBRA! A LITTLE EXTRA EXCITEMENT WILL DO YOU SOME GOOD.
NOW GET READY AND LET'S GET OUT THERE! LAST YEAR THEY RAN OUT OF FLUGELHORNS! I'M ALREADY THE PONY WITHOUT A CUTIE MARK, I WILL NOT BE THE ONE PONY WITHOUT A FLUGELHORN.
I LAID THERE AS SHE LEFT. I THOUGHT OF ALL THE THINGS WE WOULD DO. AND THEN A SLOW TERROR CREPT OVER ME.
HOPE! HOPE, HELP!
WHAT IS IT, SOMBRA?
HOPE, I CAN'T MOVE MY LEGS.

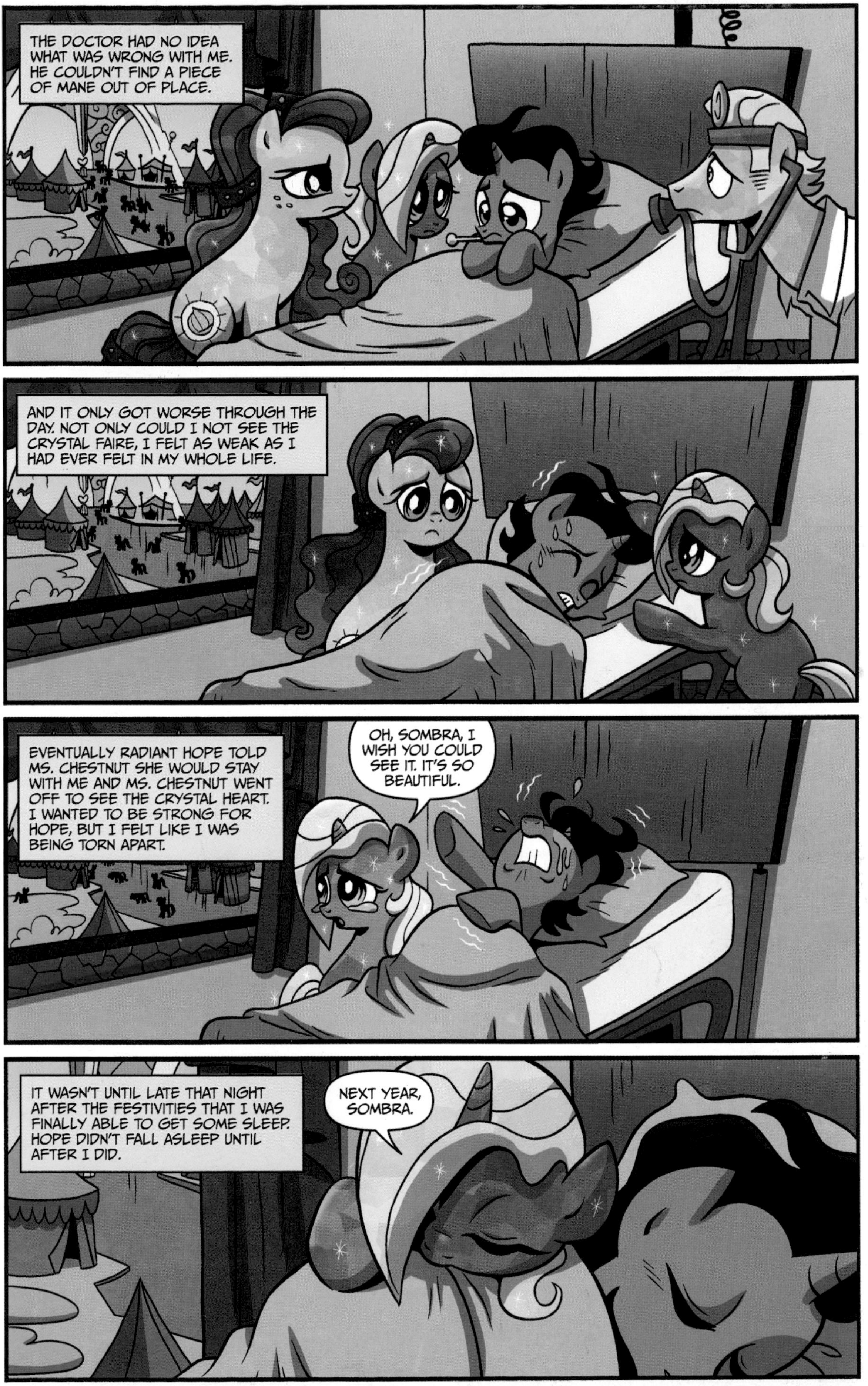
THE DOCTOR HAD NO IDEA WHAT WAS WRONG WITH ME. HE COULDN'T FIND A PIECE OF MANE OUT OF PLACE.
AND IT ONLY GOT WORSE THROUGH THE DAY. NOT ONLY COULD I NOT SEE THE CRYSTAL FAIRE, I FELT AS WEAK AS I HAD EVER FELT IN MY WHOLE LIFE.
EVENTUALLY RADIANT HOPE TOLD MS. CHESTNUT SHE WOULD STAY WITH ME AND MS. CHESTNUT WENT OFF TO SEE THE CRYSTAL HEART. I WANTED TO BE STRONG FOR HOPE, BUT I FELT LIKE I WAS BEING TORN APART.
OH, SOMBRA, I WISH YOU COULD SEE IT. IT'S SO BEAUTIFUL.
IT WASN'T UNTIL LATE THAT NIGHT AFTER THE FESTIVITIES THAT I WAS FINALLY ABLE TO GET SOME SLEEP. HOPE DIDN'T FALL ASLEEP UNTIL AFTER I DID.
NEXT YEAR, SOMBRA.

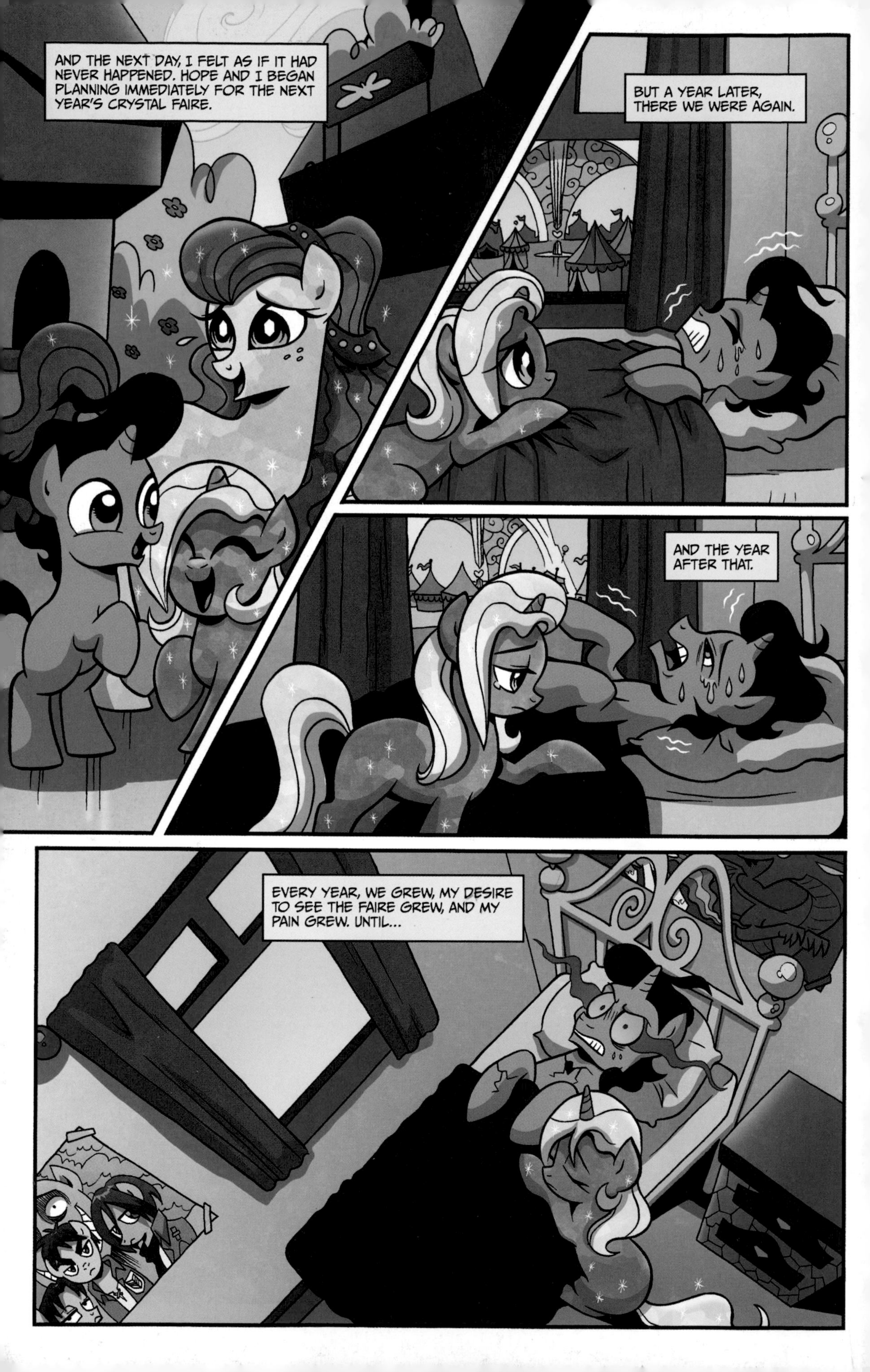
AND THE NEXT DAY, I FELT AS IF IT HAD NEVER HAPPENED. HOPE AND I BEGAN PLANNING IMMEDIATELY FOR THE NEXT YEAR'S CRYSTAL FAIRE.
BUT A YEAR LATER, THERE WE WERE AGAIN.
AND THE YEAR AFTER THAT.
EVERY YEAR, WE GREW, MY DESIRE TO SEE THE FAIRE GREW, AND MY PAIN GREW. UNTIL...

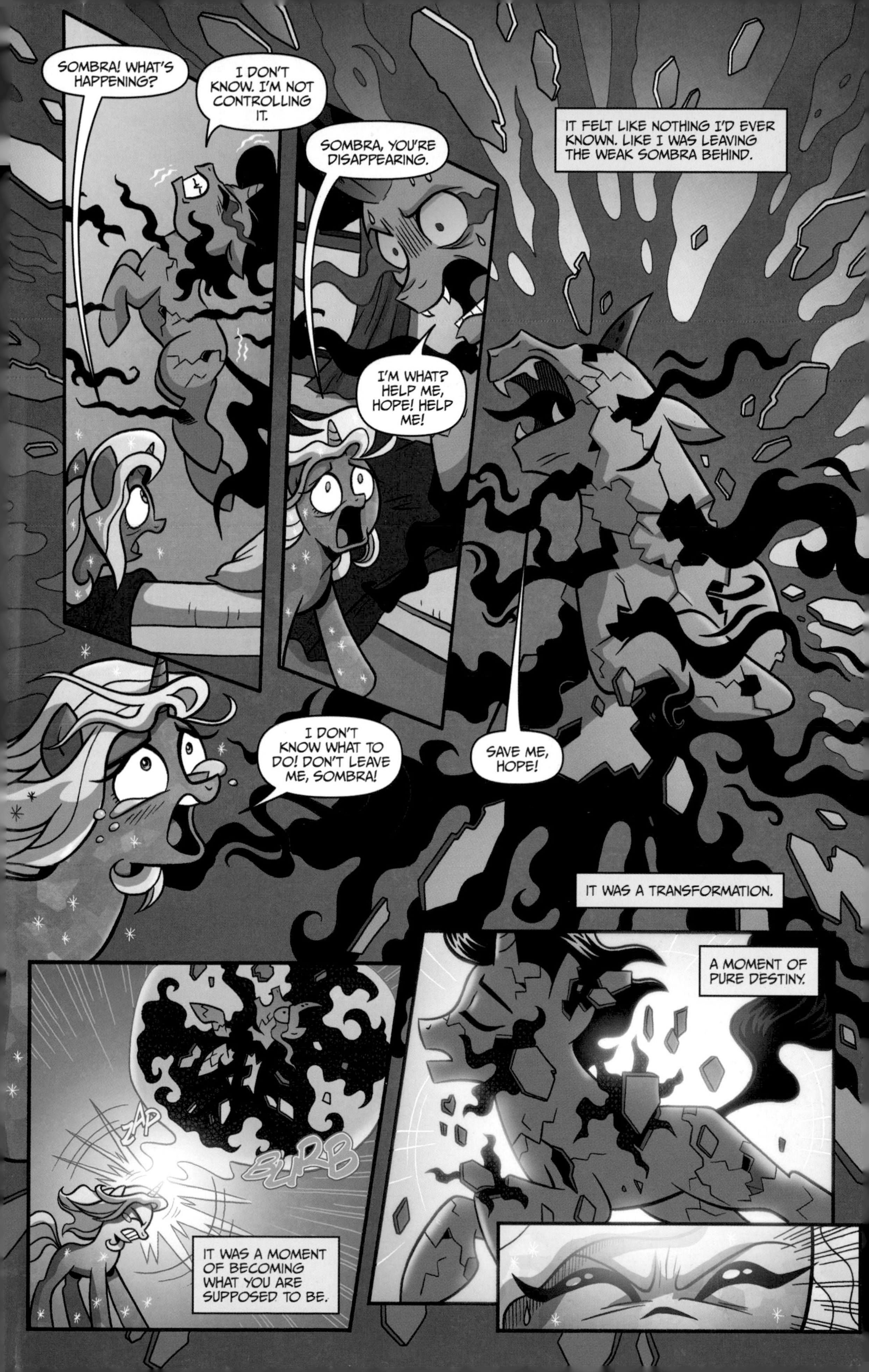

SOMBRA! WHAT'S HAPPENING?
I DON'T KNOW. I'M NOT CONTROLLING IT.
SOMBRA, YOU'RE DISAPPEARING.
I'M WHAT? HELP ME, HOPE! HELP ME!
IT FELT LIKE NOTHING I'D EVER KNOWN. LIKE I WAS LEAVING THE WEAK SOMBRA BEHIND.
I DON'T KNOW WHAT TO DO! DON'T LEAVE ME, SOMBRA!
SAVE ME, HOPE!
IT WAS A TRANSFORMATION.
ZAP
BURB
IT WAS A MOMENT OF BECOMING WHAT YOU ARE SUPPOSED TO BE.
A MOMENT OF PURE DESTINY.

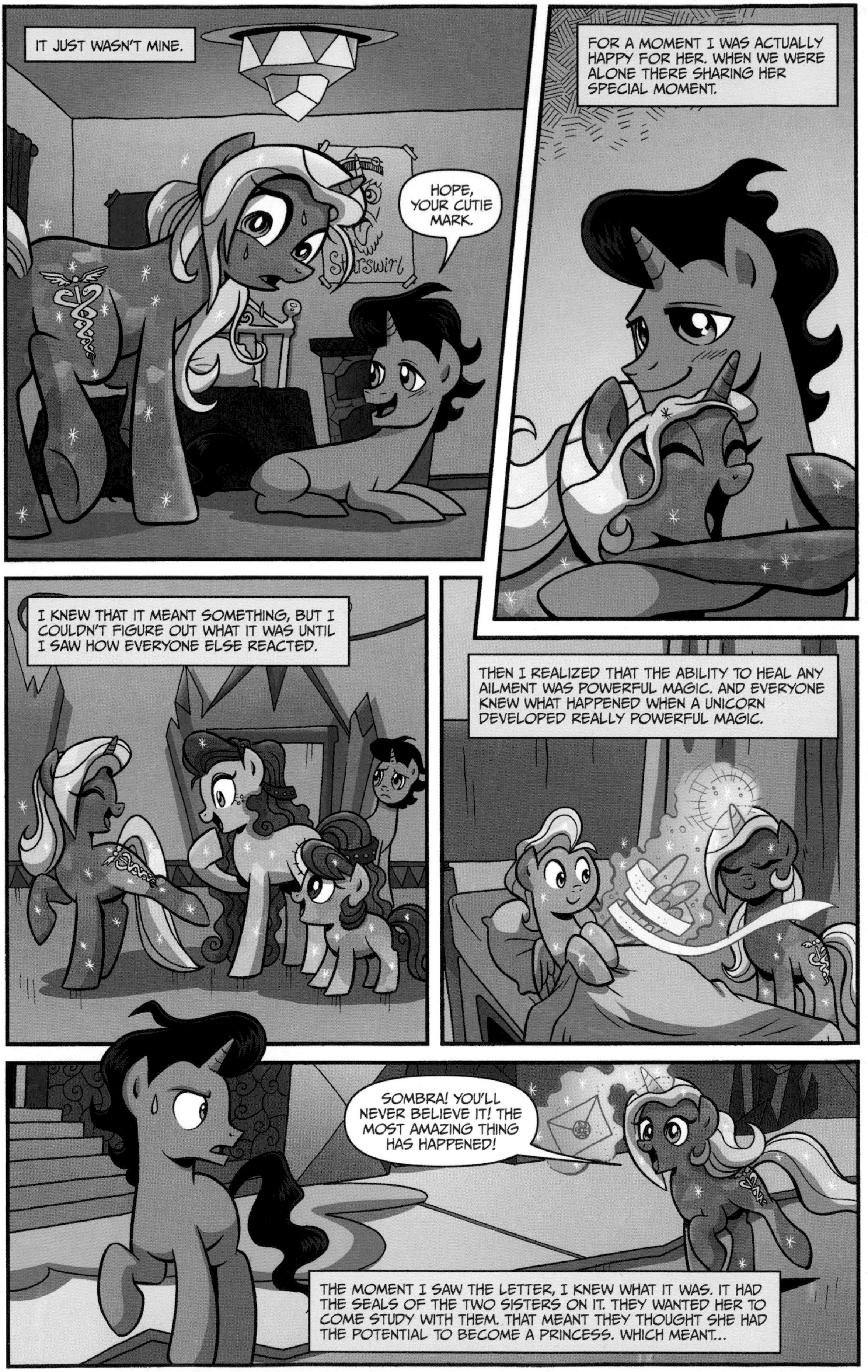
IT JUST WASN'T MINE.
HOPE, YOUR CUTIE MARK.
Starswirl
FOR A MOMENT I WAS ACTUALLY HAPPY FOR HER. WHEN WE WERE ALONE THERE SHARING HER SPECIAL MOMENT.
I KNEW THAT IT MEANT SOMETHING, BUT I COULDN'T FIGURE OUT WHAT IT WAS UNTIL I SAW HOW EVERYONE ELSE REACTED.
THEN I REALIZED THAT THE ABILITY TO HEAL ANY AILMENT WAS POWERFUL MAGIC. AND EVERYONE KNEW WHAT HAPPENED WHEN A UNICORN DEVELOPED REALLY POWERFUL MAGIC.
SOMBRA! YOU'LL NEVER BELIEVE IT! THE MOST AMAZING THING HAS HAPPENED!
THE MOMENT I SAW THE LETTER, I KNEW WHAT IT WAS. IT HAD THE SEALS OF THE TWO SISTERS ON IT. THEY WANTED HER TO COME STUDY WITH THEM. THAT MEANT THEY THOUGHT SHE HAD THE POTENTIAL TO BECOME A PRINCESS. WHICH MEANT...

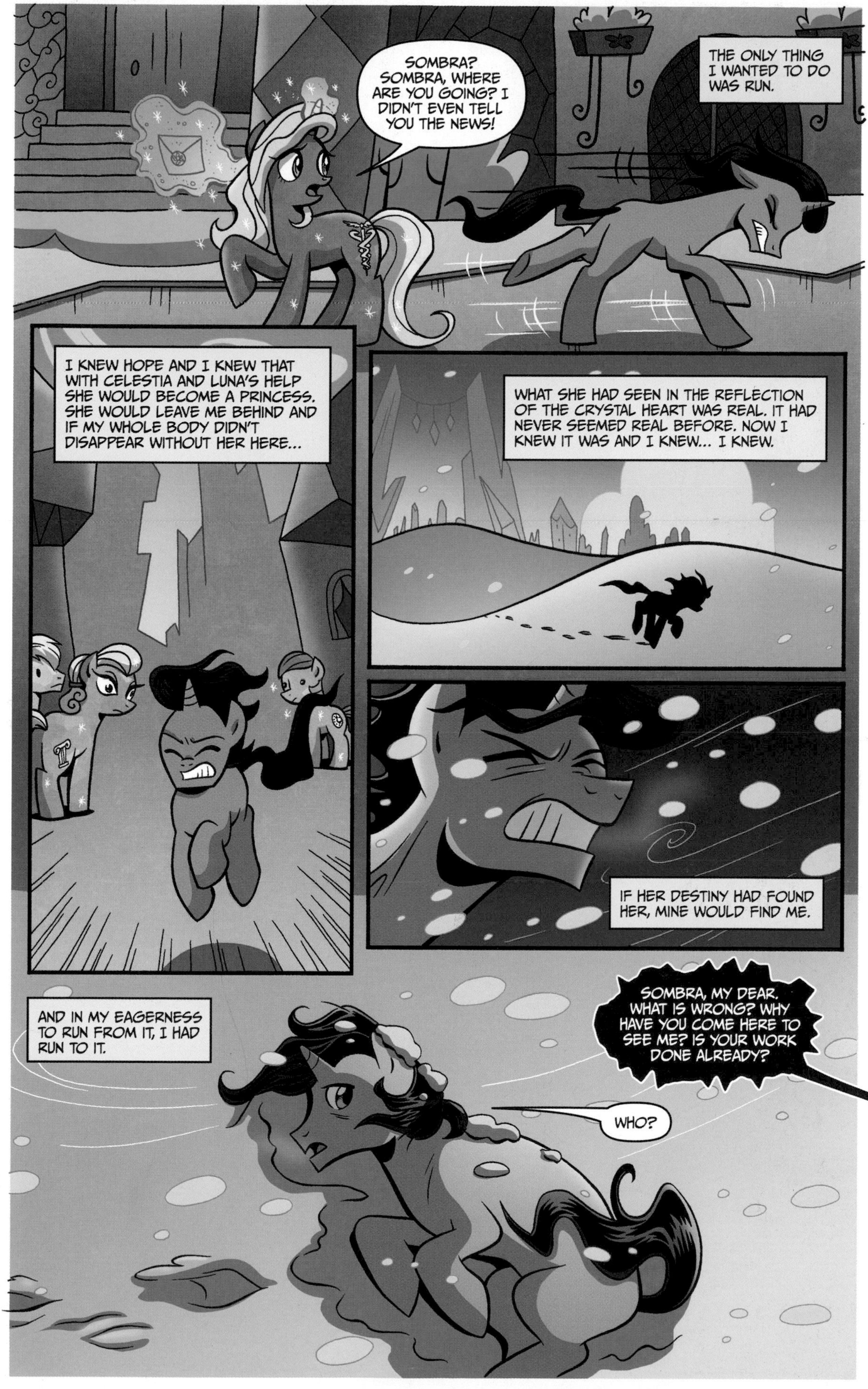
SOMBRA? SOMBRA, WHERE ARE YOU GOING? I DIDN'T EVEN TELL YOU THE NEWS!
THE ONLY THING I WANTED TO DO WAS RUN.
I KNEW HOPE AND I KNEW THAT WITH CELESTIA AND LUNA'S HELP SHE WOULD BECOME A PRINCESS. SHE WOULD LEAVE ME BEHIND AND IF MY WHOLE BODY DIDN'T DISAPPEAR WITHOUT HER HERE...
WHAT SHE HAD SEEN IN THE REFLECTION OF THE CRYSTAL HEART WAS REAL. IT HAD NEVER SEEMED REAL BEFORE. NOW I KNEW IT WAS AND I KNEW... I KNEW.
IF HER DESTINY HAD FOUND HER, MINE WOULD FIND ME.
AND IN MY EAGERNESS TO RUN FROM IT, I HAD RUN TO IT.
SOMBRA, MY DEAR. WHAT IS WRONG? WHY HAVE YOU COME HERE TO SEE ME? IS YOUR WORK DONE ALREADY?
WHO?

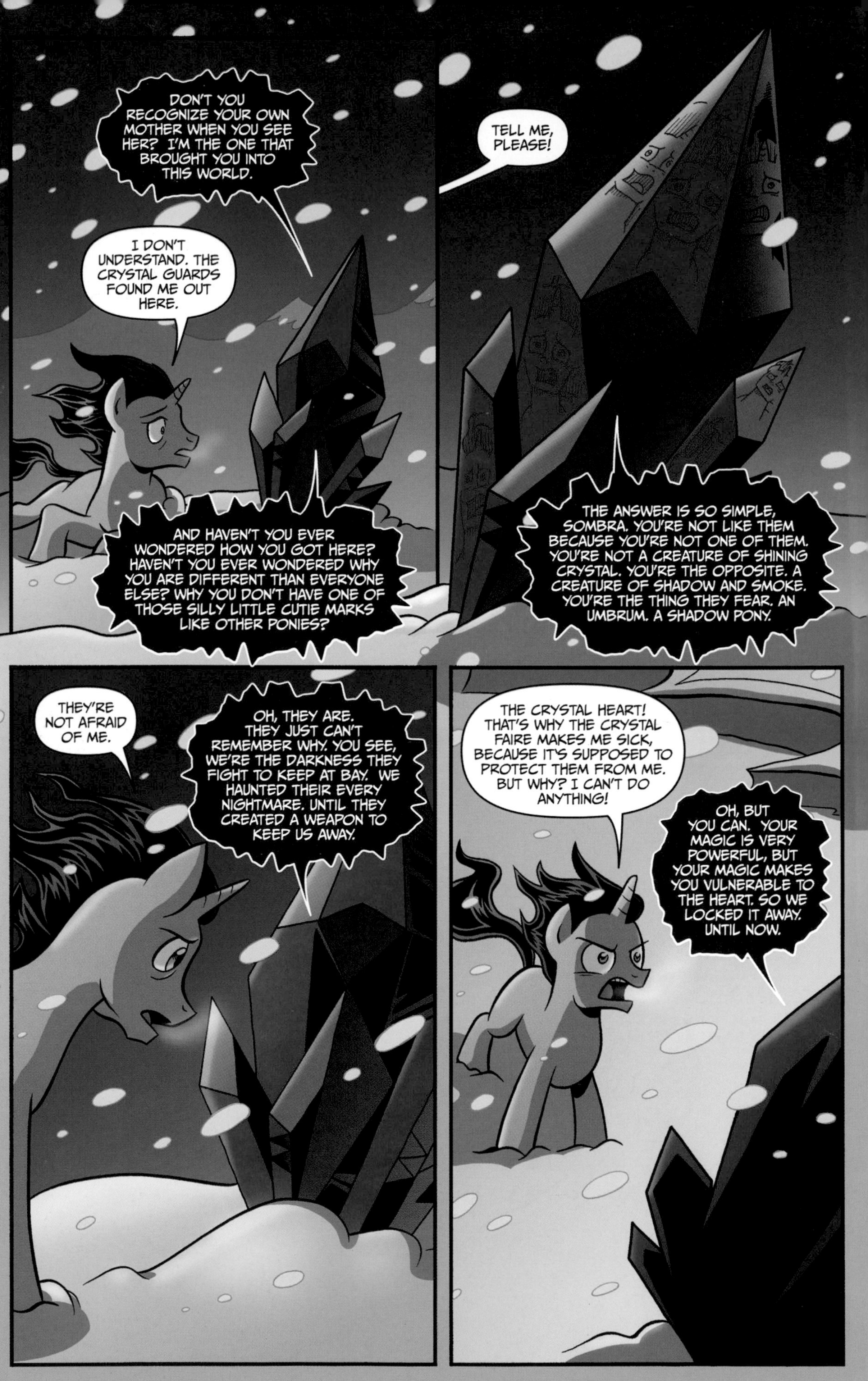
DON'T YOU RECOGNIZE YOUR OWN MOTHER WHEN YOU SEE HER? I'M THE ONE THAT BROUGHT YOU INTO THIS WORLD.
I DON'T UNDERSTAND. THE CRYSTAL GUARDS FOUND ME OUT HERE.
AND HAVEN'T YOU EVER WONDERED HOW YOU GOT HERE? HAVEN'T YOU EVER WONDERED WHY YOU ARE DIFFERENT THAN EVERYONE ELSE? WHY YOU DON'T HAVE ONE OF THOSE SILLY LITTLE CUTIE MARKS LIKE OTHER PONIES?
TELL ME, PLEASE!
THE ANSWER IS SO SIMPLE, SOMBRA. YOU'RE NOT LIKE THEM BECAUSE YOU'RE NOT ONE OF THEM. YOU'RE NOT A CREATURE OF SHINING CRYSTAL. YOU'RE THE OPPOSITE. A CREATURE OF SHADOW AND SMOKE. YOU'RE THE THING THEY FEAR. AN UMBRUM. A SHADOW PONY.
THEY'RE NOT AFRAID OF ME.
OH, THEY ARE. THEY JUST CAN'T REMEMBER WHY. YOU SEE, WE'RE THE DARKNESS THEY FIGHT TO KEEP AT BAY. WE HAUNTED THEIR EVERY NIGHTMARE. UNTIL THEY CREATED A WEAPON TO KEEP US AWAY.
THE CRYSTAL HEART! THAT'S WHY THE CRYSTAL FAIRE MAKES ME SICK, BECAUSE IT'S SUPPOSED TO PROTECT THEM FROM ME. BUT WHY? I CAN'T DO ANYTHING!
OH, BUT YOU CAN. YOUR MAGIC IS VERY POWERFUL, BUT YOUR MAGIC MAKES YOU VULNERABLE TO THE HEART. SO WE LOCKED IT AWAY. UNTIL NOW.

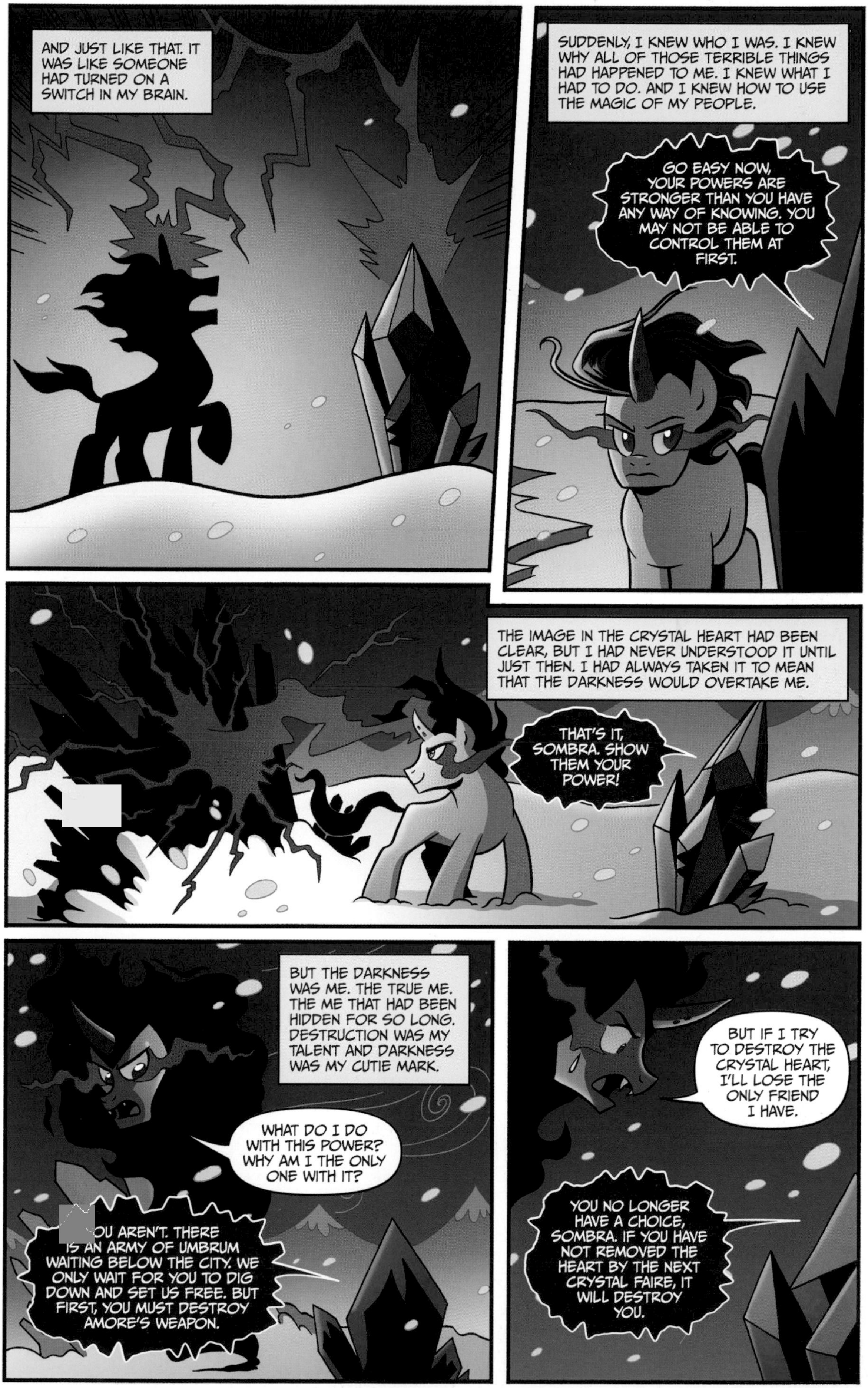
AND JUST LIKE THAT. IT WAS LIKE SOMEONE HAD TURNED ON A SWITCH IN MY BRAIN.
SUDDENLY, I KNEW WHO I WAS. I KNEW WHY ALL OF THOSE TERRIBLE THINGS HAD HAPPENED TO ME. I KNEW WHAT I HAD TO DO. AND I KNEW HOW TO USE THE MAGIC OF MY PEOPLE.
GO EASY NOW, YOUR POWERS ARE STRONGER THAN YOU HAVE ANY WAY OF KNOWING. YOU MAY NOT BE ABLE TO CONTROL THEM AT FIRST.
THE IMAGE IN THE CRYSTAL HEART HAD BEEN CLEAR, BUT I HAD NEVER UNDERSTOOD IT UNTIL JUST THEN. I HAD ALWAYS TAKEN IT TO MEAN THAT THE DARKNESS WOULD OVERTAKE ME.
THAT'S IT, SOMBRA. SHOW THEM YOUR POWER!
BUT THE DARKNESS WAS ME. THE TRUE ME. THE ME THAT HAD BEEN HIDDEN FOR SO LONG. DESTRUCTION WAS MY TALENT AND DARKNESS WAS MY CUTIE MARK.
WHAT DO I DO WITH THIS POWER? WHY AM I THE ONLY ONE WITH IT?
OU AREN'T. THERE IS AN ARMY OF UMBRUM WAITING BELOW THE CITY. WE ONLY WAIT FOR YOU TO DIG DOWN AND SET US FREE. BUT FIRST, YOU MUST DESTROY AMORE'S WEAPON.
BUT IF I TRY TO DESTROY THE CRYSTAL HEART, I'LL LOSE THE ONLY FRIEND I HAVE.
YOU NO LONGER HAVE A CHOICE, SOMBRA. IF YOU HAVE NOT REMOVED THE HEART BY THE NEXT CRYSTAL FAIRE, IT WILL DESTROY YOU.

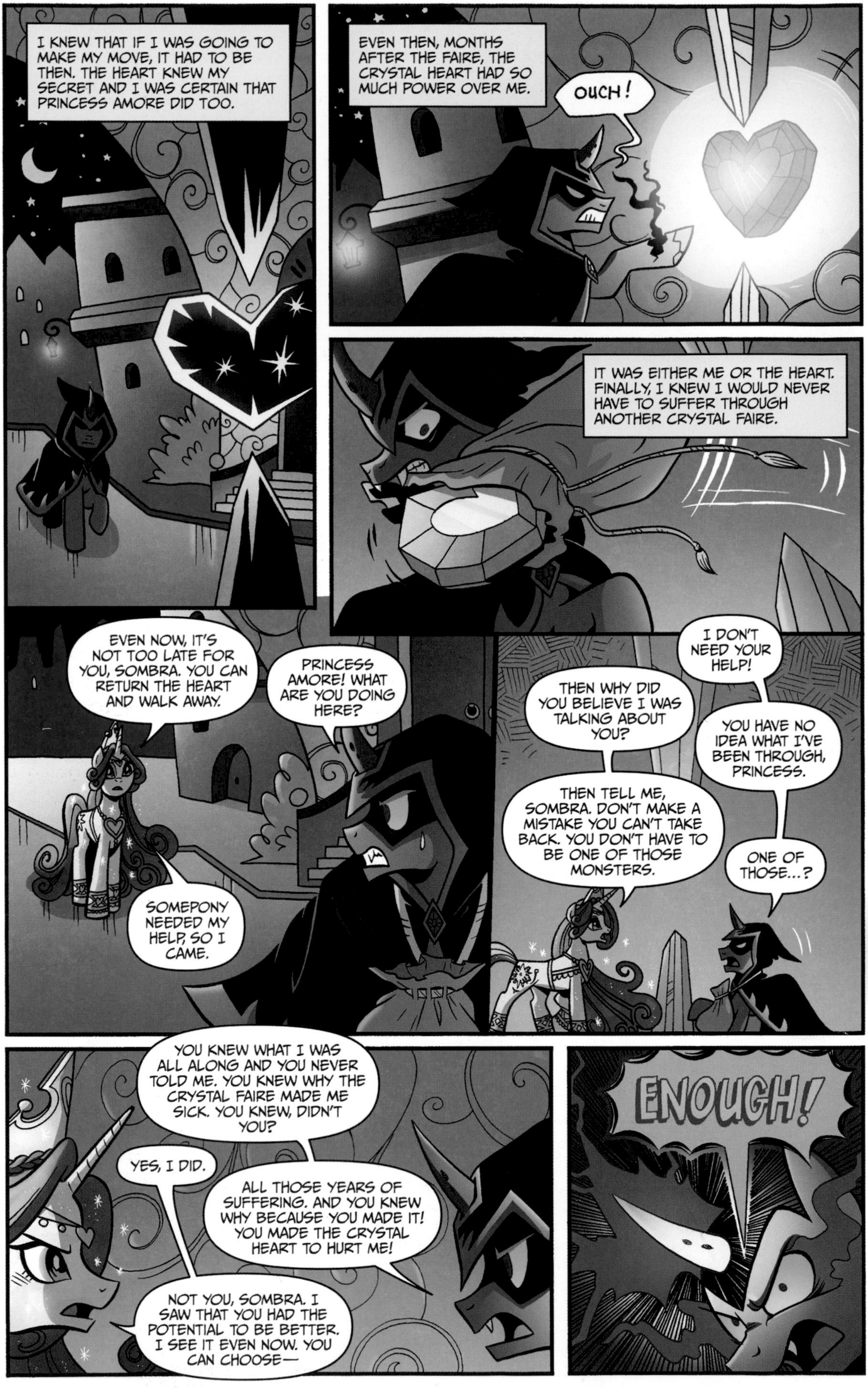
I KNEW THAT IF I WAS GOING TO MAKE MY MOVE, IT HAD TO BE THEN. THE HEART KNEW MY SECRET AND I WAS CERTAIN THAT PRINCESS AMORE DID TOO.
EVEN THEN, MONTHS AFTER THE FAIRE, THE CRYSTAL HEART HAD SO MUCH POWER OVER ME.
OUCH!
IT WAS EITHER ME OR THE HEART. FINALLY, I KNEW I WOULD NEVER HAVE TO SUFFER THROUGH ANOTHER CRYSTAL FAIRE.
EVEN NOW, IT'S NOT TOO LATE FOR YOU, SOMBRA. YOU CAN RETURN THE HEART AND WALK AWAY.
PRINCESS AMORE! WHAT ARE YOU DOING HERE?
SOMEPONY NEEDED MY HELP, SO I CAME.
I DON'T NEED YOUR HELP!
THEN WHY DID YOU BELIEVE I WAS TALKING ABOUT YOU?
YOU HAVE NO IDEA WHAT I'VE BEEN THROUGH, PRINCESS.
THEN TELL ME, SOMBRA. DON'T MAKE A MISTAKE YOU CAN'T TAKE BACK. YOU DON'T HAVE TO BE ONE OF THOSE MONSTERS.
ONE OF THOSE...?
YOU KNEW WHAT I WAS ALL ALONG AND YOU NEVER TOLD ME. YOU KNEW WHY THE CRYSTAL FAIRE MADE ME SICK. YOU KNEW, DIDN'T YOU?
YES, I DID.
ALL THOSE YEARS OF SUFFERING. AND YOU KNEW WHY BECAUSE YOU MADE IT! YOU MADE THE CRYSTAL HEART TO HURT ME!
NOT YOU, SOMBRA. I SAW THAT YOU HAD THE POTENTIAL TO BE BETTER. I SEE IT EVEN NOW. YOU CAN CHOOSE—
ENOUGH!

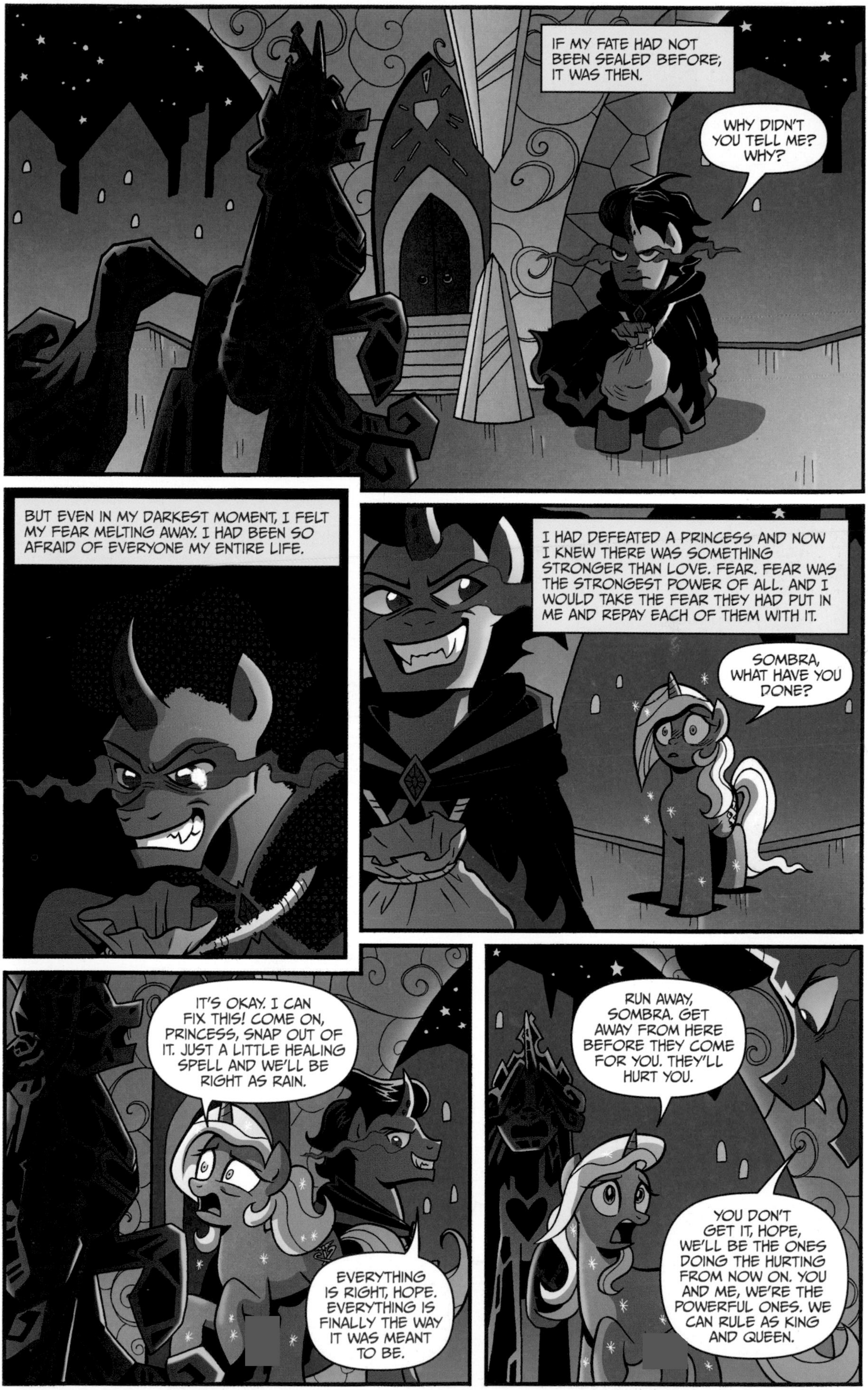
IF MY FATE HAD NOT BEEN SEALED BEFORE; IT WAS THEN.
WHY DIDN'T YOU TELL ME? WHY?
BUT EVEN IN MY DARKEST MOMENT, I FELT MY FEAR MELTING AWAY. I HAD BEEN SO AFRAID OF EVERYONE MY ENTIRE LIFE.
I HAD DEFEATED A PRINCESS AND NOW I KNEW THERE WAS SOMETHING STRONGER THAN LOVE. FEAR. FEAR WAS THE STRONGEST POWER OF ALL. AND I WOULD TAKE THE FEAR THEY HAD PUT IN ME AND REPAY EACH OF THEM WITH IT.
SOMBRA, WHAT HAVE YOU DONE?
IT'S OKAY. I CAN FIX THIS! COME ON, PRINCESS, SNAP OUT OF IT. JUST A LITTLE HEALING SPELL AND WE'LL BE RIGHT AS RAIN.
EVERYTHING IS RIGHT, HOPE. EVERYTHING IS FINALLY THE WAY IT WAS MEANT TO BE.
RUN AWAY, SOMBRA. GET AWAY FROM HERE BEFORE THEY COME FOR YOU. THEY'LL HURT YOU.
YOU DON'T GET IT, HOPE, WE'LL BE THE ONES DOING THE HURTING FROM NOW ON. YOU AND ME, WE'RE THE POWERFUL ONES. WE CAN RULE AS KING AND QUEEN.

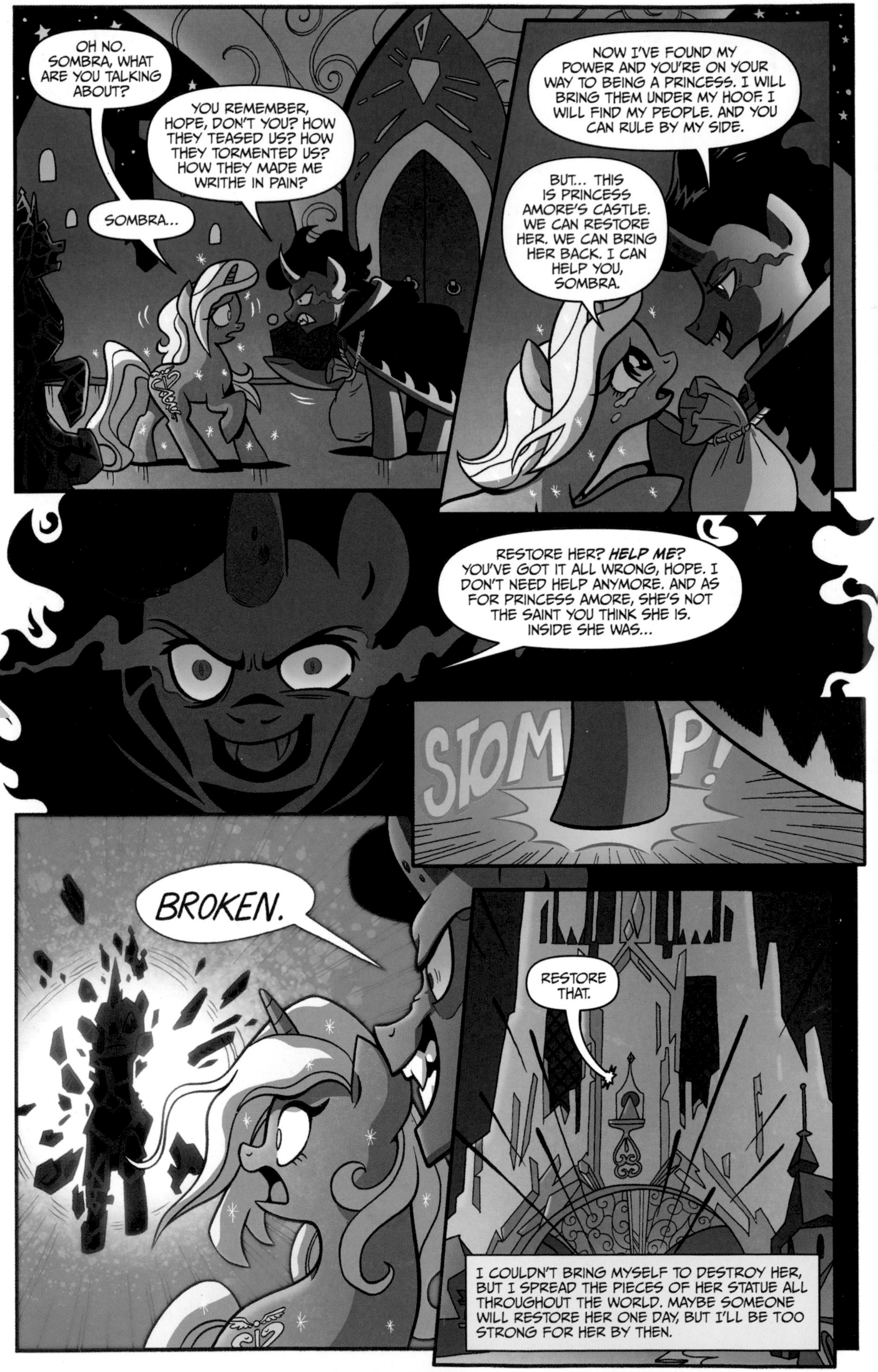
OH NO. SOMBRA, WHAT ARE YOU TALKING ABOUT?
YOU REMEMBER, HOPE, DON'T YOU? HOW THEY TEASED US? HOW THEY TORMENTED US? HOW THEY MADE ME WRITHE IN PAIN?
SOMBRA...
NOW I'VE FOUND MY POWER AND YOU'RE ON YOUR WAY TO BEING A PRINCESS. I WILL BRING THEM UNDER MY HOOF. I WILL FIND MY PEOPLE. AND YOU CAN RULE BY MY SIDE.
BUT... THIS IS PRINCESS AMORE'S CASTLE. WE CAN RESTORE HER. WE CAN BRING HER BACK. I CAN HELP YOU, SOMBRA.
RESTORE HER? HELP ME? YOU'VE GOT IT ALL WRONG, HOPE. I DON'T NEED HELP ANYMORE. AND AS FOR PRINCESS AMORE, SHE'S NOT THE SAINT YOU THINK SHE IS. INSIDE SHE WAS...
STOM P!
BROKEN.
RESTORE THAT.
I COULDN'T BRING MYSELF TO DESTROY HER, BUT I SPREAD THE PIECES OF HER STATUE ALL THROUGHOUT THE WORLD. MAYBE SOMEONE WILL RESTORE HER ONE DAY, BUT I'LL BE TOO STRONG FOR HER BY THEN.

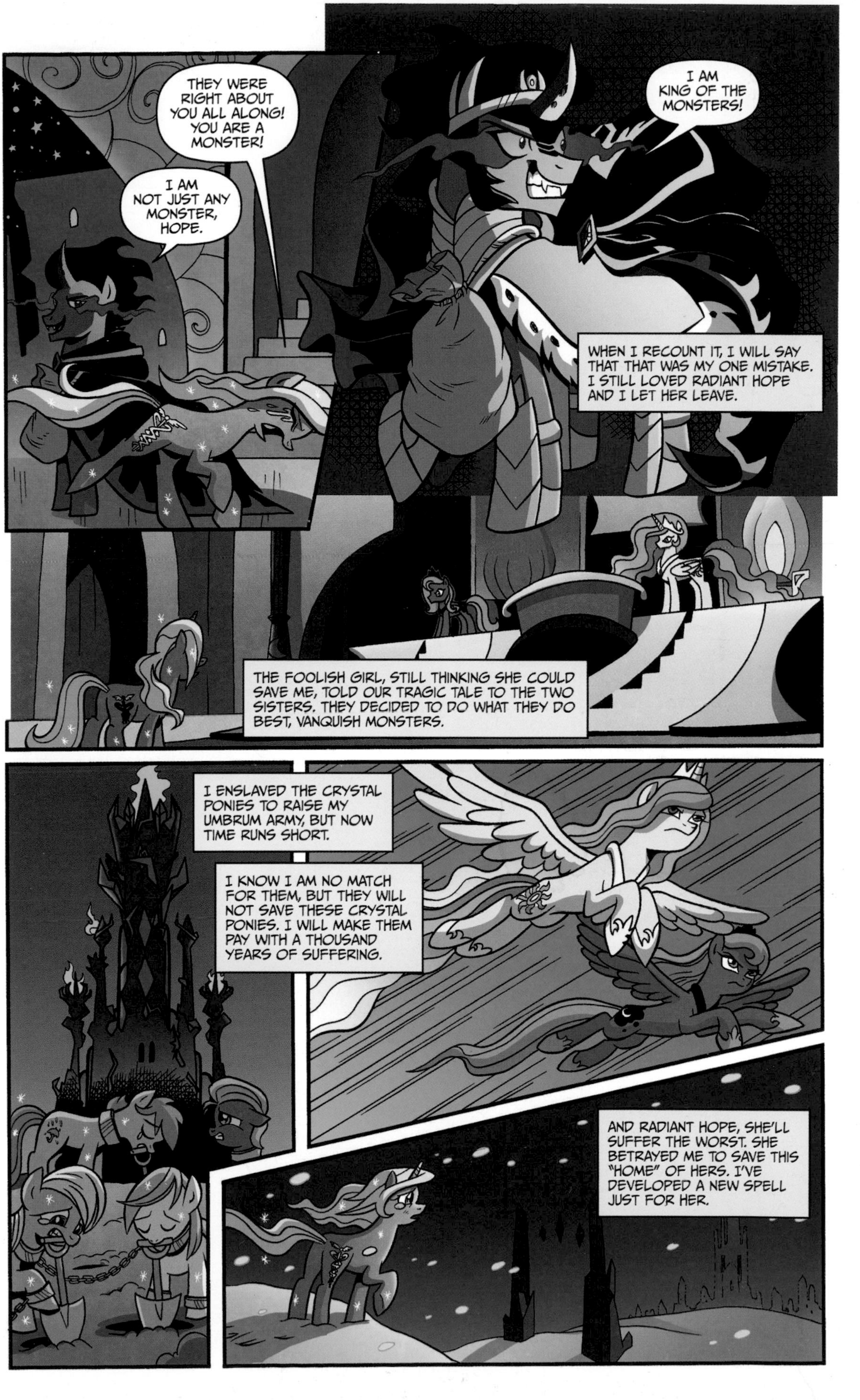
THEY WERE RIGHT ABOUT YOU ALL ALONG! YOU ARE A MONSTER!
I AM NOT JUST ANY MONSTER, HOPE.
I AM KING OF THE MONSTERS!
WHEN I RECOUNT IT, I WILL SAY THAT THAT WAS MY ONE MISTAKE. I STILL LOVED RADIANT HOPE AND I LET HER LEAVE.
THE FOOLISH GIRL, STILL THINKING SHE COULD SAVE ME, TOLD OUR TRAGIC TALE TO THE TWO SISTERS. THEY DECIDED TO DO WHAT THEY DO BEST, VANQUISH MONSTERS.
I ENSLAVED THE CRYSTAL PONIES TO RAISE MY UMBRUM ARMY, BUT NOW TIME RUNS SHORT.
I KNOW I AM NO MATCH FOR THEM, BUT THEY WILL NOT SAVE THESE CRYSTAL PONIES. I WILL MAKE THEM PAY WITH A THOUSAND YEARS OF SUFFERING.
AND RADIANT HOPE, SHE'LL SUFFER THE WORST. SHE BETRAYED ME TO SAVE THIS "HOME" OF HERS. I'VE DEVELOPED A NEW SPELL JUST FOR HER.

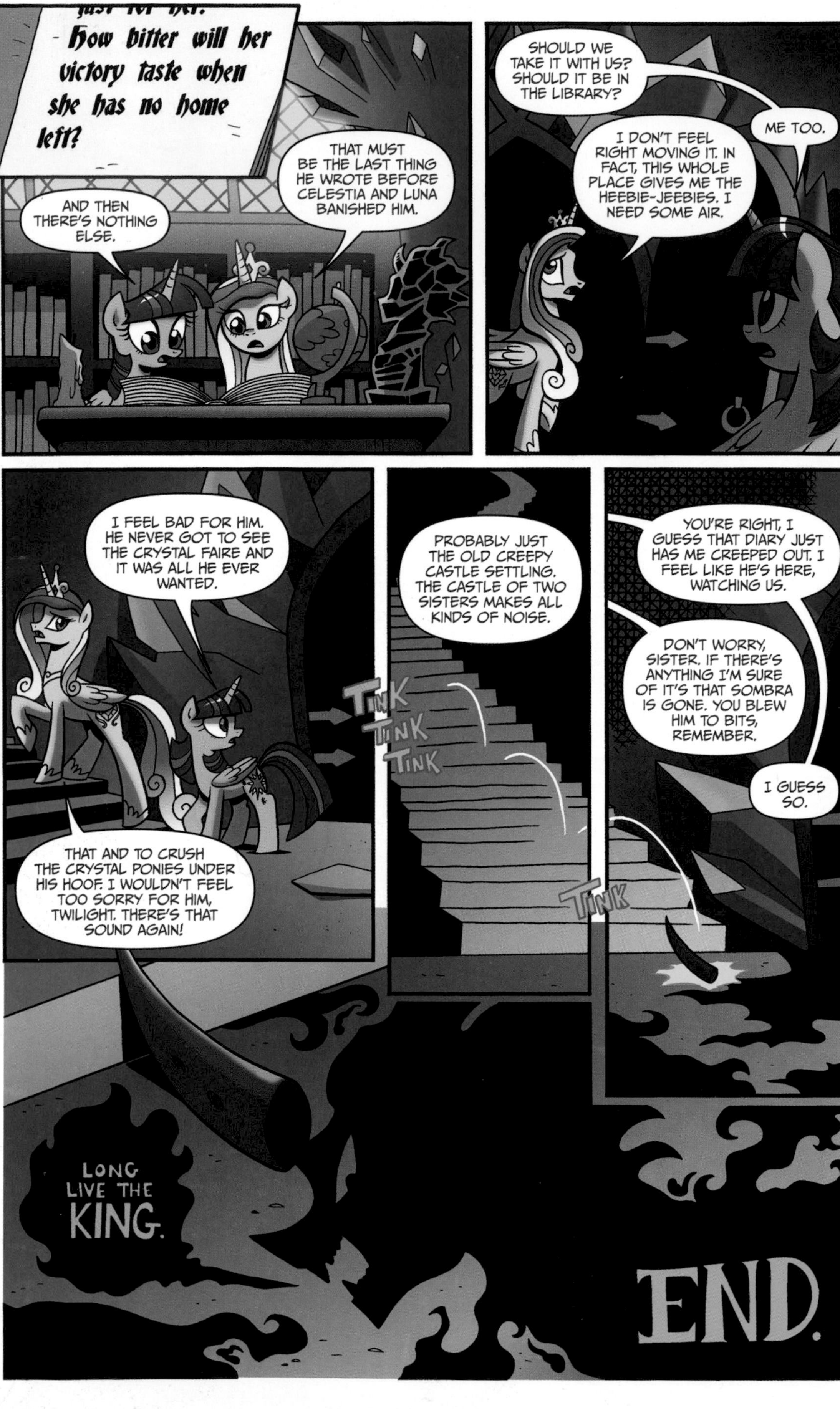
just for her.
How bitter will her victory taste when she has no home left?
AND THEN THERE'S NOTHING ELSE.
THAT MUST BE THE LAST THING HE WROTE BEFORE CELESTIA AND LUNA BANISHED HIM.
SHOULD WE TAKE IT WITH US? SHOULD IT BE IN THE LIBRARY?
I DON'T FEEL RIGHT MOVING IT. IN FACT, THIS WHOLE PLACE GIVES ME THE HEEBIE-JEEBIES. I NEED SOME AIR.
ME TOO.
I FEEL BAD FOR HIM. HE NEVER GOT TO SEE THE CRYSTAL FAIRE AND IT WAS ALL HE EVER WANTED.
THAT AND TO CRUSH THE CRYSTAL PONIES UNDER HIS HOOF. I WOULDN'T FEEL TOO SORRY FOR HIM, TWILIGHT. THERE'S THAT SOUND AGAIN!
TINK
TINK
TINK
PROBABLY JUST THE OLD CREEPY CASTLE SETTLING. THE CASTLE OF TWO SISTERS MAKES ALL KINDS OF NOISE.
TINK
YOU'RE RIGHT, I GUESS THAT DIARY JUST HAS ME CREEPED OUT. I FEEL LIKE HE'S HERE, WATCHING US.
DON'T WORRY, SISTER. IF THERE'S ANYTHING I'M SURE OF IT'S THAT SOMBRA IS GONE. YOU BLEW HIM TO BITS, REMEMBER.
I GUESS SO.
LONG LIVE THE KING.
END.

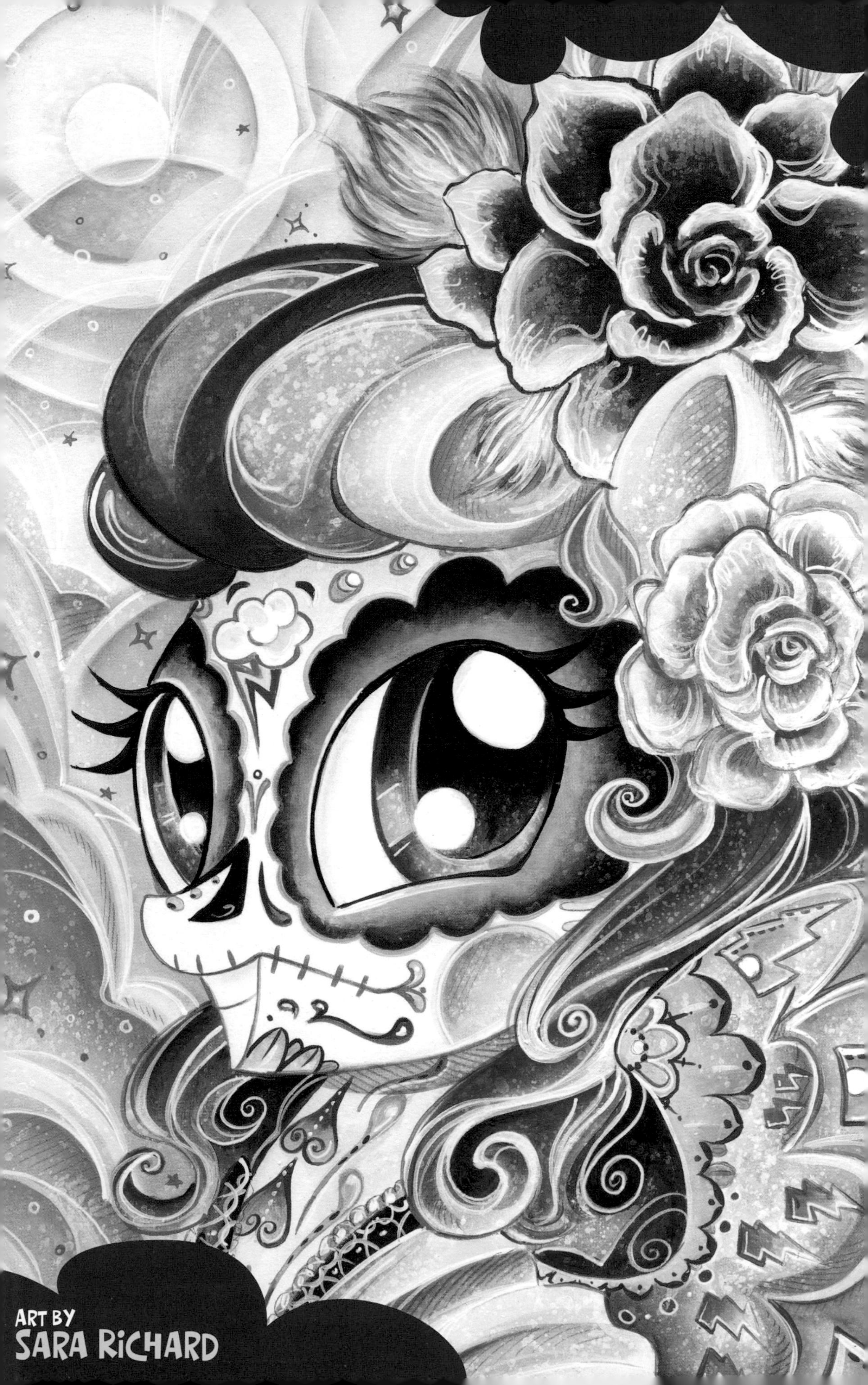
ART BY
SARA RICHARD

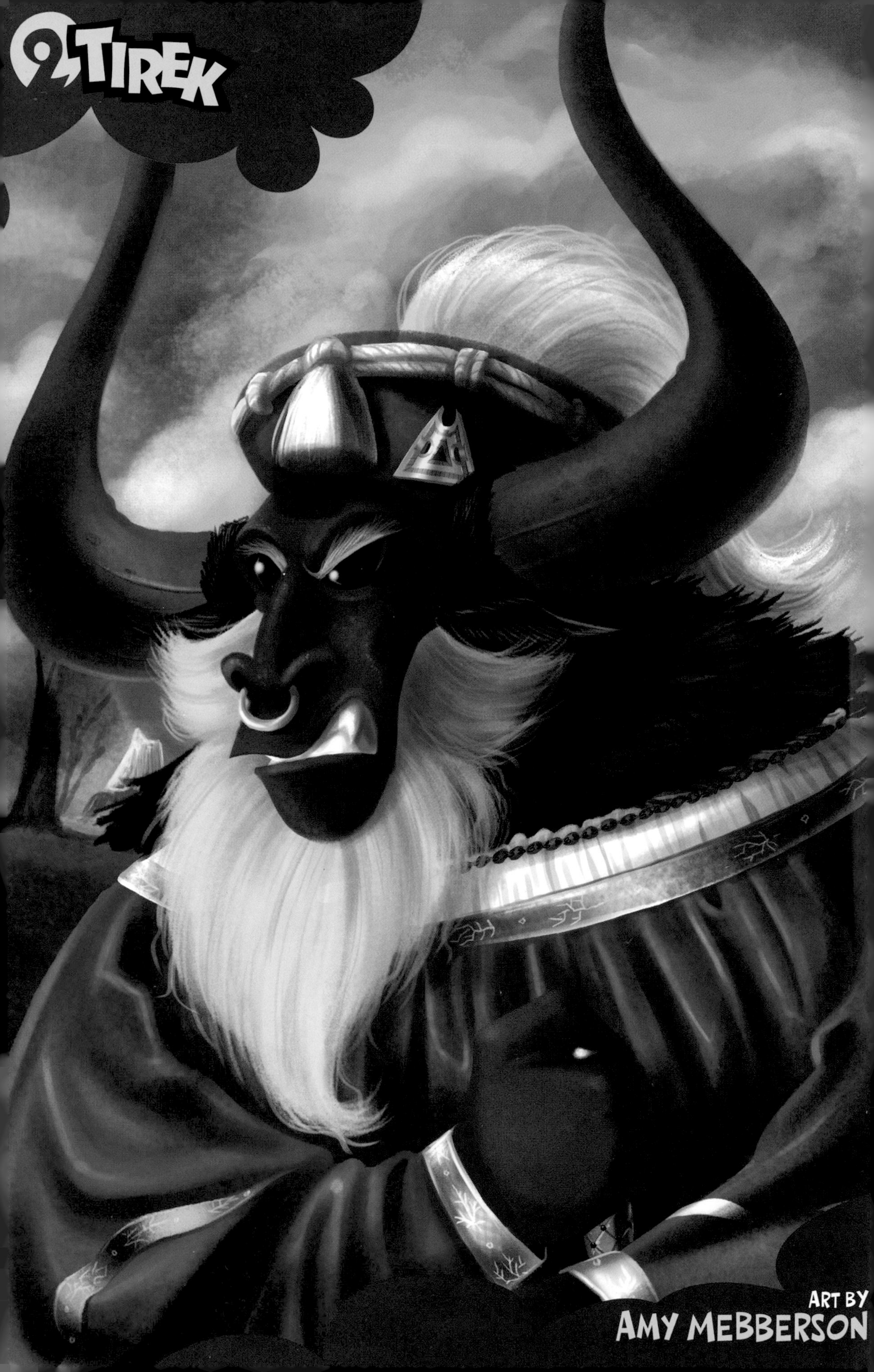
TIREK
ART BY
AMY MEBBERSON

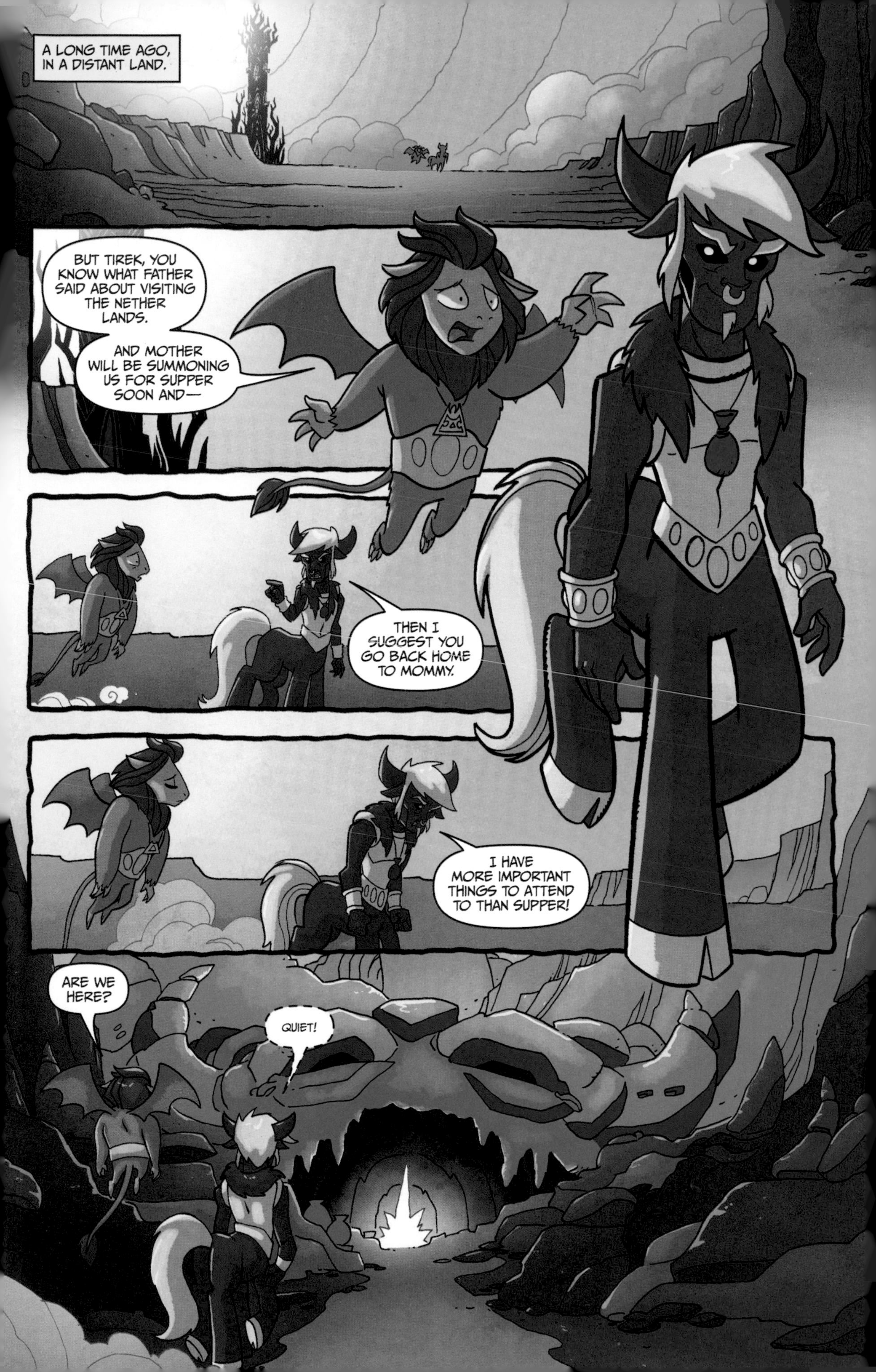
A LONG TIME AGO, IN A DISTANT LAND.
BUT TIREK, YOU KNOW WHAT FATHER SAID ABOUT VISITING THE NETHER LANDS.
AND MOTHER WILL BE SUMMONING US FOR SUPPER SOON AND—
THEN I SUGGEST YOU GO BACK HOME TO MOMMY.
I HAVE MORE IMPORTANT THINGS TO ATTEND TO THAN SUPPER!
ARE WE HERE?
QUIET!

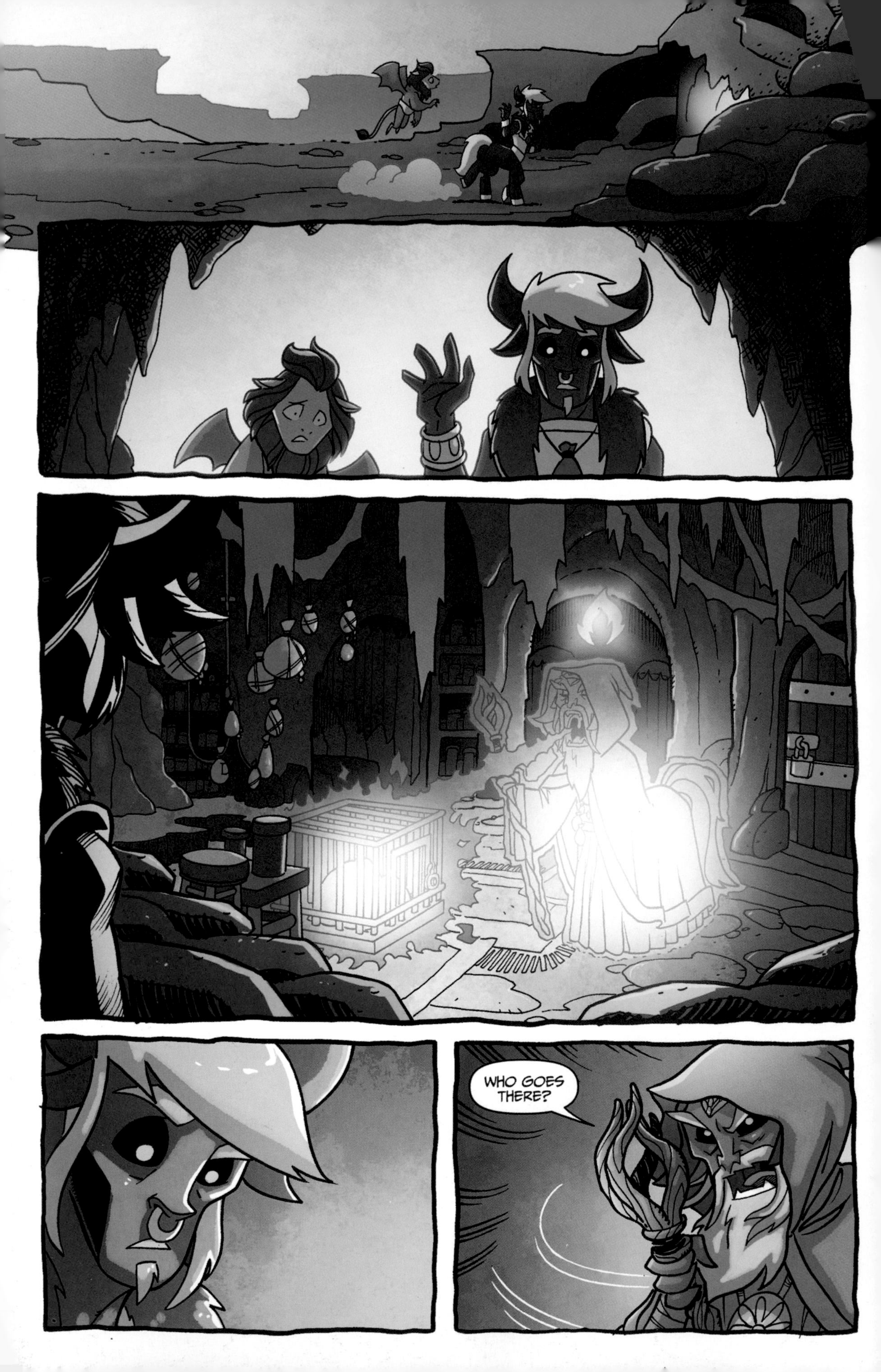
WHO GOES THERE?

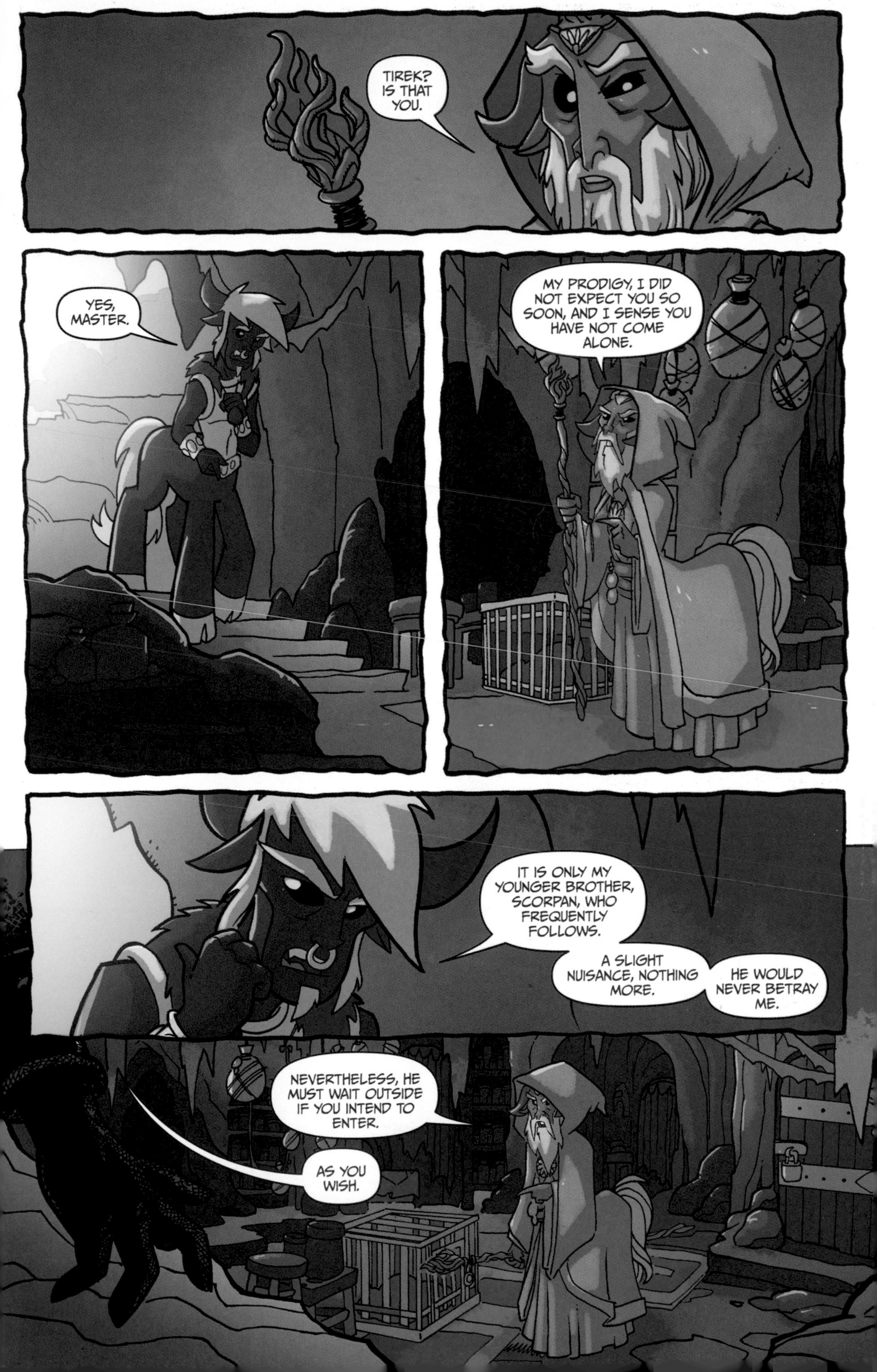
TIREK? IS THAT YOU.
YES, MASTER.
MY PRODIGY, I DID NOT EXPECT YOU SO SOON, AND I SENSE YOU HAVE NOT COME ALONE.
IT IS ONLY MY YOUNGER BROTHER, SCORPAN, WHO FREQUENTLY FOLLOWS.
A SLIGHT NUISANCE, NOTHING MORE.
HE WOULD NEVER BETRAY ME.
NEVERTHELESS, HE MUST WAIT OUTSIDE IF YOU INTEND TO ENTER.
AS YOU WISH.

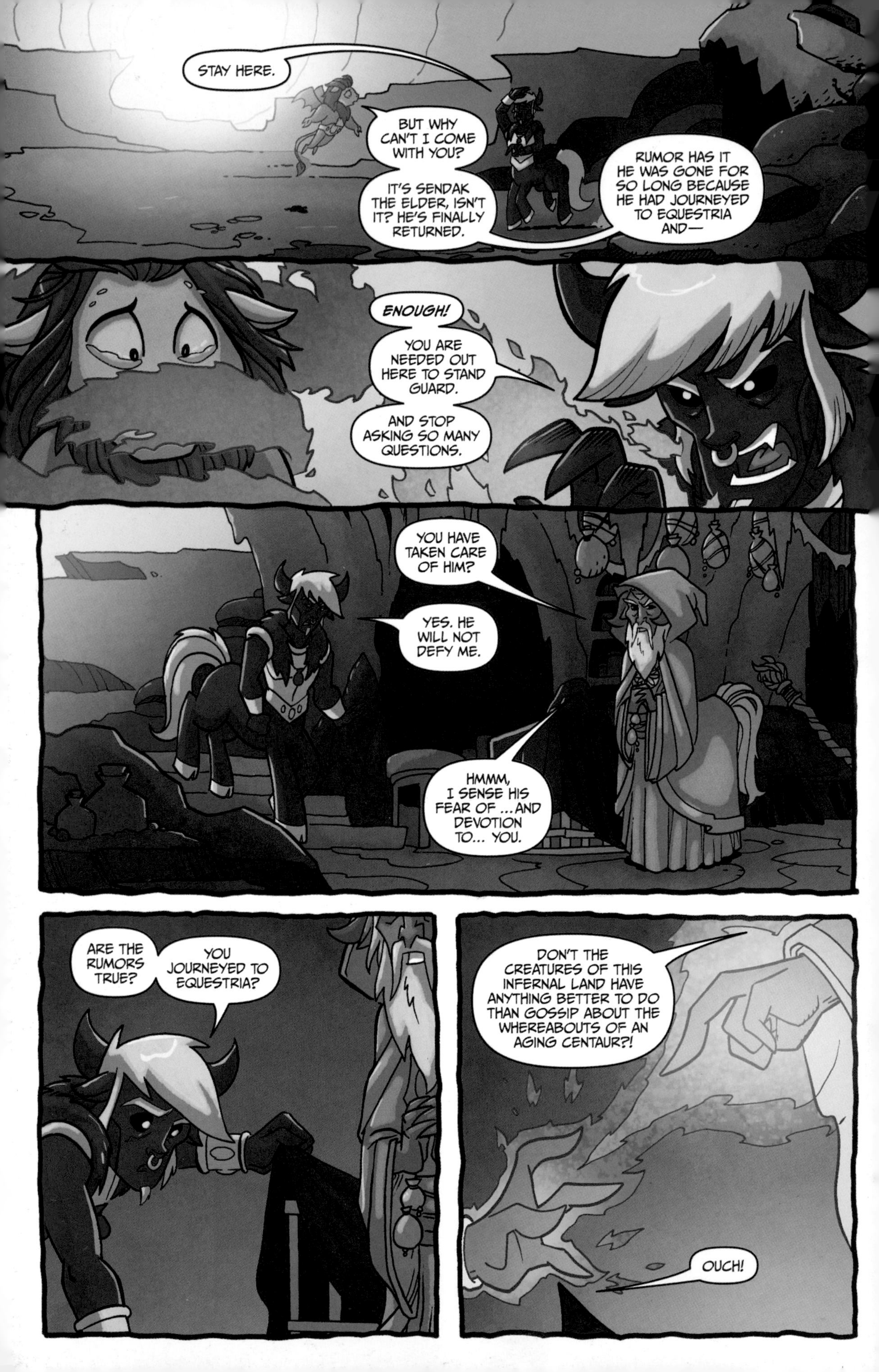
STAY HERE.
BUT WHY CAN'T I COME WITH YOU?
IT'S SENDAK THE ELDER, ISN'T IT? HE'S FINALLY RETURNED.
RUMOR HAS IT HE WAS GONE FOR SO LONG BECAUSE HE HAD JOURNEYED TO EQUESTRIA AND—
ENOUGH!
YOU ARE NEEDED OUT HERE TO STAND GUARD.
AND STOP ASKING SO MANY QUESTIONS.
YOU HAVE TAKEN CARE OF HIM?
YES. HE WILL NOT DEFY ME.
HMMM, I SENSE HIS FEAR OF ...AND DEVOTION TO... YOU.
ARE THE RUMORS TRUE?
YOU JOURNEYED TO EQUESTRIA?
DON'T THE CREATURES OF THIS INFERNAL LAND HAVE ANYTHING BETTER TO DO THAN GOSSIP ABOUT THE WHEREABOUTS OF AN AGING CENTAUR?!
OUCH!

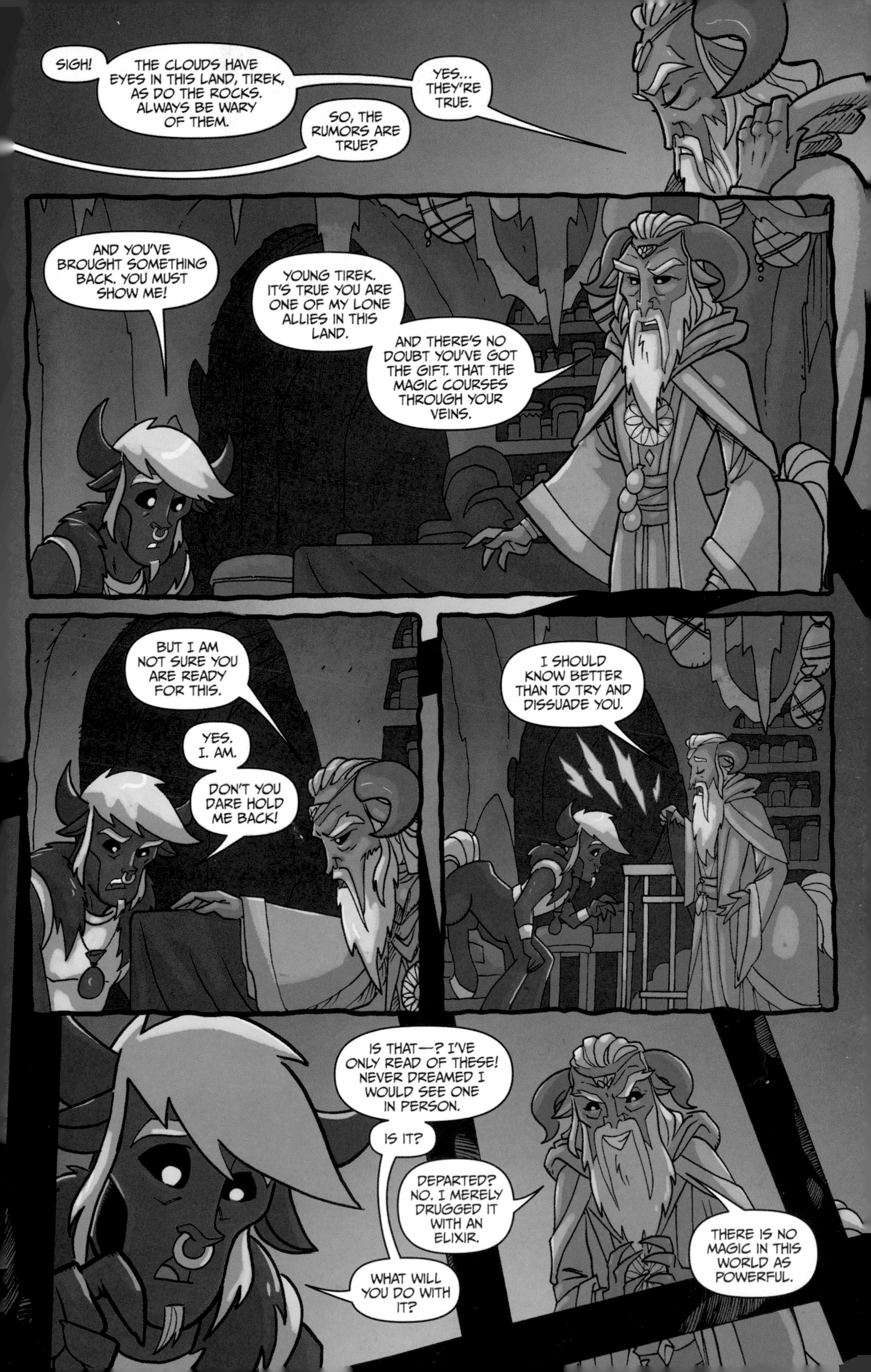
SIGH!
THE CLOUDS HAVE EYES IN THIS LAND, TIREK, AS DO THE ROCKS. ALWAYS BE WARY OF THEM.
SO, THE RUMORS ARE TRUE?
YES... THEY'RE TRUE.
AND YOU'VE BROUGHT SOMETHING BACK. YOU MUST SHOW ME!
YOUNG TIREK. IT'S TRUE YOU ARE ONE OF MY LONE ALLIES IN THIS LAND.
AND THERE'S NO DOUBT YOU'VE GOT THE GIFT. THAT THE MAGIC COURSES THROUGH YOUR VEINS.
BUT I AM NOT SURE YOU ARE READY FOR THIS.
YES. I. AM.
DON'T YOU DARE HOLD ME BACK!
I SHOULD KNOW BETTER THAN TO TRY AND DISSUADE YOU.
IS THAT—? I'VE ONLY READ OF THESE! NEVER DREAMED I WOULD SEE ONE IN PERSON.
IS IT?
DEPARTED? NO. I MERELY DRUGGED IT WITH AN ELIXIR.
WHAT WILL YOU DO WITH IT?
THERE IS NO MAGIC IN THIS WORLD AS POWERFUL.

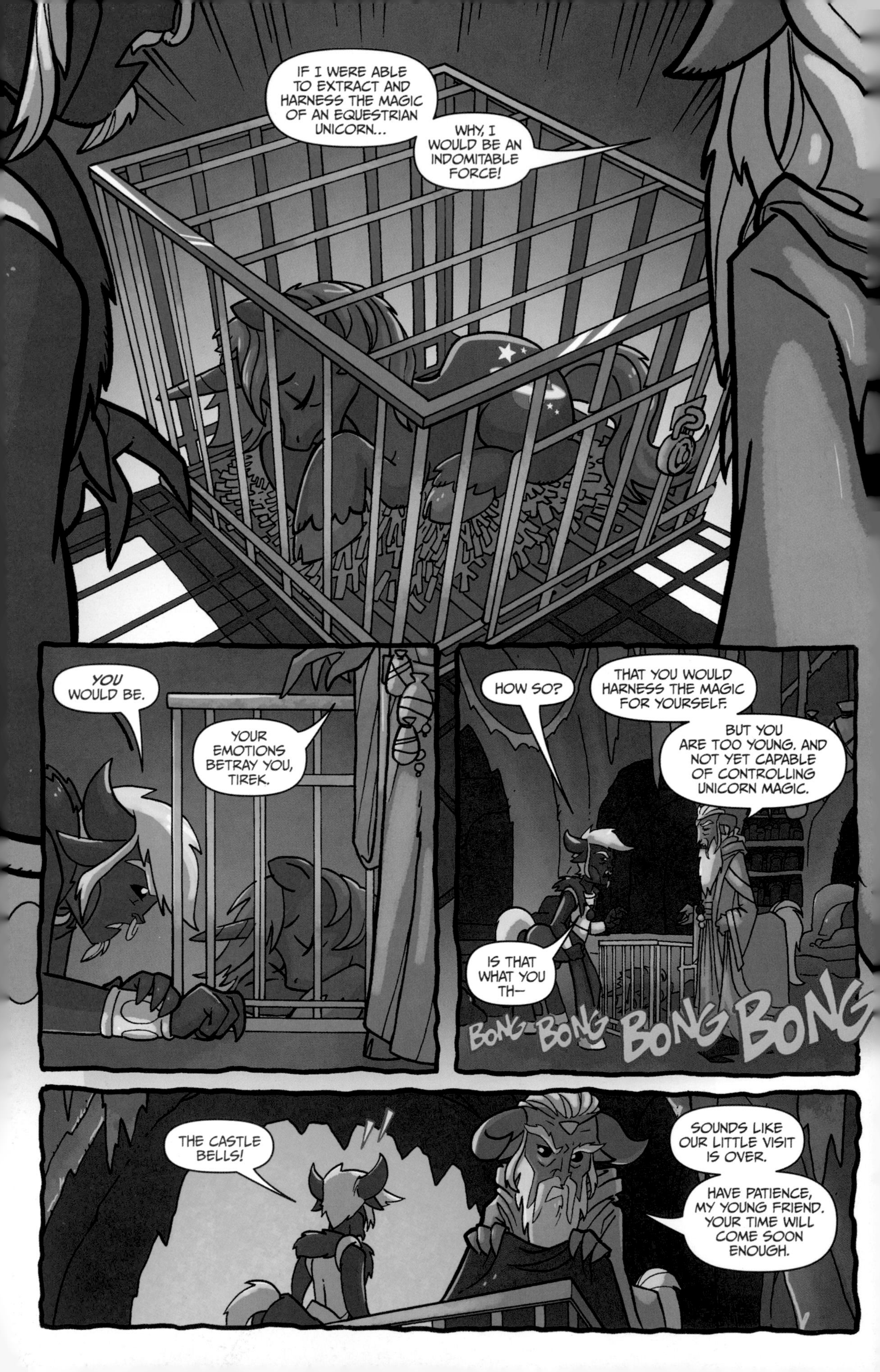
IF I WERE ABLE TO EXTRACT AND HARNESS THE MAGIC OF AN EQUESTRIAN UNICORN...
WHY, I WOULD BE AN INDOMITABLE FORCE!
YOU WOULD BE.
YOUR EMOTIONS BETRAY YOU, TIREK.
HOW SO?
THAT YOU WOULD HARNESS THE MAGIC FOR YOURSELF.
BUT YOU ARE TOO YOUNG. AND NOT YET CAPABLE OF CONTROLLING UNICORN MAGIC.
IS THAT WHAT YOU TH—
BONG BONG BONG BONG
THE CASTLE BELLS!
SOUNDS LIKE OUR LITTLE VISIT IS OVER.
HAVE PATIENCE, MY YOUNG FRIEND. YOUR TIME WILL COME SOON ENOUGH.

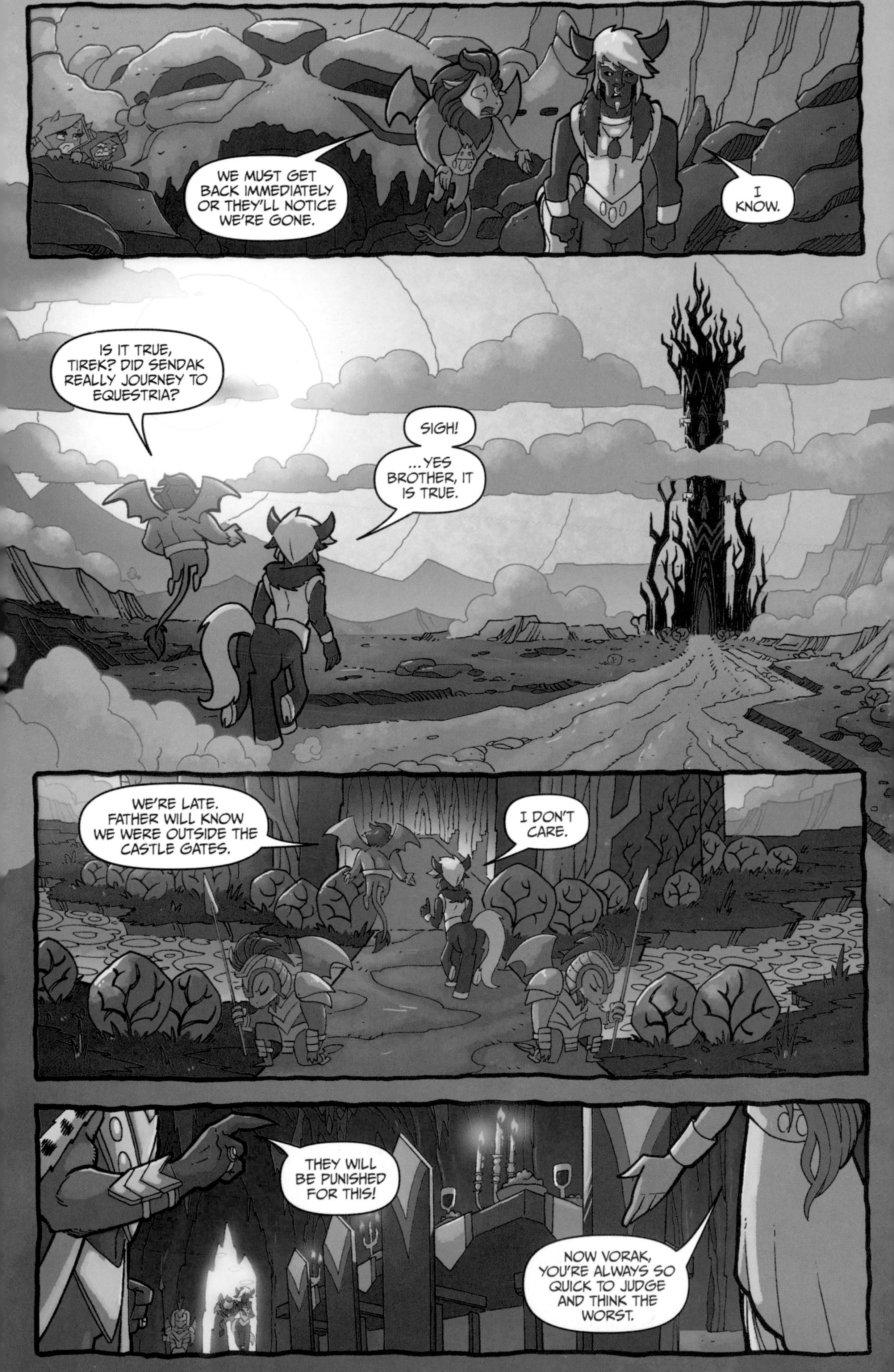
WE MUST GET BACK IMMEDIATELY OR THEY'LL NOTICE WE'RE GONE.
I KNOW.
IS IT TRUE, TIREK? DID SENDAK REALLY JOURNEY TO EQUESTRIA?
SIGH!
...YES BROTHER, IT IS TRUE.
WE'RE LATE. FATHER WILL KNOW WE WERE OUTSIDE THE CASTLE GATES.
I DON'T CARE.
THEY WILL BE PUNISHED FOR THIS!
NOW VORAK, YOU'RE ALWAYS SO QUICK TO JUDGE AND THINK THE WORST.

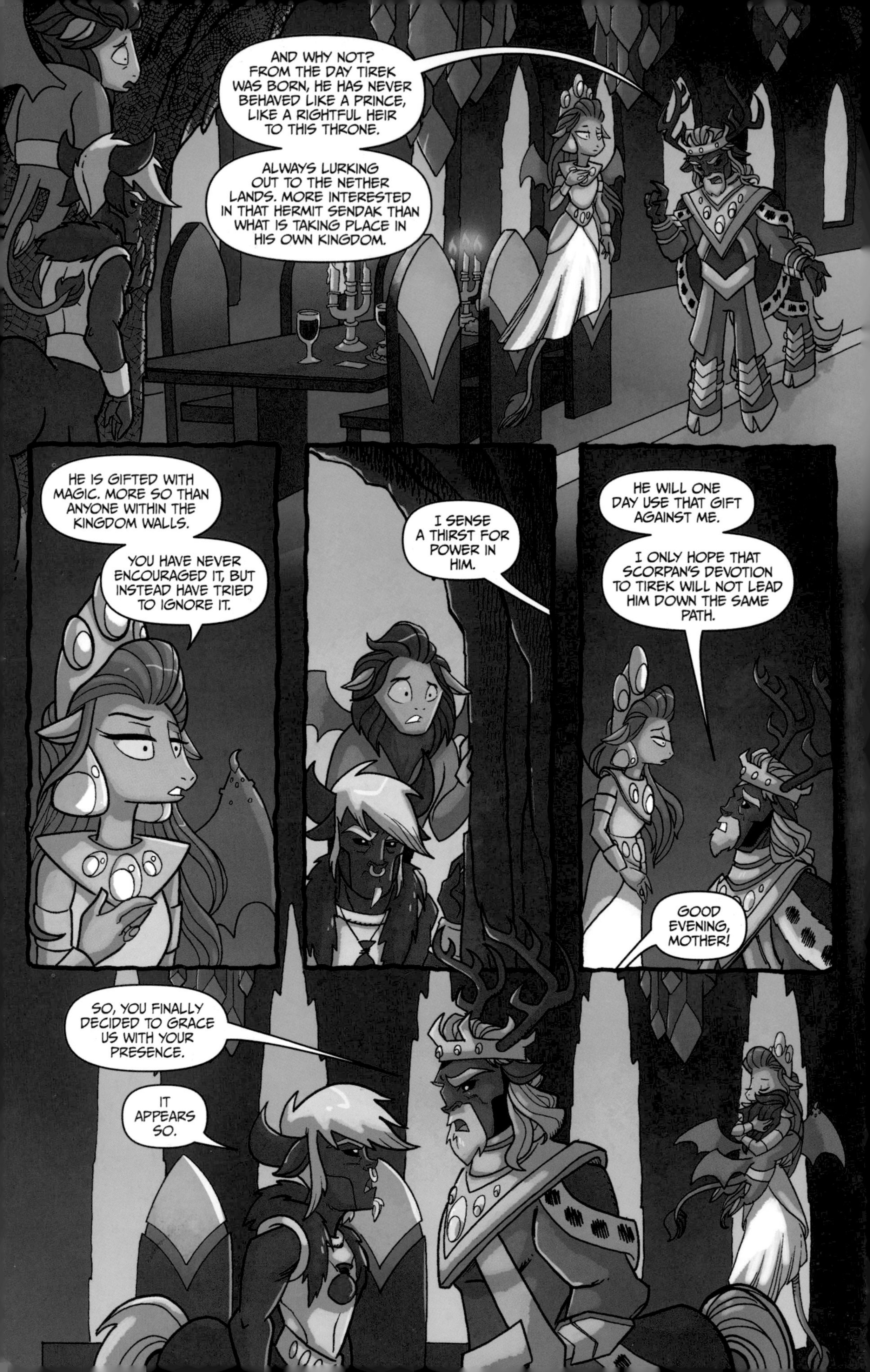
AND WHY NOT? FROM THE DAY TIREK WAS BORN, HE HAS NEVER BEHAVED LIKE A PRINCE, LIKE A RIGHTFUL HEIR TO THIS THRONE.
ALWAYS LURKING OUT TO THE NETHER LANDS. MORE INTERESTED IN THAT HERMIT SENDAK THAN WHAT IS TAKING PLACE IN HIS OWN KINGDOM.
HE IS GIFTED WITH MAGIC. MORE SO THAN ANYONE WITHIN THE KINGDOM WALLS.
YOU HAVE NEVER ENCOURAGED IT, BUT INSTEAD HAVE TRIED TO IGNORE IT.
I SENSE A THIRST FOR POWER IN HIM.
HE WILL ONE DAY USE THAT GIFT AGAINST ME.
I ONLY HOPE THAT SCORPAN'S DEVOTION TO TIREK WILL NOT LEAD HIM DOWN THE SAME PATH.
GOOD EVENING, MOTHER!
SO, YOU FINALLY DECIDED TO GRACE US WITH YOUR PRESENCE.
IT APPEARS SO.

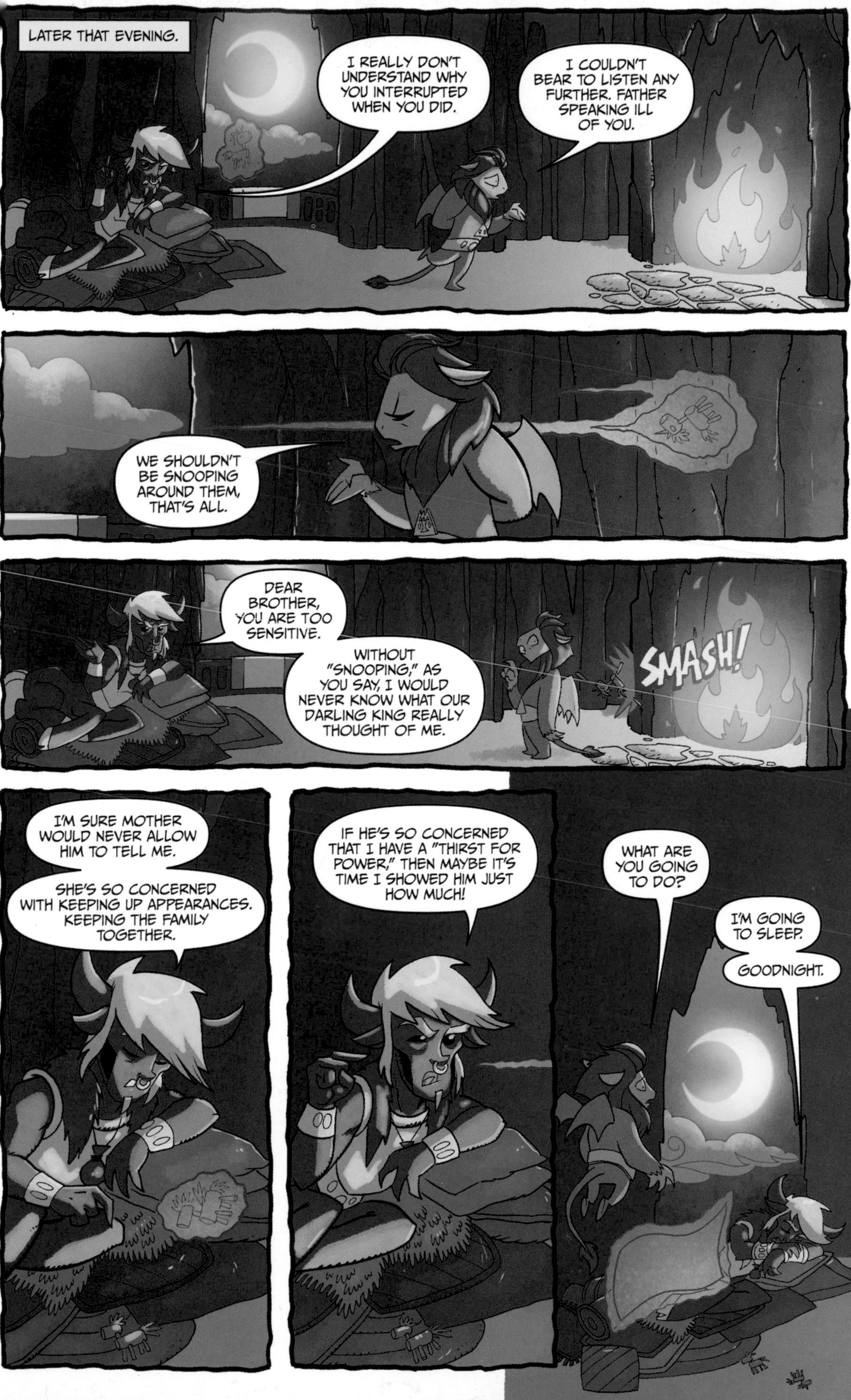
LATER THAT EVENING.
I REALLY DON'T UNDERSTAND WHY YOU INTERRUPTED WHEN YOU DID.
I COULDN'T BEAR TO LISTEN ANY FURTHER. FATHER SPEAKING ILL OF YOU.
WE SHOULDN'T BE SNOOPING AROUND THEM, THAT'S ALL.
DEAR BROTHER, YOU ARE TOO SENSITIVE.
WITHOUT "SNOOPING," AS YOU SAY, I WOULD NEVER KNOW WHAT OUR DARLING KING REALLY THOUGHT OF ME.
SMASH!
I'M SURE MOTHER WOULD NEVER ALLOW HIM TO TELL ME.
SHE'S SO CONCERNED WITH KEEPING UP APPEARANCES. KEEPING THE FAMILY TOGETHER.
IF HE'S SO CONCERNED THAT I HAVE A "THIRST FOR POWER," THEN MAYBE IT'S TIME I SHOWED HIM JUST HOW MUCH!
WHAT ARE YOU GOING TO DO?
I'M GOING TO SLEEP.
GOODNIGHT.

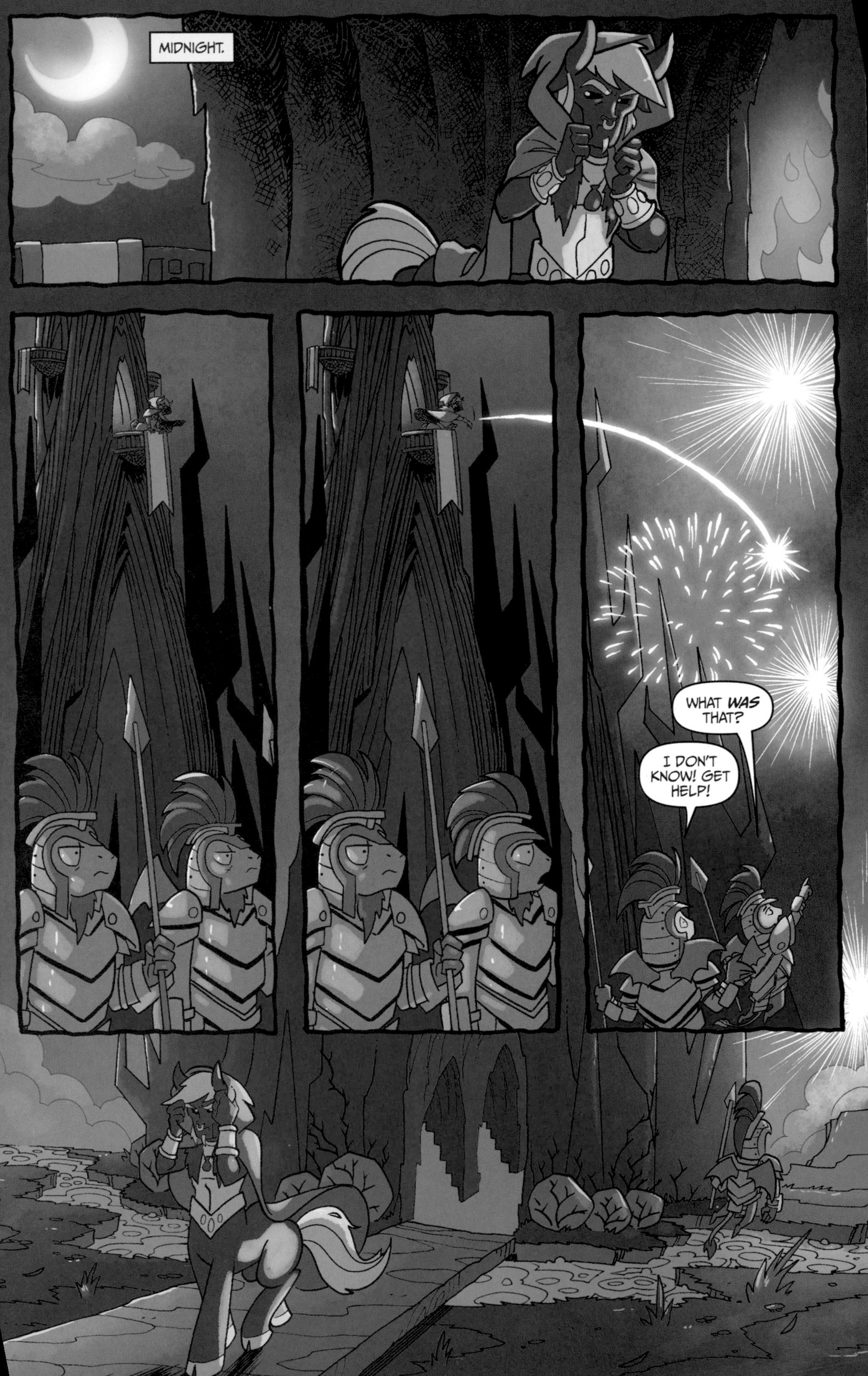
MIDNIGHT.
WHAT WAS THAT?
I DON'T KNOW! GET HELP!

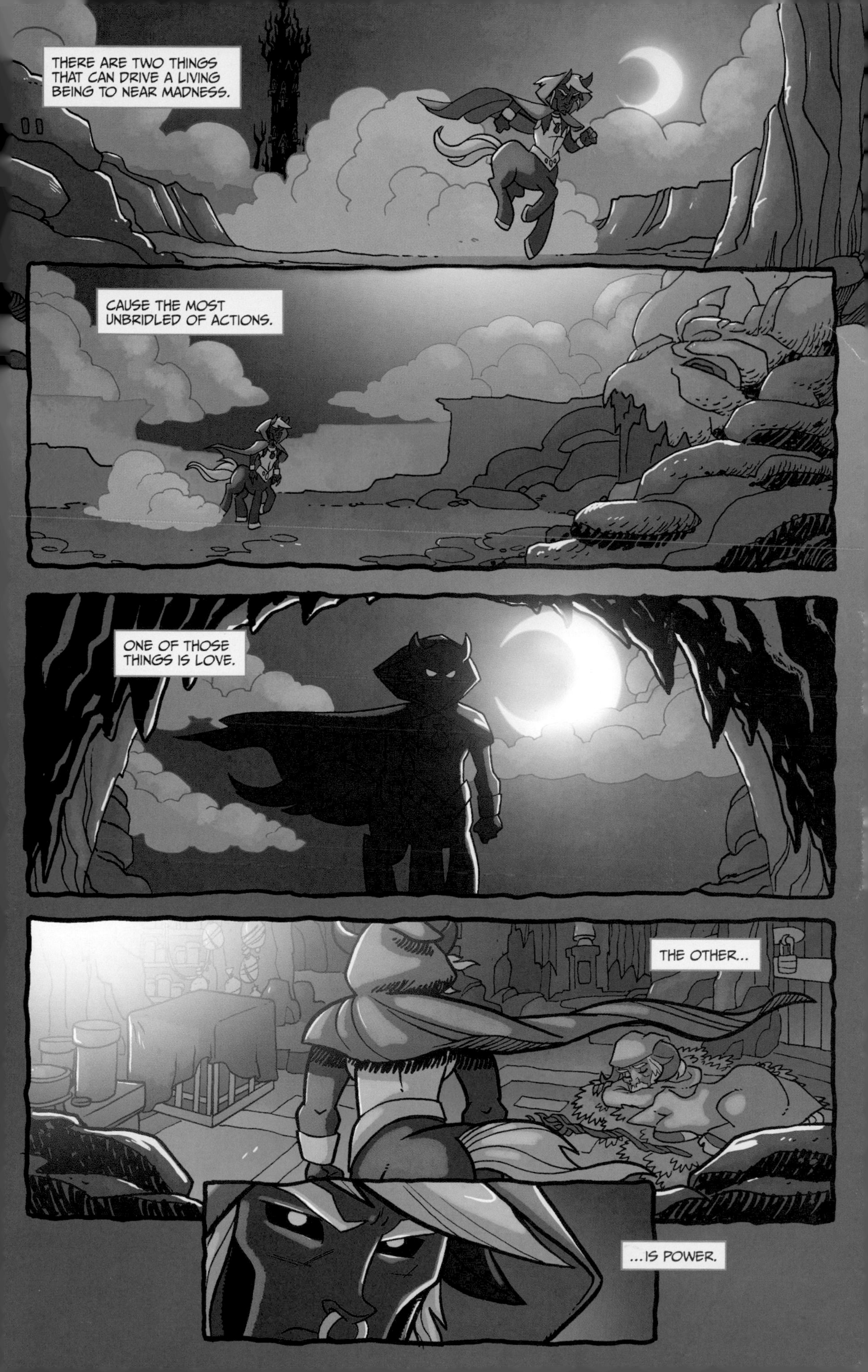

THERE ARE TWO THINGS THAT CAN DRIVE A LIVING BEING TO NEAR MADNESS.
CAUSE THE MOST UNBRIDLED OF ACTIONS.
ONE OF THOSE THINGS IS LOVE.
THE OTHER...
...IS POWER.

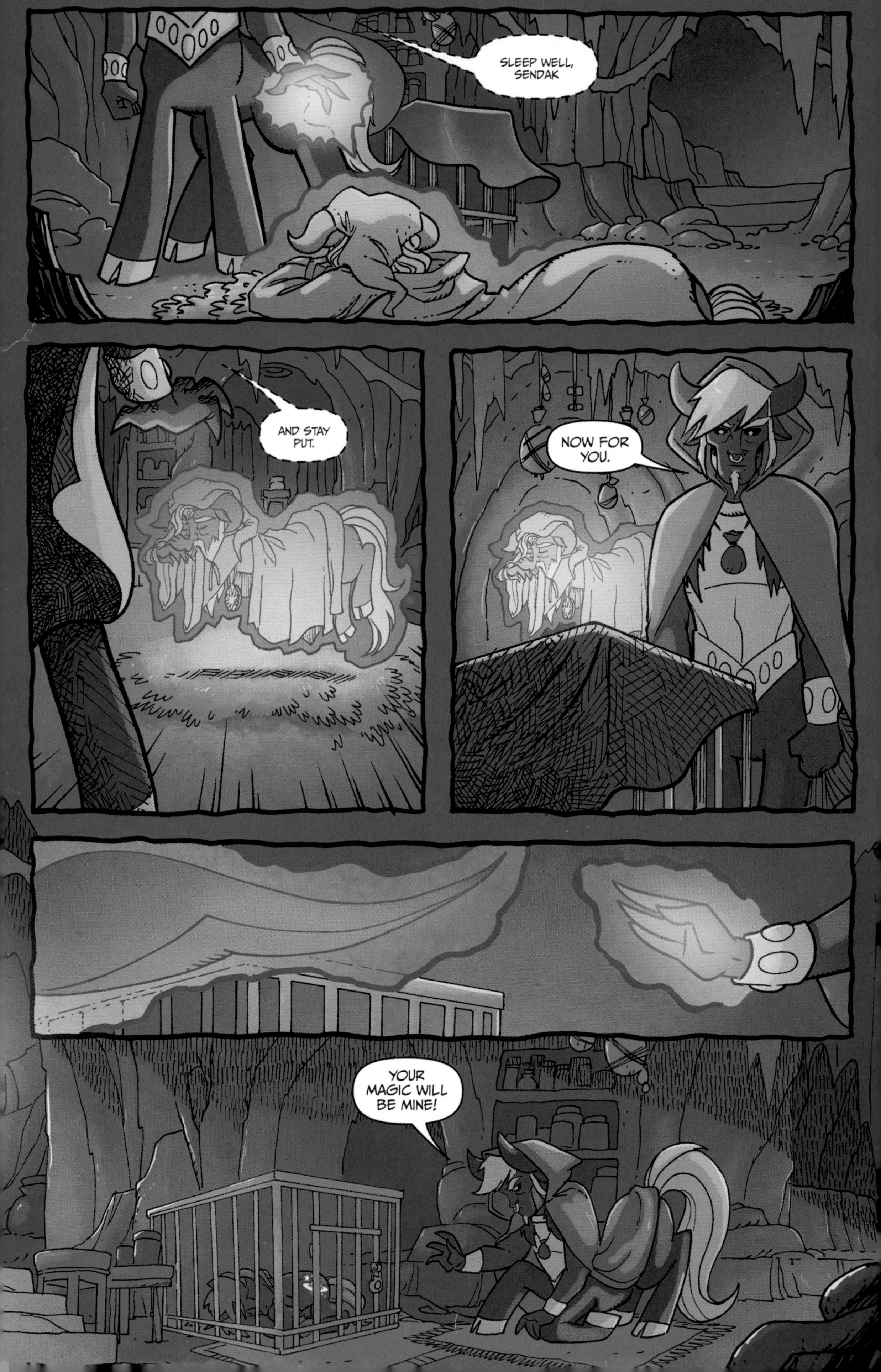
SLEEP WELL, SENDAK
AND STAY PUT.
NOW FOR YOU.
YOUR MAGIC WILL BE MINE!

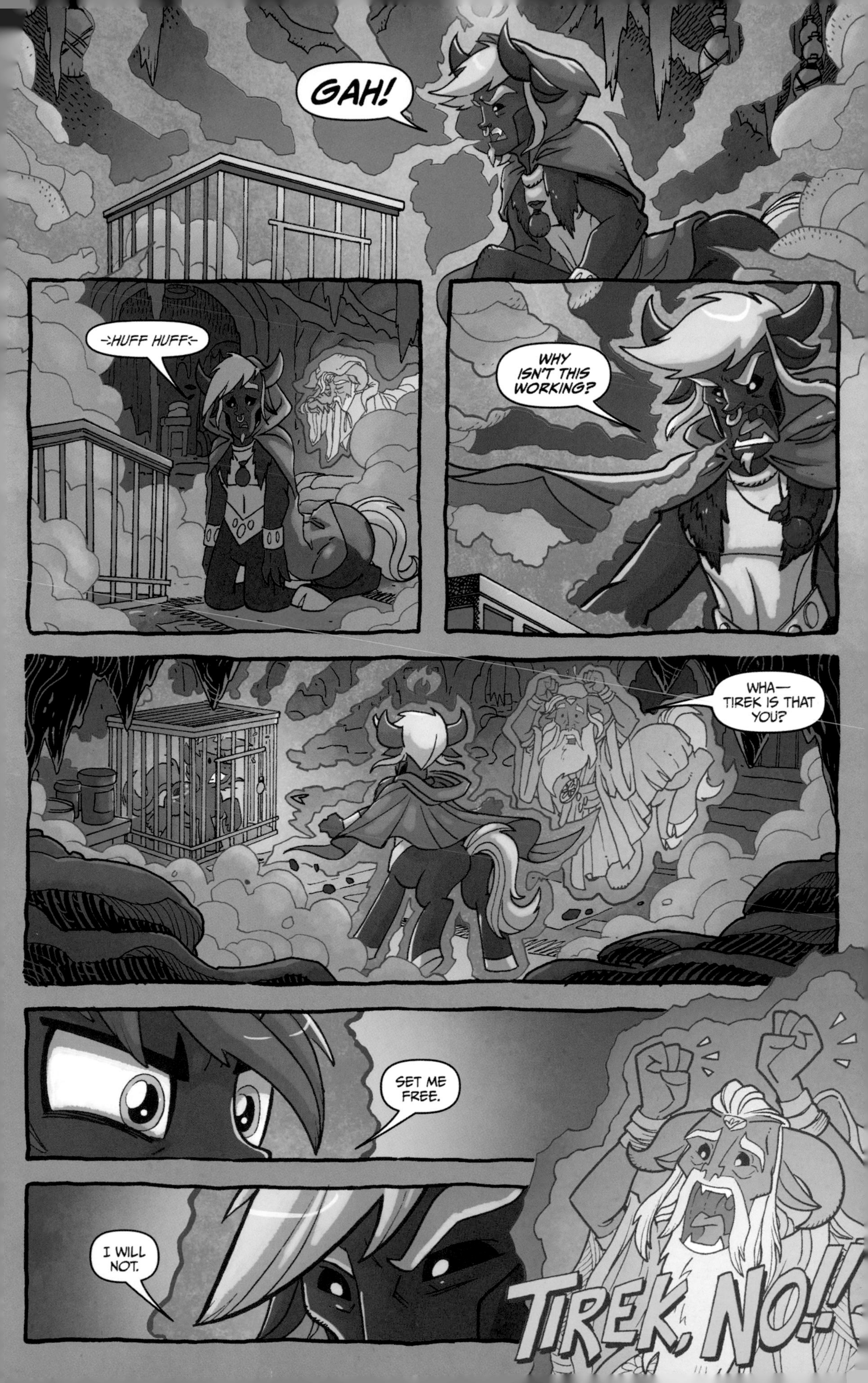
GAH!
~HUFF HUFF~
WHY ISN'T THIS WORKING?
WHA— TIREK IS THAT YOU?
SET ME FREE.
I WILL NOT.
TIREK, NO!!

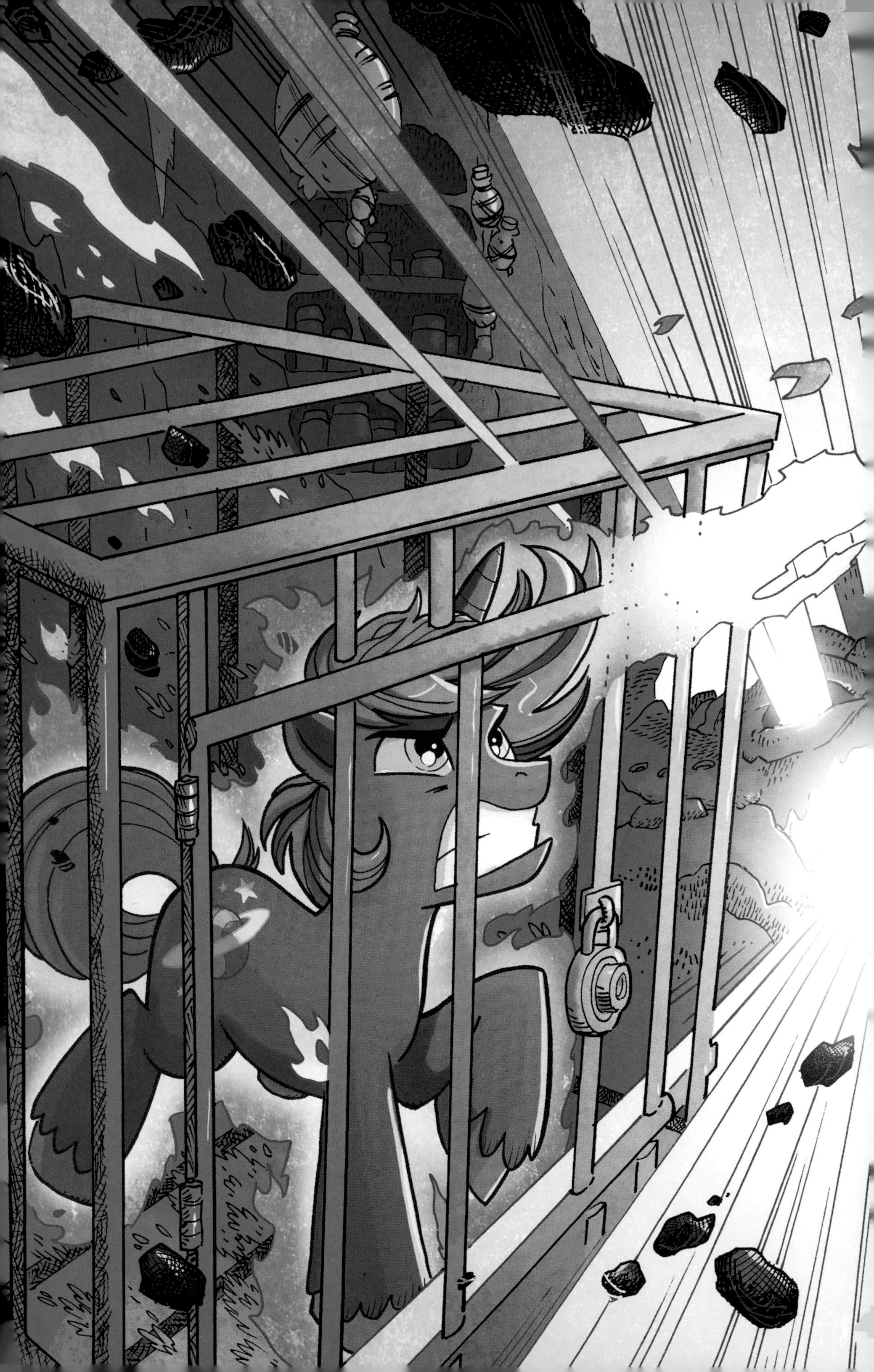

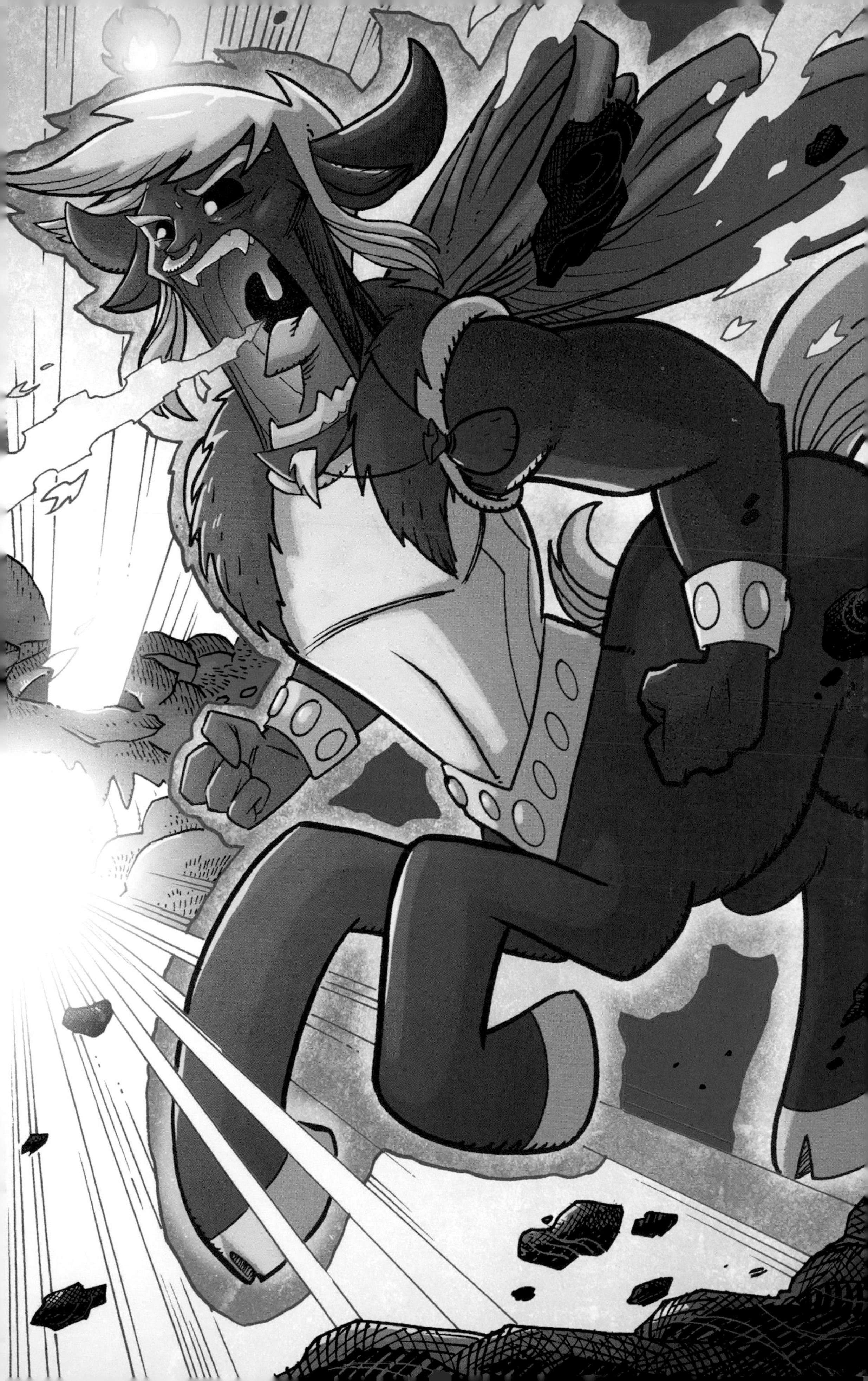

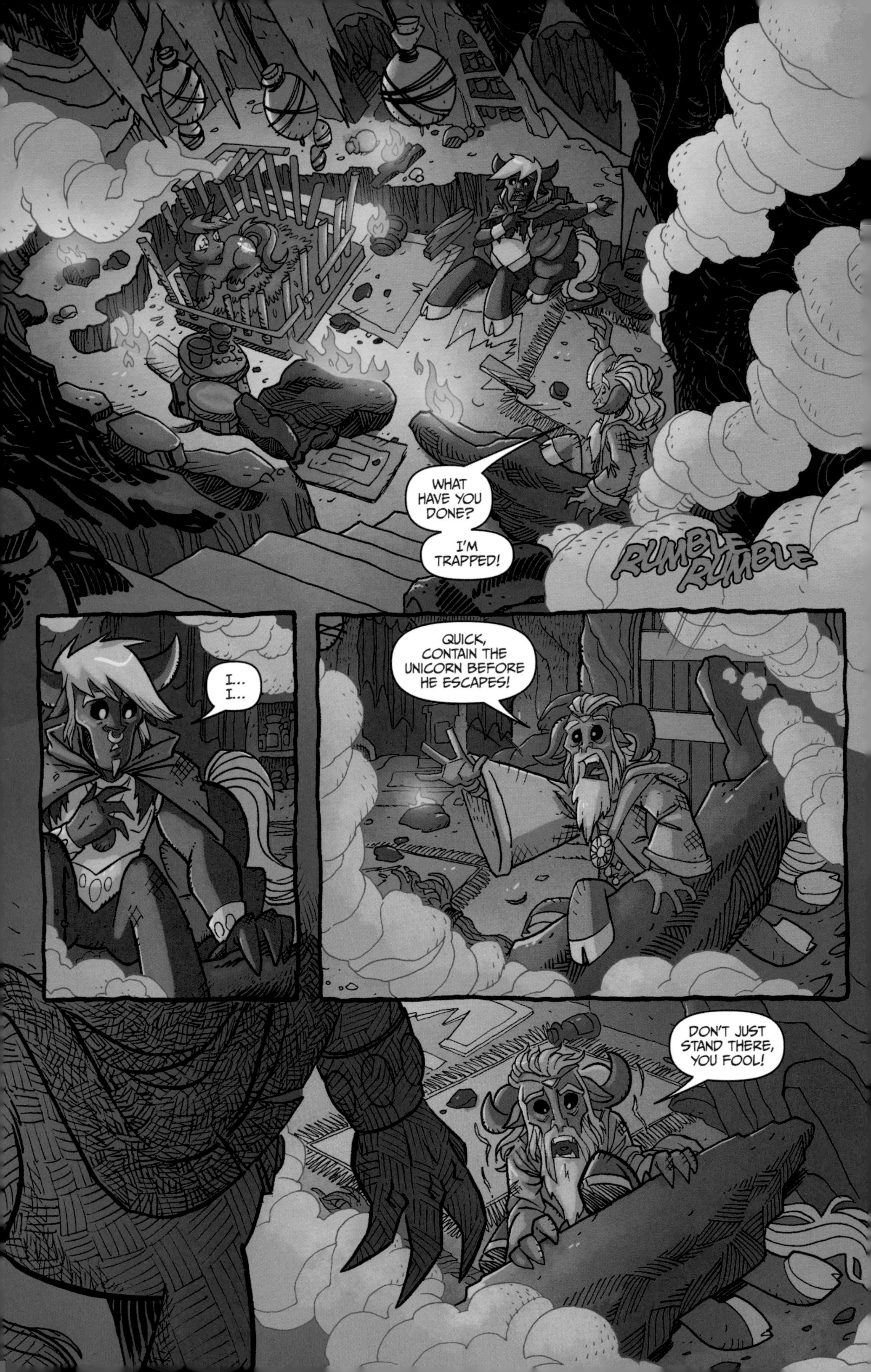
WHAT HAVE YOU DONE?
I'M TRAPPED!
RUMBLE RUMBLE
I... I...
QUICK, CONTAIN THE UNICORN BEFORE HE ESCAPES!
DON'T JUST STAND THERE, YOU FOOL!

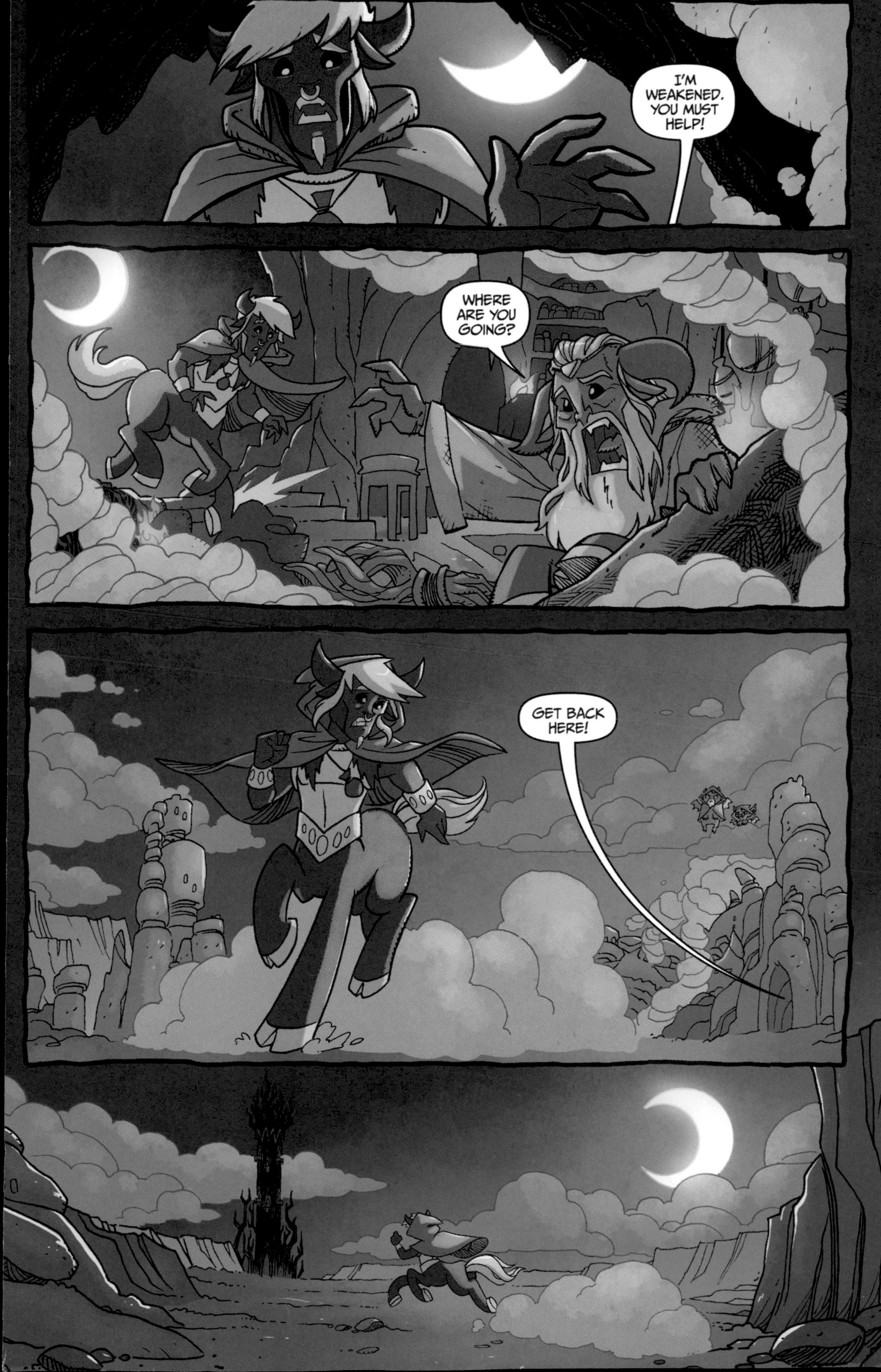
I'M WEAKENED. YOU MUST HELP!
WHERE ARE YOU GOING?
GET BACK HERE!

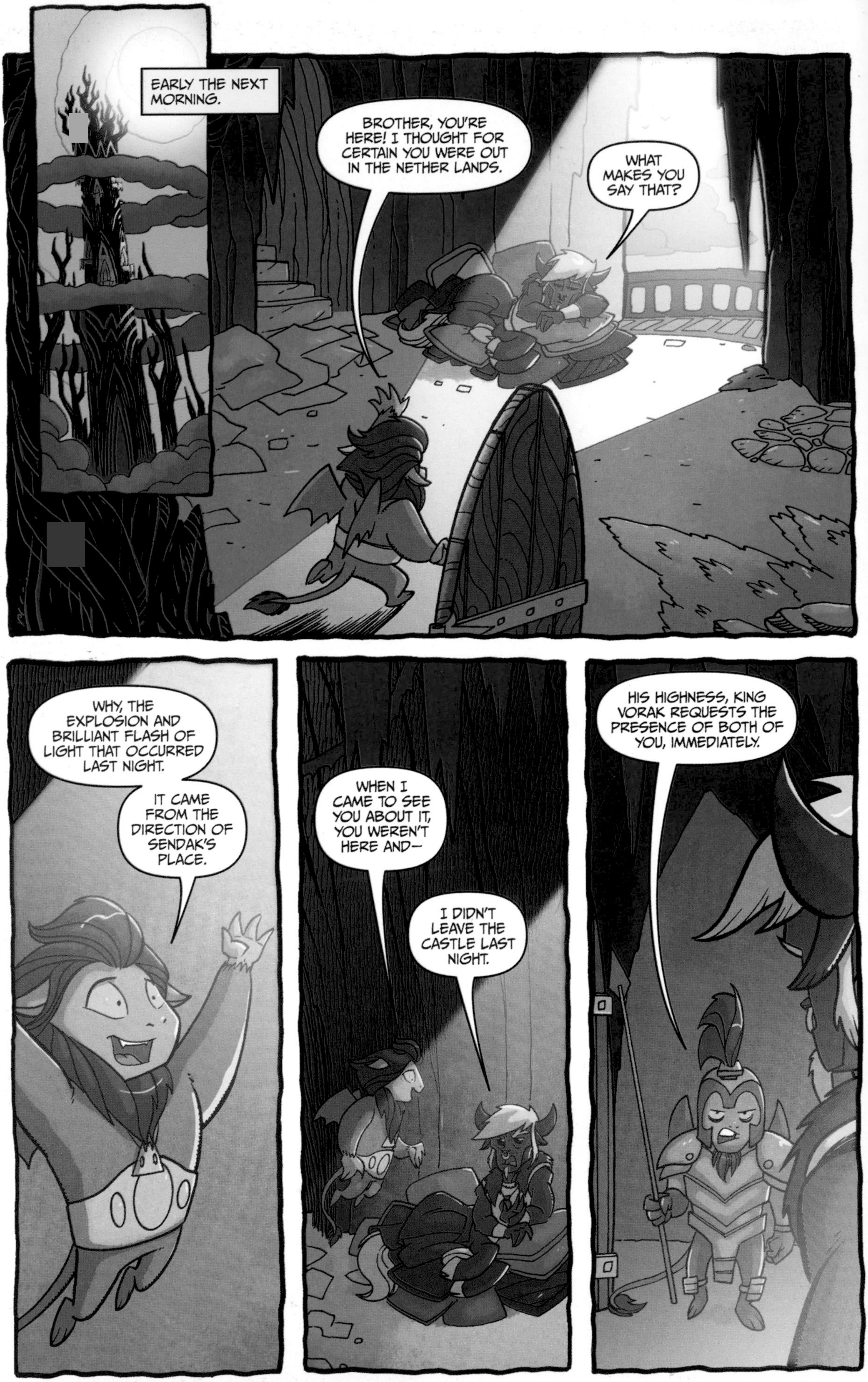

EARLY THE NEXT MORNING.
BROTHER, YOU'RE HERE! I THOUGHT FOR CERTAIN YOU WERE OUT IN THE NETHER LANDS.
WHAT MAKES YOU SAY THAT?
WHY, THE EXPLOSION AND BRILLIANT FLASH OF LIGHT THAT OCCURRED LAST NIGHT.
IT CAME FROM THE DIRECTION OF SENDAK'S PLACE.
WHEN I CAME TO SEE YOU ABOUT IT, YOU WEREN'T HERE AND—
I DIDN'T LEAVE THE CASTLE LAST NIGHT.
HIS HIGHNESS, KING VORAK REQUESTS THE PRESENCE OF BOTH OF YOU, IMMEDIATELY.

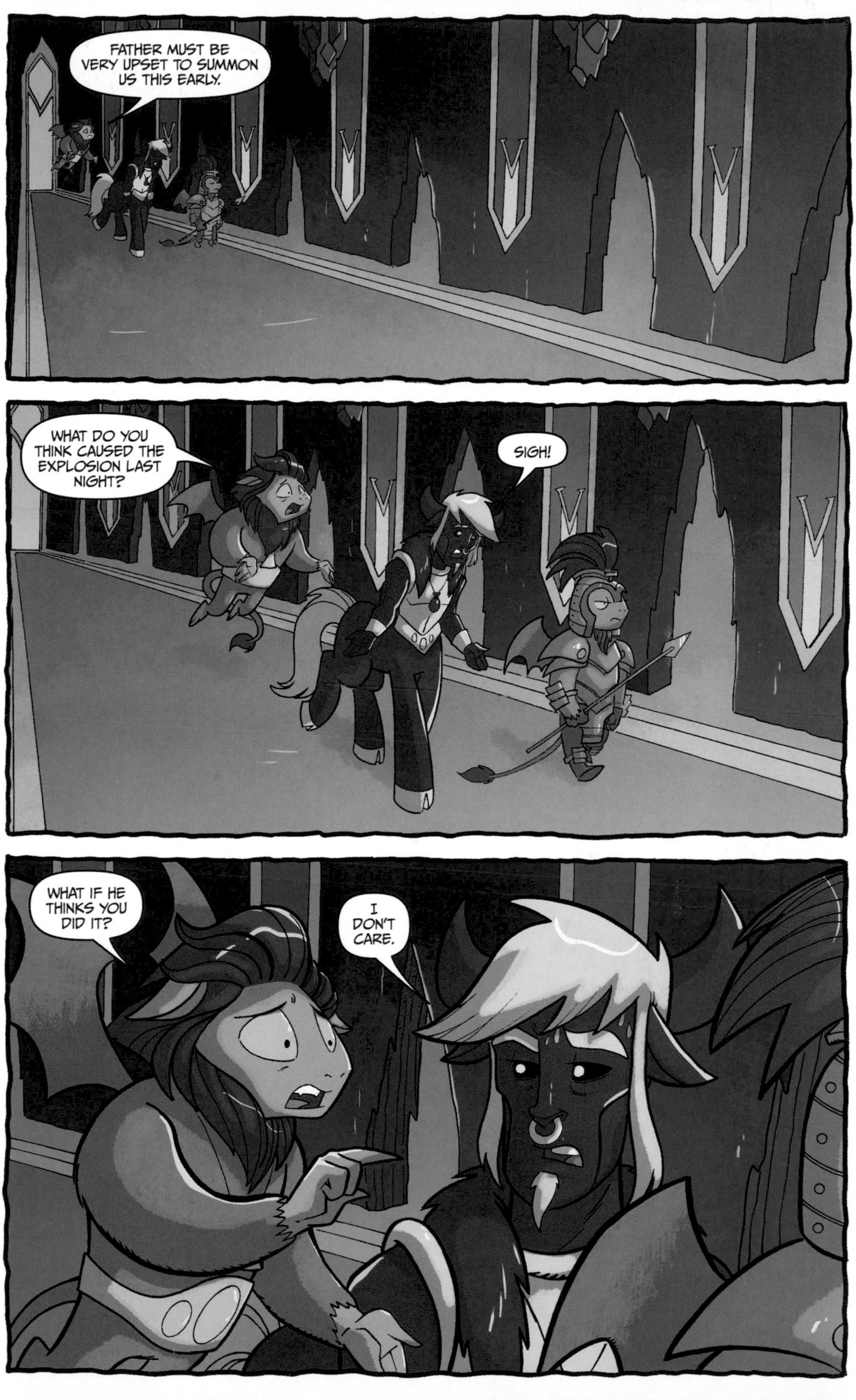
FATHER MUST BE VERY UPSET TO SUMMON US THIS EARLY.
WHAT DO YOU THINK CAUSED THE EXPLOSION LAST NIGHT?
SIGH!
WHAT IF HE THINKS YOU DID IT?
I DON'T CARE.

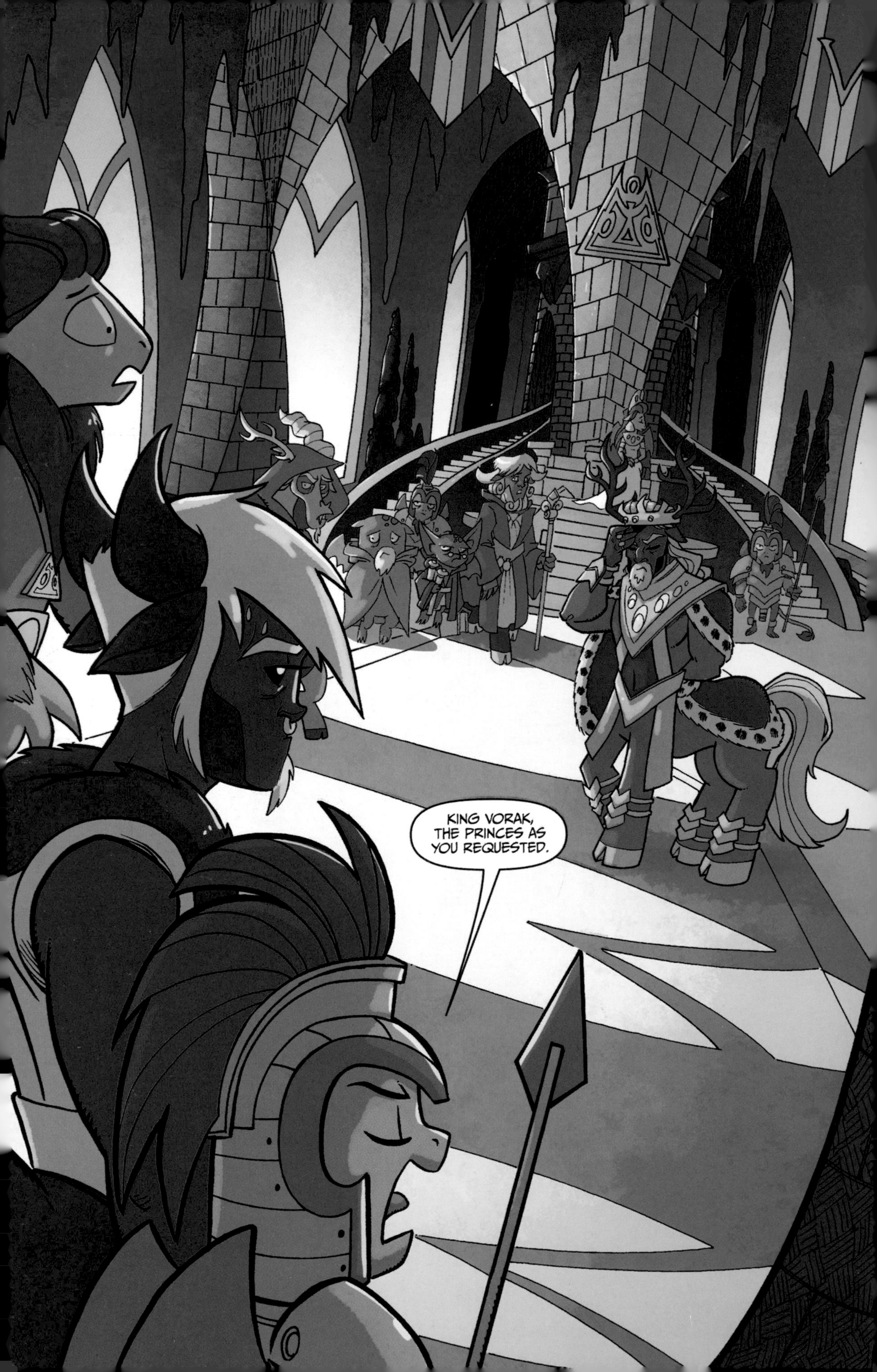
KING VORAK, THE PRINCES AS YOU REQUESTED.

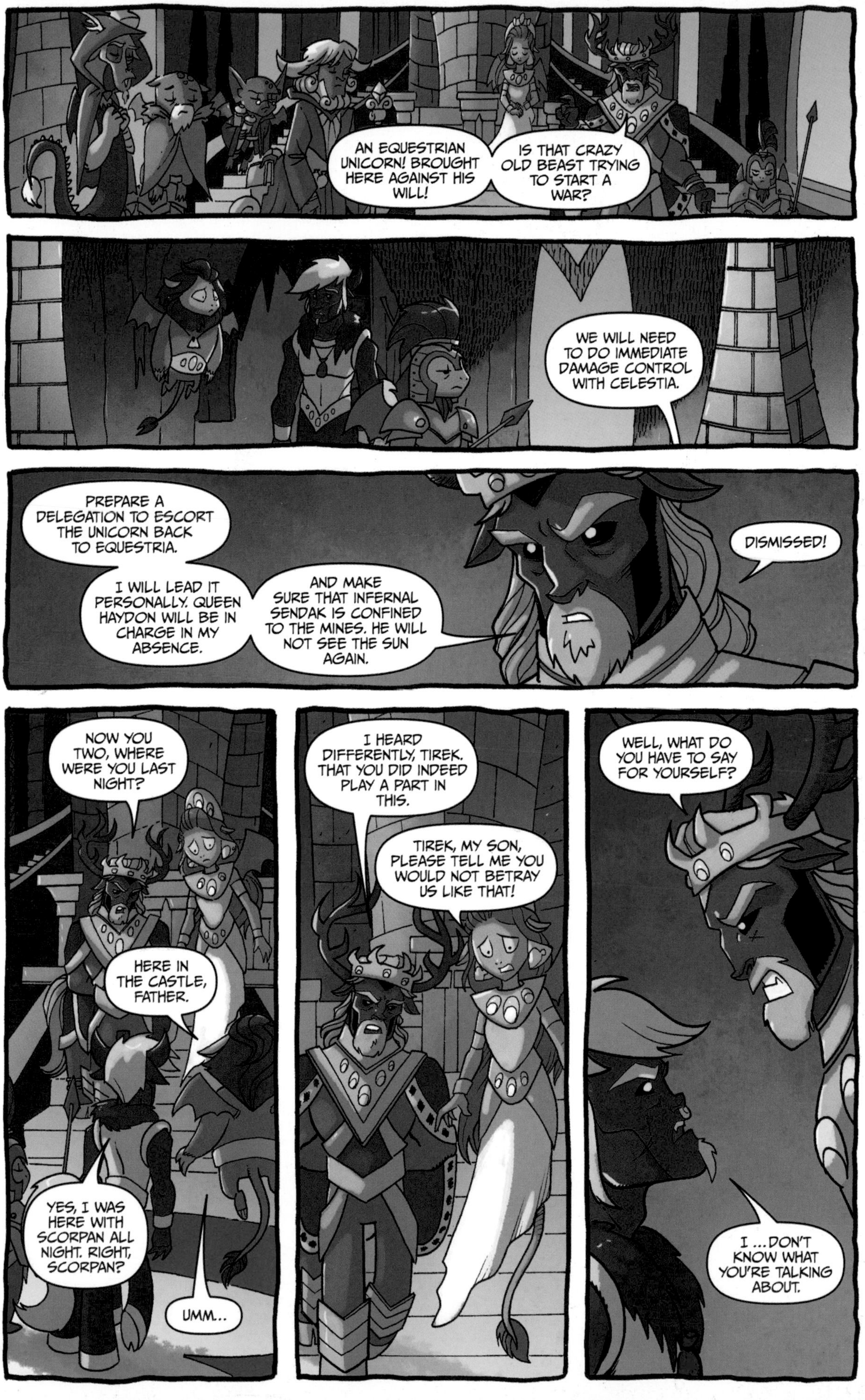
AN EQUESTRIAN UNICORN! BROUGHT HERE AGAINST HIS WILL!
IS THAT CRAZY OLD BEAST TRYING TO START A WAR?
WE WILL NEED TO DO IMMEDIATE DAMAGE CONTROL WITH CELESTIA.
PREPARE A DELEGATION TO ESCORT THE UNICORN BACK TO EQUESTRIA.
I WILL LEAD IT PERSONALLY. QUEEN HAYDON WILL BE IN CHARGE IN MY ABSENCE.
AND MAKE SURE THAT INFERNAL SENDAK IS CONFINED TO THE MINES. HE WILL NOT SEE THE SUN AGAIN.
DISMISSED!
NOW YOU TWO, WHERE WERE YOU LAST NIGHT?
HERE IN THE CASTLE, FATHER.
YES, I WAS HERE WITH SCORPAN ALL NIGHT. RIGHT, SCORPAN?
UMM...
I HEARD DIFFERENTLY, TIREK. THAT YOU DID INDEED PLAY A PART IN THIS.
TIREK, MY SON, PLEASE TELL ME YOU WOULD NOT BETRAY US LIKE THAT!
WELL, WHAT DO YOU HAVE TO SAY FOR YOURSELF?
I ...DON'T KNOW WHAT YOU'RE TALKING ABOUT.

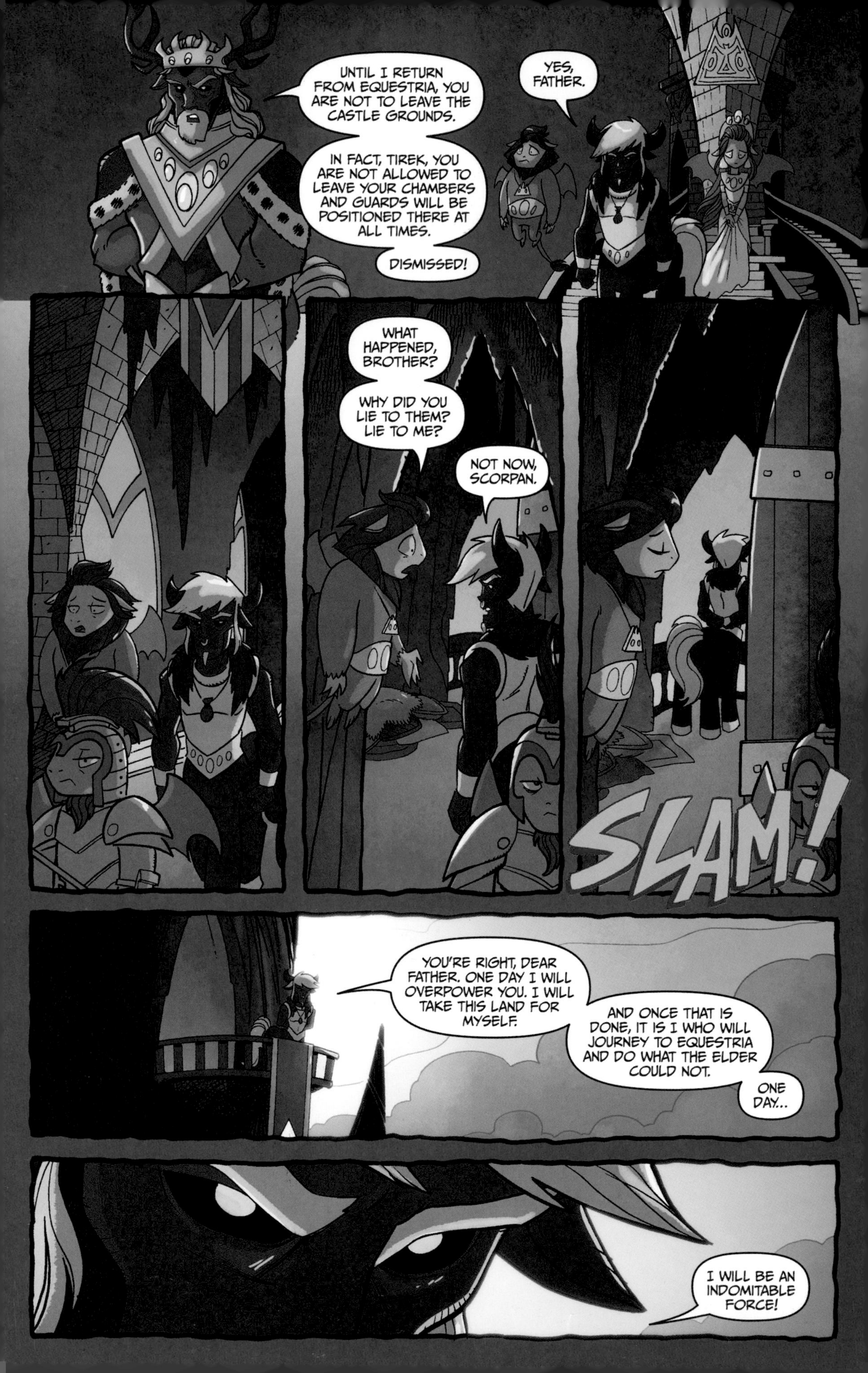
UNTIL I RETURN FROM EQUESTRIA, YOU ARE NOT TO LEAVE THE CASTLE GROUNDS.
IN FACT, TIREK, YOU ARE NOT ALLOWED TO LEAVE YOUR CHAMBERS AND GUARDS WILL BE POSITIONED THERE AT ALL TIMES.
DISMISSED!
YES, FATHER.
WHAT HAPPENED, BROTHER?
WHY DID YOU LIE TO THEM? LIE TO ME?
NOT NOW, SCORPAN.
SLAM!
YOU'RE RIGHT, DEAR FATHER. ONE DAY I WILL OVERPOWER YOU. I WILL TAKE THIS LAND FOR MYSELF.
AND ONCE THAT IS DONE, IT IS I WHO WILL JOURNEY TO EQUESTRIA AND DO WHAT THE ELDER COULD NOT.
ONE DAY...
I WILL BE AN INDOMITABLE FORCE!

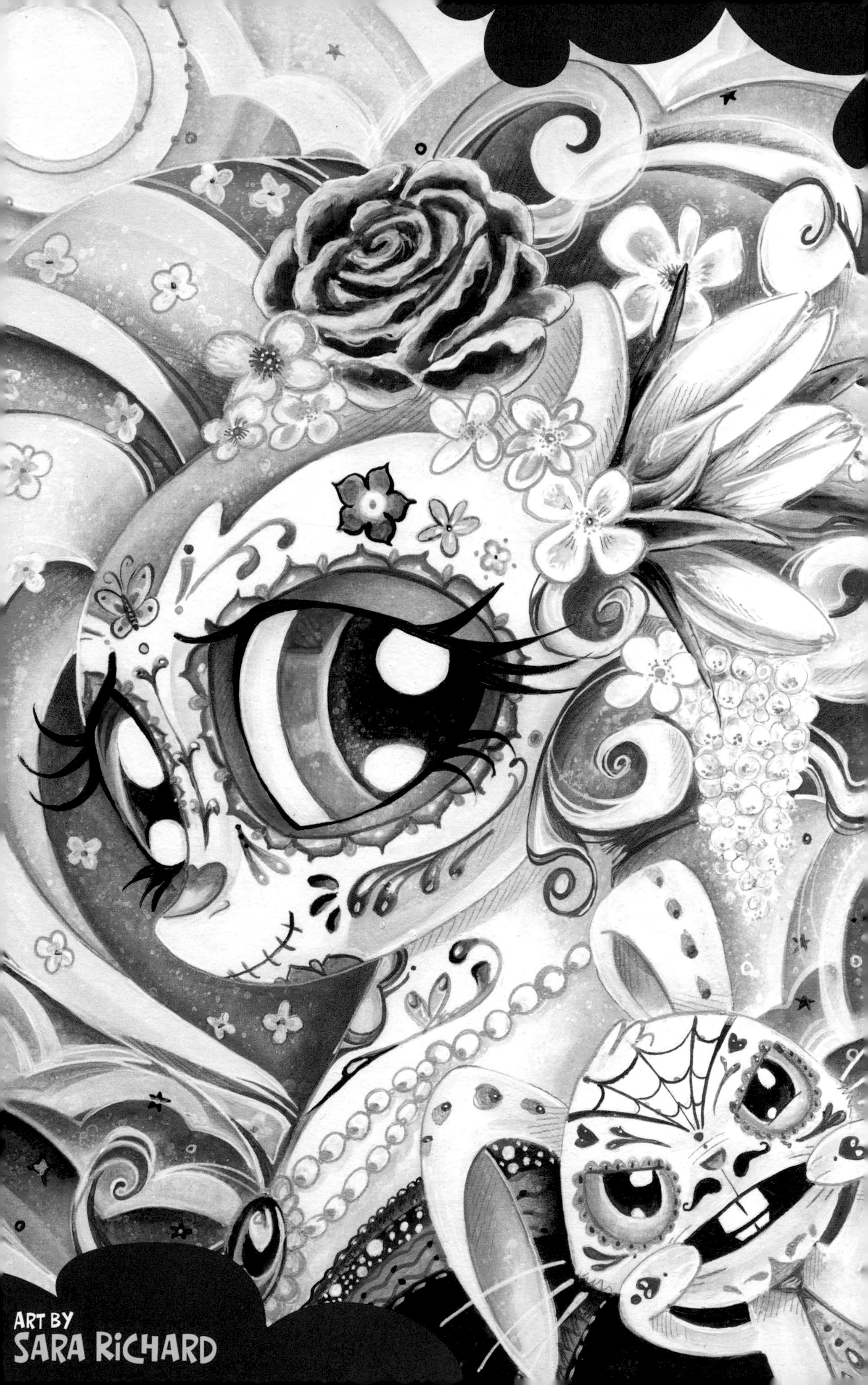

ART BY
SARA RICHARD

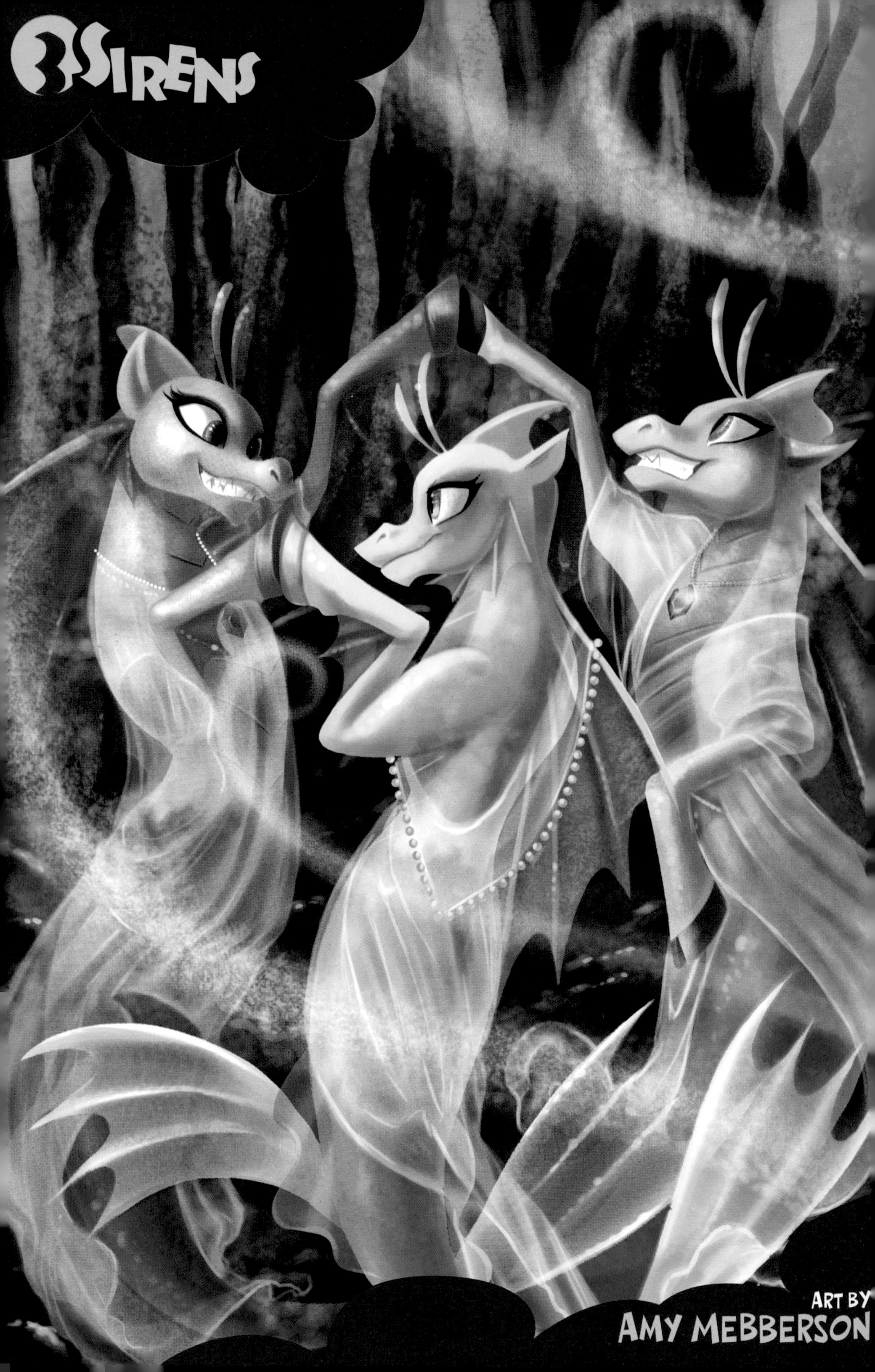
SIRENS
ART BY
AMY MEBBERSON

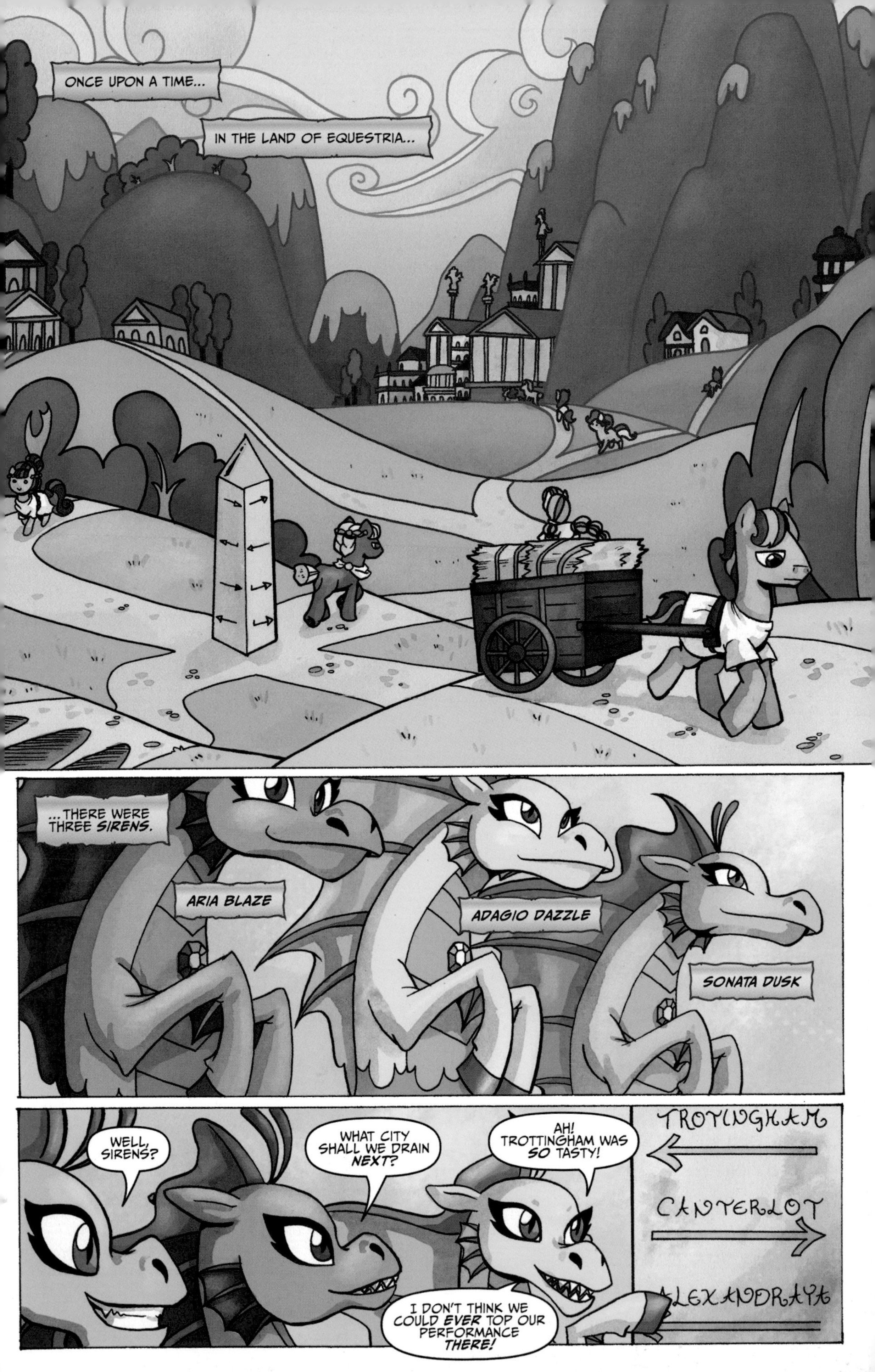
ONCE UPON A TIME...
IN THE LAND OF EQUESTRIA...
...THERE WERE THREE *SIRENS.*
ARIA BLAZE
ADAGIO DAZZLE
SONATA DUSK
WELL, SIRENS?
WHAT CITY SHALL WE DRAIN *NEXT?*
AH! TROTTINGHAM WAS *SO* TASTY!
I DON'T THINK WE COULD *EVER* TOP OUR PERFORMANCE *THERE!*
TROTINGHAM
CANTERLOT

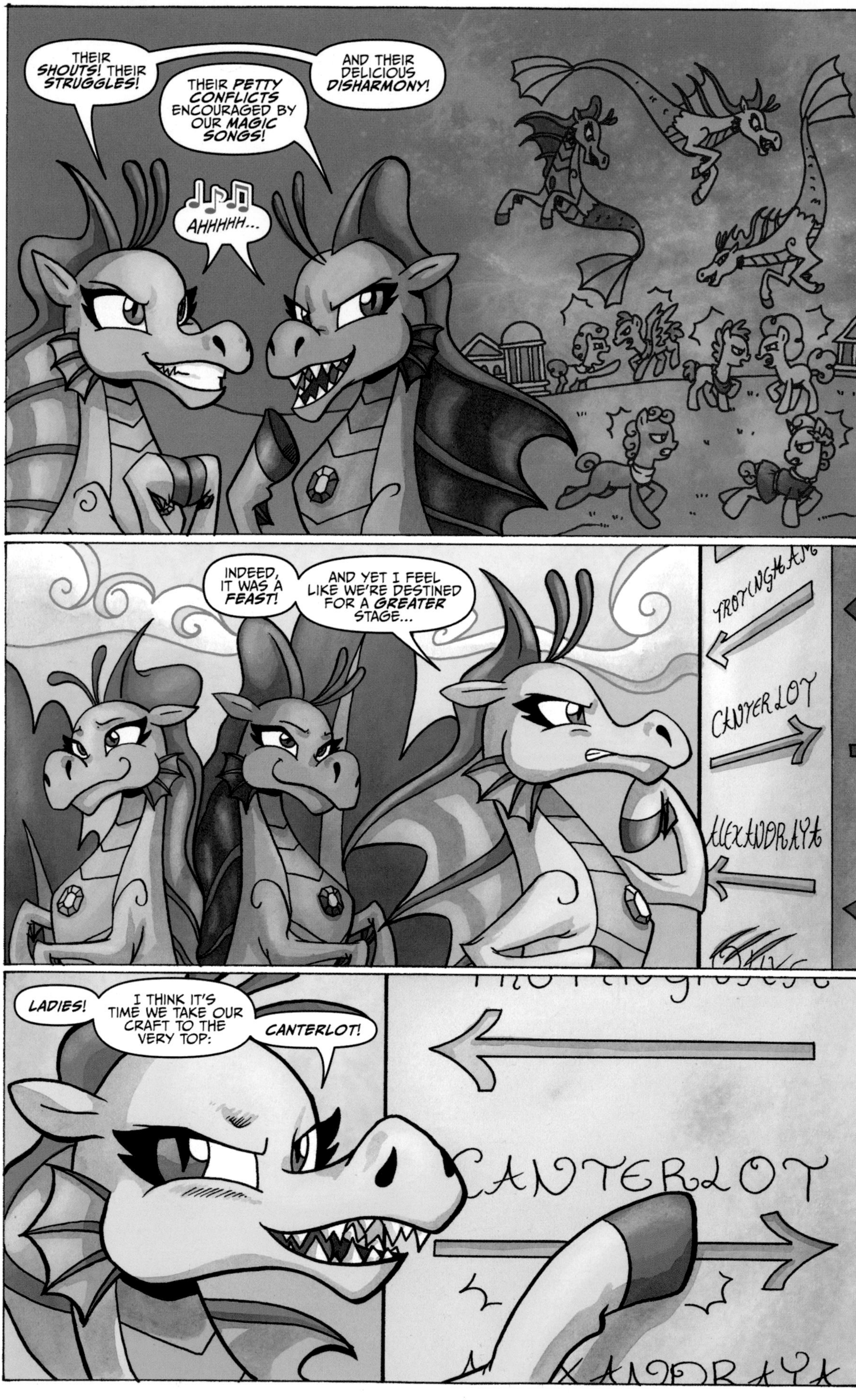
THEIR SHOUTS! THEIR STRUGGLES!
THEIR PETTY CONFLICTS ENCOURAGED BY OUR MAGIC SONGS!
AND THEIR DELICIOUS DISHARMONY!
AHHHHH...
INDEED, IT WAS A FEAST!
AND YET I FEEL LIKE WE'RE DESTINED FOR A GREATER STAGE...
TROTTINGHAM
CANTERLOT
ALEXANDRAYA
LADIES!
I THINK IT'S TIME WE TAKE OUR CRAFT TO THE VERY TOP:
CANTERLOT!
CANTERLOT

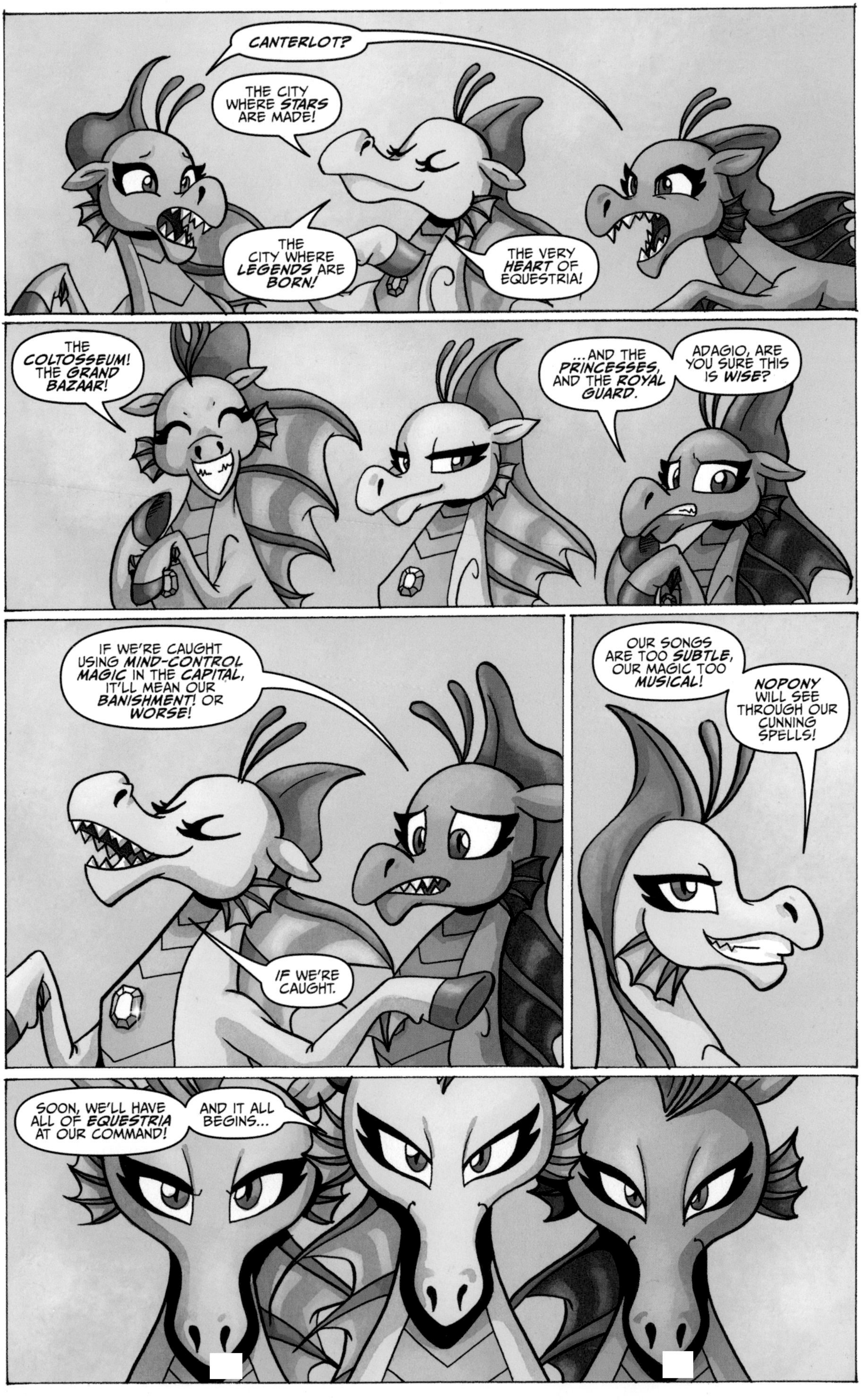
CANTERLOT?
THE CITY WHERE STARS ARE MADE!
THE CITY WHERE LEGENDS ARE BORN!
THE VERY HEART OF EQUESTRIA!
THE COLTOSSEUM! THE GRAND BAZAAR!
...AND THE PRINCESSES, AND THE ROYAL GUARD.
ADAGIO, ARE YOU SURE THIS IS WISE?
IF WE'RE CAUGHT USING MIND-CONTROL MAGIC IN THE CAPITAL, IT'LL MEAN OUR BANISHMENT! OR WORSE!
IF WE'RE CAUGHT.
OUR SONGS ARE TOO SUBTLE, OUR MAGIC TOO MUSICAL!
NOPONY WILL SEE THROUGH OUR CUNNING SPELLS!
SOON, WE'LL HAVE ALL OF EQUESTRIA AT OUR COMMAND!
AND IT ALL BEGINS...

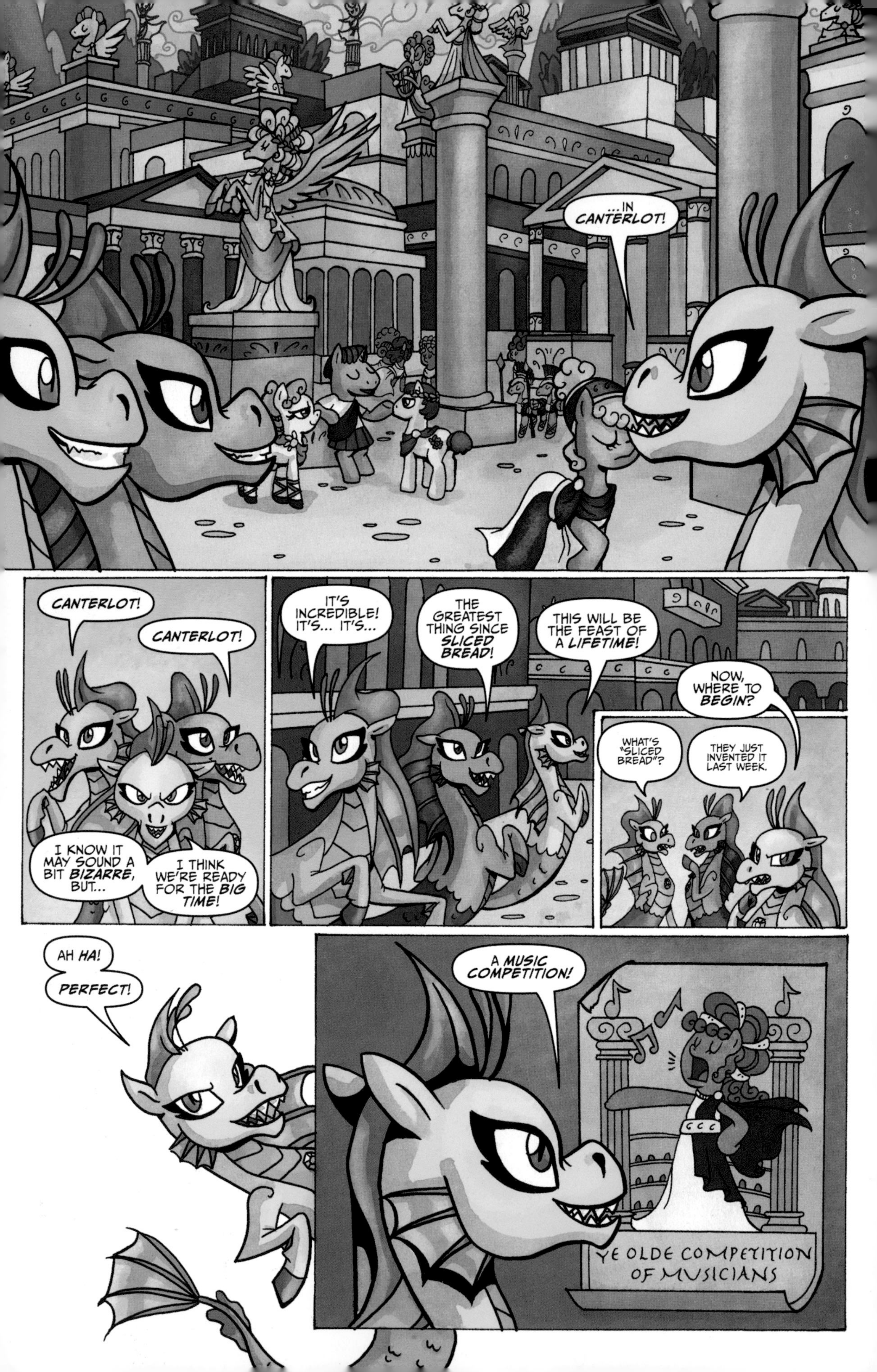
...IN CANTERLOT!
CANTERLOT!
CANTERLOT!
I KNOW IT MAY SOUND A BIT BIZARRE, BUT...
I THINK WE'RE READY FOR THE BIG TIME!
IT'S INCREDIBLE! IT'S... IT'S...
THE GREATEST THING SINCE SLICED BREAD!
THIS WILL BE THE FEAST OF A LIFETIME!
NOW, WHERE TO BEGIN?
WHAT'S "SLICED BREAD"?
THEY JUST INVENTED IT LAST WEEK.
AH HA!
PERFECT!
A MUSIC COMPETITION!
YE OLDE COMPETITION OF MUSICIANS

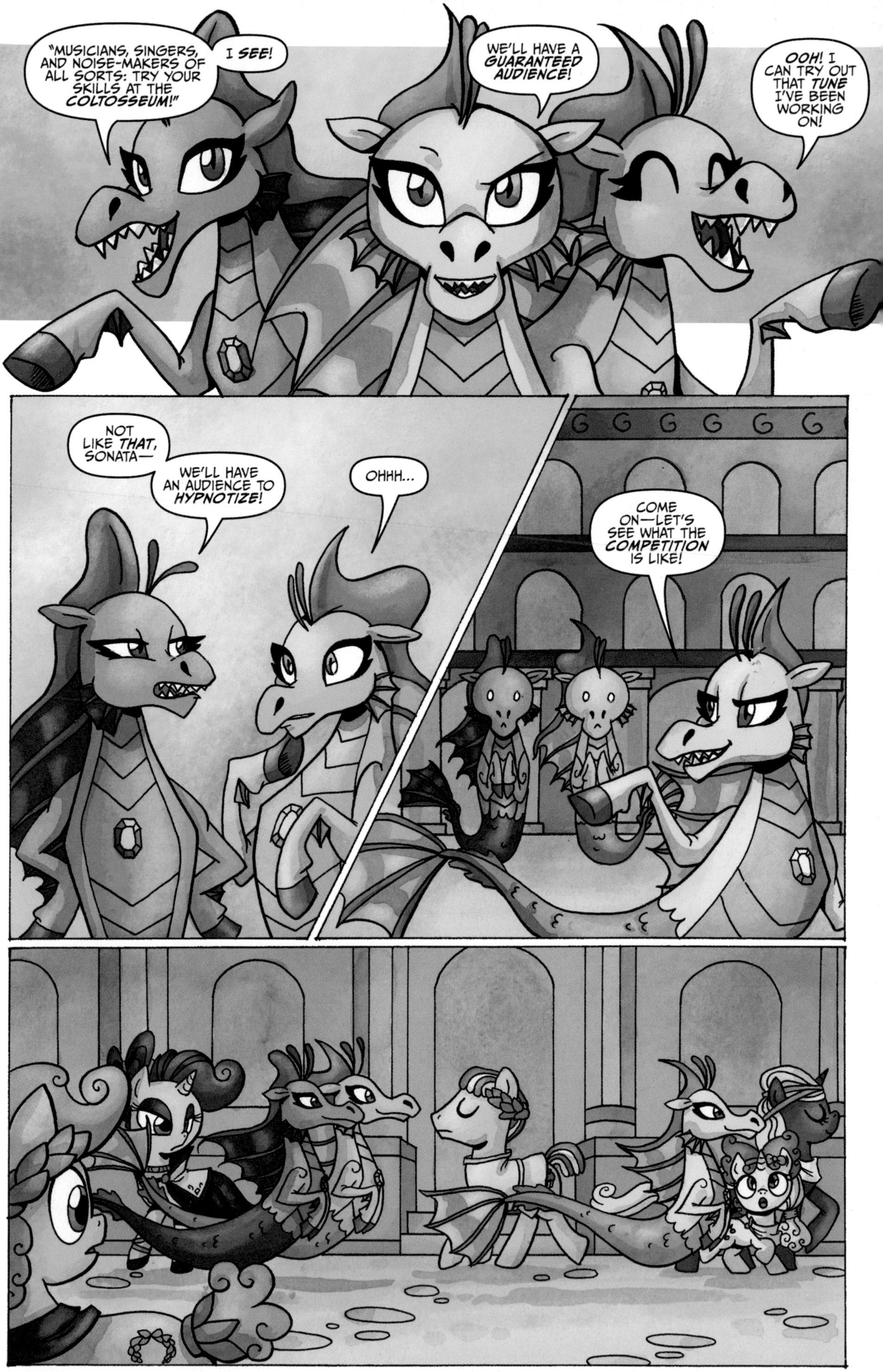
"MUSICIANS, SINGERS, AND NOISE-MAKERS OF ALL SORTS: TRY YOUR SKILLS AT THE COLTOSSEUM!"
I SEE!
WE'LL HAVE A GUARANTEED AUDIENCE!
OOH! I CAN TRY OUT THAT TUNE I'VE BEEN WORKING ON!
NOT LIKE THAT, SONATA—
WE'LL HAVE AN AUDIENCE TO HYPNOTIZE!
OHHH...
COME ON—LET'S SEE WHAT THE COMPETITION IS LIKE!

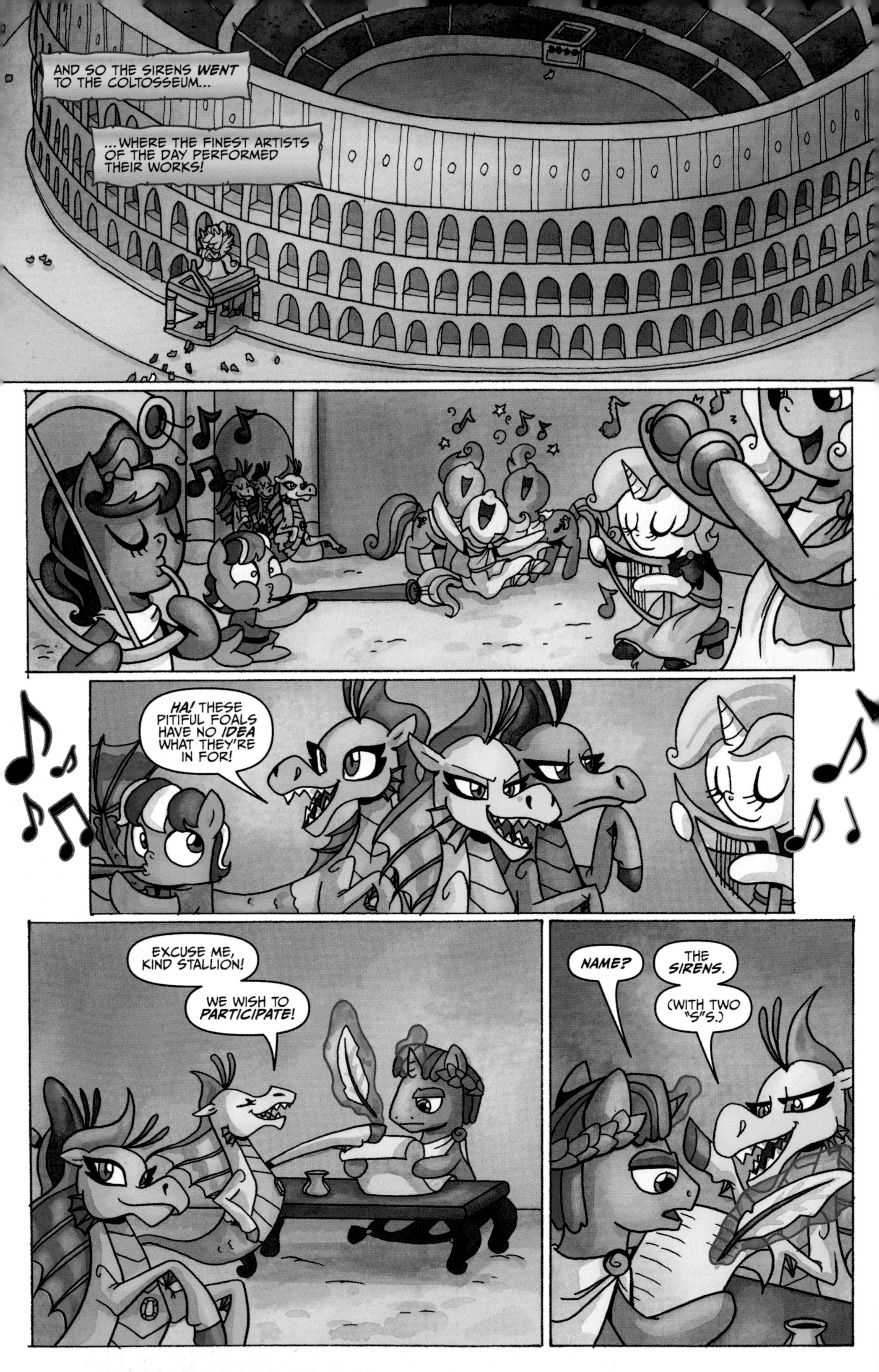
AND SO THE SIRENS WENT TO THE COLTOSSEUM...
...WHERE THE FINEST ARTISTS OF THE DAY PERFORMED THEIR WORKS!
HA! THESE PITIFUL FOALS HAVE NO IDEA WHAT THEY'RE IN FOR!
EXCUSE ME, KIND STALLION!
WE WISH TO PARTICIPATE!
NAME?
THE SIRENS.
(WITH TWO "S"S.)

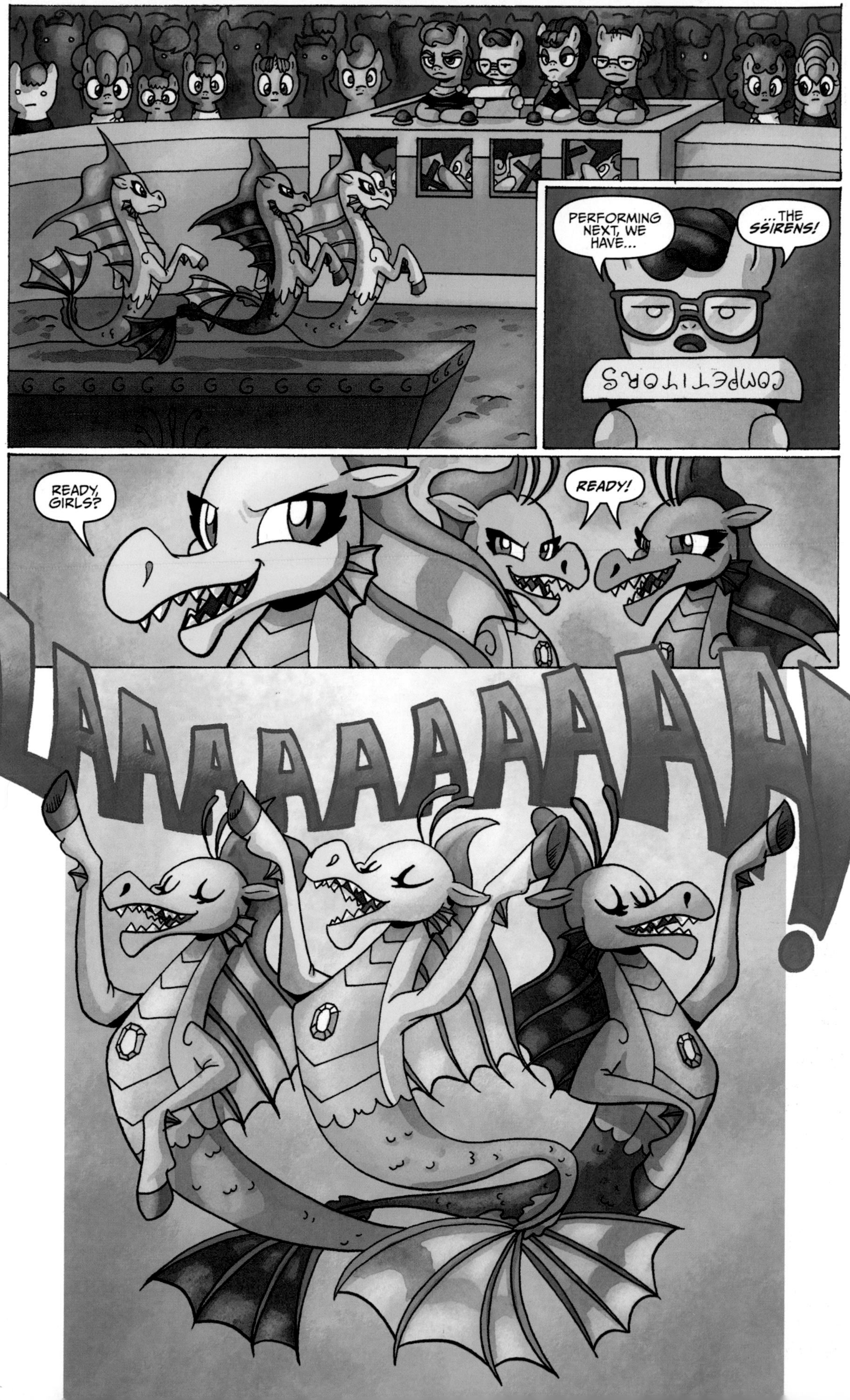
PERFORMING NEXT, WE HAVE...
...THE SSIRENS!
COMPETITORS
READY, GIRLS?
READY!
LAAAAAAAAAA!

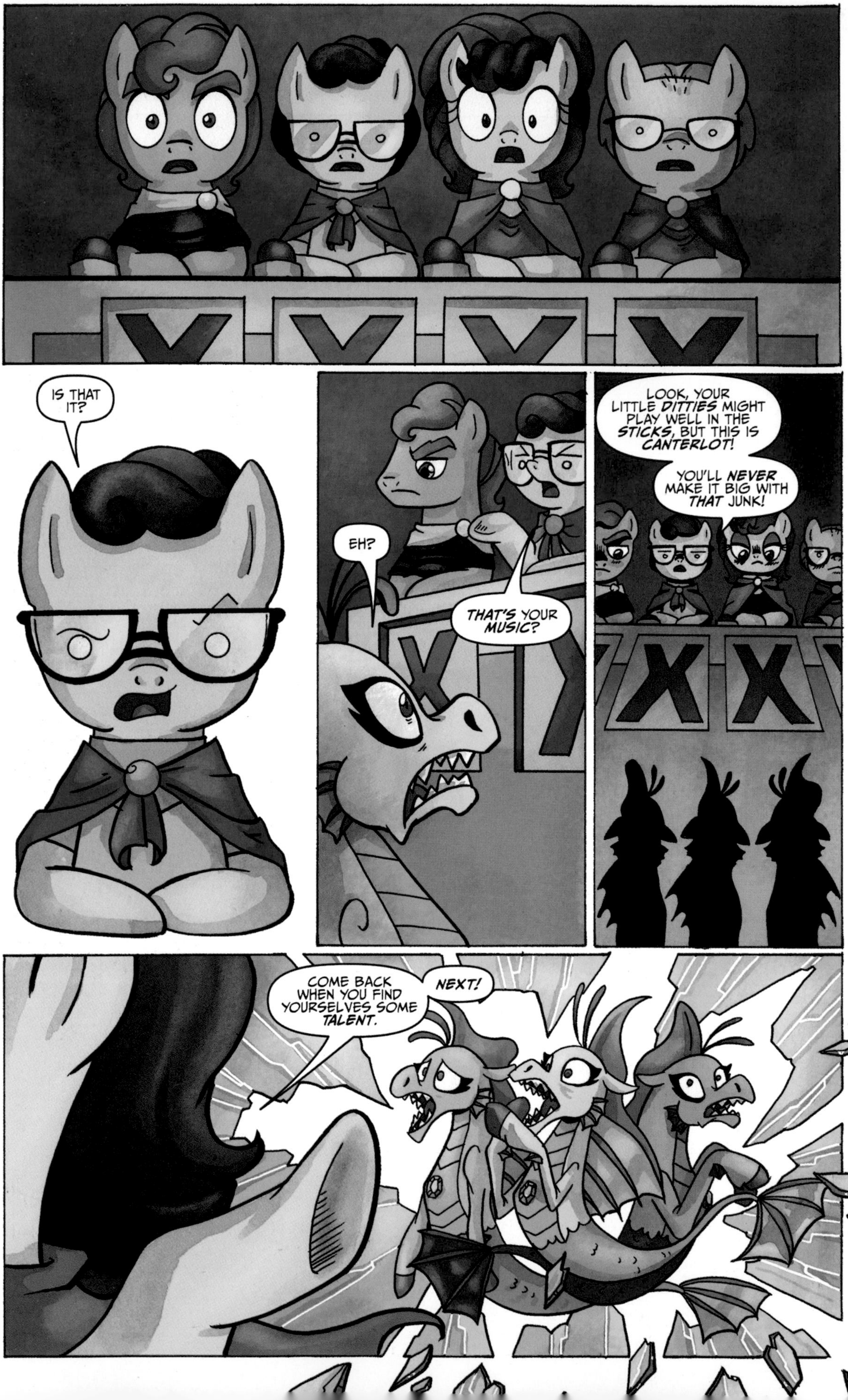
IS THAT IT?
EH?
THAT'S YOUR MUSIC?
LOOK, YOUR LITTLE DITTIES MIGHT PLAY WELL IN THE STICKS, BUT THIS IS CANTERLOT!
YOU'LL NEVER MAKE IT BIG WITH THAT JUNK!
COME BACK WHEN YOU FIND YOURSELVES SOME TALENT.
NEXT!

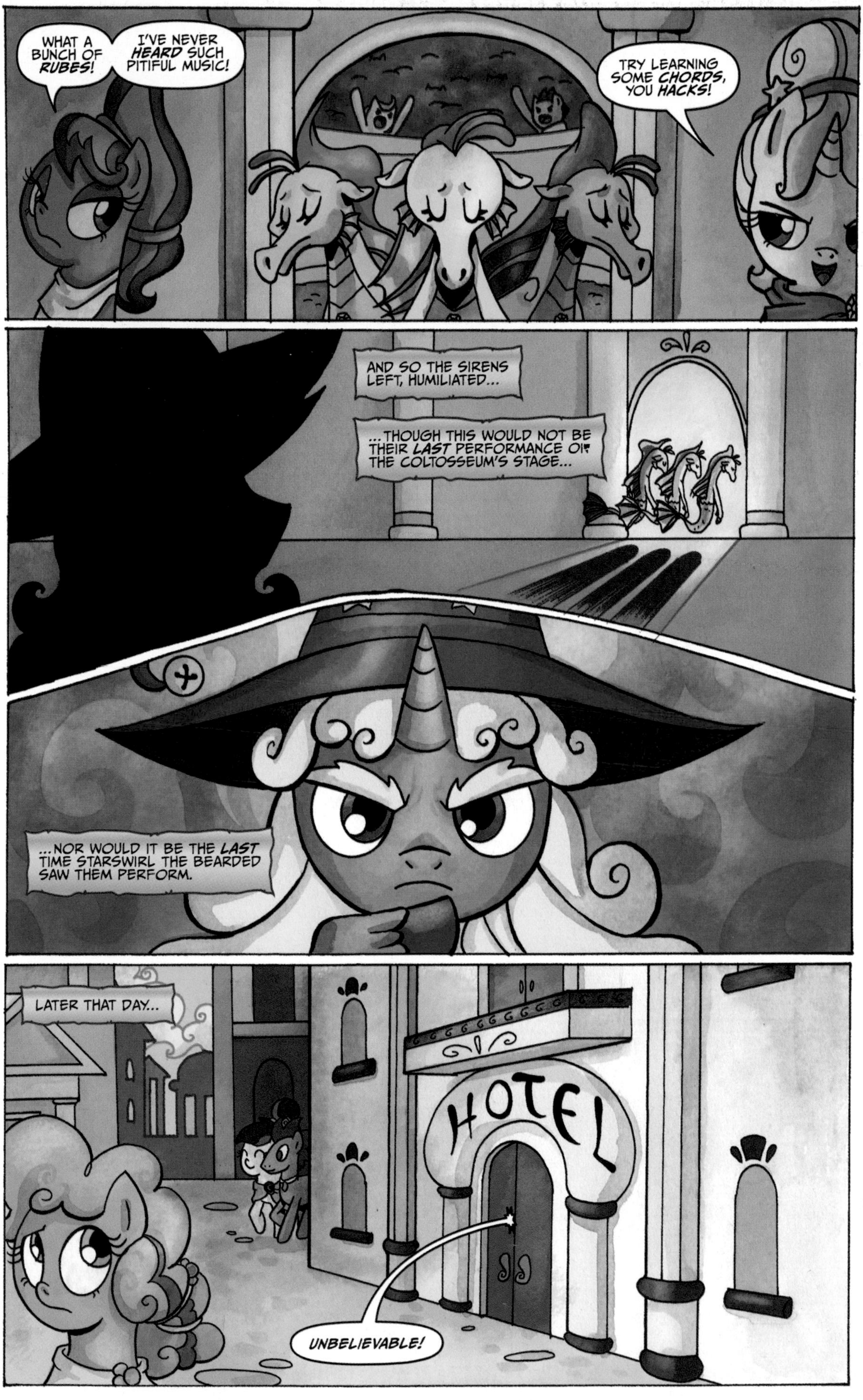
WHAT A BUNCH OF RUBES!
I'VE NEVER HEARD SUCH PITIFUL MUSIC!
TRY LEARNING SOME CHORDS, YOU HACKS!
AND SO THE SIRENS LEFT, HUMILIATED...
...THOUGH THIS WOULD NOT BE THEIR LAST PERFORMANCE ON THE COLTOSSEUM'S STAGE...
...NOR WOULD IT BE THE LAST TIME STARSWIRL THE BEARDED SAW THEM PERFORM.
LATER THAT DAY...
HOTEL
UNBELIEVABLE!

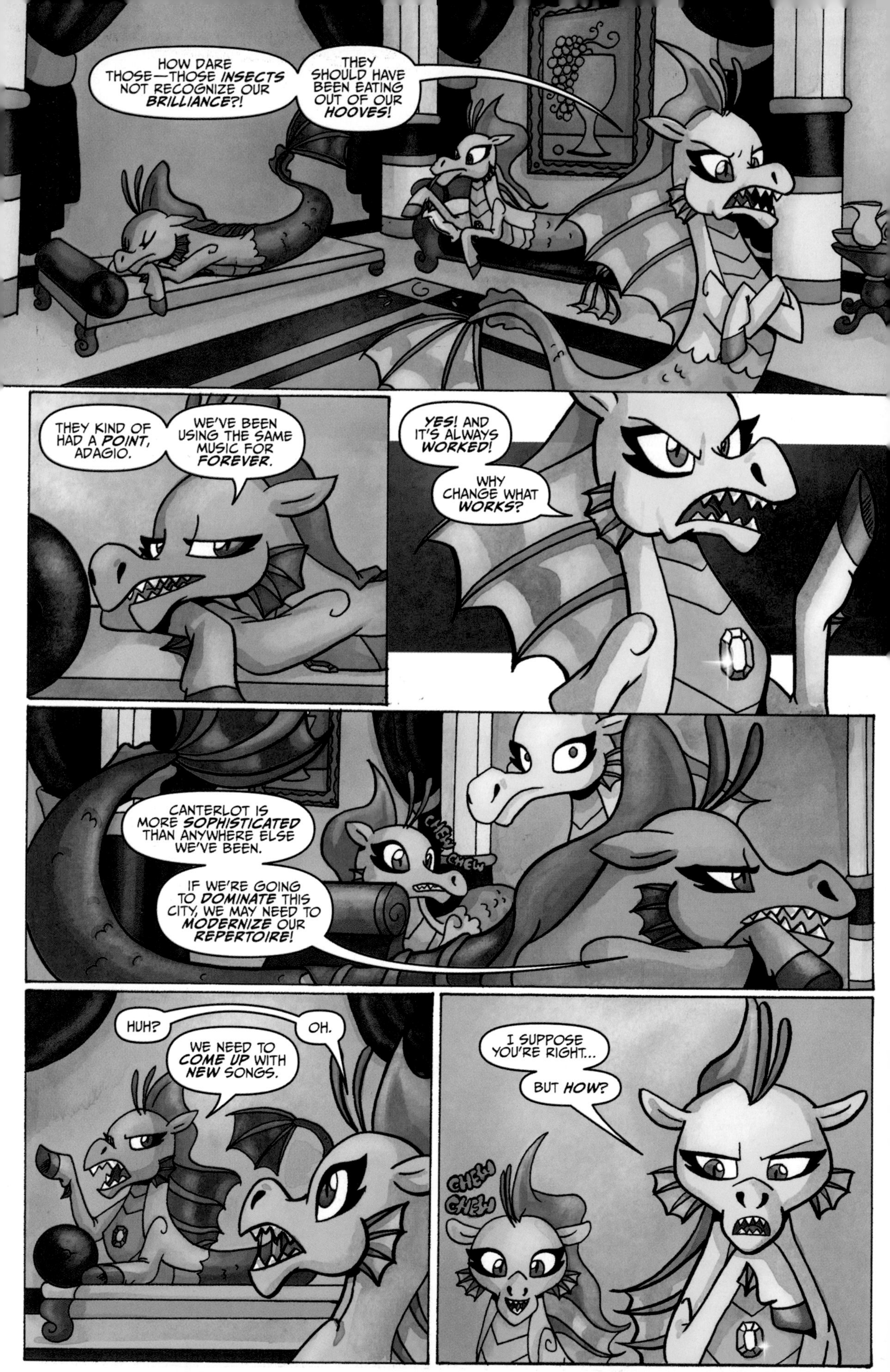
HOW DARE THOSE—THOSE *INSECTS* NOT RECOGNIZE OUR *BRILLIANCE*?!
THEY SHOULD HAVE BEEN EATING OUT OF OUR *HOOVES*!
THEY KIND OF HAD A *POINT*, ADAGIO.
WE'VE BEEN USING THE SAME MUSIC FOR *FOREVER*.
YES! AND IT'S ALWAYS *WORKED*!
WHY CHANGE WHAT *WORKS*?
CANTERLOT IS MORE *SOPHISTICATED* THAN ANYWHERE ELSE WE'VE BEEN.
CHEW CHEW
IF WE'RE GOING TO *DOMINATE* THIS CITY, WE MAY NEED TO *MODERNIZE* OUR *REPERTOIRE*!
HUH?
OH.
WE NEED TO *COME UP* WITH *NEW* SONGS.
I SUPPOSE YOU'RE RIGHT...
BUT *HOW*?
CHEW CHEW

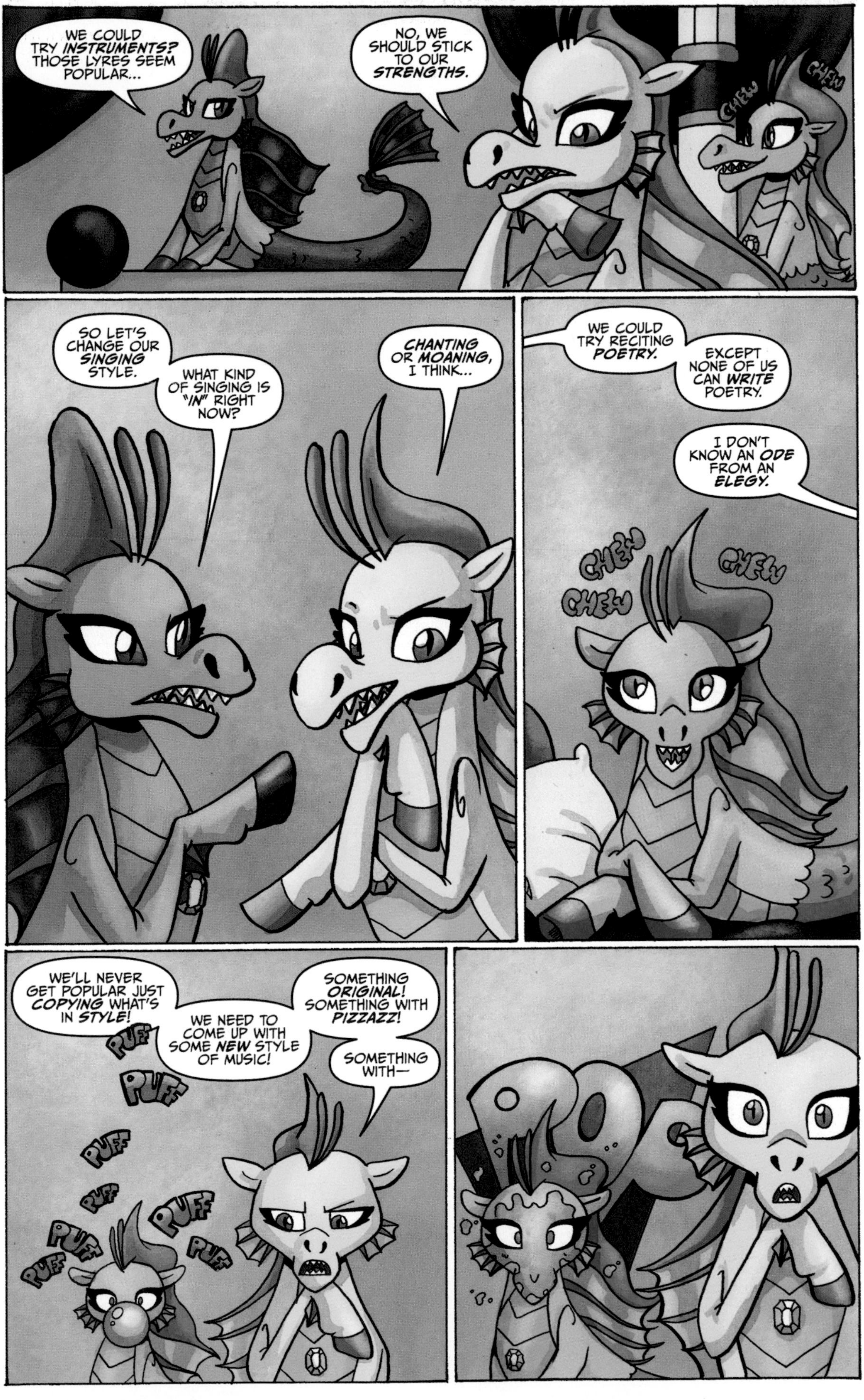

WE COULD TRY INSTRUMENTS? THOSE LYRES SEEM POPULAR...
NO, WE SHOULD STICK TO OUR STRENGTHS.
CHEW
CHEW
SO LET'S CHANGE OUR SINGING STYLE.
WHAT KIND OF SINGING IS "IN" RIGHT NOW?
CHANTING OR MOANING, I THINK...
WE COULD TRY RECITING POETRY.
EXCEPT NONE OF US CAN WRITE POETRY.
I DON'T KNOW AN ODE FROM AN ELEGY.
CHEW
CHEW
CHEW
WE'LL NEVER GET POPULAR JUST COPYING WHAT'S IN STYLE!
WE NEED TO COME UP WITH SOME NEW STYLE OF MUSIC!
SOMETHING ORIGINAL! SOMETHING WITH PIZZAZZ!
SOMETHING WITH—
PUFF
PUFF
PUFF
PUFF
PUFF
PUFF
PUFF
PUFF

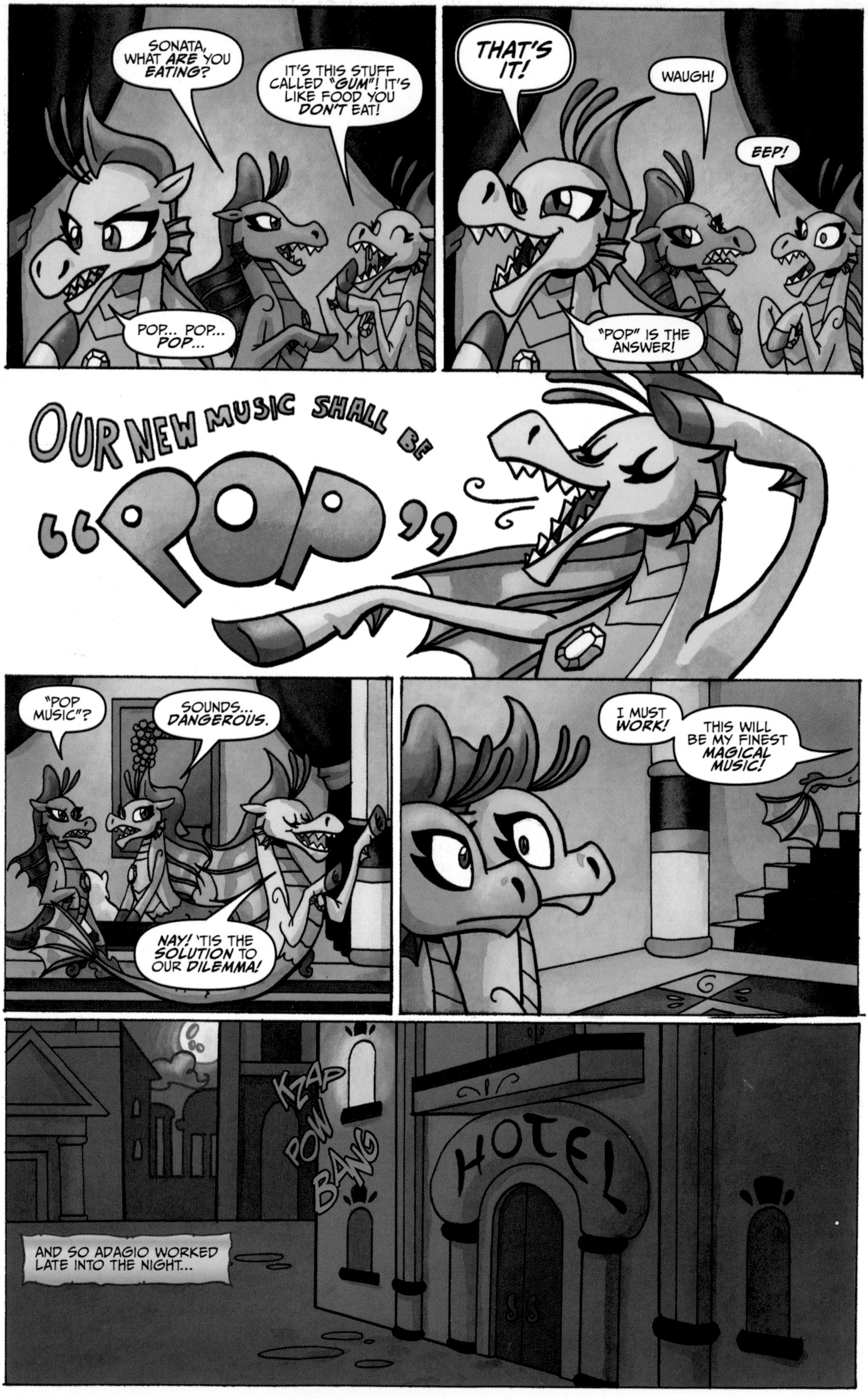
SONATA, WHAT ARE YOU EATING?
IT'S THIS STUFF CALLED "GUM"! IT'S LIKE FOOD YOU DON'T EAT!
POP... POP... POP...
THAT'S IT!
WAUGH!
EEP!
"POP" IS THE ANSWER!
OUR NEW MUSIC SHALL BE "POP"
"POP MUSIC"?
SOUNDS... DANGEROUS.
NAY! 'TIS THE SOLUTION TO OUR DILEMMA!
I MUST WORK!
THIS WILL BE MY FINEST MAGICAL MUSIC!
KZAP
POW
BANG
HOTEL
AND SO ADAGIO WORKED LATE INTO THE NIGHT...

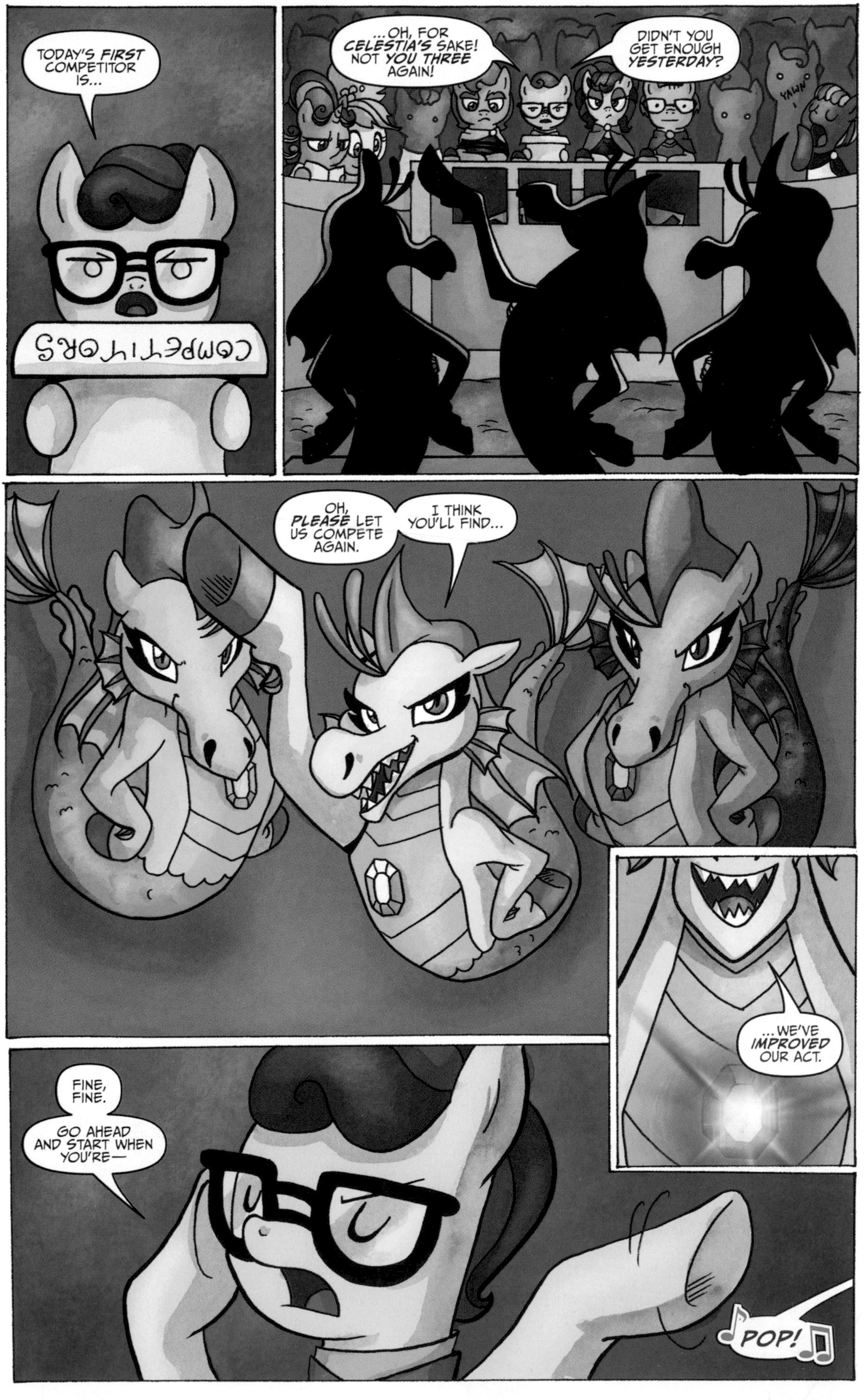

TODAY'S *FIRST* COMPETITOR IS...
COMPETITORS
...OH, FOR *CELESTIA'S* SAKE! NOT *YOU THREE* AGAIN!
DIDN'T YOU GET ENOUGH *YESTERDAY?*
YAWN
OH, *PLEASE* LET US COMPETE AGAIN.
I THINK YOU'LL FIND...
...WE'VE *IMPROVED* OUR ACT.
FINE, FINE.
GO AHEAD AND START WHEN YOU'RE—
POP!

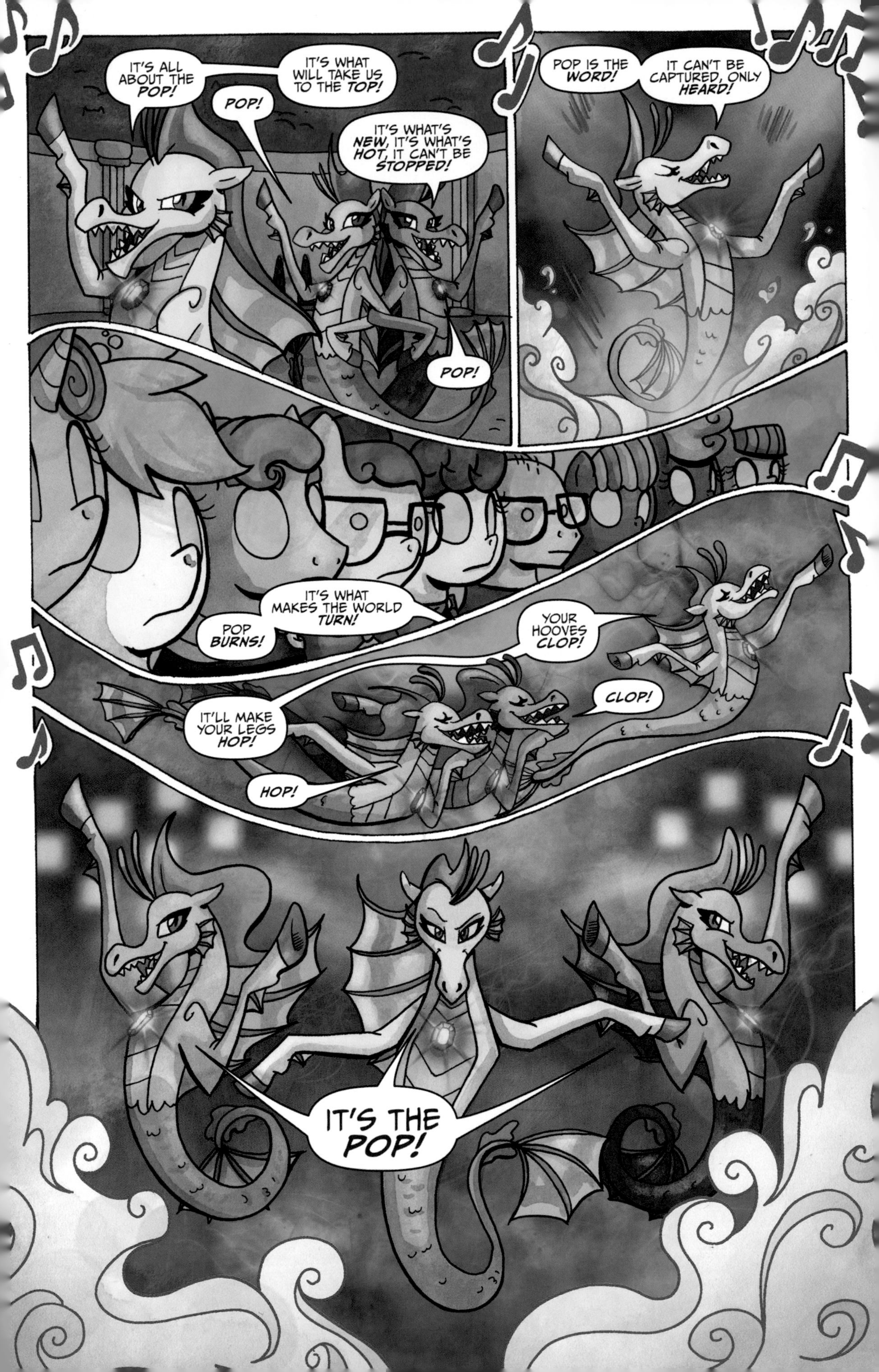
IT'S ALL ABOUT THE POP!
IT'S WHAT WILL TAKE US TO THE TOP!
POP!
IT'S WHAT'S NEW, IT'S WHAT'S HOT, IT CAN'T BE STOPPED!
POP!
POP IS THE WORD!
IT CAN'T BE CAPTURED, ONLY HEARD!
POP BURNS!
IT'S WHAT MAKES THE WORLD TURN!
YOUR HOOVES CLOP!
CLOP!
IT'LL MAKE YOUR LEGS HOP!
HOP!
IT'S THE POP!

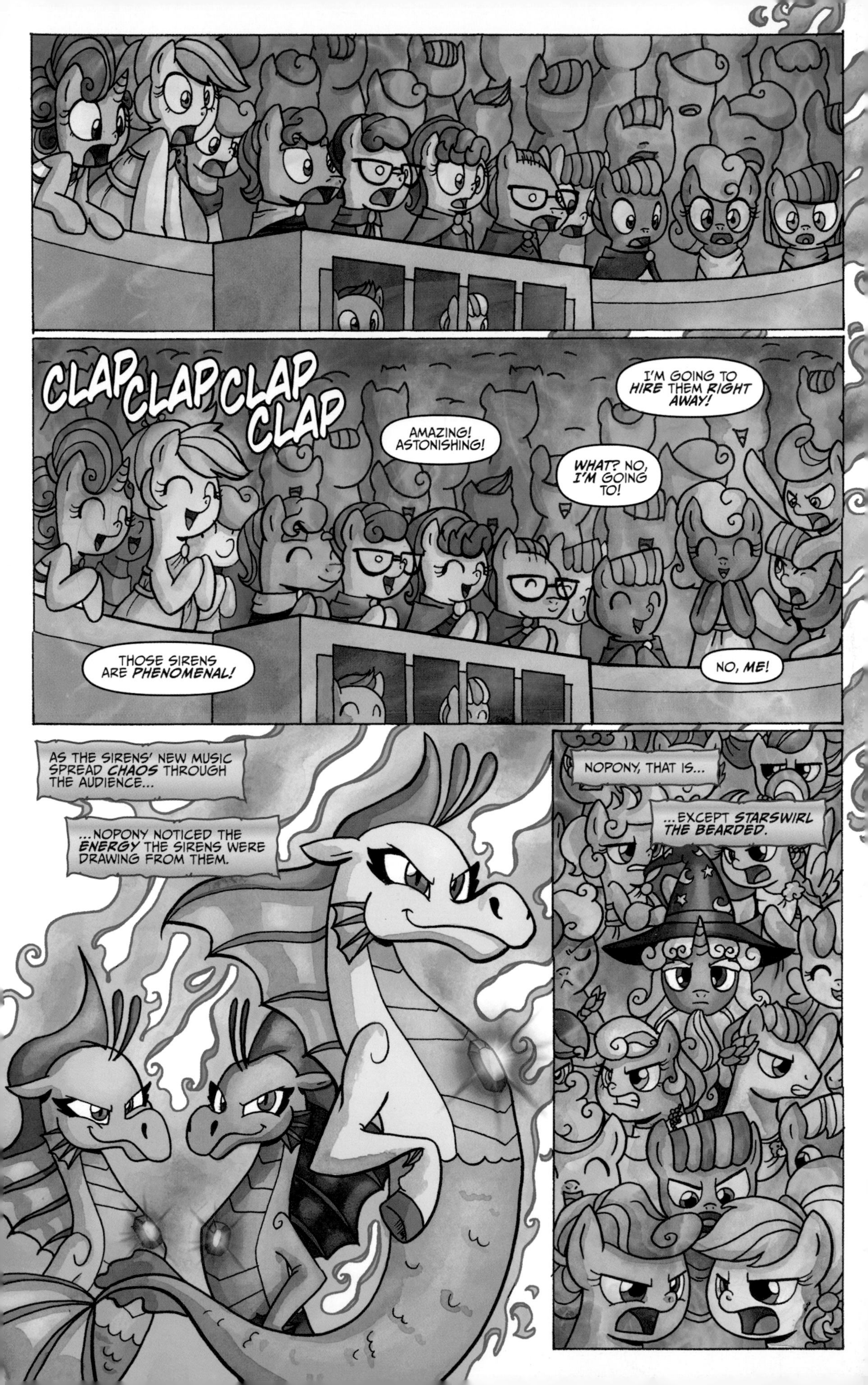
CLAP CLAP CLAP CLAP
AMAZING! ASTONISHING!
I'M GOING TO HIRE THEM RIGHT AWAY!
WHAT? NO, I'M GOING TO!
THOSE SIRENS ARE PHENOMENAL!
NO, ME!
AS THE SIRENS' NEW MUSIC SPREAD CHAOS THROUGH THE AUDIENCE...
...NOPONY NOTICED THE ENERGY THE SIRENS WERE DRAWING FROM THEM.
NOPONY, THAT IS...
...EXCEPT STARSWIRL THE BEARDED.

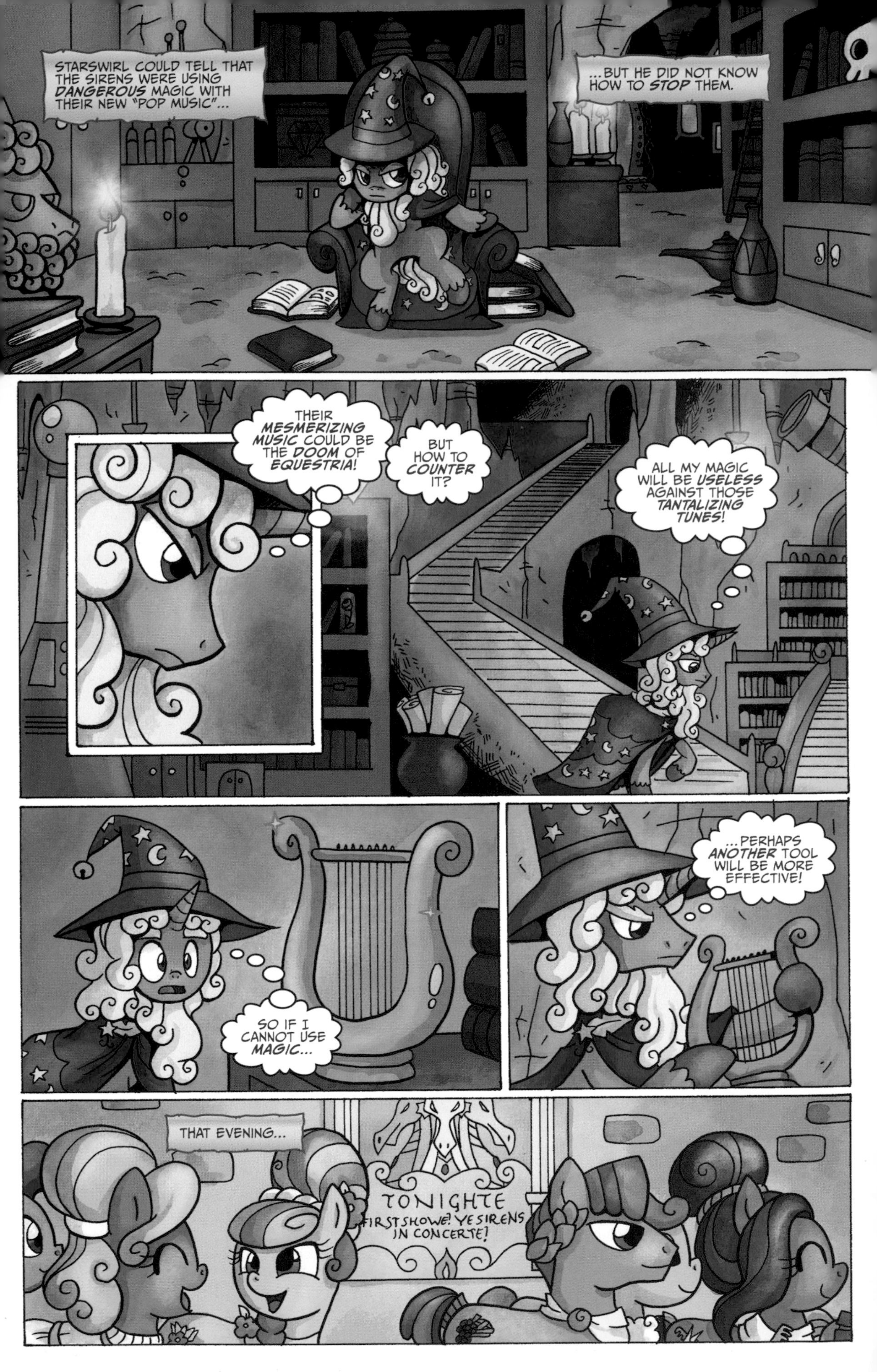
STARSWIRL COULD TELL THAT THE SIRENS WERE USING DANGEROUS MAGIC WITH THEIR NEW "POP MUSIC"...
...BUT HE DID NOT KNOW HOW TO STOP THEM.
THEIR MESMERIZING MUSIC COULD BE THE DOOM OF EQUESTRIA!
BUT HOW TO COUNTER IT?
ALL MY MAGIC WILL BE USELESS AGAINST THOSE TANTALIZING TUNES!
SO IF I CANNOT USE MAGIC...
...PERHAPS ANOTHER TOOL WILL BE MORE EFFECTIVE!
THAT EVENING...
TONIGHTE
FIRST SHOWE! YE SIRENS IN CONCERTE!

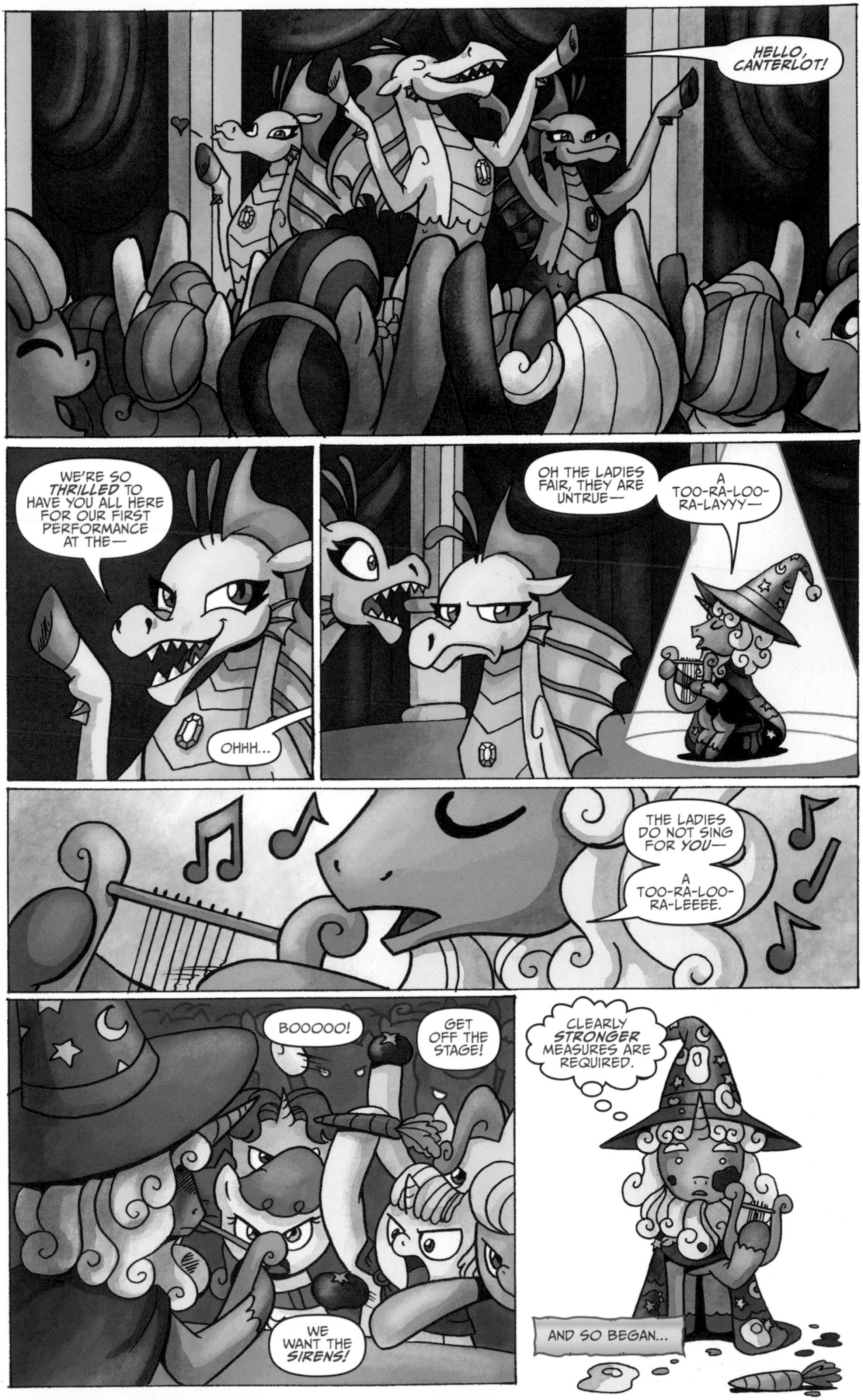
HELLO, CANTERLOT!
WE'RE SO THRILLED TO HAVE YOU ALL HERE FOR OUR FIRST PERFORMANCE AT THE—
OHHH...
OH THE LADIES FAIR, THEY ARE UNTRUE—
A TOO-RA-LOO-RA-LAYYY—
THE LADIES DO NOT SING FOR YOU—
A TOO-RA-LOO-RA-LEEEE.
BOOOOO!
GET OFF THE STAGE!
WE WANT THE SIRENS!
CLEARLY STRONGER MEASURES ARE REQUIRED.
AND SO BEGAN...

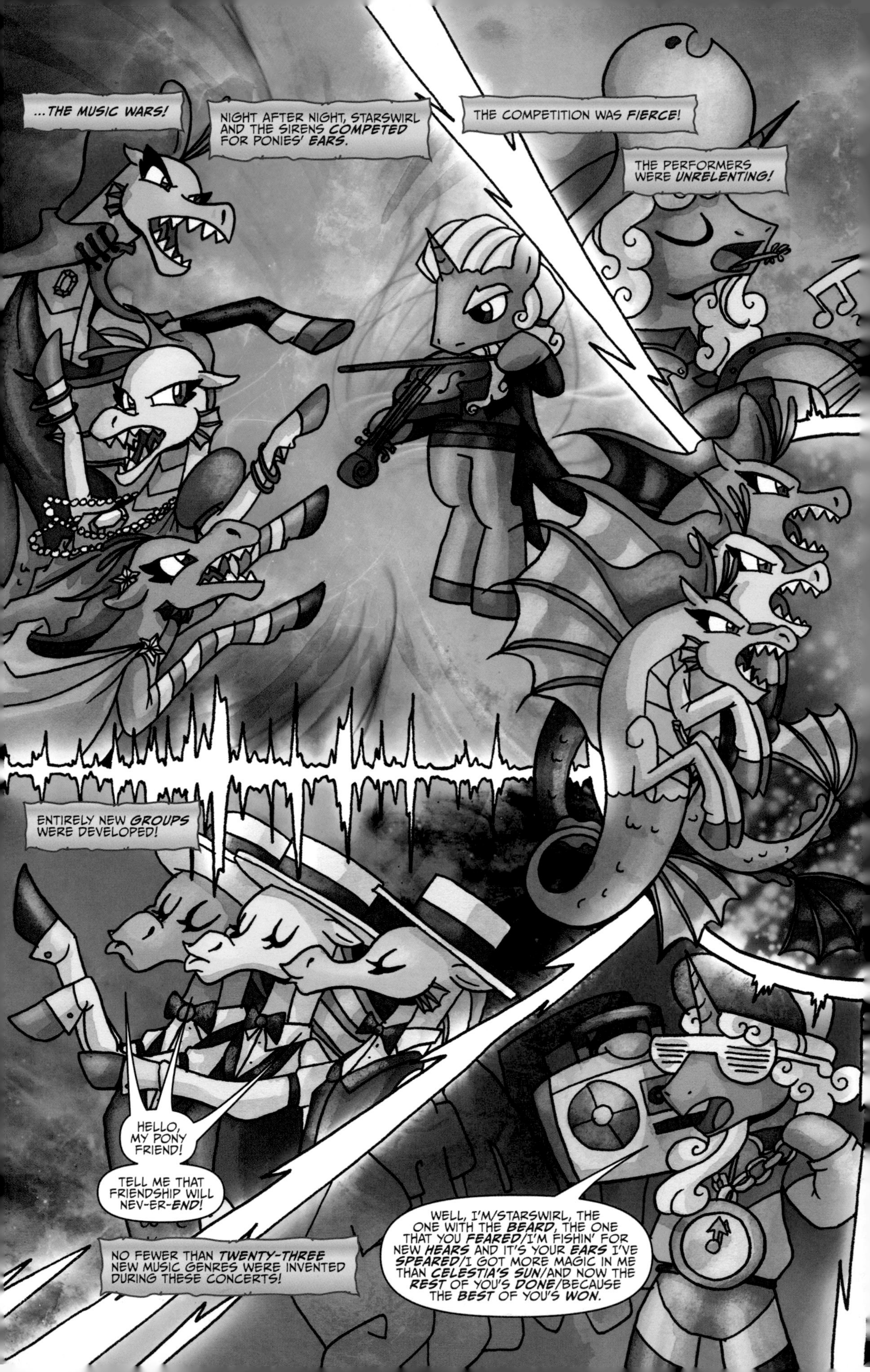
...THE MUSIC WARS!
NIGHT AFTER NIGHT, STARSWIRL AND THE SIRENS COMPETED FOR PONIES' EARS.
THE COMPETITION WAS FIERCE!
THE PERFORMERS WERE UNRELENTING!
ENTIRELY NEW GROUPS WERE DEVELOPED!
HELLO, MY PONY FRIEND!
TELL ME THAT FRIENDSHIP WILL NEV-ER-END!
NO FEWER THAN TWENTY-THREE NEW MUSIC GENRES WERE INVENTED DURING THESE CONCERTS!
WELL, I'M/STARSWIRL, THE ONE WITH THE BEARD, THE ONE THAT YOU FEARED/I'M FISHIN' FOR NEW HEARS AND IT'S YOUR EARS I'VE SPEARED/I GOT MORE MAGIC IN ME THAN CELESTIA'S SUN/AND NOW THE REST OF YOU'S DONE/BECAUSE THE BEST OF YOU'S WON.

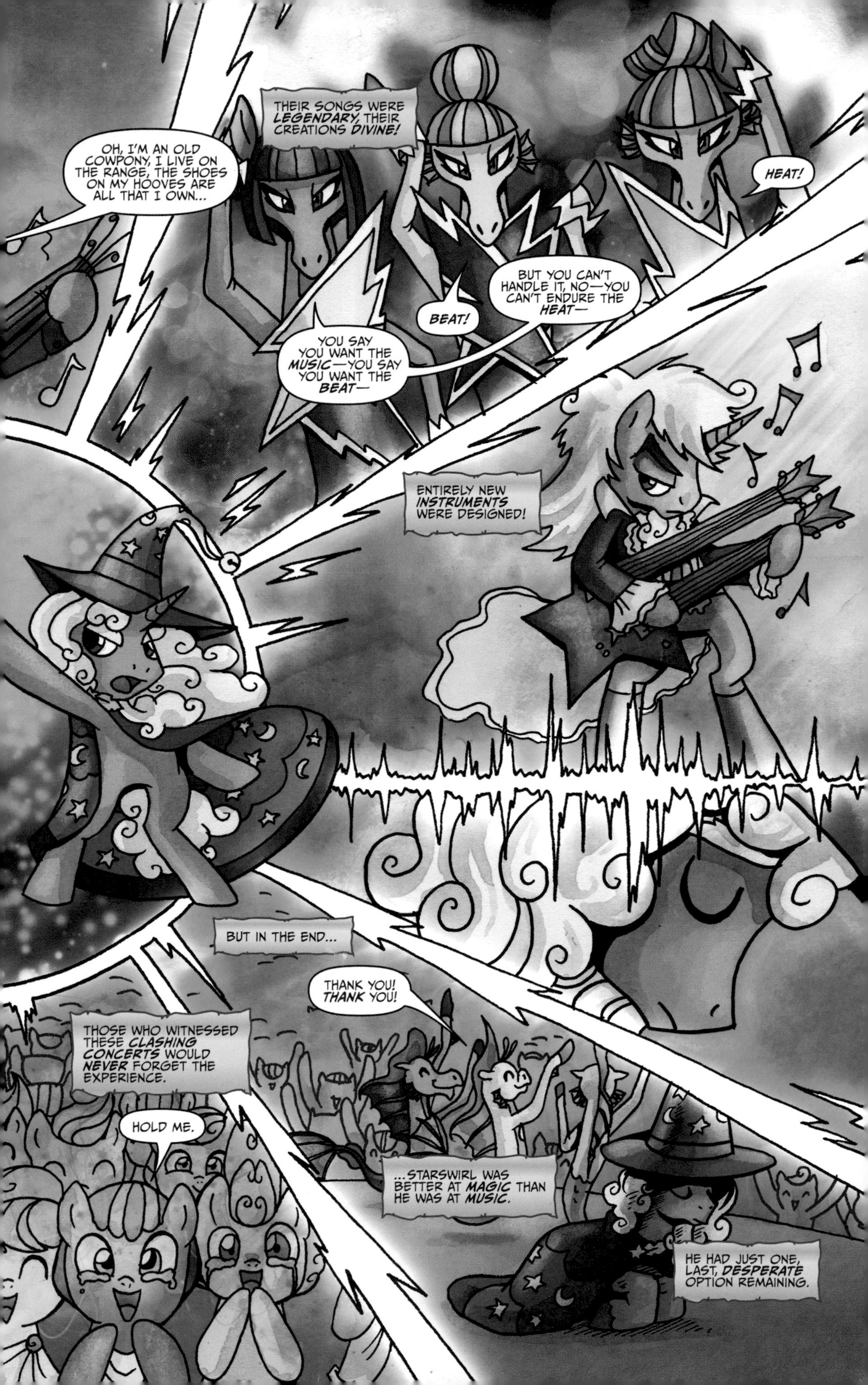
THEIR SONGS WERE LEGENDARY, THEIR CREATIONS DIVINE!
OH, I'M AN OLD COWPONY, I LIVE ON THE RANGE, THE SHOES ON MY HOOVES ARE ALL THAT I OWN...
HEAT!
BUT YOU CAN'T HANDLE IT, NO—YOU CAN'T ENDURE THE HEAT—
BEAT!
YOU SAY YOU WANT THE MUSIC—YOU SAY YOU WANT THE BEAT—
ENTIRELY NEW INSTRUMENTS WERE DESIGNED!
BUT IN THE END...
THANK YOU! THANK YOU!
THOSE WHO WITNESSED THESE CLASHING CONCERTS WOULD NEVER FORGET THE EXPERIENCE.
HOLD ME.
...STARSWIRL WAS BETTER AT MAGIC THAN HE WAS AT MUSIC.
HE HAD JUST ONE, LAST, DESPERATE OPTION REMAINING.

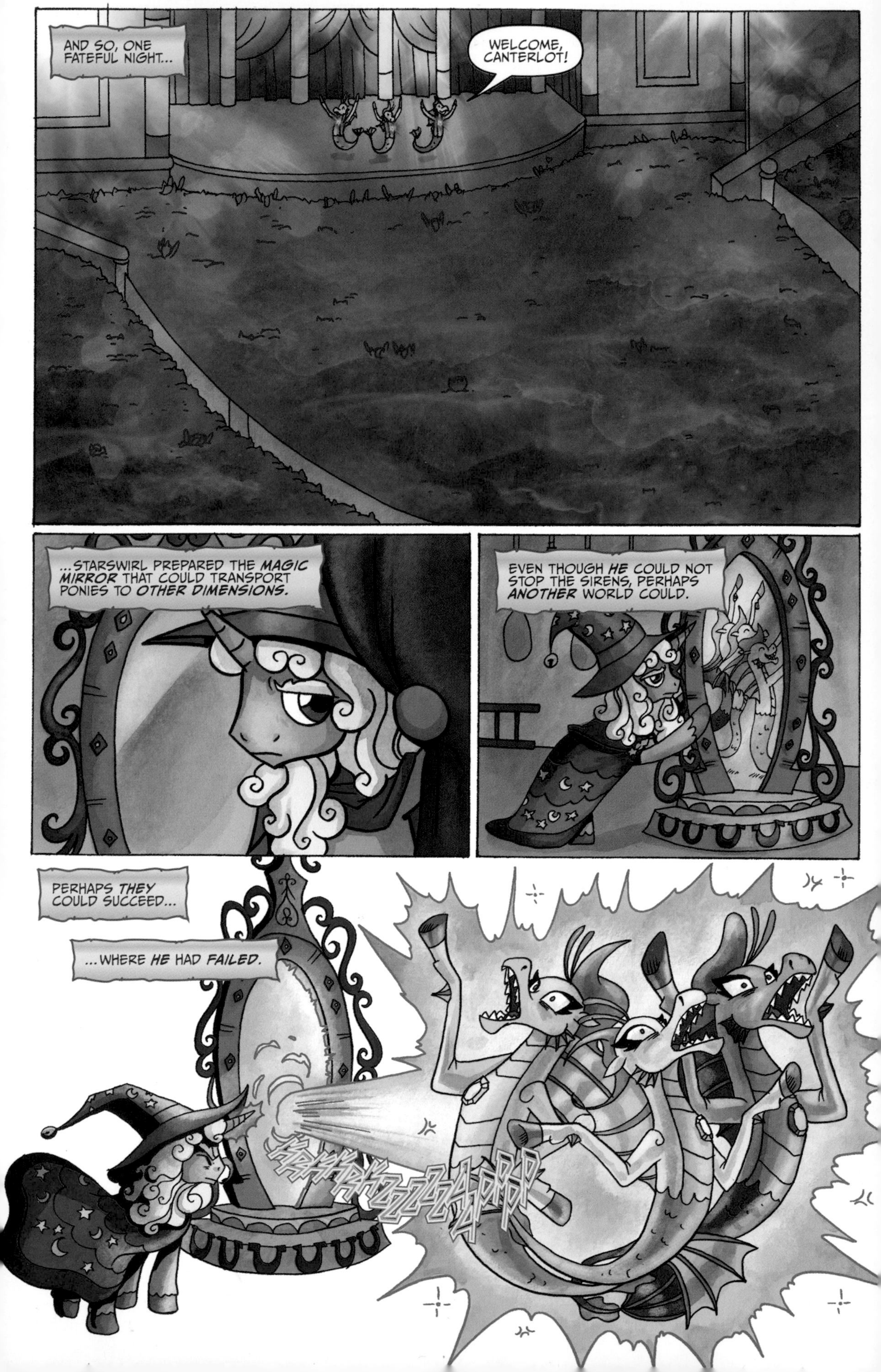
AND SO, ONE FATEFUL NIGHT...
WELCOME, CANTERLOT!
...STARSWIRL PREPARED THE MAGIC MIRROR THAT COULD TRANSPORT PONIES TO OTHER DIMENSIONS.
EVEN THOUGH HE COULD NOT STOP THE SIRENS, PERHAPS ANOTHER WORLD COULD.
PERHAPS THEY COULD SUCCEED...
...WHERE HE HAD FAILED.

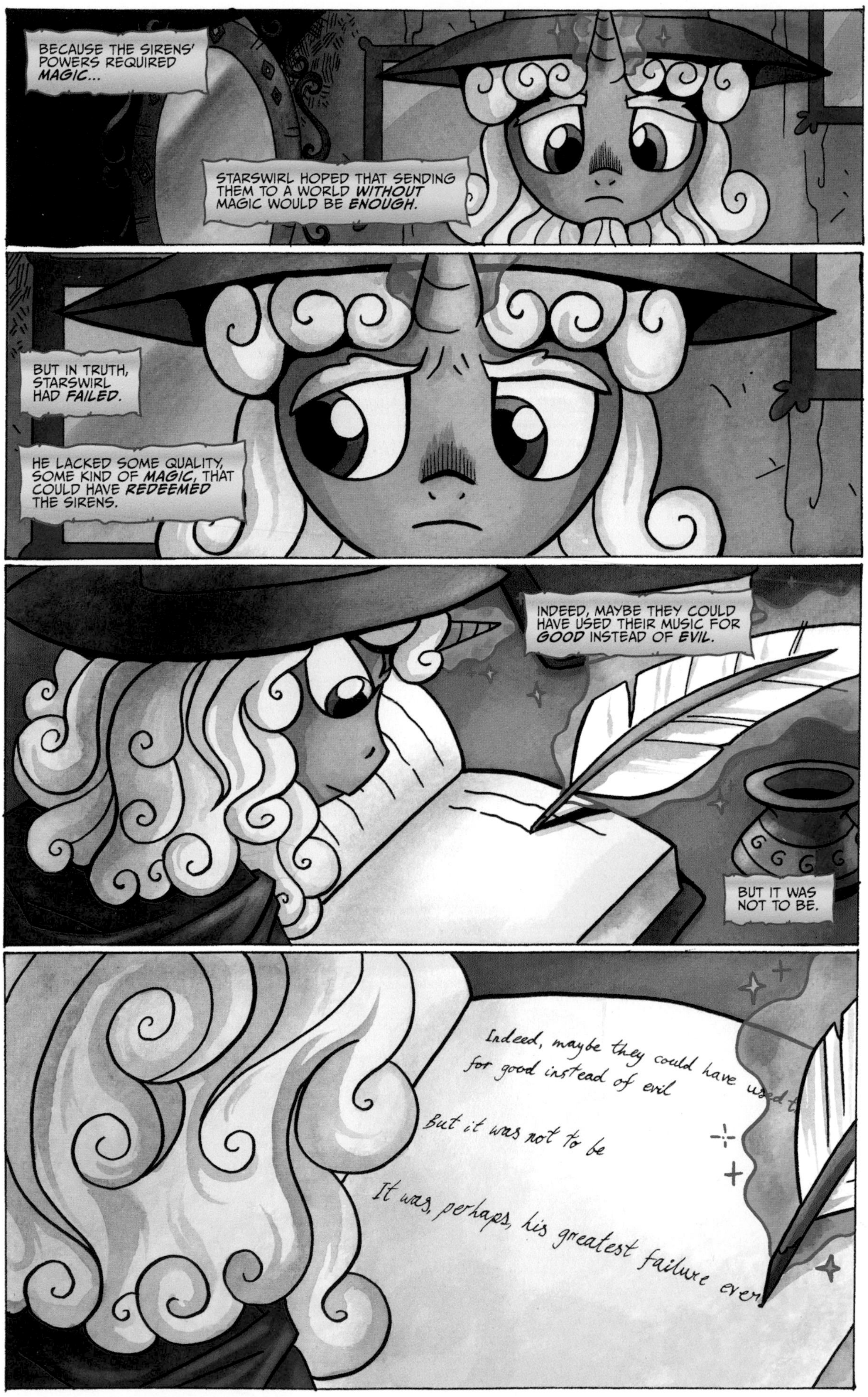
BECAUSE THE SIRENS' POWERS REQUIRED MAGIC...
STARSWIRL HOPED THAT SENDING THEM TO A WORLD WITHOUT MAGIC WOULD BE ENOUGH.
BUT IN TRUTH, STARSWIRL HAD FAILED.
HE LACKED SOME QUALITY, SOME KIND OF MAGIC, THAT COULD HAVE REDEEMED THE SIRENS.
INDEED, MAYBE THEY COULD HAVE USED THEIR MUSIC FOR GOOD INSTEAD OF EVIL.
BUT IT WAS NOT TO BE.
Indeed, maybe they could have used t
for good instead of evil
But it was not to be
It was, perhaps, his greatest failure ever

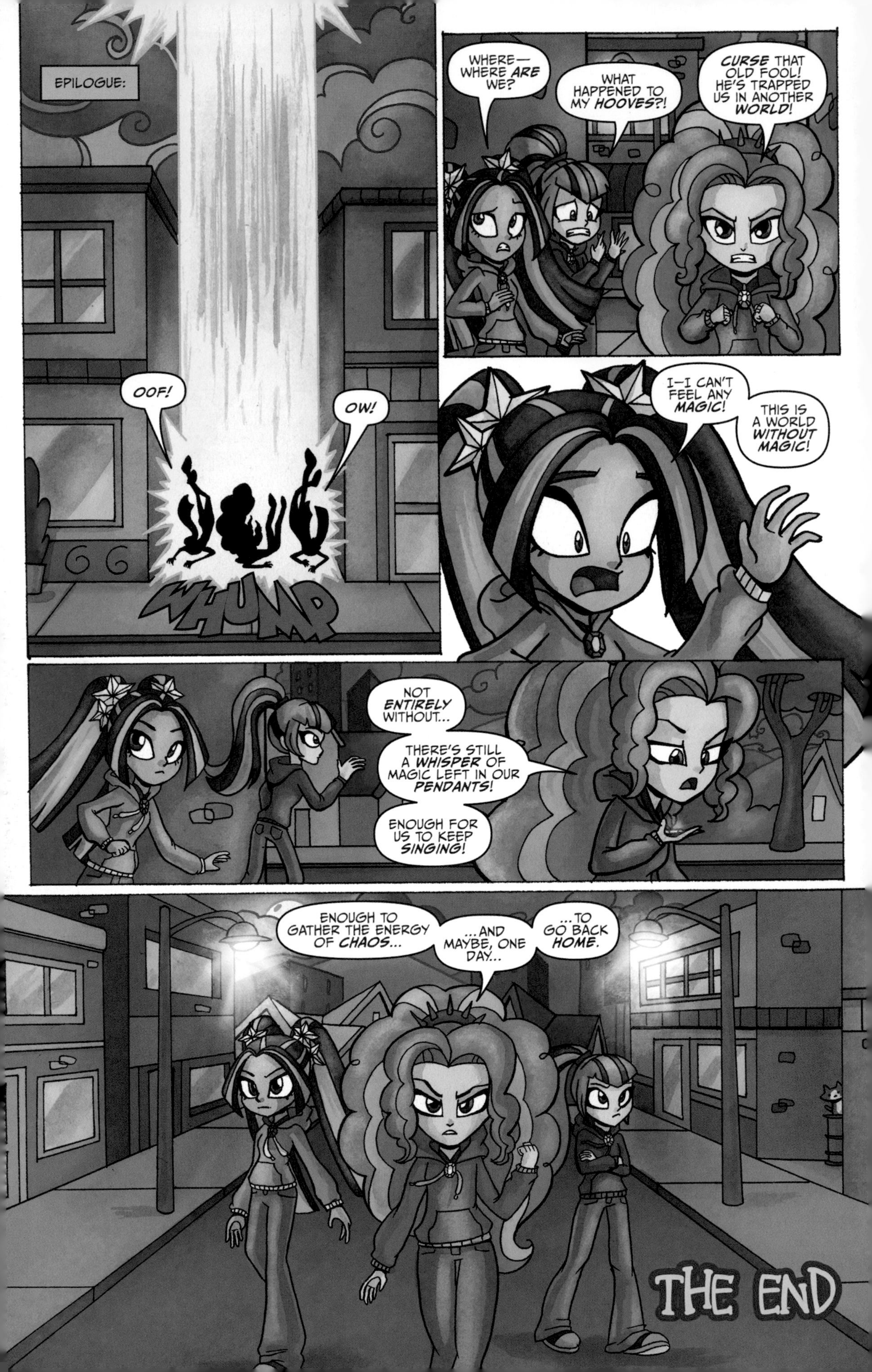
EPILOGUE:
OOF!
OW!
WHUMP
WHERE— WHERE ARE WE?
WHAT HAPPENED TO MY HOOVES?!
CURSE THAT OLD FOOL! HE'S TRAPPED US IN ANOTHER WORLD!
I—I CAN'T FEEL ANY MAGIC!
THIS IS A WORLD WITHOUT MAGIC!
NOT ENTIRELY WITHOUT...
THERE'S STILL A WHISPER OF MAGIC LEFT IN OUR PENDANTS!
ENOUGH FOR US TO KEEP SINGING!
ENOUGH TO GATHER THE ENERGY OF CHAOS...
...AND MAYBE, ONE DAY...
...TO GO BACK HOME.
THE END

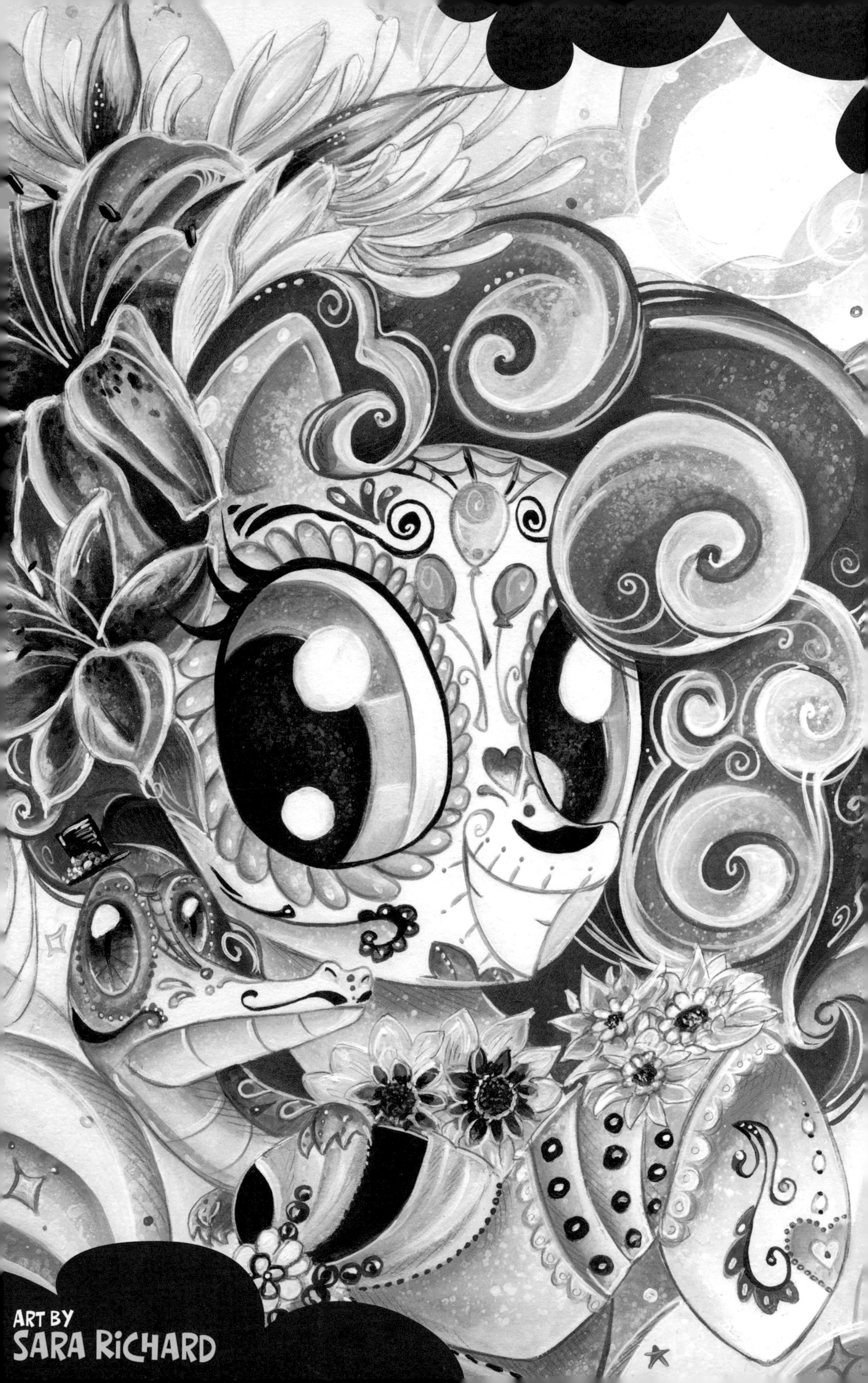
ART BY
SARA RICHARD

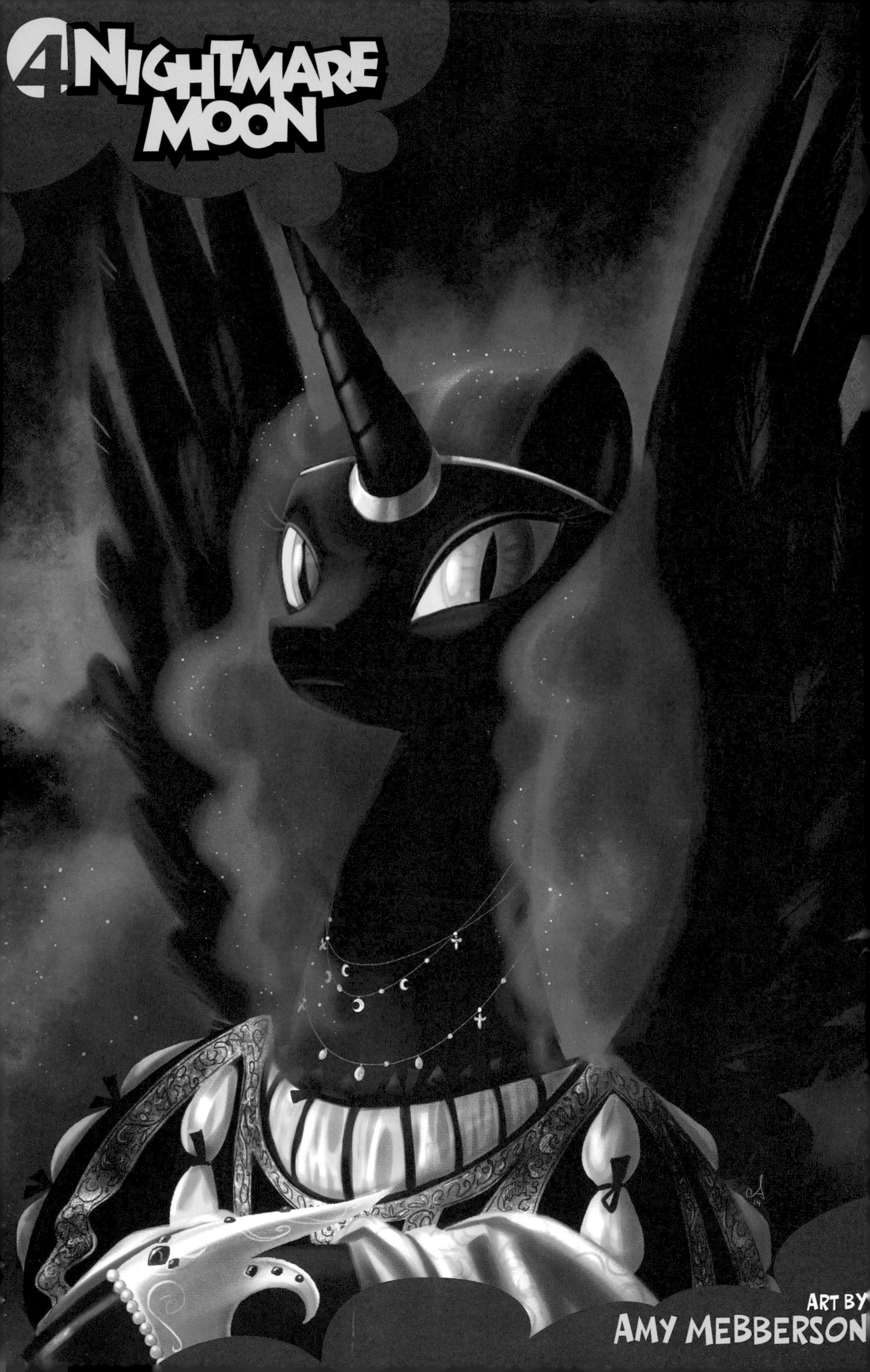
4 NIGHTMARE MOON
ART BY
AMY MEBBERSON

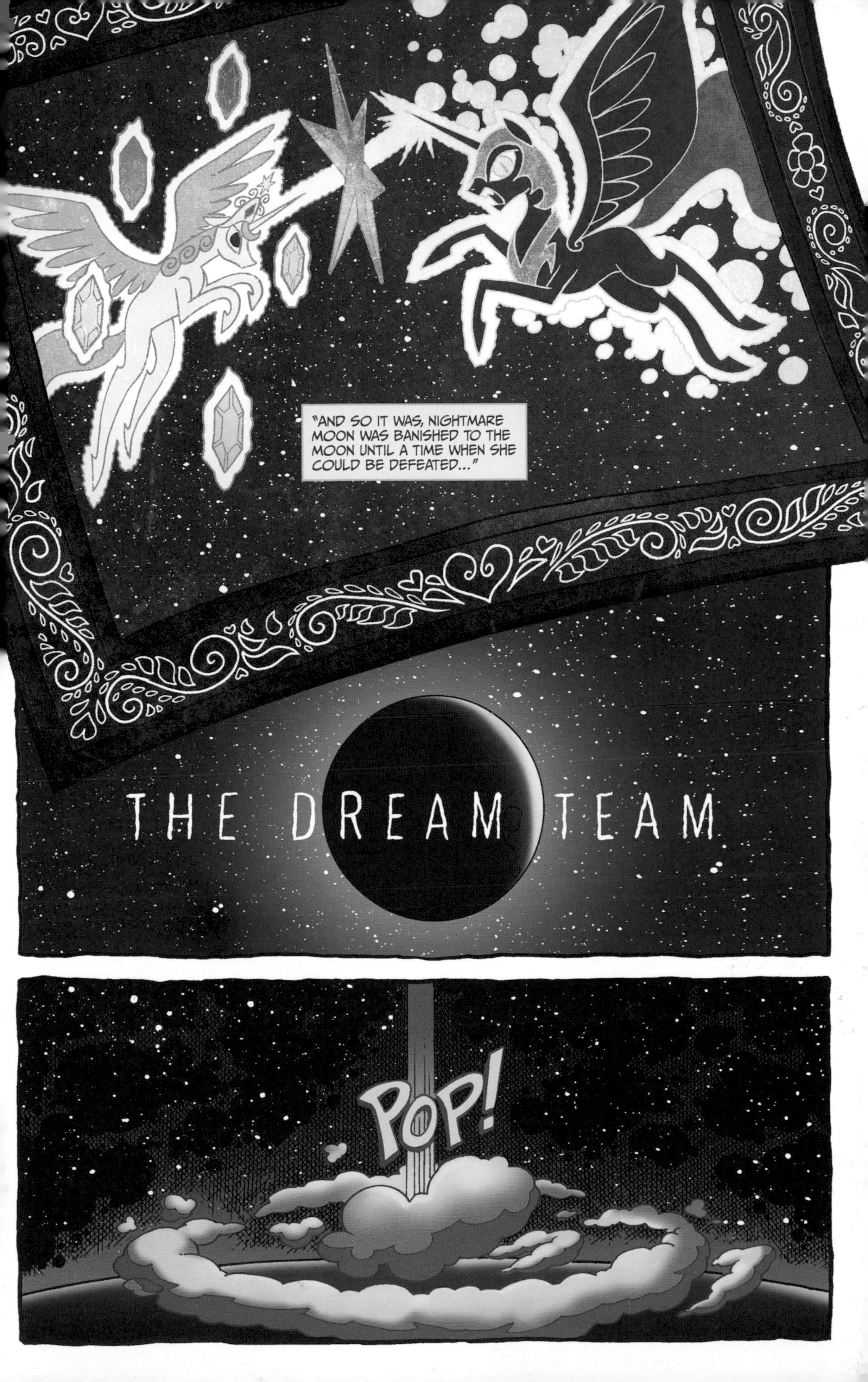
"AND SO IT WAS, NIGHTMARE MOON WAS BANISHED TO THE MOON UNTIL A TIME WHEN SHE COULD BE DEFEATED..."
THE DREAM TEAM
POP!

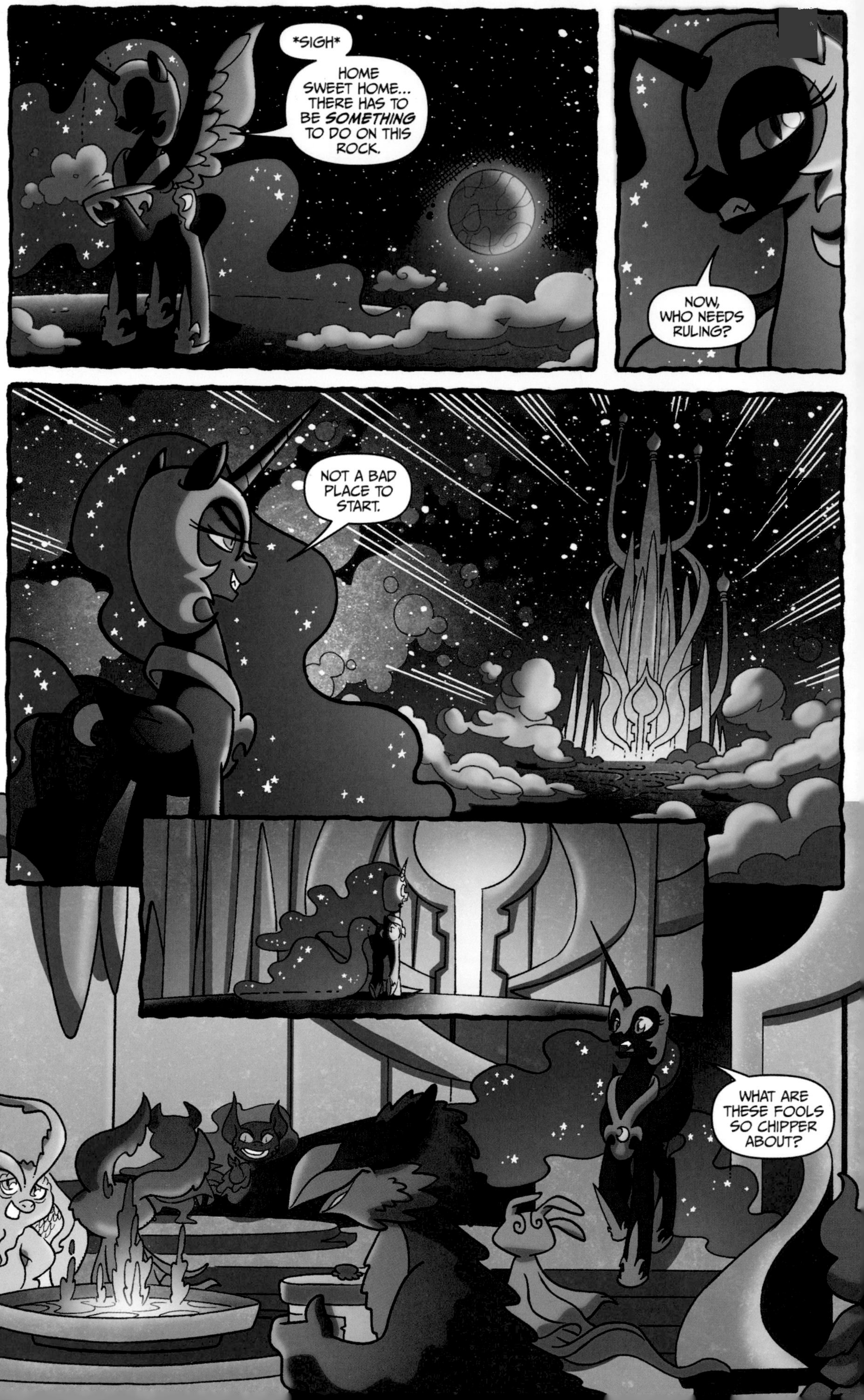
SIGH
HOME SWEET HOME... THERE HAS TO BE SOMETHING TO DO ON THIS ROCK.
NOW, WHO NEEDS RULING?
NOT A BAD PLACE TO START.
WHAT ARE THESE FOOLS SO CHIPPER ABOUT?

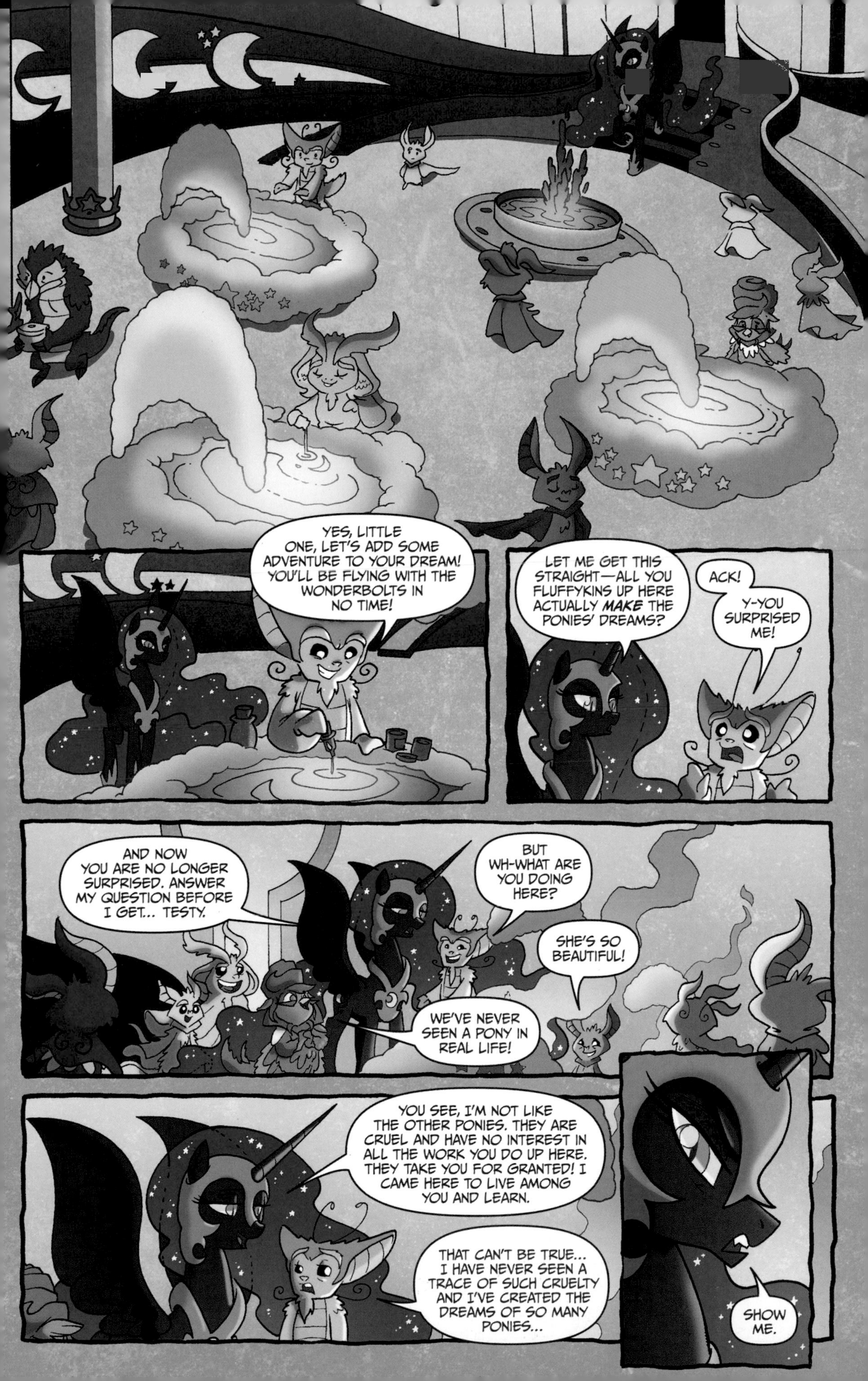

YES, LITTLE ONE, LET'S ADD SOME ADVENTURE TO YOUR DREAM! YOU'LL BE FLYING WITH THE WONDERBOLTS IN NO TIME!
LET ME GET THIS STRAIGHT—ALL YOU FLUFFYKINS UP HERE ACTUALLY *MAKE* THE PONIES' DREAMS?
ACK!
Y-YOU SURPRISED ME!
AND NOW YOU ARE NO LONGER SURPRISED. ANSWER MY QUESTION BEFORE I GET... TESTY.
BUT WH-WHAT ARE YOU DOING HERE?
SHE'S SO BEAUTIFUL!
WE'VE NEVER SEEN A PONY IN REAL LIFE!
YOU SEE, I'M NOT LIKE THE OTHER PONIES. THEY ARE CRUEL AND HAVE NO INTEREST IN ALL THE WORK YOU DO UP HERE. THEY TAKE YOU FOR GRANTED! I CAME HERE TO LIVE AMONG YOU AND LEARN.
THAT CAN'T BE TRUE... I HAVE NEVER SEEN A TRACE OF SUCH CRUELTY AND I'VE CREATED THE DREAMS OF SO MANY PONIES...
SHOW ME.

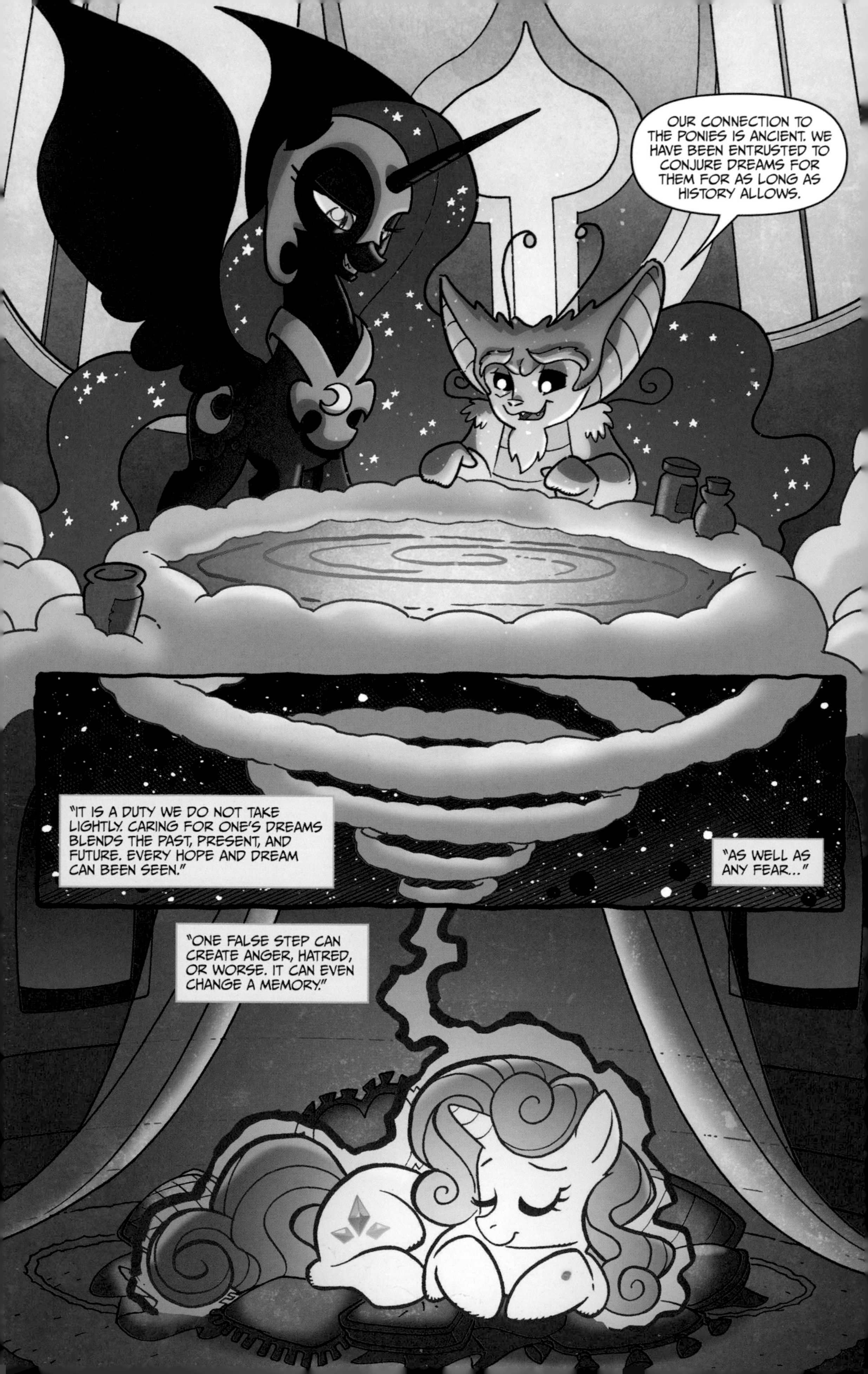
OUR CONNECTION TO THE PONIES IS ANCIENT. WE HAVE BEEN ENTRUSTED TO CONJURE DREAMS FOR THEM FOR AS LONG AS HISTORY ALLOWS.
"IT IS A DUTY WE DO NOT TAKE LIGHTLY. CARING FOR ONE'S DREAMS BLENDS THE PAST, PRESENT, AND FUTURE. EVERY HOPE AND DREAM CAN BEEN SEEN."
"AS WELL AS ANY FEAR..."
"ONE FALSE STEP CAN CREATE ANGER, HATRED, OR WORSE. IT CAN EVEN CHANGE A MEMORY."

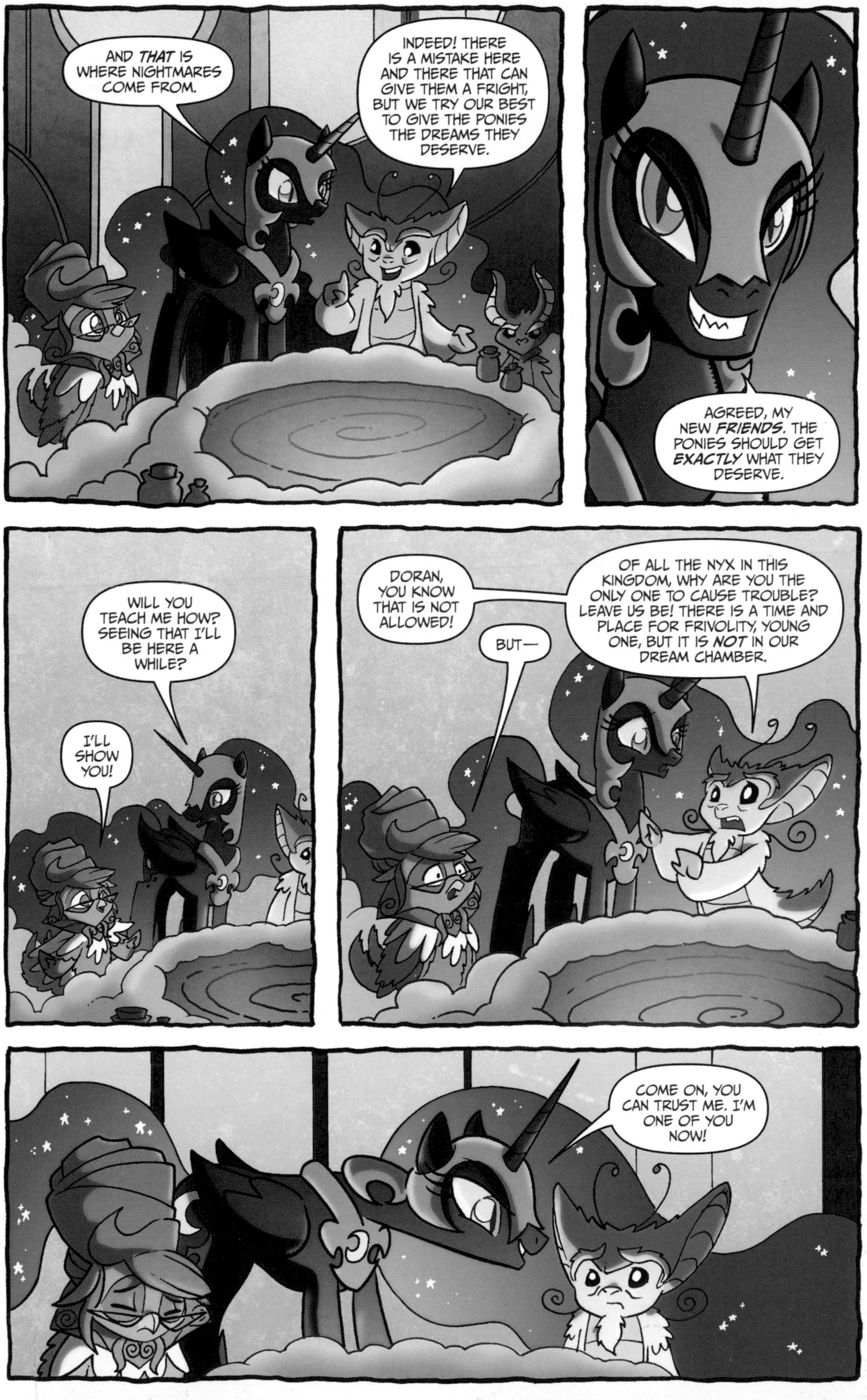
AND *THAT* IS WHERE NIGHTMARES COME FROM.
INDEED! THERE IS A MISTAKE HERE AND THERE THAT CAN GIVE THEM A FRIGHT, BUT WE TRY OUR BEST TO GIVE THE PONIES THE DREAMS THEY DESERVE.
AGREED, MY NEW ***FRIENDS***. THE PONIES SHOULD GET ***EXACTLY*** WHAT THEY DESERVE.
WILL YOU TEACH ME HOW? SEEING THAT I'LL BE HERE A WHILE?
I'LL SHOW YOU!
DORAN, YOU KNOW THAT IS NOT ALLOWED!
OF ALL THE NYX IN THIS KINGDOM, WHY ARE YOU THE ONLY ONE TO CAUSE TROUBLE? LEAVE US BE! THERE IS A TIME AND PLACE FOR FRIVOLITY, YOUNG ONE, BUT IT IS ***NOT*** IN OUR DREAM CHAMBER.
BUT—
COME ON, YOU CAN TRUST ME. I'M ONE OF YOU NOW!

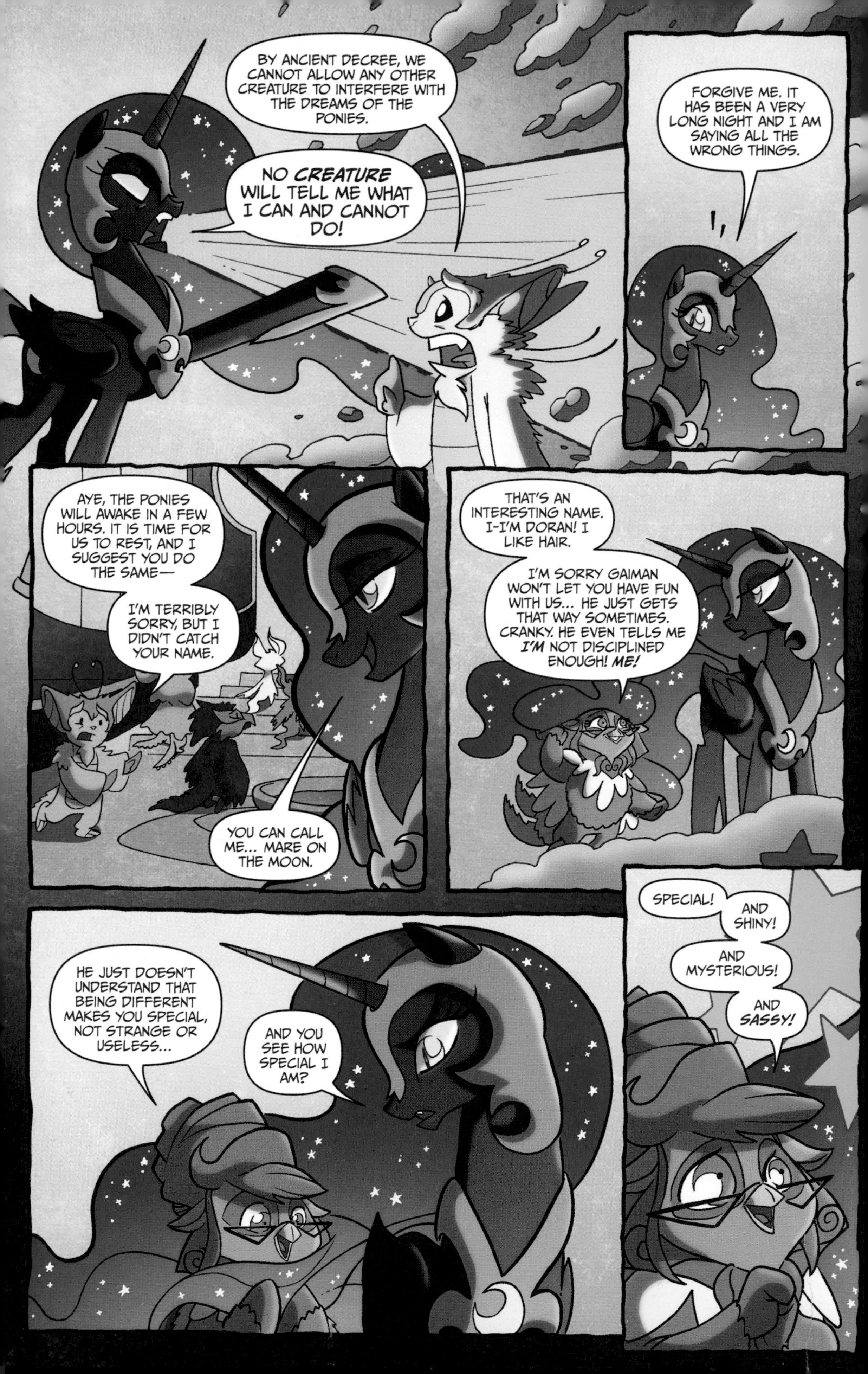
BY ANCIENT DECREE, WE CANNOT ALLOW ANY OTHER CREATURE TO INTERFERE WITH THE DREAMS OF THE PONIES.
NO *CREATURE* WILL TELL ME WHAT I CAN AND CANNOT DO!
FORGIVE ME. IT HAS BEEN A VERY LONG NIGHT AND I AM SAYING ALL THE WRONG THINGS.
AYE, THE PONIES WILL AWAKE IN A FEW HOURS. IT IS TIME FOR US TO REST, AND I SUGGEST YOU DO THE SAME—
I'M TERRIBLY SORRY, BUT I DIDN'T CATCH YOUR NAME.
YOU CAN CALL ME... MARE ON THE MOON.
THAT'S AN INTERESTING NAME. I-I'M DORAN! I LIKE HAIR.
I'M SORRY GAIMAN WON'T LET YOU HAVE FUN WITH US... HE JUST GETS THAT WAY SOMETIMES. CRANKY. HE EVEN TELLS ME *I'M* NOT DISCIPLINED ENOUGH! *ME!*
HE JUST DOESN'T UNDERSTAND THAT BEING DIFFERENT MAKES YOU SPECIAL, NOT STRANGE OR USELESS...
AND YOU SEE HOW SPECIAL I AM?
SPECIAL!
AND SHINY!
AND MYSTERIOUS!
AND *SASSY!*

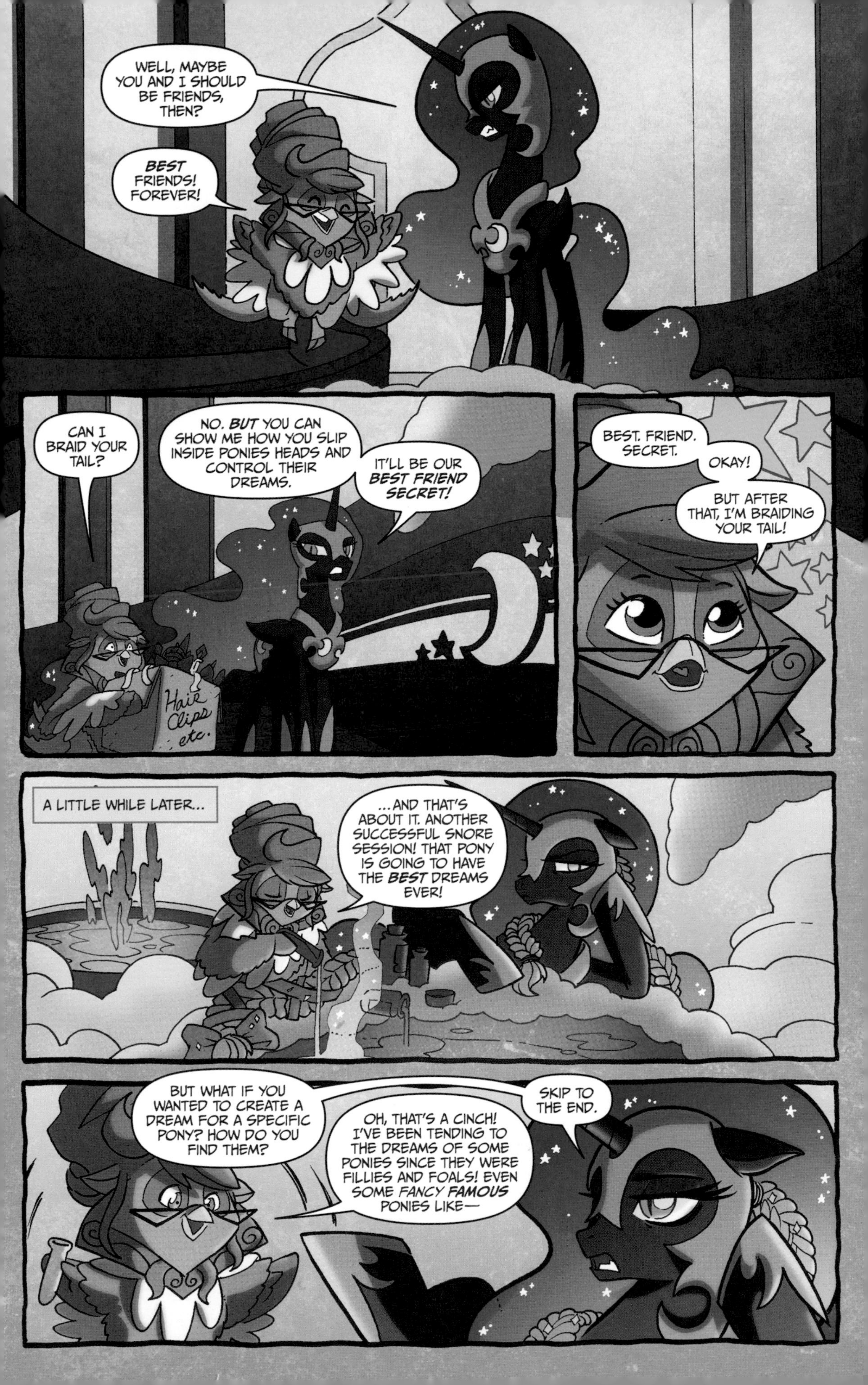

WELL, MAYBE YOU AND I SHOULD BE FRIENDS, THEN?
BEST FRIENDS! FOREVER!
CAN I BRAID YOUR TAIL?
NO. BUT YOU CAN SHOW ME HOW YOU SLIP INSIDE PONIES HEADS AND CONTROL THEIR DREAMS.
IT'LL BE OUR BEST FRIEND SECRET!
Hair Clips etc.
BEST. FRIEND. SECRET.
OKAY!
BUT AFTER THAT, I'M BRAIDING YOUR TAIL!
A LITTLE WHILE LATER...
...AND THAT'S ABOUT IT. ANOTHER SUCCESSFUL SNORE SESSION! THAT PONY IS GOING TO HAVE THE BEST DREAMS EVER!
BUT WHAT IF YOU WANTED TO CREATE A DREAM FOR A SPECIFIC PONY? HOW DO YOU FIND THEM?
OH, THAT'S A CINCH! I'VE BEEN TENDING TO THE DREAMS OF SOME PONIES SINCE THEY WERE FILLIES AND FOALS! EVEN SOME FANCY FAMOUS PONIES LIKE—
SKIP TO THE END.

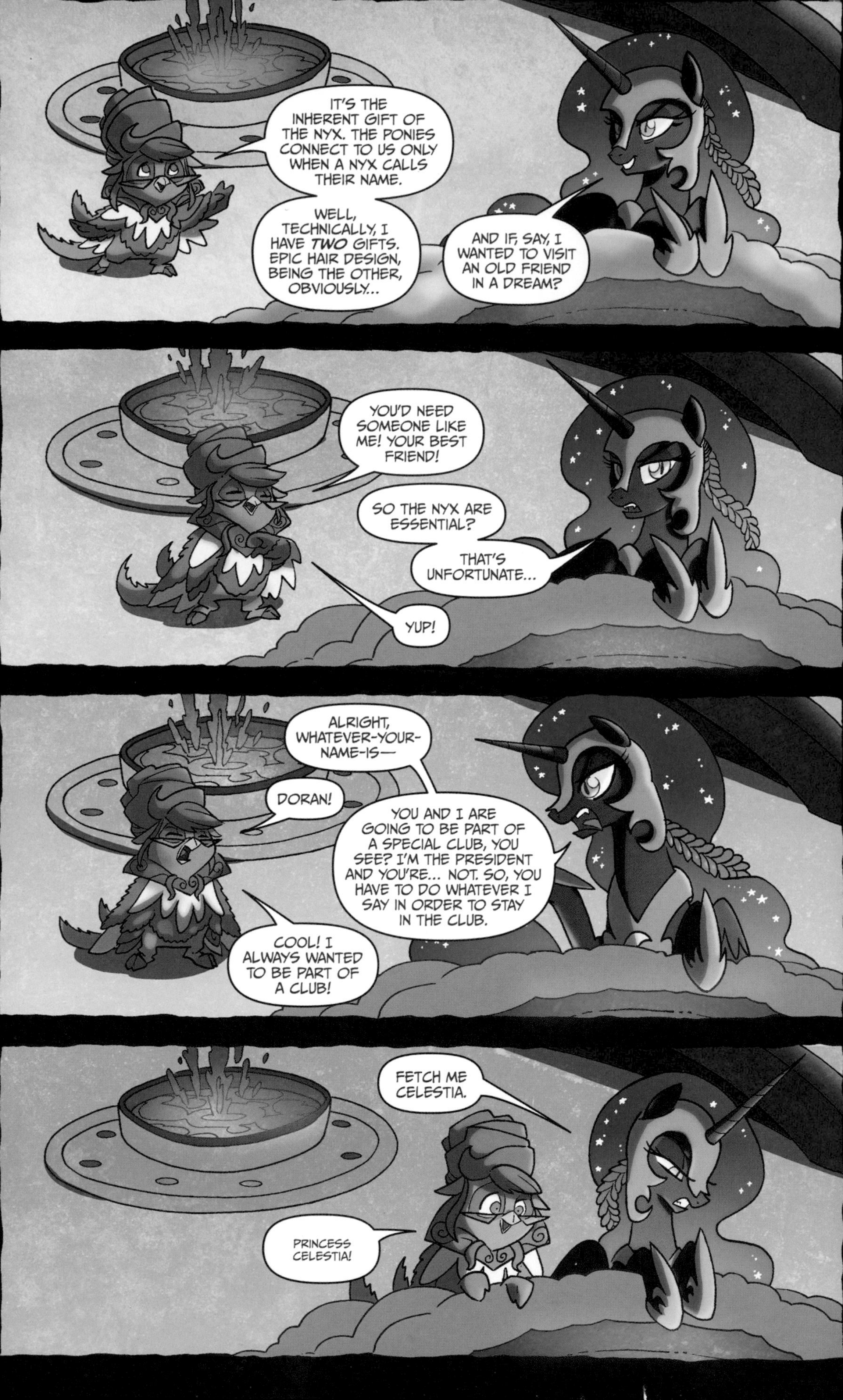
IT'S THE INHERENT GIFT OF THE NYX. THE PONIES CONNECT TO US ONLY WHEN A NYX CALLS THEIR NAME.
WELL, TECHNICALLY, I HAVE *TWO* GIFTS. EPIC HAIR DESIGN, BEING THE OTHER, OBVIOUSLY...
AND IF, SAY, I WANTED TO VISIT AN OLD FRIEND IN A DREAM?
YOU'D NEED SOMEONE LIKE ME! YOUR BEST FRIEND!
SO THE NYX ARE ESSENTIAL?
THAT'S UNFORTUNATE...
YUP!
ALRIGHT, WHATEVER-YOUR-NAME-IS—
DORAN!
YOU AND I ARE GOING TO BE PART OF A SPECIAL CLUB, YOU SEE? I'M THE PRESIDENT AND YOU'RE... NOT. SO, YOU HAVE TO DO WHATEVER I SAY IN ORDER TO STAY IN THE CLUB.
COOL! I ALWAYS WANTED TO BE PART OF A CLUB!
FETCH ME CELESTIA.
PRINCESS CELESTIA!

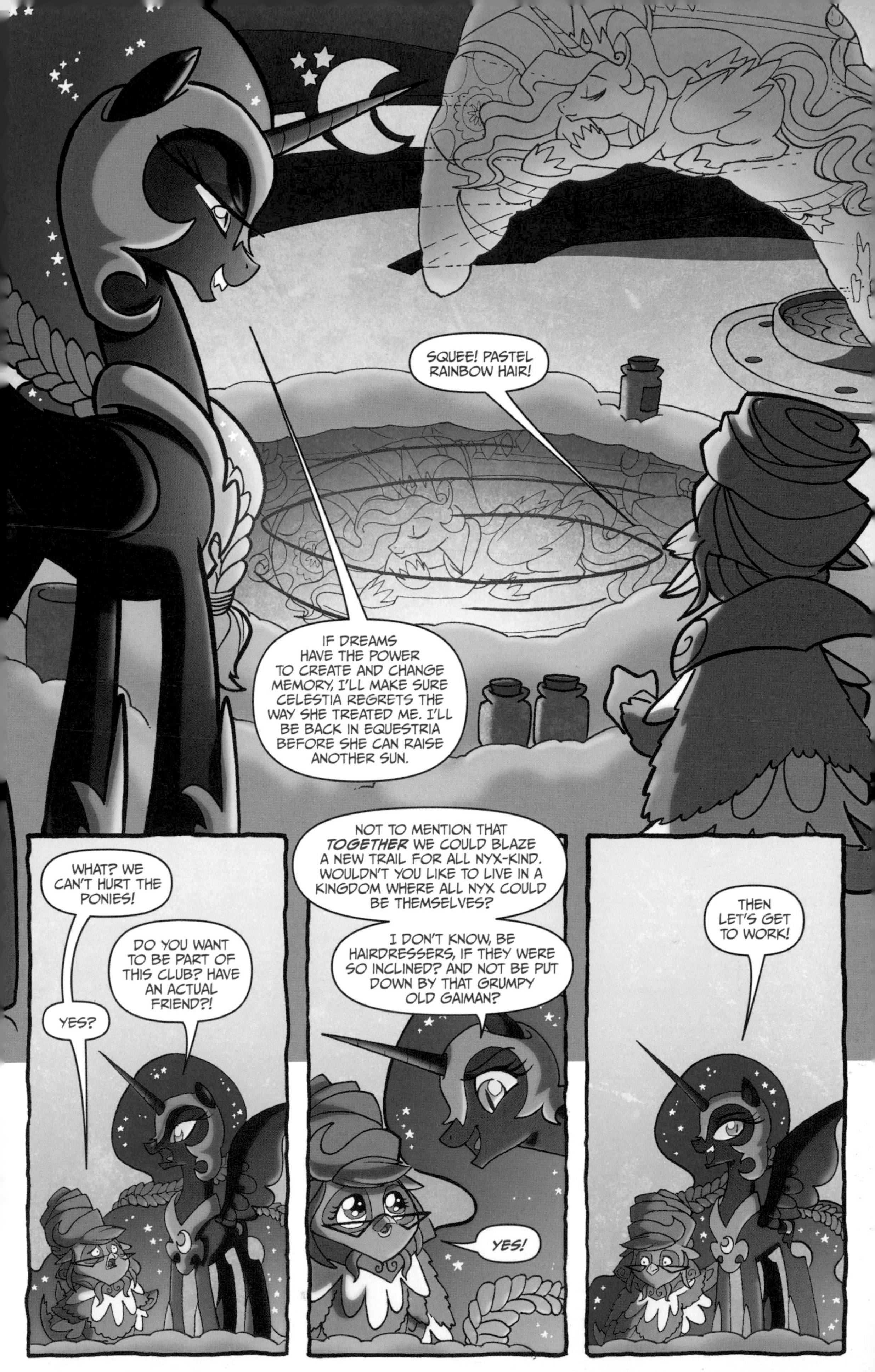
SQUEE! PASTEL RAINBOW HAIR!
IF DREAMS HAVE THE POWER TO CREATE AND CHANGE MEMORY, I'LL MAKE SURE CELESTIA REGRETS THE WAY SHE TREATED ME. I'LL BE BACK IN EQUESTRIA BEFORE SHE CAN RAISE ANOTHER SUN.
WHAT? WE CAN'T HURT THE PONIES!
DO YOU WANT TO BE PART OF THIS CLUB? HAVE AN ACTUAL FRIEND?!
YES?
NOT TO MENTION THAT TOGETHER WE COULD BLAZE A NEW TRAIL FOR ALL NYX-KIND. WOULDN'T YOU LIKE TO LIVE IN A KINGDOM WHERE ALL NYX COULD BE THEMSELVES?
I DON'T KNOW, BE HAIRDRESSERS, IF THEY WERE SO INCLINED? AND NOT BE PUT DOWN BY THAT GRUMPY OLD GAIMAN?
YES!
THEN LET'S GET TO WORK!

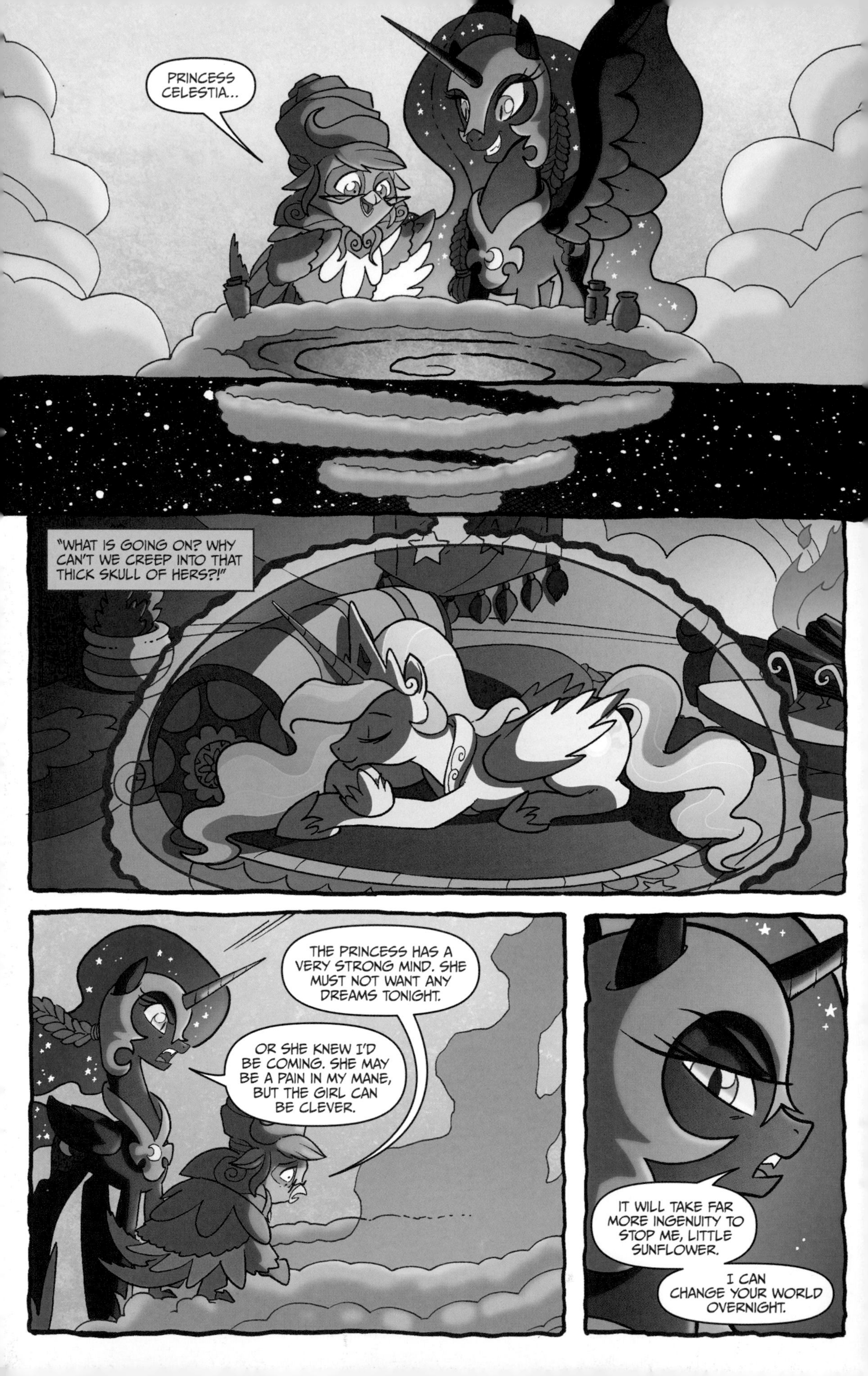
PRINCESS CELESTIA...
"WHAT IS GOING ON? WHY CAN'T WE CREEP INTO THAT THICK SKULL OF HERS?!"
THE PRINCESS HAS A VERY STRONG MIND. SHE MUST NOT WANT ANY DREAMS TONIGHT.
OR SHE KNEW I'D BE COMING. SHE MAY BE A PAIN IN MY MANE, BUT THE GIRL CAN BE CLEVER.
IT WILL TAKE FAR MORE INGENUITY TO STOP ME, LITTLE SUNFLOWER.
I CAN CHANGE YOUR WORLD OVERNIGHT.

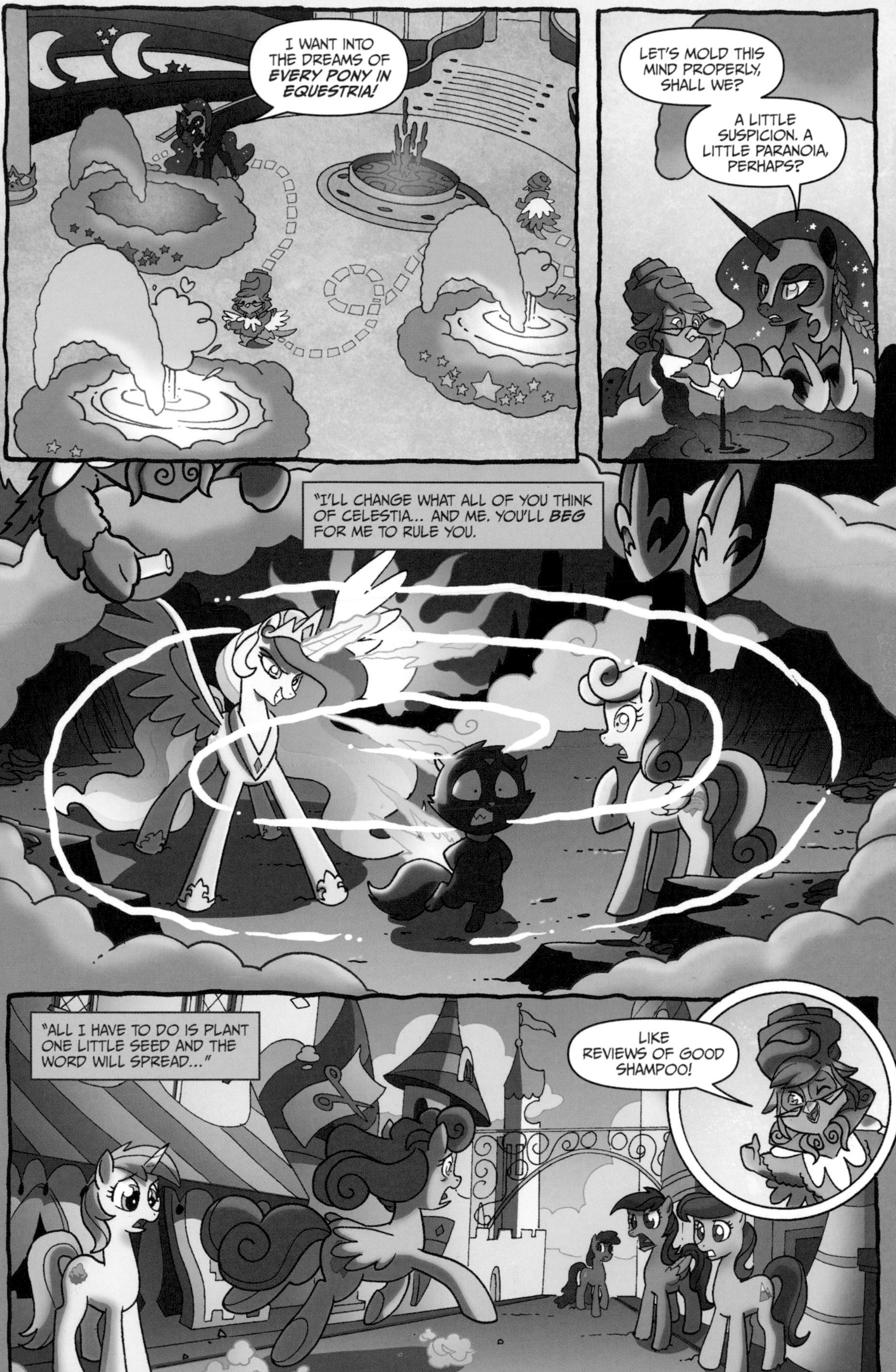
I WANT INTO THE DREAMS OF EVERY PONY IN EQUESTRIA!
LET'S MOLD THIS MIND PROPERLY, SHALL WE?
A LITTLE SUSPICION. A LITTLE PARANOIA, PERHAPS?
"I'LL CHANGE WHAT ALL OF YOU THINK OF CELESTIA... AND ME. YOU'LL BEG FOR ME TO RULE YOU.
"ALL I HAVE TO DO IS PLANT ONE LITTLE SEED AND THE WORD WILL SPREAD..."
LIKE REVIEWS OF GOOD SHAMPOO!

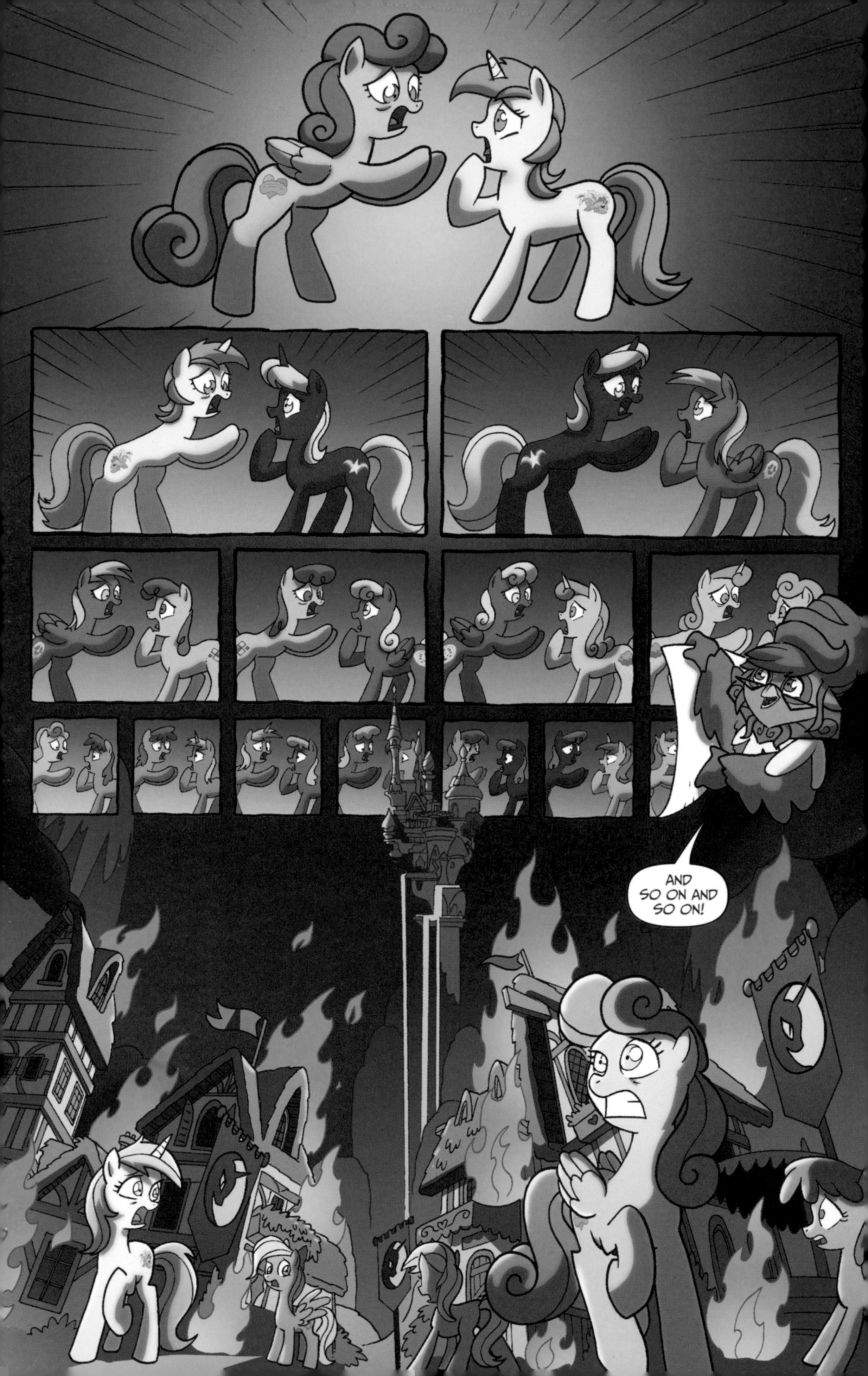
AND SO ON AND SO ON!

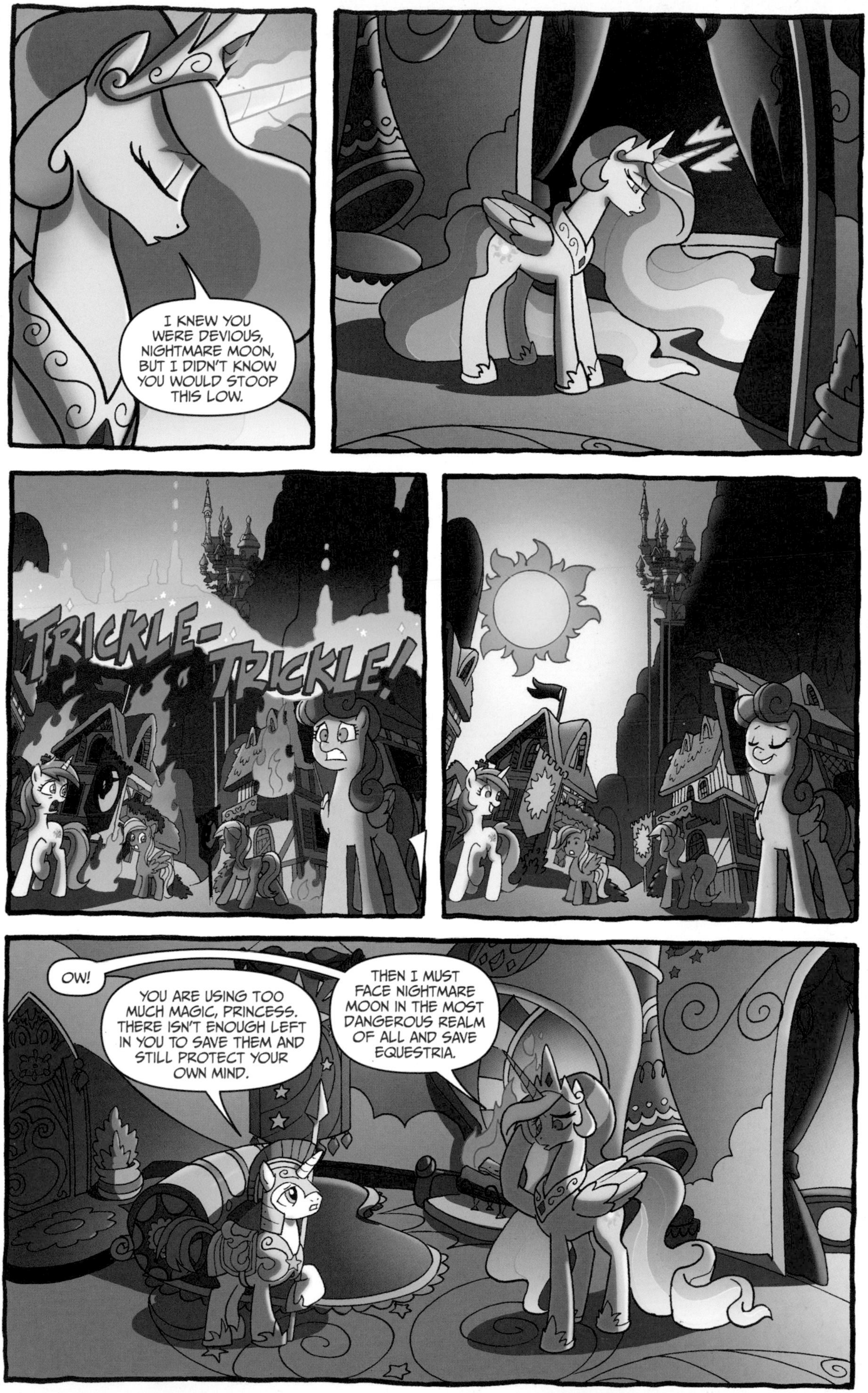
I KNEW YOU WERE DEVIOUS, NIGHTMARE MOON, BUT I DIDN'T KNOW YOU WOULD STOOP THIS LOW.
TRICKLE-TRICKLE!
OW!
YOU ARE USING TOO MUCH MAGIC, PRINCESS. THERE ISN'T ENOUGH LEFT IN YOU TO SAVE THEM AND STILL PROTECT YOUR OWN MIND.
THEN I MUST FACE NIGHTMARE MOON IN THE MOST DANGEROUS REALM OF ALL AND SAVE EQUESTRIA.

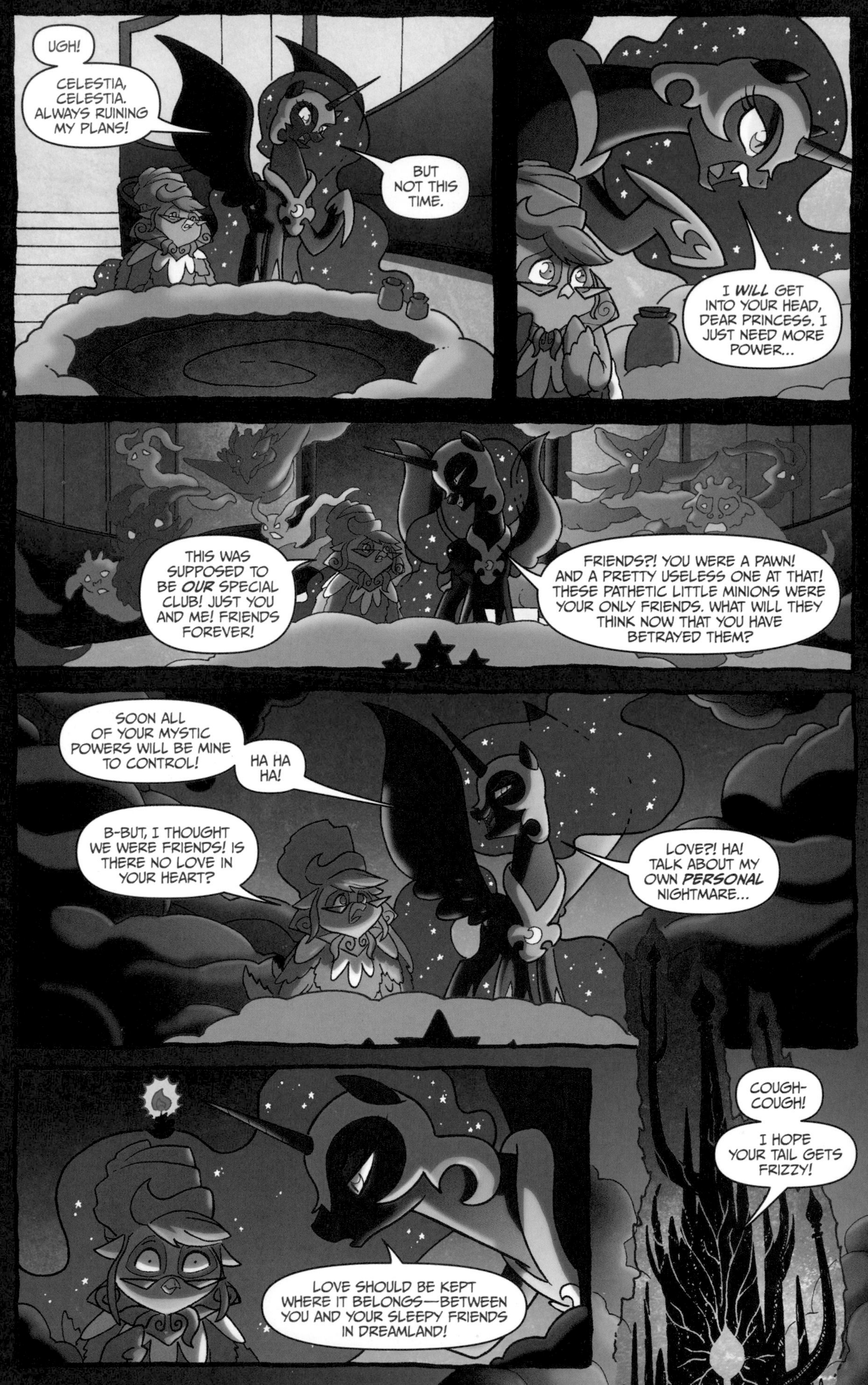
UGH!
CELESTIA, CELESTIA. ALWAYS RUINING MY PLANS!
BUT NOT THIS TIME.
I WILL GET INTO YOUR HEAD, DEAR PRINCESS. I JUST NEED MORE POWER...
THIS WAS SUPPOSED TO BE OUR SPECIAL CLUB! JUST YOU AND ME! FRIENDS FOREVER!
FRIENDS?! YOU WERE A PAWN! AND A PRETTY USELESS ONE AT THAT! THESE PATHETIC LITTLE MINIONS WERE YOUR ONLY FRIENDS. WHAT WILL THEY THINK NOW THAT YOU HAVE BETRAYED THEM?
SOON ALL OF YOUR MYSTIC POWERS WILL BE MINE TO CONTROL!
HA HA HA!
B-BUT, I THOUGHT WE WERE FRIENDS! IS THERE NO LOVE IN YOUR HEART?
LOVE?! HA! TALK ABOUT MY OWN PERSONAL NIGHTMARE...
LOVE SHOULD BE KEPT WHERE IT BELONGS—BETWEEN YOU AND YOUR SLEEPY FRIENDS IN DREAMLAND!
COUGH-COUGH!
I HOPE YOUR TAIL GETS FRIZZY!

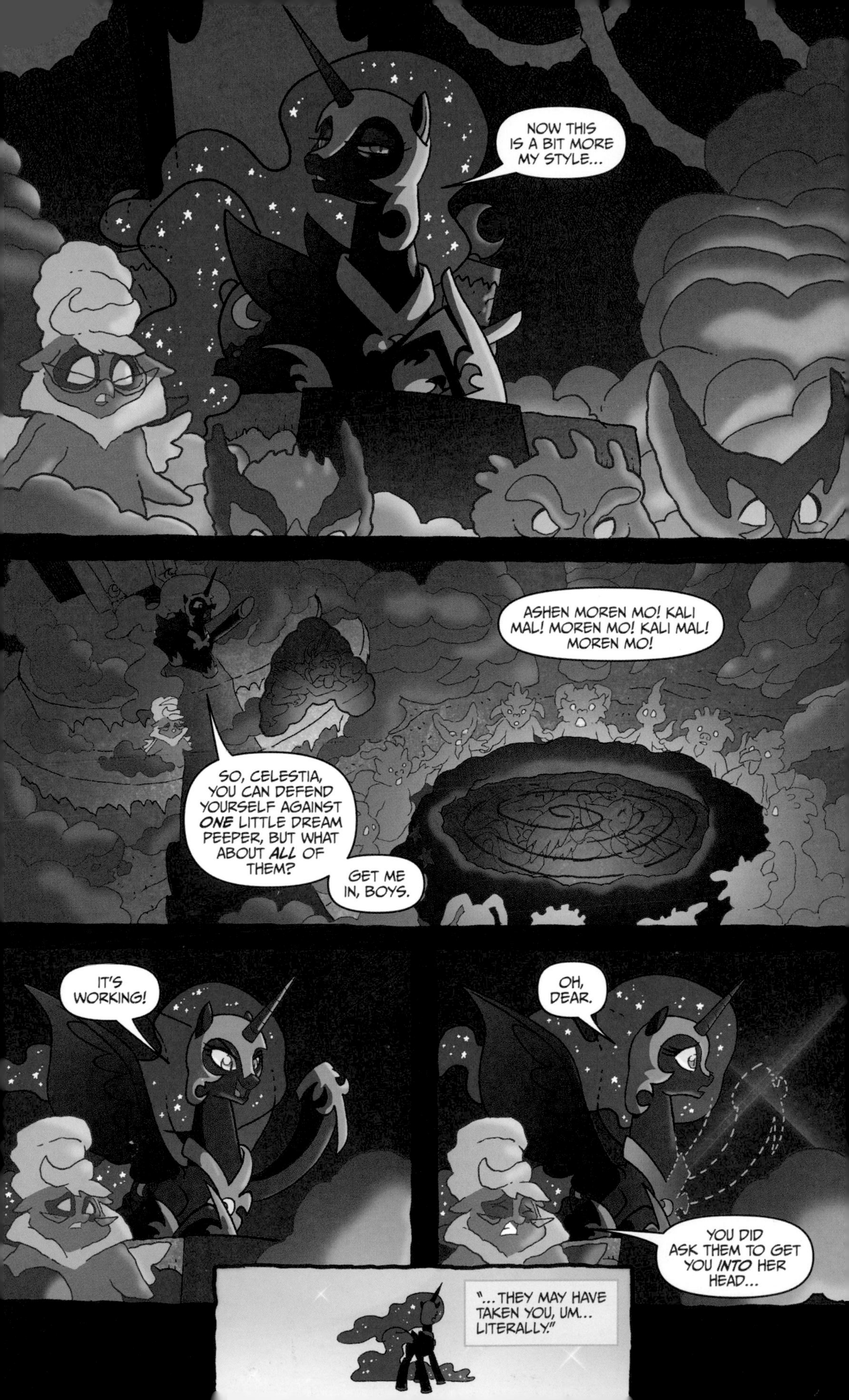
NOW THIS IS A BIT MORE MY STYLE...
ASHEN MOREN MO! KALI MAL! MOREN MO! KALI MAL! MOREN MO!
SO, CELESTIA, YOU CAN DEFEND YOURSELF AGAINST ONE LITTLE DREAM PEEPER, BUT WHAT ABOUT ALL OF THEM?
GET ME IN, BOYS.
IT'S WORKING!
OH, DEAR.
YOU DID ASK THEM TO GET YOU INTO HER HEAD...
"...THEY MAY HAVE TAKEN YOU, UM... LITERALLY."

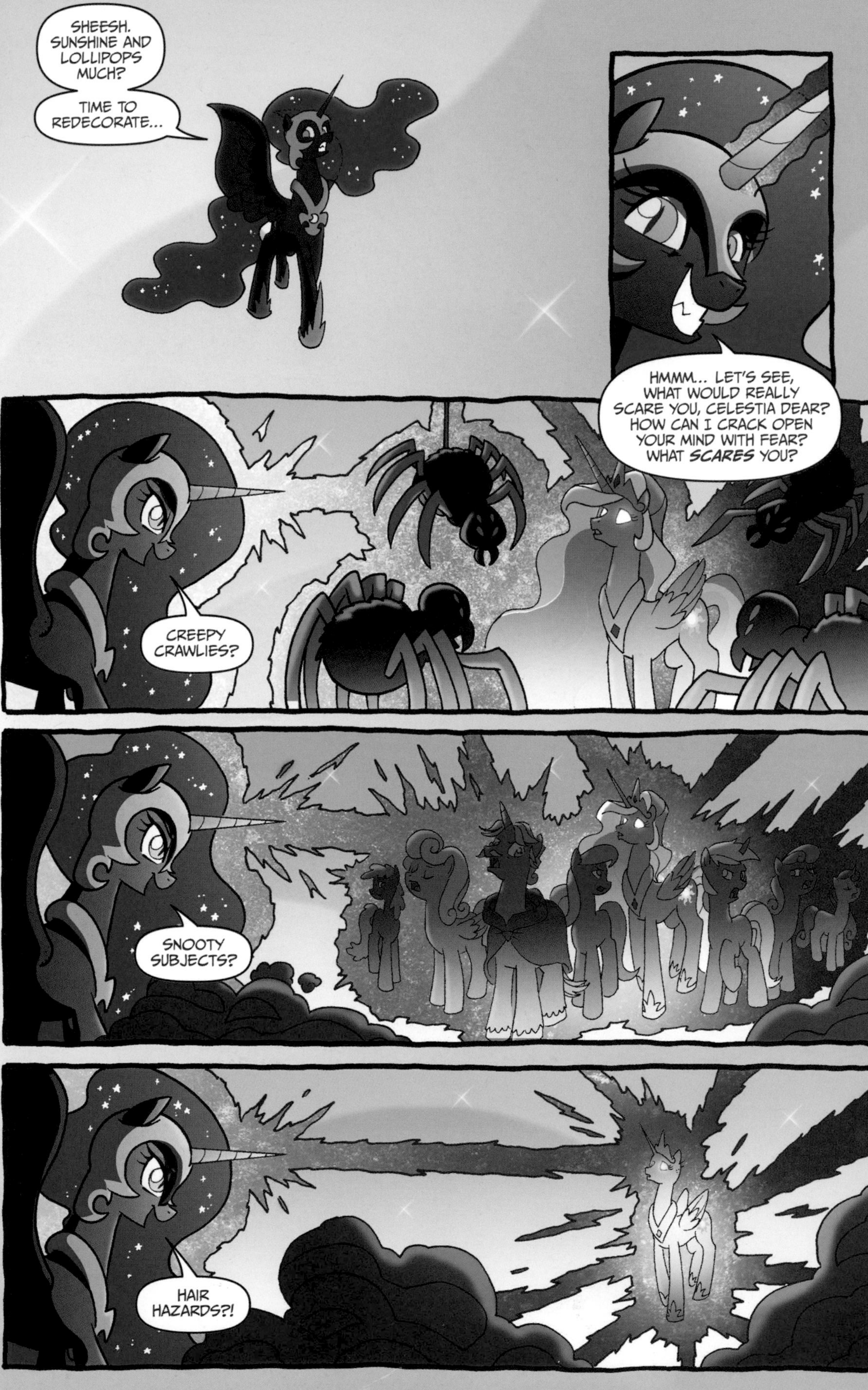
SHEESH. SUNSHINE AND LOLLIPOPS MUCH?
TIME TO REDECORATE...
HMMM... LET'S SEE, WHAT WOULD REALLY SCARE YOU, CELESTIA DEAR? HOW CAN I CRACK OPEN YOUR MIND WITH FEAR? WHAT SCARES YOU?
CREEPY CRAWLIES?
SNOOTY SUBJECTS?
HAIR HAZARDS?!

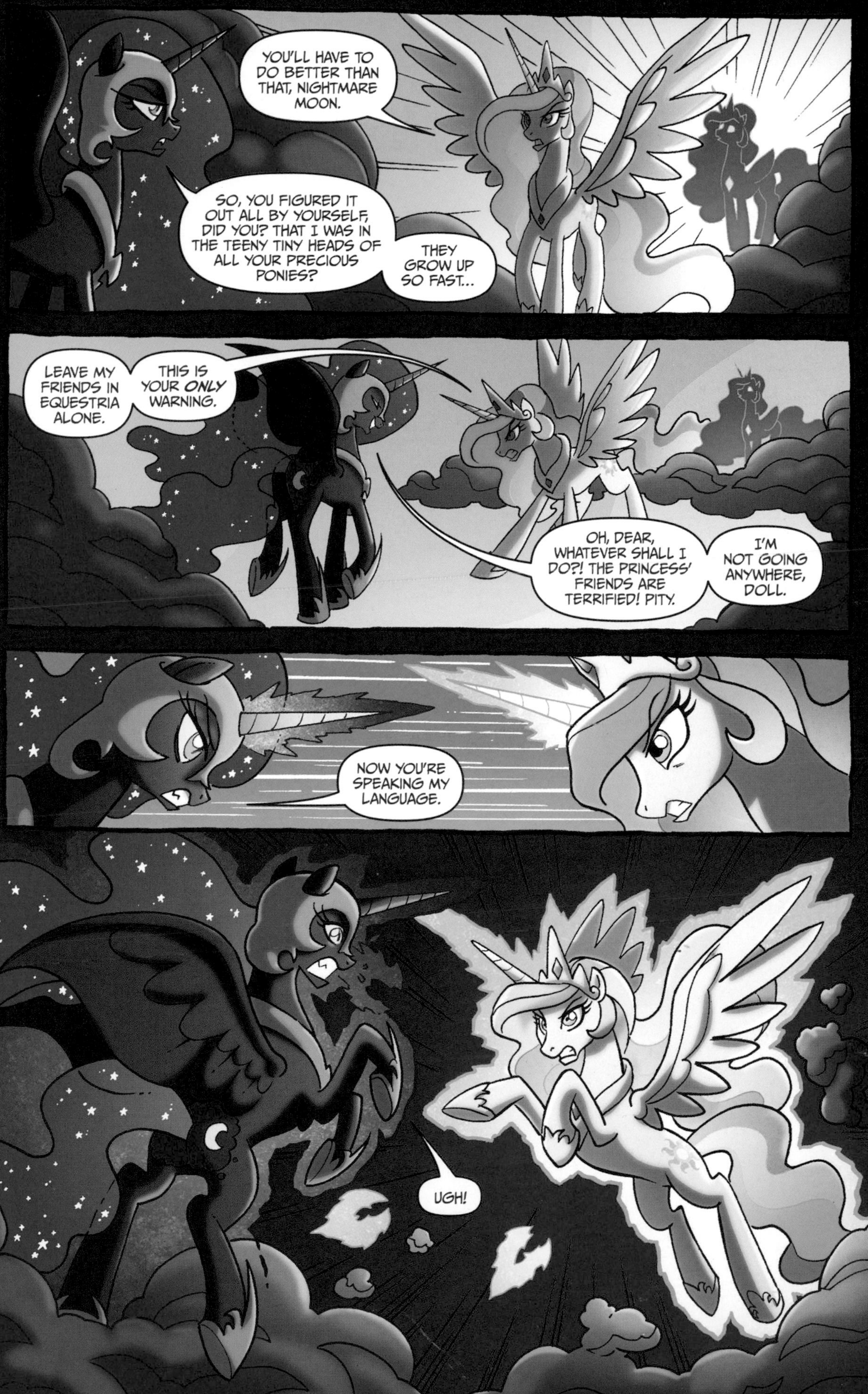
YOU'LL HAVE TO DO BETTER THAN THAT, NIGHTMARE MOON.
SO, YOU FIGURED IT OUT ALL BY YOURSELF, DID YOU? THAT I WAS IN THE TEENY TINY HEADS OF ALL YOUR PRECIOUS PONIES?
THEY GROW UP SO FAST...
LEAVE MY FRIENDS IN EQUESTRIA ALONE.
THIS IS YOUR *ONLY* WARNING.
OH, DEAR, WHATEVER SHALL I DO?! THE PRINCESS' FRIENDS ARE TERRIFIED! PITY.
I'M NOT GOING ANYWHERE, DOLL.
NOW YOU'RE SPEAKING MY LANGUAGE.
UGH!

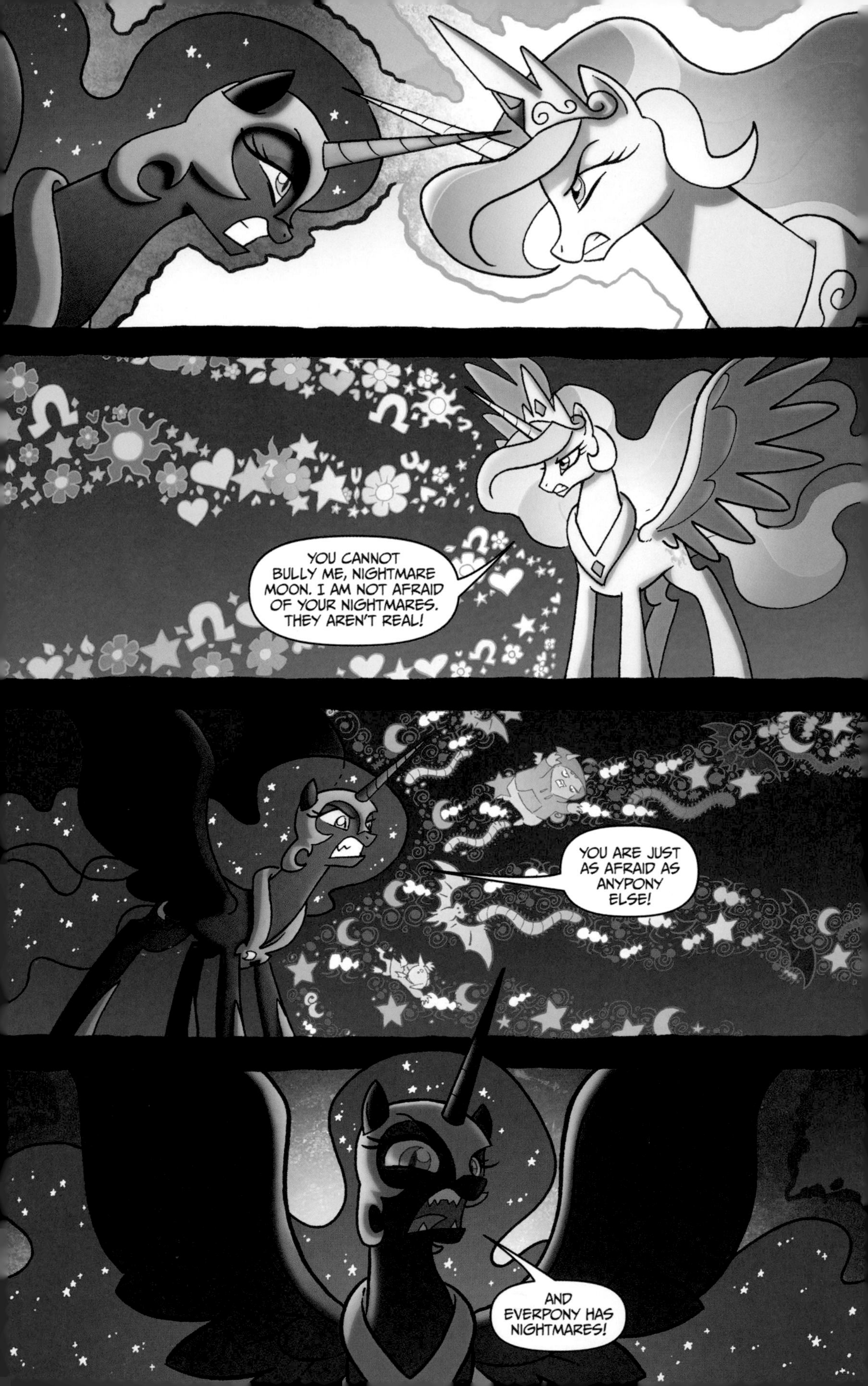
YOU CANNOT BULLY ME, NIGHTMARE MOON. I AM NOT AFRAID OF YOUR NIGHTMARES. THEY AREN'T REAL!
YOU ARE JUST AS AFRAID AS ANYPONY ELSE!
AND EVERPONY HAS NIGHTMARES!

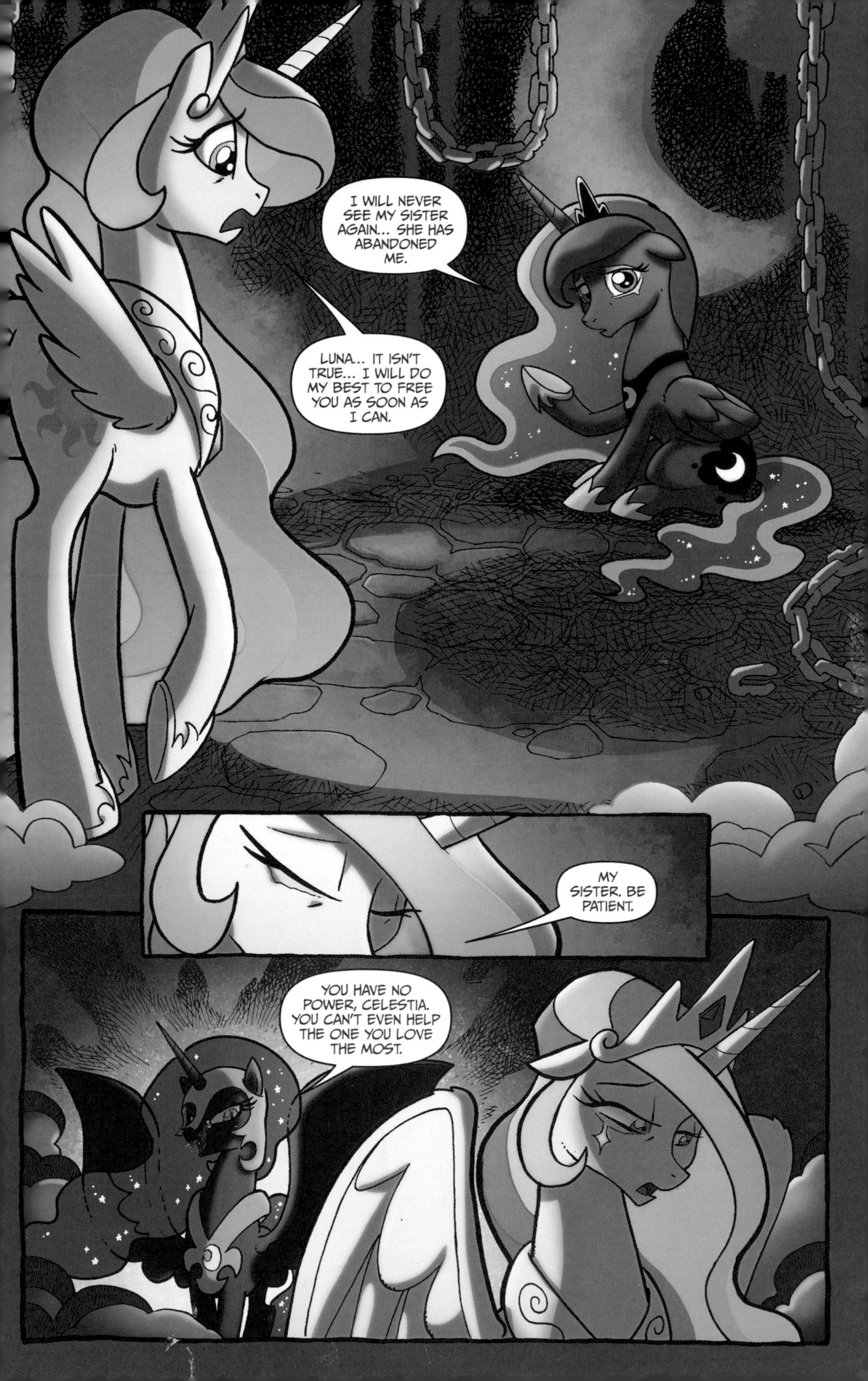
I WILL NEVER SEE MY SISTER AGAIN... SHE HAS ABANDONED ME.
LUNA... IT ISN'T TRUE... I WILL DO MY BEST TO FREE YOU AS SOON AS I CAN.
MY SISTER. BE PATIENT.
YOU HAVE NO POWER, CELESTIA. YOU CAN'T EVEN HELP THE ONE YOU LOVE THE MOST.

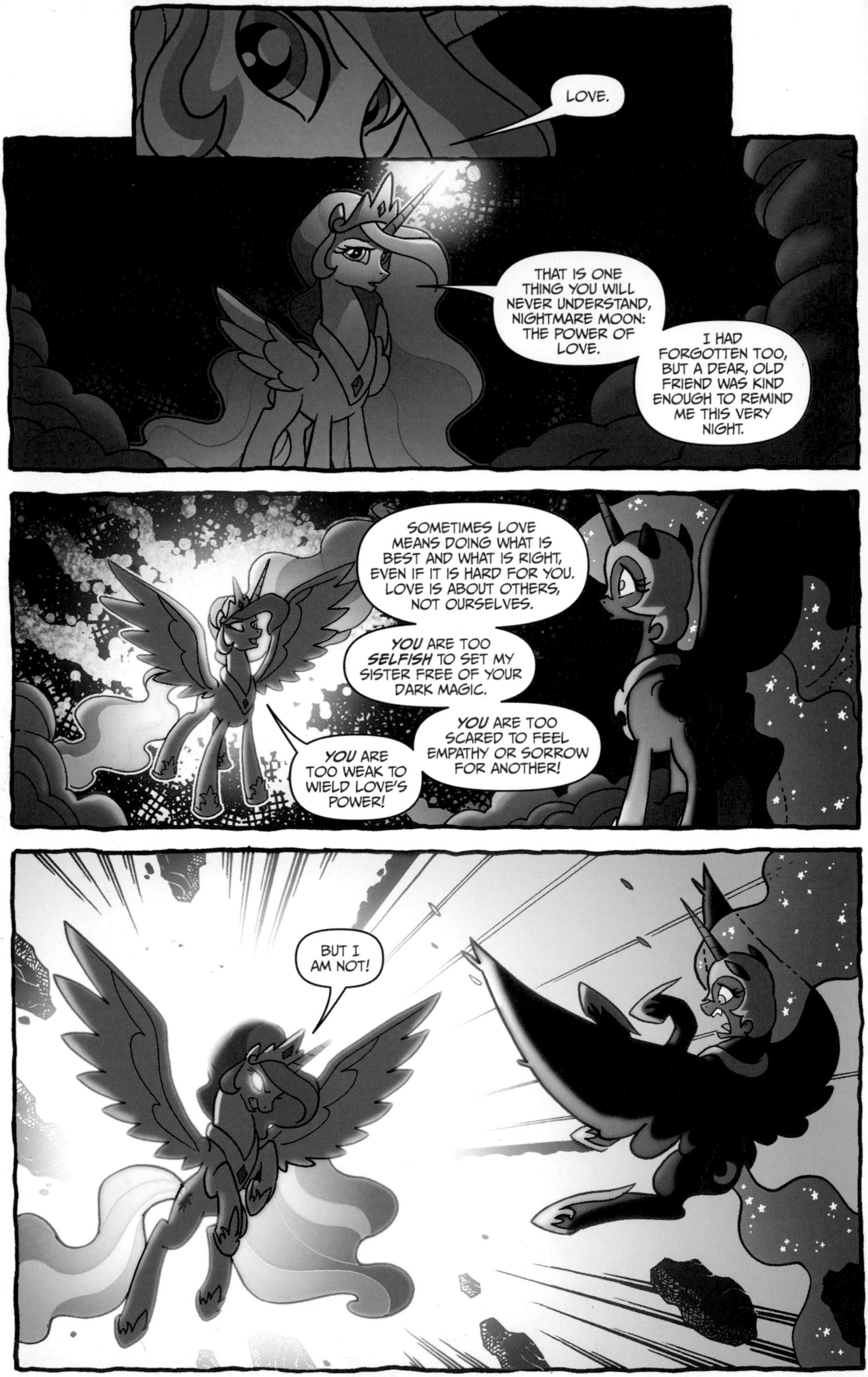
LOVE.
THAT IS ONE THING YOU WILL NEVER UNDERSTAND, NIGHTMARE MOON: THE POWER OF LOVE.
I HAD FORGOTTEN TOO, BUT A DEAR, OLD FRIEND WAS KIND ENOUGH TO REMIND ME THIS VERY NIGHT.
SOMETIMES LOVE MEANS DOING WHAT IS BEST AND WHAT IS RIGHT, EVEN IF IT IS HARD FOR YOU. LOVE IS ABOUT OTHERS, NOT OURSELVES.
YOU ARE TOO SELFISH TO SET MY SISTER FREE OF YOUR DARK MAGIC.
YOU ARE TOO SCARED TO FEEL EMPATHY OR SORROW FOR ANOTHER!
YOU ARE TOO WEAK TO WIELD LOVE'S POWER!
BUT I AM NOT!

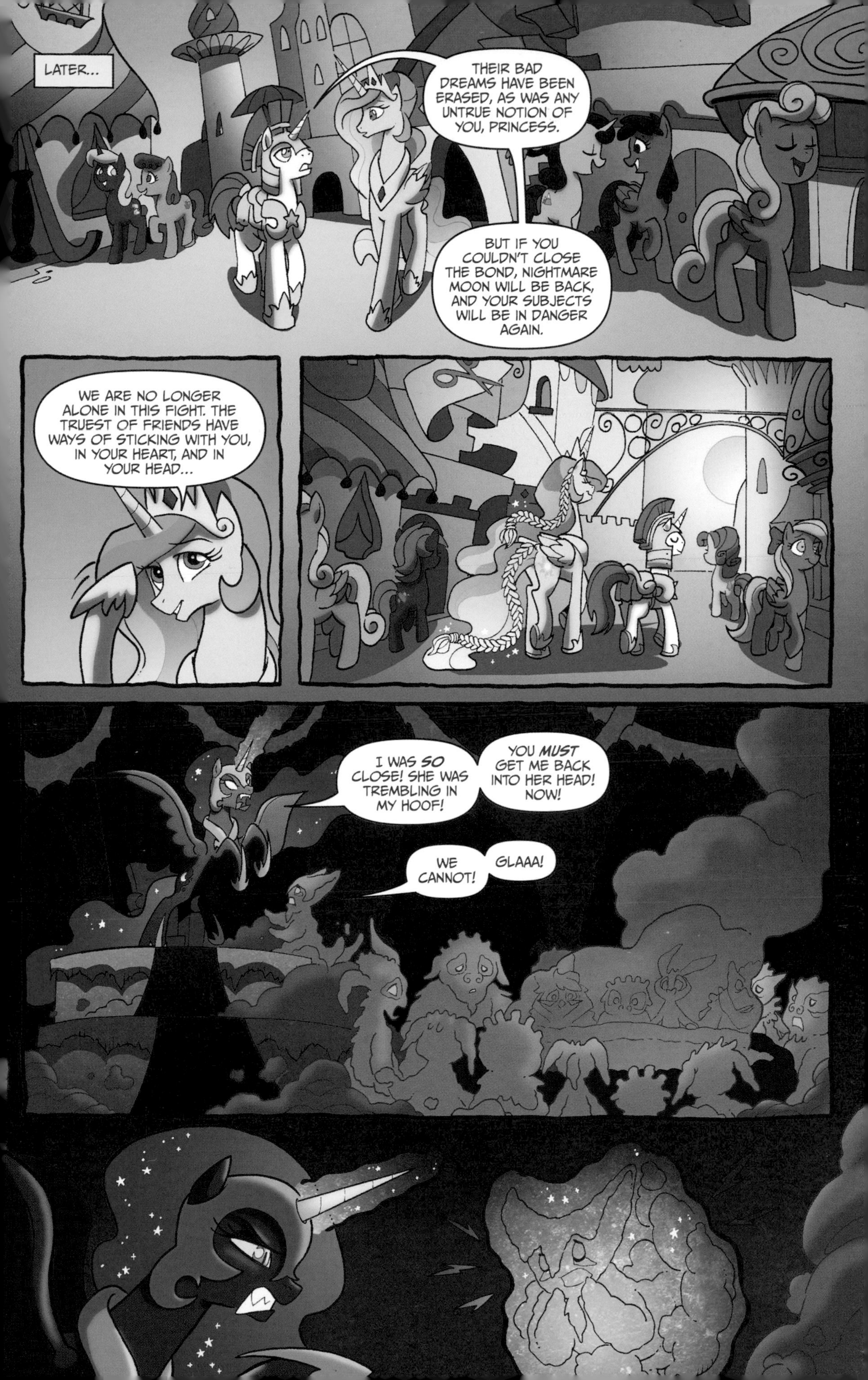
LATER...
THEIR BAD DREAMS HAVE BEEN ERASED, AS WAS ANY UNTRUE NOTION OF YOU, PRINCESS.
BUT IF YOU COULDN'T CLOSE THE BOND, NIGHTMARE MOON WILL BE BACK, AND YOUR SUBJECTS WILL BE IN DANGER AGAIN.
WE ARE NO LONGER ALONE IN THIS FIGHT. THE TRUEST OF FRIENDS HAVE WAYS OF STICKING WITH YOU, IN YOUR HEART, AND IN YOUR HEAD...
I WAS SO CLOSE! SHE WAS TREMBLING IN MY HOOF!
YOU MUST GET ME BACK INTO HER HEAD! NOW!
WE CANNOT!
GLAAA!

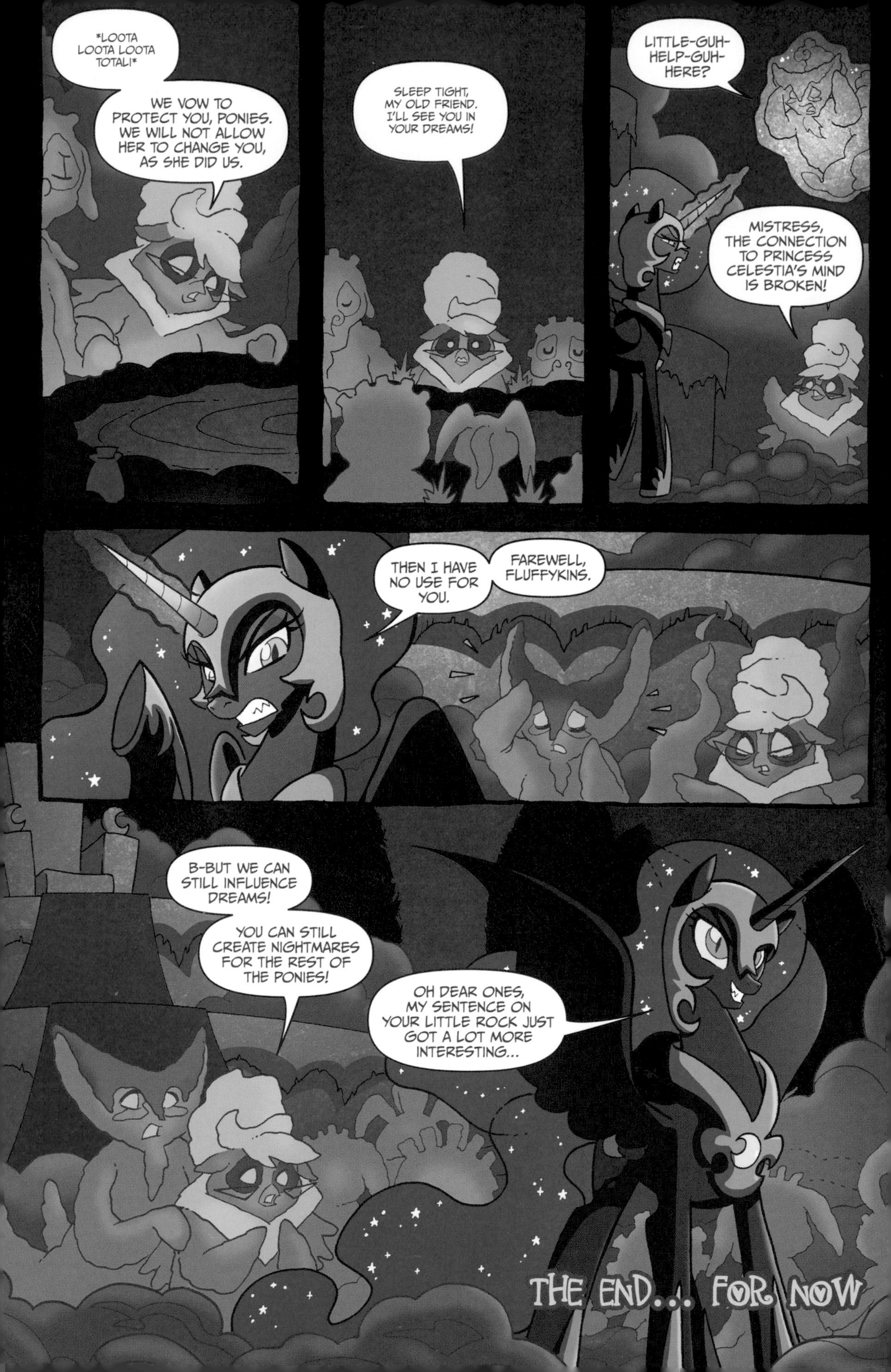
LOOTA LOOTA LOOTA TOTAL!
WE VOW TO PROTECT YOU, PONIES. WE WILL NOT ALLOW HER TO CHANGE YOU, AS SHE DID US.
SLEEP TIGHT, MY OLD FRIEND. I'LL SEE YOU IN YOUR DREAMS!
LITTLE-GUH-HELP-GUH-HERE?
MISTRESS, THE CONNECTION TO PRINCESS CELESTIA'S MIND IS BROKEN!
THEN I HAVE NO USE FOR YOU.
FAREWELL, FLUFFYKINS.
B-BUT WE CAN STILL INFLUENCE DREAMS!
YOU CAN STILL CREATE NIGHTMARES FOR THE REST OF THE PONIES!
OH DEAR ONES, MY SENTENCE ON YOUR LITTLE ROCK JUST GOT A LOT MORE INTERESTING...
THE END... FOR NOW

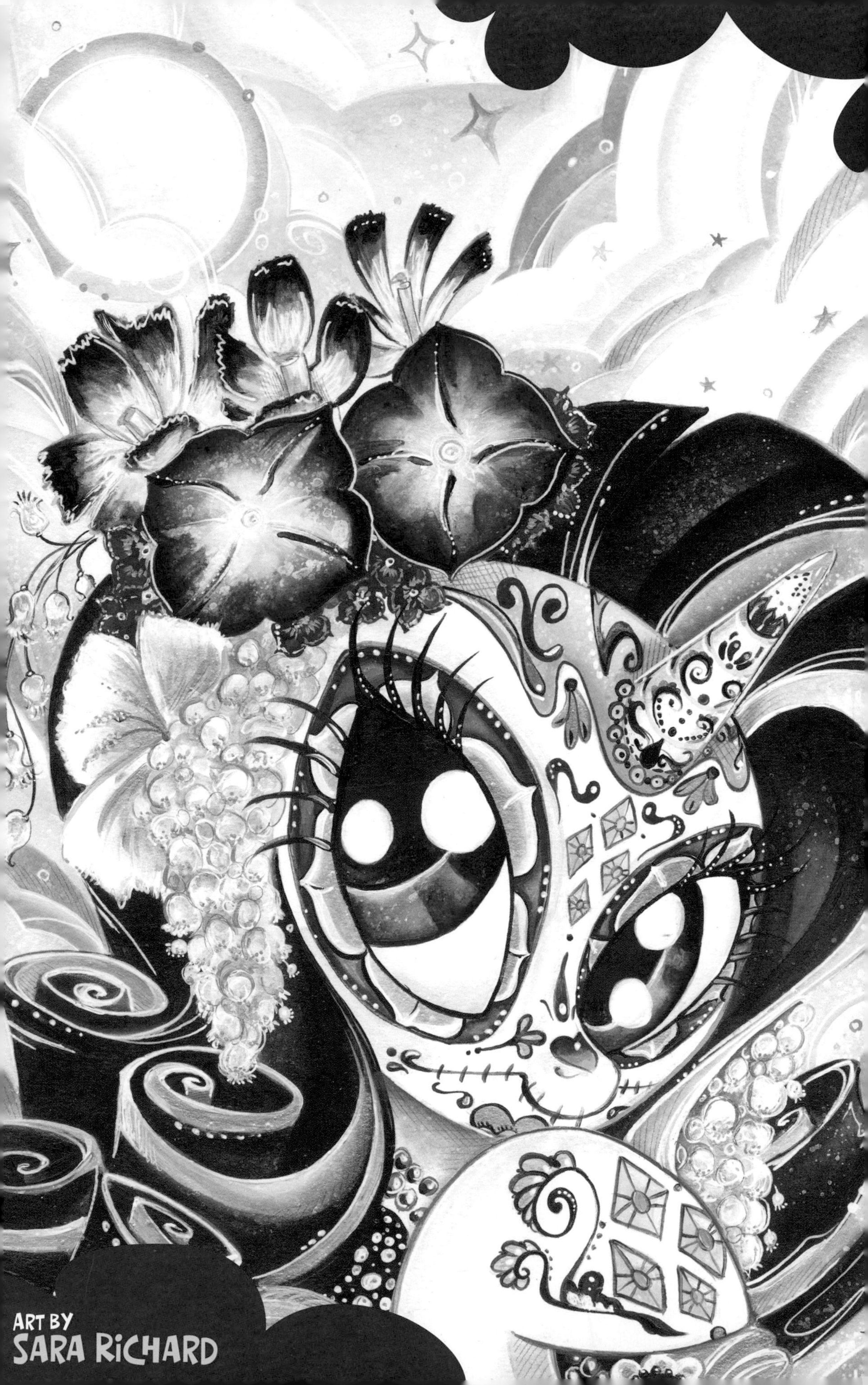
ART BY
SARA RICHARD

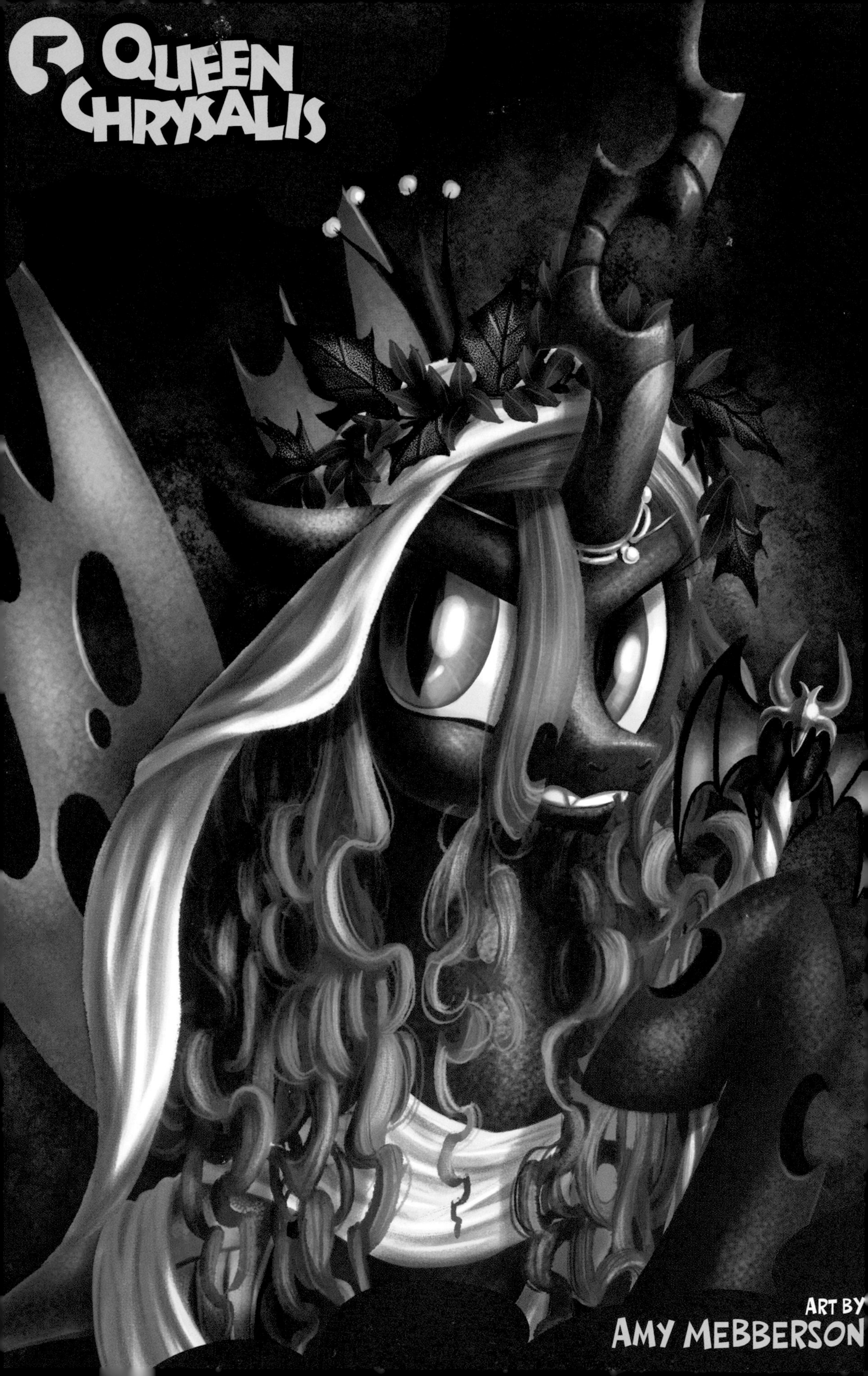
QUEEN CHRYSALIS
ART BY
AMY MEBBERSON

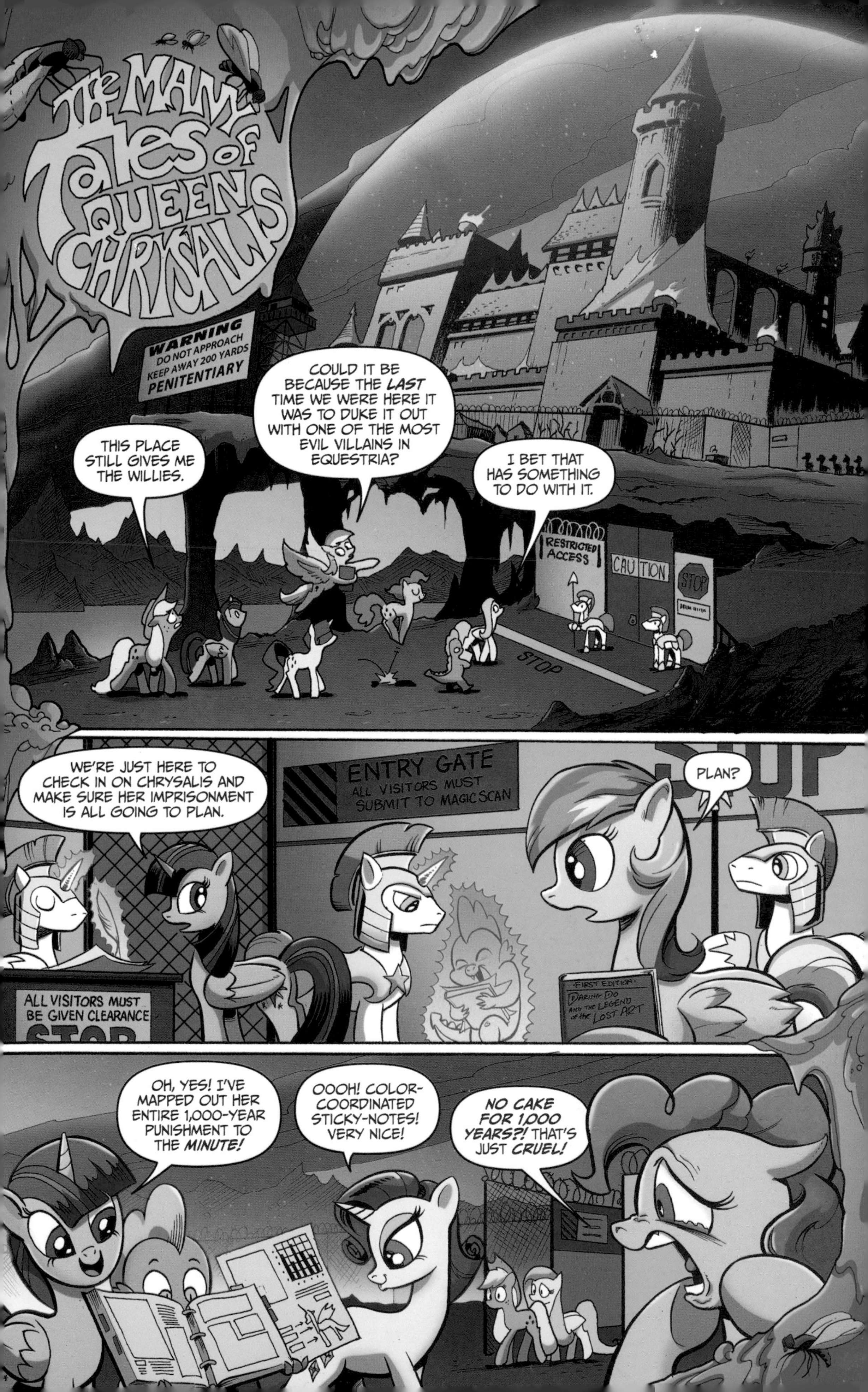
The Many Tales of Queen Chrysalis
WARNING DO NOT APPROACH KEEP AWAY 200 YARDS PENITENTIARY
THIS PLACE STILL GIVES ME THE WILLIES.
COULD IT BE BECAUSE THE *LAST* TIME WE WERE HERE IT WAS TO DUKE IT OUT WITH ONE OF THE MOST EVIL VILLAINS IN EQUESTRIA?
I BET THAT HAS SOMETHING TO DO WITH IT.
RESTRICTED ACCESS
CAUTION
STOP
STOP
WE'RE JUST HERE TO CHECK IN ON CHRYSALIS AND MAKE SURE HER IMPRISONMENT IS ALL GOING TO PLAN.
ENTRY GATE ALL VISITORS MUST SUBMIT TO MAGICSCAN
PLAN?
ALL VISITORS MUST BE GIVEN CLEARANCE
FIRST EDITION DARING DO AND THE LEGEND OF THE LOST ART
OH, YES! I'VE MAPPED OUT HER ENTIRE 1,000-YEAR PUNISHMENT TO THE *MINUTE!*
OOOH! COLOR-COORDINATED STICKY-NOTES! VERY NICE!
NO CAKE FOR 1,000 YEARS?! THAT'S JUST ***CRUEL!***

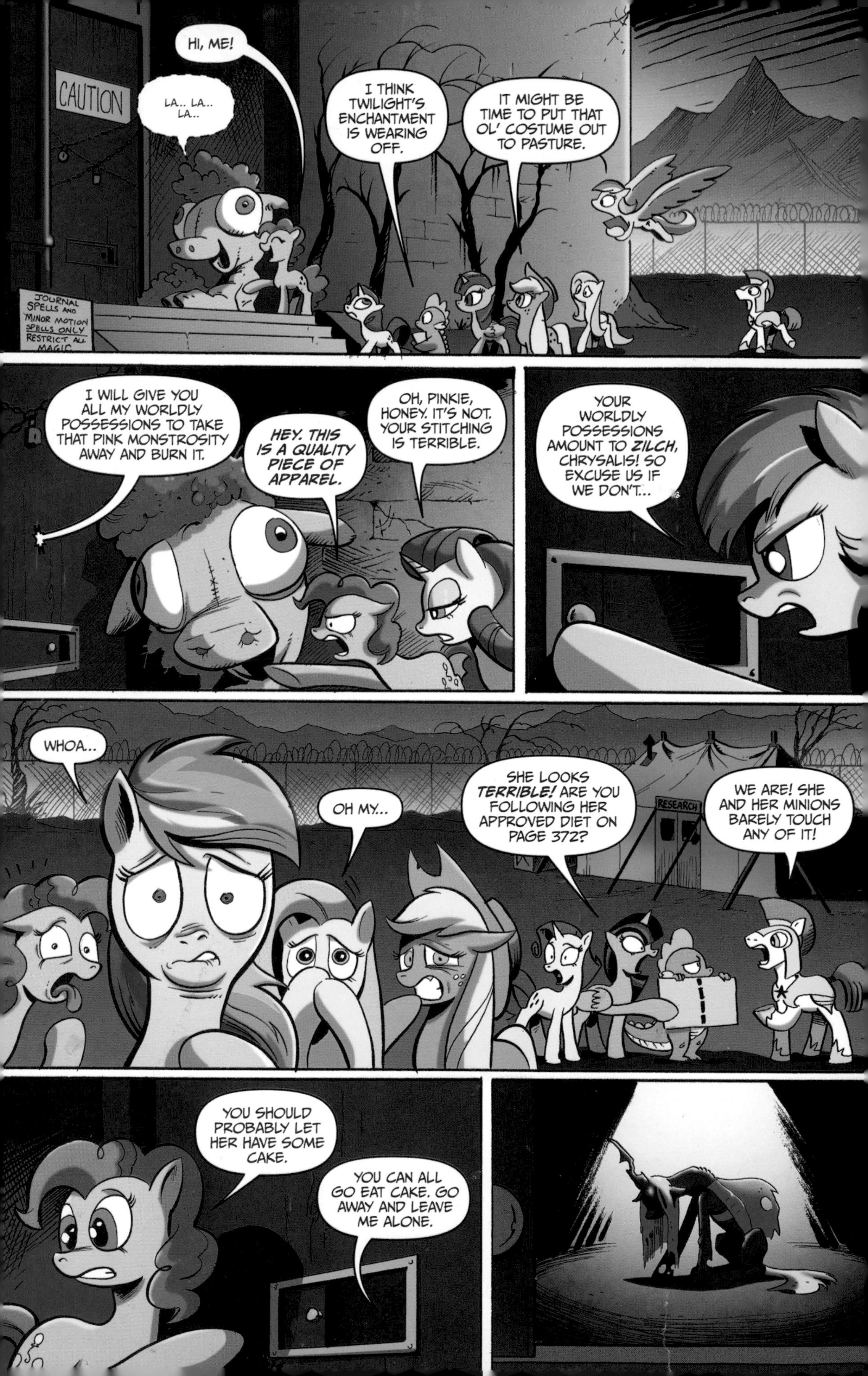
CAUTION
JOURNAL SPELLS AND MINOR MOTION SPELLS ONLY RESTRICT ALL MAGIC
HI, ME!
LA... LA.. LA...
I THINK TWILIGHT'S ENCHANTMENT IS WEARING OFF.
IT MIGHT BE TIME TO PUT THAT OL' COSTUME OUT TO PASTURE.
I WILL GIVE YOU ALL MY WORLDLY POSSESSIONS TO TAKE THAT PINK MONSTROSITY AWAY AND BURN IT.
HEY. THIS IS A QUALITY PIECE OF APPAREL.
OH, PINKIE, HONEY. IT'S NOT. YOUR STITCHING IS TERRIBLE.
YOUR WORLDLY POSSESSIONS AMOUNT TO ZILCH, CHRYSALIS! SO EXCUSE US IF WE DON'T...
WHOA...
OH MY...
SHE LOOKS TERRIBLE! ARE YOU FOLLOWING HER APPROVED DIET ON PAGE 372?
RESEARCH
WE ARE! SHE AND HER MINIONS BARELY TOUCH ANY OF IT!
YOU SHOULD PROBABLY LET HER HAVE SOME CAKE.
YOU CAN ALL GO EAT CAKE. GO AWAY AND LEAVE ME ALONE.

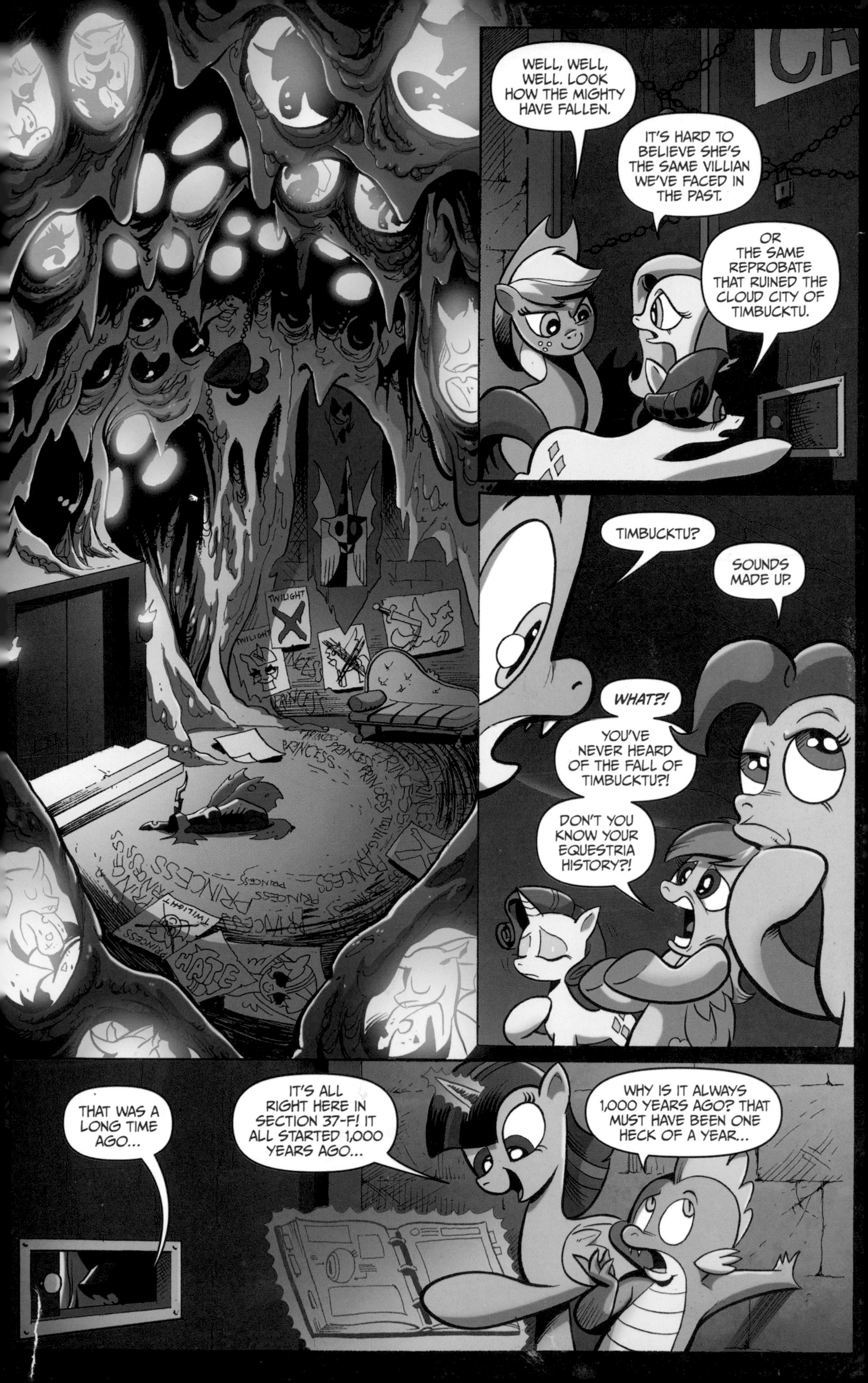
WELL, WELL, WELL. LOOK HOW THE MIGHTY HAVE FALLEN.
IT'S HARD TO BELIEVE SHE'S THE SAME VILLIAN WE'VE FACED IN THE PAST.
OR THE SAME REPROBATE THAT RUINED THE CLOUD CITY OF TIMBUCKTU.
TIMBUCKTU?
SOUNDS MADE UP.
WHAT?!
YOU'VE NEVER HEARD OF THE FALL OF TIMBUCKTU?!
DON'T YOU KNOW YOUR EQUESTRIA HISTORY?!
THAT WAS A LONG TIME AGO...
IT'S ALL RIGHT HERE IN SECTION 37-F! IT ALL STARTED 1,000 YEARS AGO...
WHY IS IT ALWAYS 1,000 YEARS AGO? THAT MUST HAVE BEEN ONE HECK OF A YEAR...

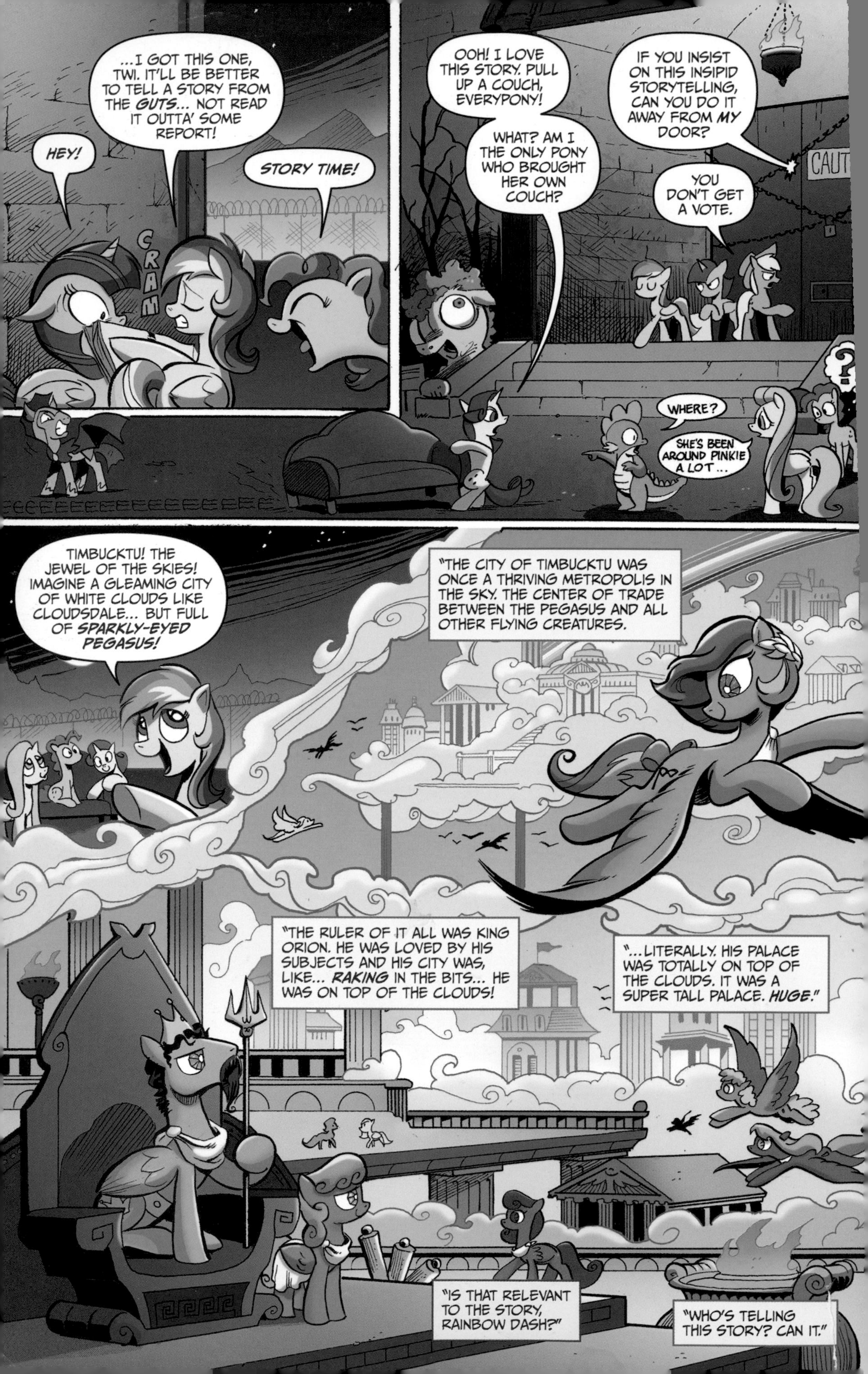
...I GOT THIS ONE, TWI. IT'LL BE BETTER TO TELL A STORY FROM THE GUTS... NOT READ IT OUTTA' SOME REPORT!
HEY!
STORY TIME!
CRAM
OOH! I LOVE THIS STORY. PULL UP A COUCH, EVERYPONY!
WHAT? AM I THE ONLY PONY WHO BROUGHT HER OWN COUCH?
IF YOU INSIST ON THIS INSIPID STORYTELLING, CAN YOU DO IT AWAY FROM MY DOOR?
YOU DON'T GET A VOTE.
CAUT
WHERE?
SHE'S BEEN AROUND PINKIE A LOT...
TIMBUCKTU! THE JEWEL OF THE SKIES! IMAGINE A GLEAMING CITY OF WHITE CLOUDS LIKE CLOUDSDALE... BUT FULL OF SPARKLY-EYED PEGASUS!
"THE CITY OF TIMBUCKTU WAS ONCE A THRIVING METROPOLIS IN THE SKY. THE CENTER OF TRADE BETWEEN THE PEGASUS AND ALL OTHER FLYING CREATURES.
"THE RULER OF IT ALL WAS KING ORION. HE WAS LOVED BY HIS SUBJECTS AND HIS CITY WAS, LIKE... RAKING IN THE BITS... HE WAS ON TOP OF THE CLOUDS!
"...LITERALLY. HIS PALACE WAS TOTALLY ON TOP OF THE CLOUDS. IT WAS A SUPER TALL PALACE. HUGE."
"IS THAT RELEVANT TO THE STORY, RAINBOW DASH?"
"WHO'S TELLING THIS STORY? CAN IT."

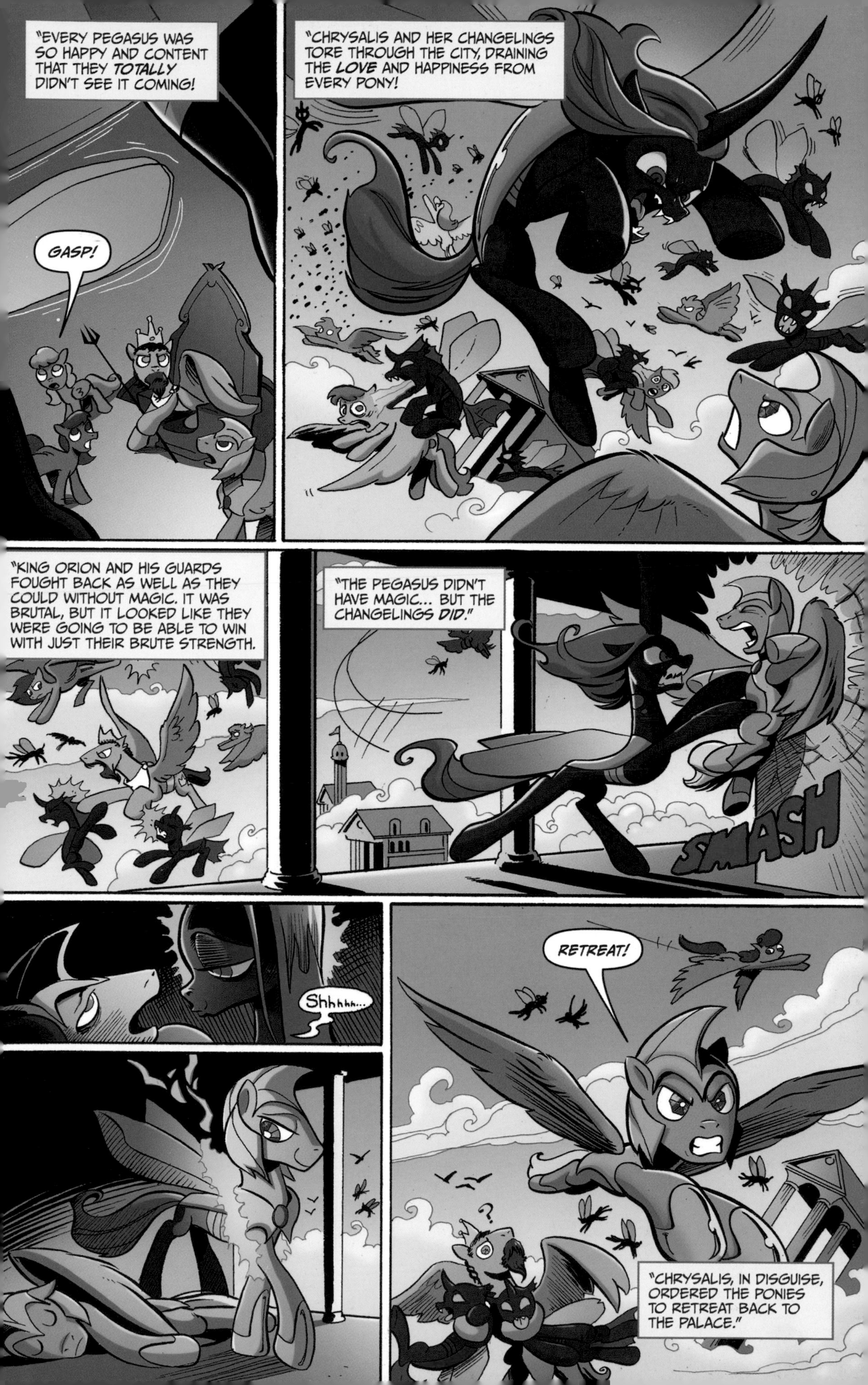
"EVERY PEGASUS WAS SO HAPPY AND CONTENT THAT THEY TOTALLY DIDN'T SEE IT COMING!
GASP!
"CHRYSALIS AND HER CHANGELINGS TORE THROUGH THE CITY, DRAINING THE LOVE AND HAPPINESS FROM EVERY PONY!
"KING ORION AND HIS GUARDS FOUGHT BACK AS WELL AS THEY COULD WITHOUT MAGIC. IT WAS BRUTAL, BUT IT LOOKED LIKE THEY WERE GOING TO BE ABLE TO WIN WITH JUST THEIR BRUTE STRENGTH.
"THE PEGASUS DIDN'T HAVE MAGIC... BUT THE CHANGELINGS DID."
SMASH
Shhhhh...
RETREAT!
?
"CHRYSALIS, IN DISGUISE, ORDERED THE PONIES TO RETREAT BACK TO THE PALACE."

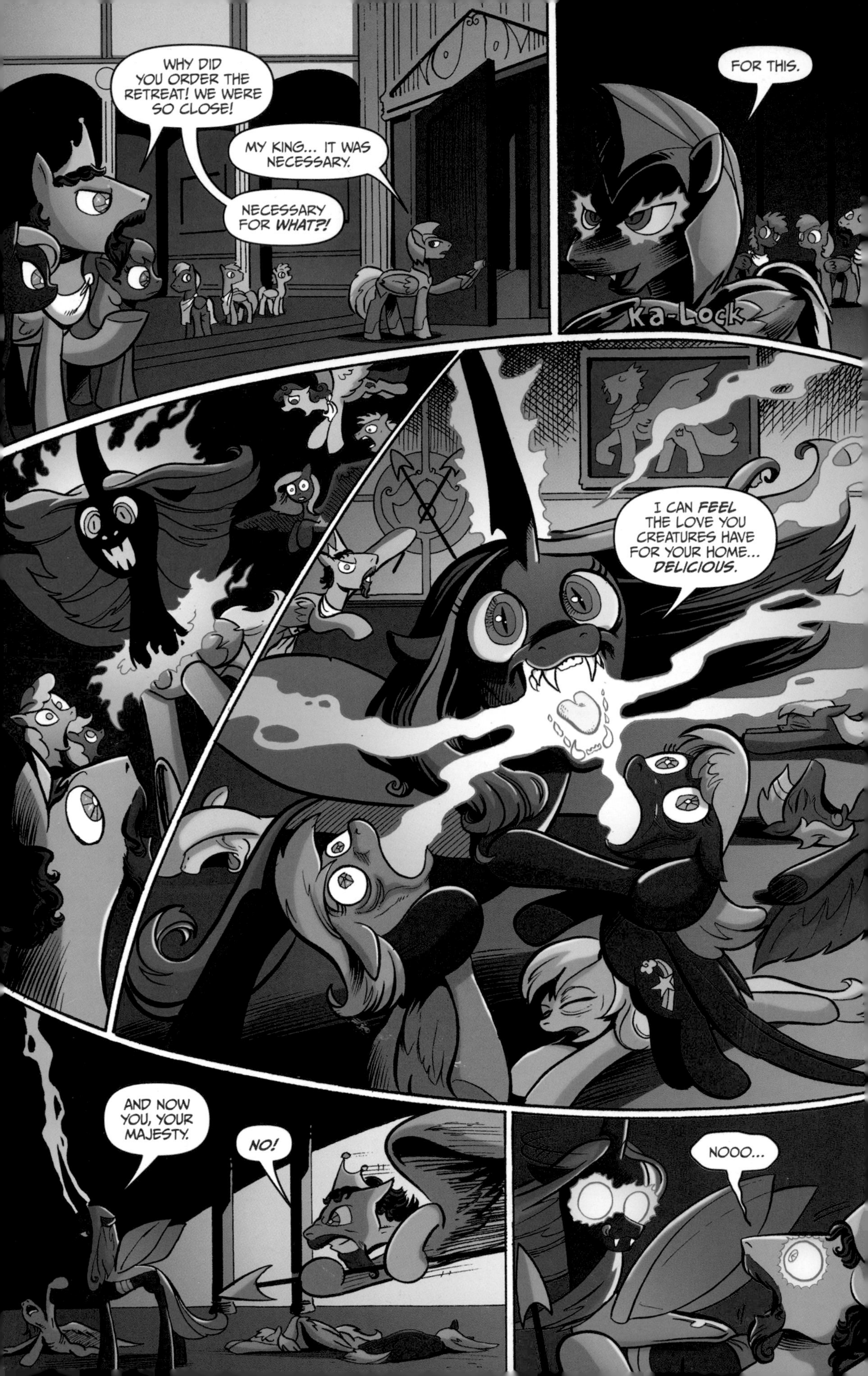

WHY DID YOU ORDER THE RETREAT! WE WERE SO CLOSE!
MY KING... IT WAS NECESSARY.
NECESSARY FOR WHAT?!
FOR THIS.
KA-LOCK
I CAN FEEL THE LOVE YOU CREATURES HAVE FOR YOUR HOME... DELICIOUS.
AND NOW YOU, YOUR MAJESTY.
NO!
NOOO...

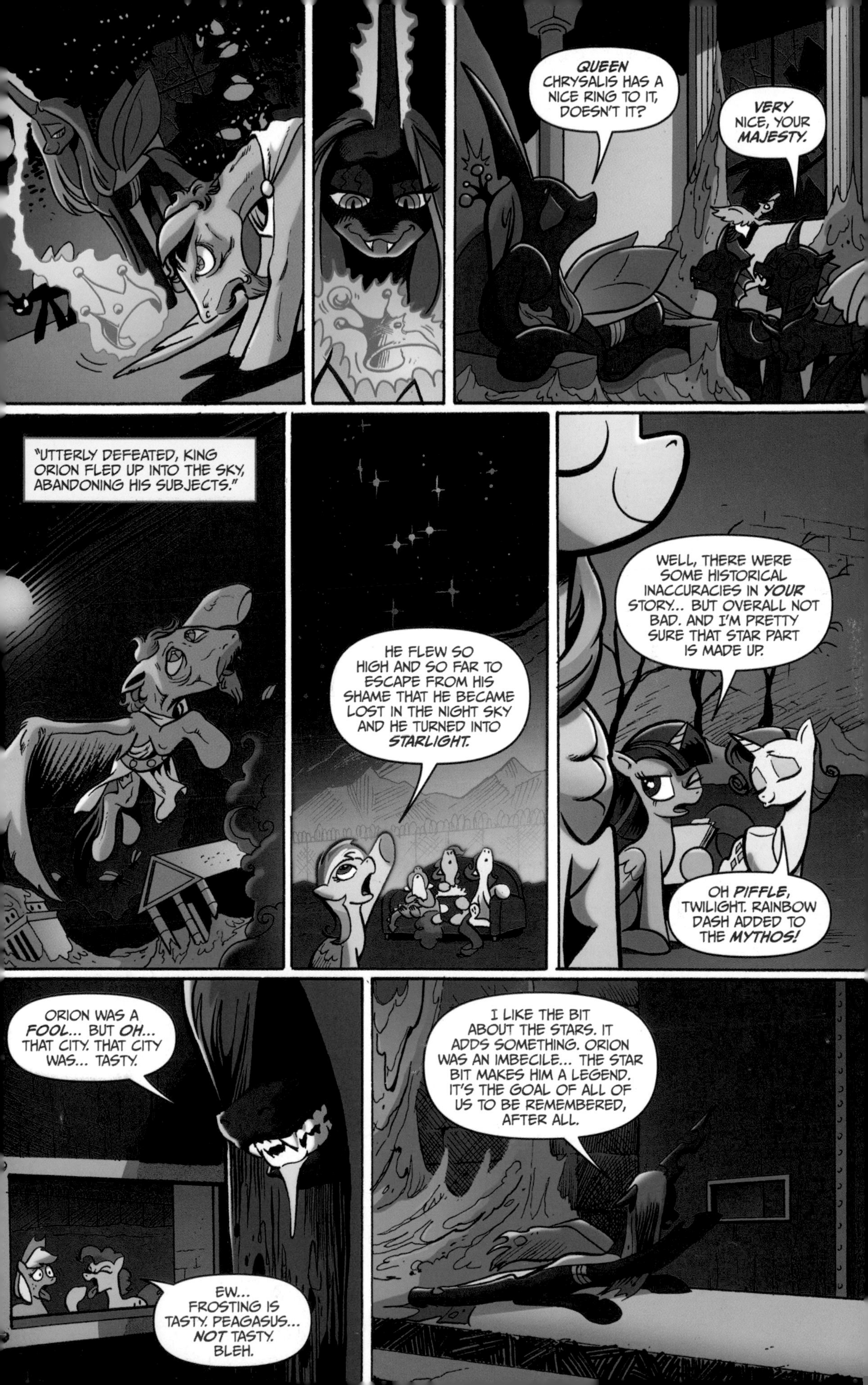
QUEEN CHRYSALIS HAS A NICE RING TO IT, DOESN'T IT?
VERY NICE, YOUR MAJESTY.
"UTTERLY DEFEATED, KING ORION FLED UP INTO THE SKY, ABANDONING HIS SUBJECTS."
HE FLEW SO HIGH AND SO FAR TO ESCAPE FROM HIS SHAME THAT HE BECAME LOST IN THE NIGHT SKY AND HE TURNED INTO STARLIGHT.
WELL, THERE WERE SOME HISTORICAL INACCURACIES IN YOUR STORY... BUT OVERALL NOT BAD. AND I'M PRETTY SURE THAT STAR PART IS MADE UP.
OH PIFFLE, TWILIGHT. RAINBOW DASH ADDED TO THE MYTHOS!
ORION WAS A FOOL... BUT OH... THAT CITY. THAT CITY WAS... TASTY.
EW... FROSTING IS TASTY. PEAGASUS... NOT TASTY. BLEH.
I LIKE THE BIT ABOUT THE STARS. IT ADDS SOMETHING. ORION WAS AN IMBECILE... THE STAR BIT MAKES HIM A LEGEND. IT'S THE GOAL OF ALL OF US TO BE REMEMBERED, AFTER ALL.

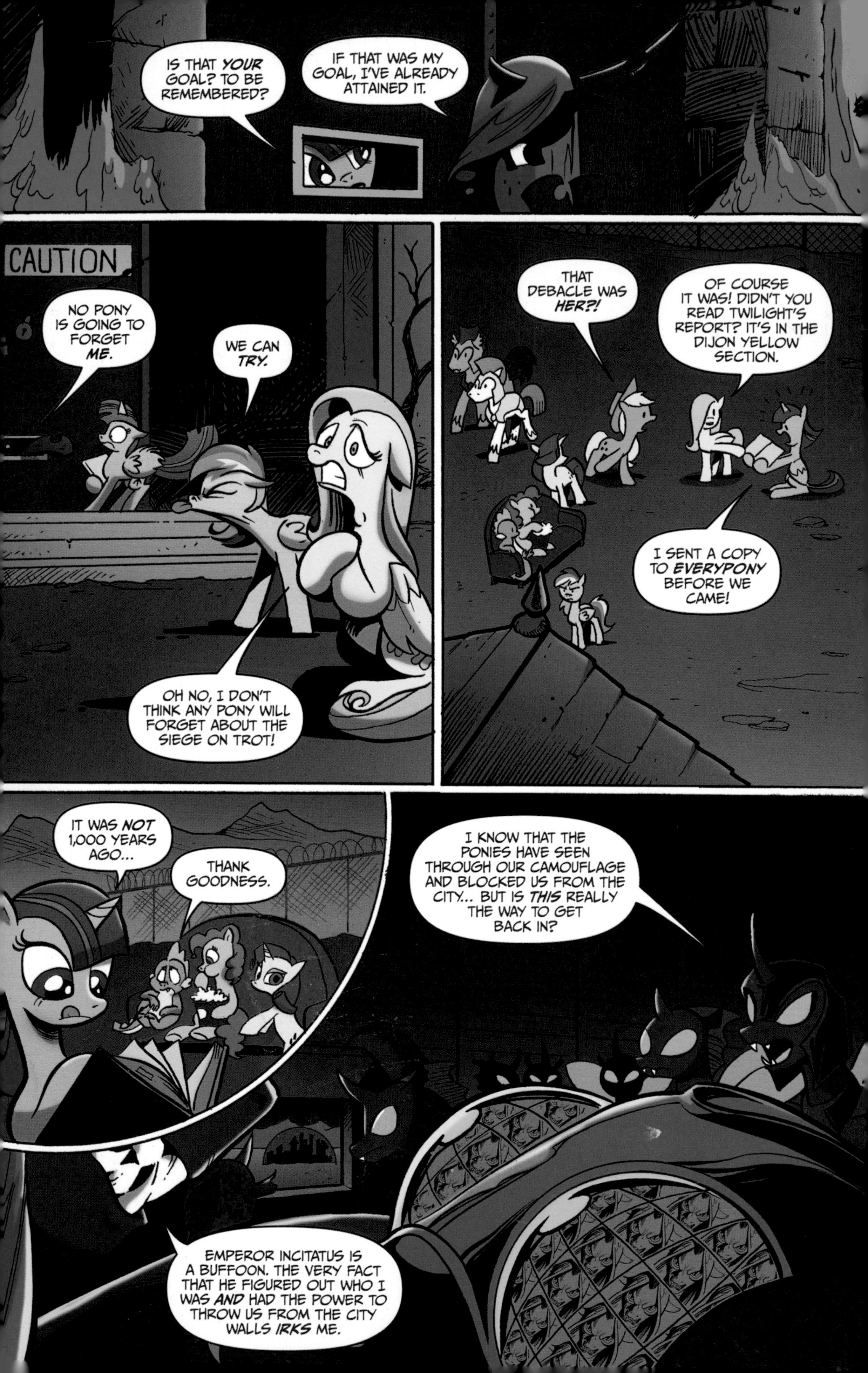
IS THAT *YOUR* GOAL? TO BE REMEMBERED?
IF THAT WAS MY GOAL, I'VE ALREADY ATTAINED IT.
CAUTION
NO PONY IS GOING TO FORGET *ME*.
WE CAN *TRY*.
OH NO, I DON'T THINK ANY PONY WILL FORGET ABOUT THE SIEGE ON TROT!
THAT DEBACLE WAS *HER?!*
OF COURSE IT WAS! DIDN'T YOU READ TWILIGHT'S REPORT? IT'S IN THE DIJON YELLOW SECTION.
I SENT A COPY TO *EVERYPONY* BEFORE WE CAME!
IT WAS *NOT* 1,000 YEARS AGO...
THANK GOODNESS.
I KNOW THAT THE PONIES HAVE SEEN THROUGH OUR CAMOUFLAGE AND BLOCKED US FROM THE CITY... BUT IS *THIS* REALLY THE WAY TO GET BACK IN?
EMPEROR INCITATUS IS A BUFFOON. THE VERY FACT THAT HE FIGURED OUT WHO I WAS *AND* HAD THE POWER TO THROW US FROM THE CITY WALLS *IRKS* ME.

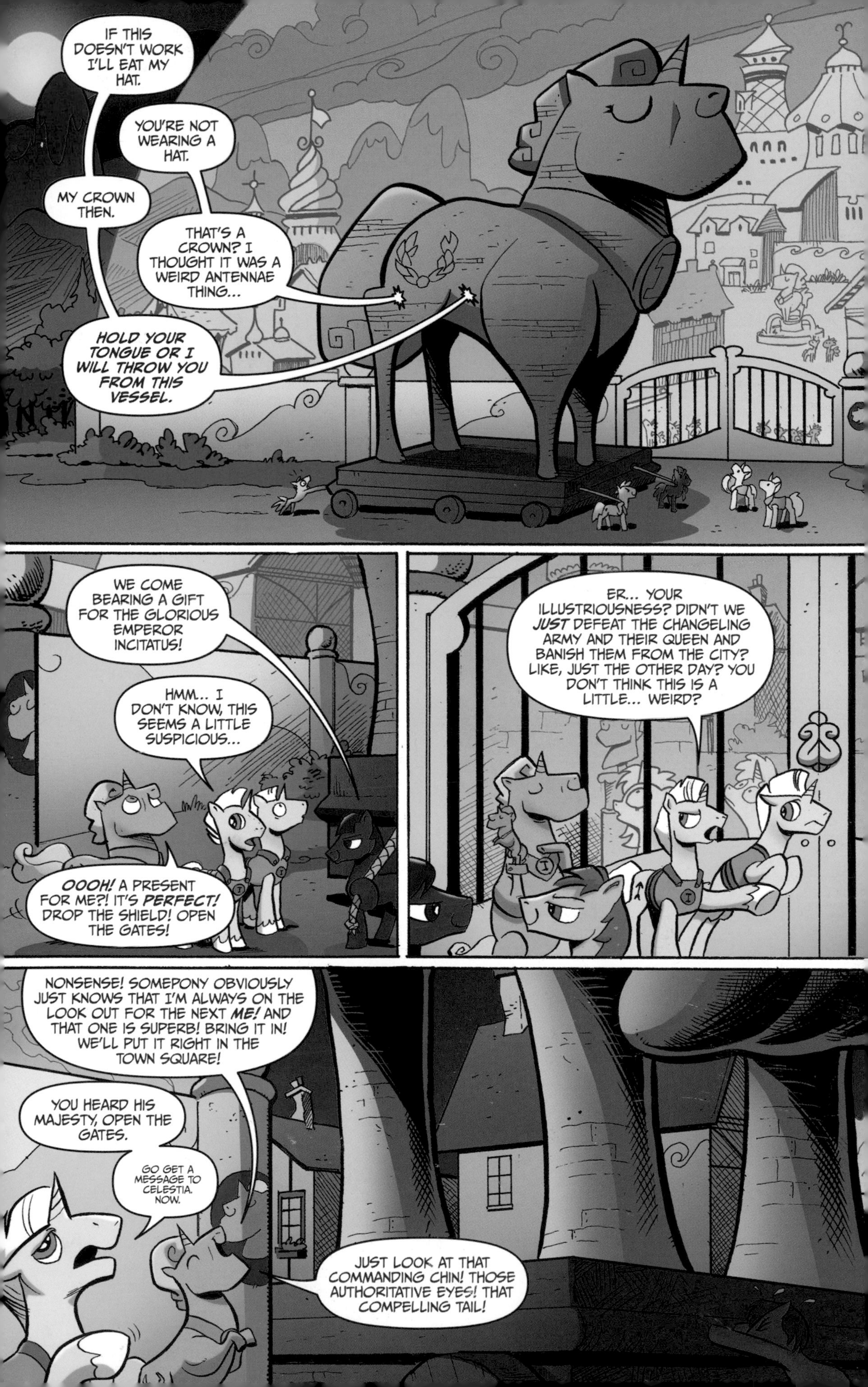
IF THIS DOESN'T WORK I'LL EAT MY HAT.
YOU'RE NOT WEARING A HAT.
MY CROWN THEN.
THAT'S A CROWN? I THOUGHT IT WAS A WEIRD ANTENNAE THING...
HOLD YOUR TONGUE OR I WILL THROW YOU FROM THIS VESSEL.
WE COME BEARING A GIFT FOR THE GLORIOUS EMPEROR INCITATUS!
HMM... I DON'T KNOW, THIS SEEMS A LITTLE SUSPICIOUS...
OOOH! A PRESENT FOR ME?! IT'S PERFECT! DROP THE SHIELD! OPEN THE GATES!
ER... YOUR ILLUSTRIOUSNESS? DIDN'T WE JUST DEFEAT THE CHANGELING ARMY AND THEIR QUEEN AND BANISH THEM FROM THE CITY? LIKE, JUST THE OTHER DAY? YOU DON'T THINK THIS IS A LITTLE... WEIRD?
NONSENSE! SOMEPONY OBVIOUSLY JUST KNOWS THAT I'M ALWAYS ON THE LOOK OUT FOR THE NEXT ME! AND THAT ONE IS SUPERB! BRING IT IN! WE'LL PUT IT RIGHT IN THE TOWN SQUARE!
YOU HEARD HIS MAJESTY, OPEN THE GATES.
GO GET A MESSAGE TO CELESTIA. NOW.
JUST LOOK AT THAT COMMANDING CHIN! THOSE AUTHORITATIVE EYES! THAT COMPELLING TAIL!

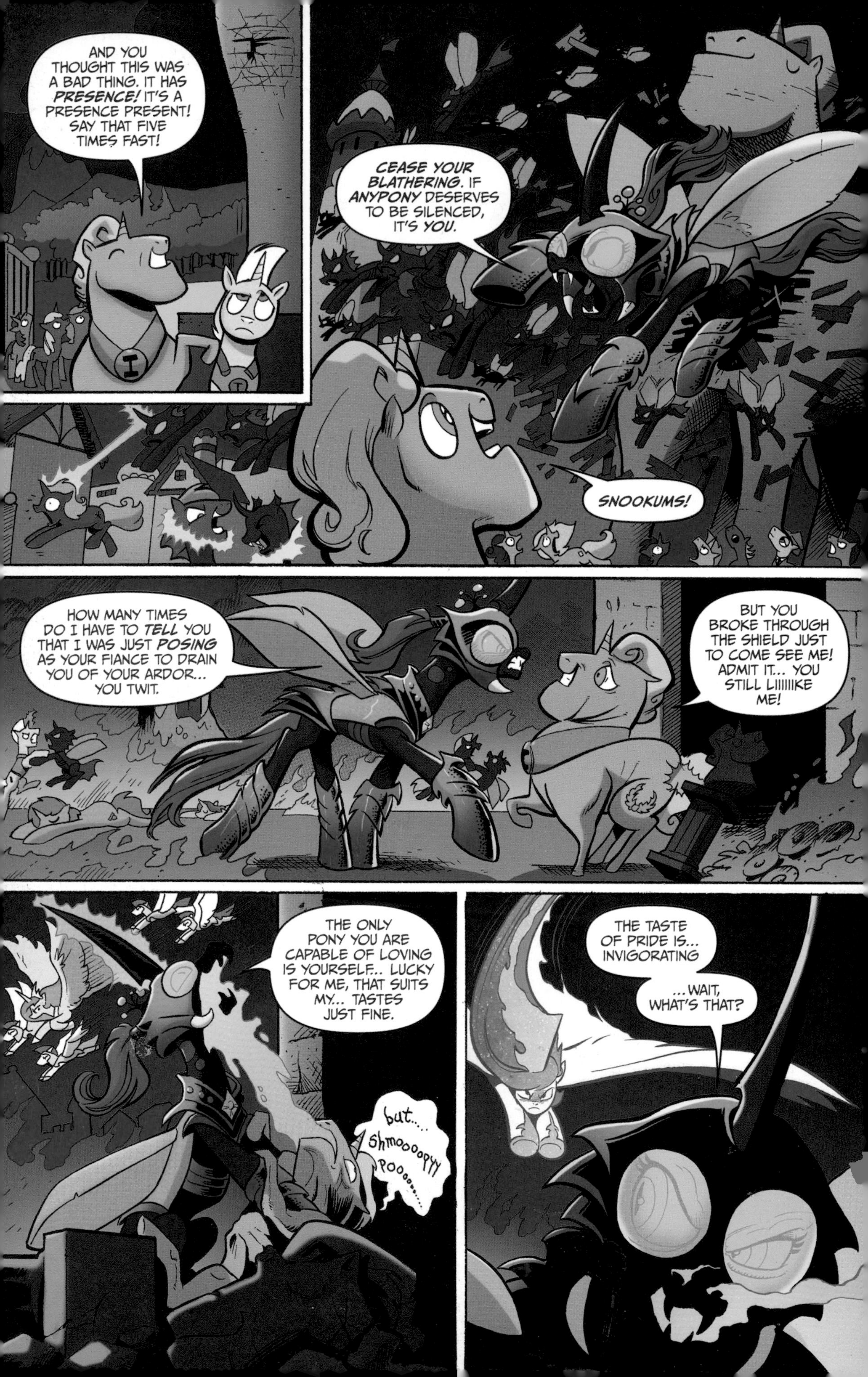
AND YOU THOUGHT THIS WAS A BAD THING. IT HAS *PRESENCE!* IT'S A PRESENCE PRESENT! SAY THAT FIVE TIMES FAST!
CEASE YOUR BLATHERING. IF *ANYPONY* DESERVES TO BE SILENCED, IT'S *YOU.*
SNOOKUMS!
HOW MANY TIMES DO I HAVE TO *TELL* YOU THAT I WAS JUST *POSING* AS YOUR FIANCE TO DRAIN YOU OF YOUR ARDOR... YOU TWIT.
BUT YOU BROKE THROUGH THE SHIELD JUST TO COME SEE ME! ADMIT IT... YOU STILL LIIIIIIKE ME!
THE ONLY PONY YOU ARE CAPABLE OF LOVING IS YOURSELF... LUCKY FOR ME, THAT SUITS MY... TASTES JUST FINE.
but.... shmoooopyy poo......
THE TASTE OF PRIDE IS... INVIGORATING
...WAIT, WHAT'S THAT?

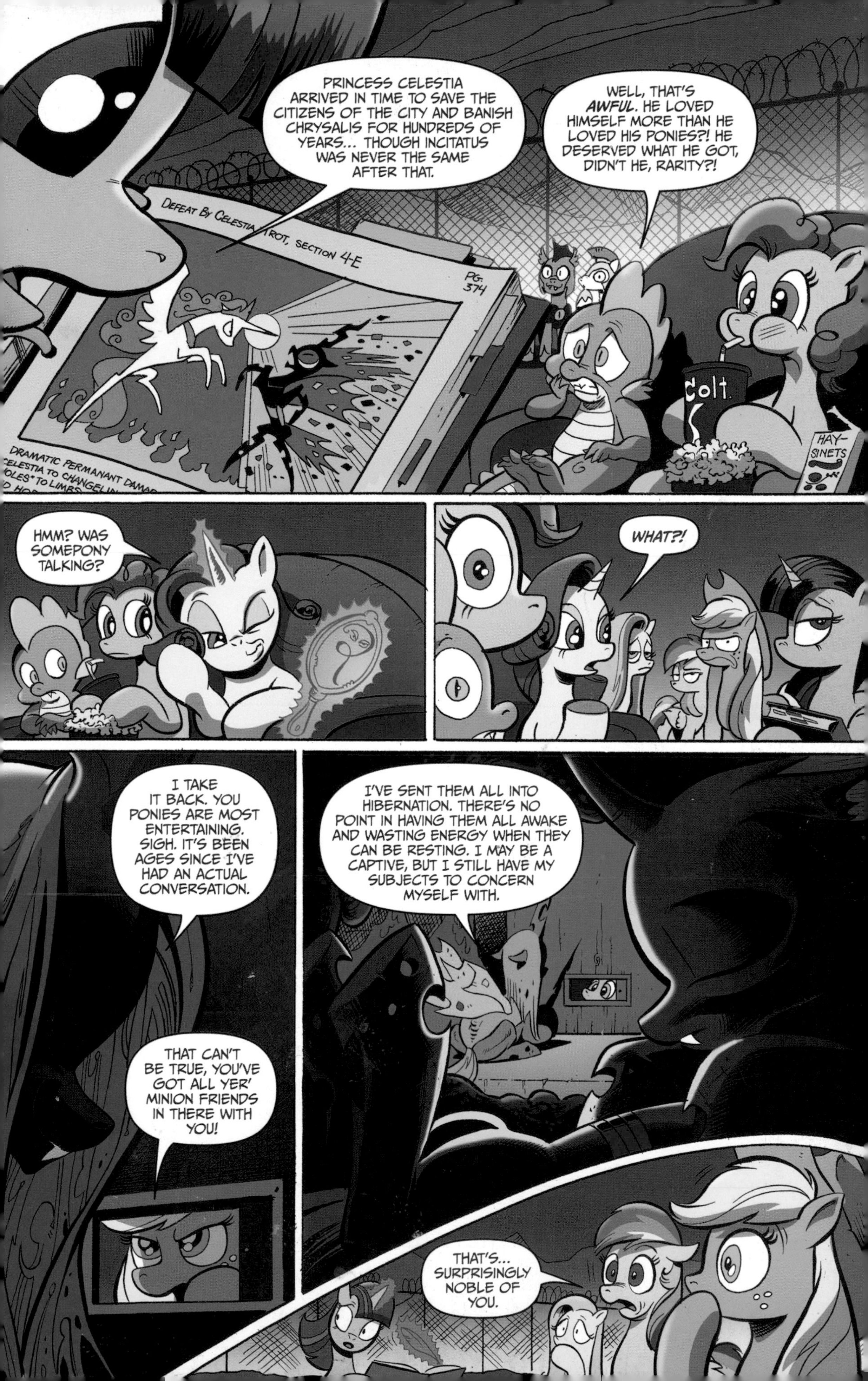

PRINCESS CELESTIA ARRIVED IN TIME TO SAVE THE CITIZENS OF THE CITY AND BANISH CHRYSALIS FOR HUNDREDS OF YEARS... THOUGH INCITATUS WAS NEVER THE SAME AFTER THAT.
WELL, THAT'S *AWFUL*. HE LOVED HIMSELF MORE THAN HE LOVED HIS PONIES?! HE DESERVED WHAT HE GOT, DIDN'T HE, RARITY?!
DEFEAT BY CELESTIA TROT, SECTION 4E
PG. 374
DRAMATIC PERMANANT DAMAG
CELESTIA TO CHANGELIN
HOLES* TO LIMBS
COLT.
HAY-SINETS
HMM? WAS SOMEPONY TALKING?
WHAT?!
I TAKE IT BACK. YOU PONIES ARE MOST ENTERTAINING. SIGH. IT'S BEEN AGES SINCE I'VE HAD AN ACTUAL CONVERSATION.
THAT CAN'T BE TRUE, YOU'VE GOT ALL YER' MINION FRIENDS IN THERE WITH YOU!
I'VE SENT THEM ALL INTO HIBERNATION. THERE'S NO POINT IN HAVING THEM ALL AWAKE AND WASTING ENERGY WHEN THEY CAN BE RESTING. I MAY BE A CAPTIVE, BUT I STILL HAVE MY SUBJECTS TO CONCERN MYSELF WITH.
THAT'S... SURPRISINGLY NOBLE OF YOU.

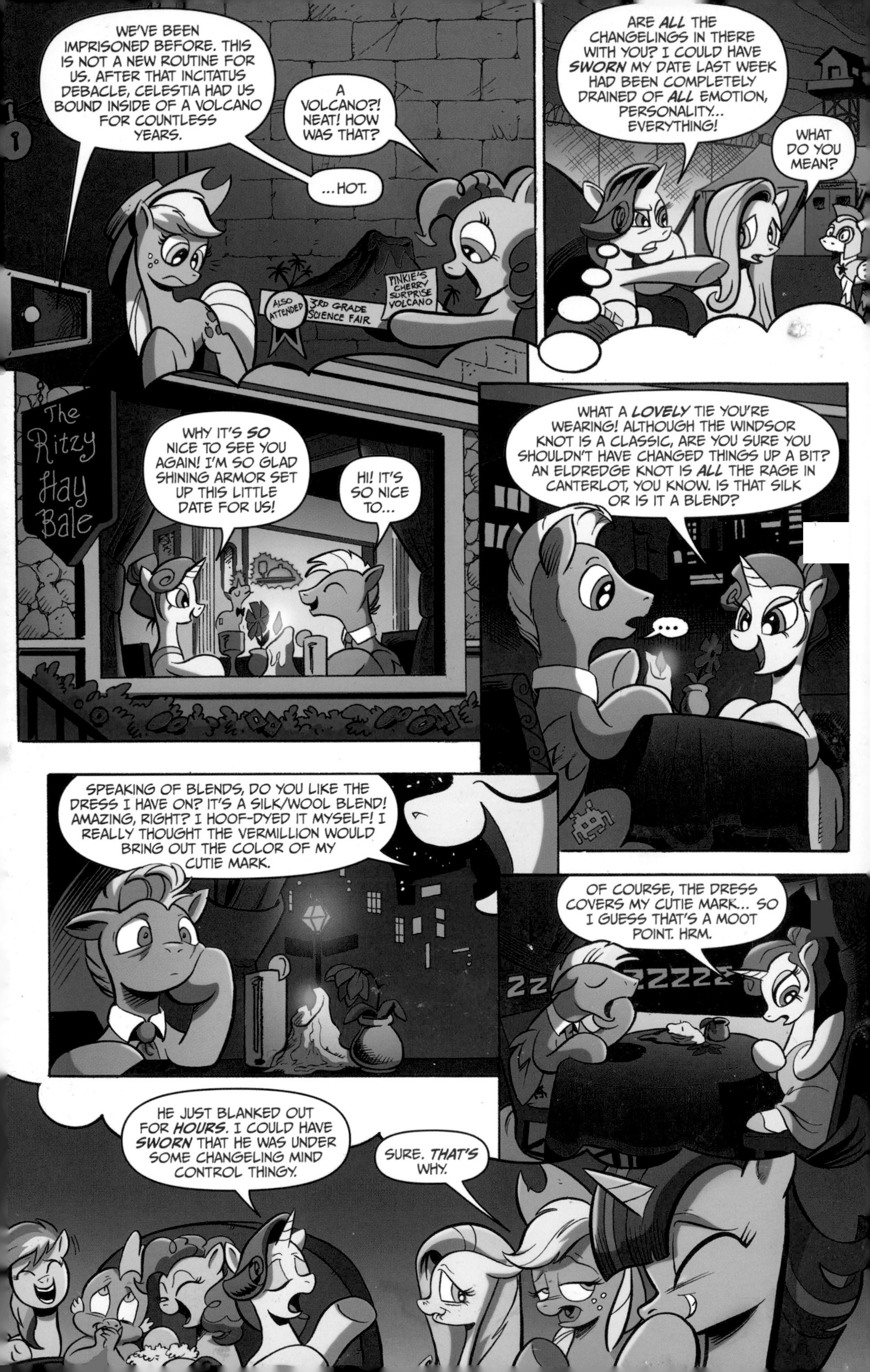

WE'VE BEEN IMPRISONED BEFORE. THIS IS NOT A NEW ROUTINE FOR US. AFTER THAT INCITATUS DEBACLE, CELESTIA HAD US BOUND INSIDE OF A VOLCANO FOR COUNTLESS YEARS.
A VOLCANO?! NEAT! HOW WAS THAT?
...HOT.
ALSO ATTENDED
3RD GRADE SCIENCE FAIR
PINKIE'S CHERRY SURPRISE VOLCANO
ARE ALL THE CHANGELINGS IN THERE WITH YOU? I COULD HAVE SWORN MY DATE LAST WEEK HAD BEEN COMPLETELY DRAINED OF ALL EMOTION, PERSONALITY... EVERYTHING!
WHAT DO YOU MEAN?
The Ritzy Hay Bale
WHY IT'S SO NICE TO SEE YOU AGAIN! I'M SO GLAD SHINING ARMOR SET UP THIS LITTLE DATE FOR US!
HI! IT'S SO NICE TO...
WHAT A LOVELY TIE YOU'RE WEARING! ALTHOUGH THE WINDSOR KNOT IS A CLASSIC, ARE YOU SURE YOU SHOULDN'T HAVE CHANGED THINGS UP A BIT? AN ELDREDGE KNOT IS ALL THE RAGE IN CANTERLOT, YOU KNOW. IS THAT SILK OR IS IT A BLEND?
...
SPEAKING OF BLENDS, DO YOU LIKE THE DRESS I HAVE ON? IT'S A SILK/WOOL BLEND! AMAZING, RIGHT? I HOOF-DYED IT MYSELF! I REALLY THOUGHT THE VERMILLION WOULD BRING OUT THE COLOR OF MY CUTIE MARK.
OF COURSE, THE DRESS COVERS MY CUTIE MARK... SO I GUESS THAT'S A MOOT POINT. HRM.
ZZ ZZZZZZ
HE JUST BLANKED OUT FOR HOURS. I COULD HAVE SWORN THAT HE WAS UNDER SOME CHANGELING MIND CONTROL THINGY.
SURE. THAT'S WHY.

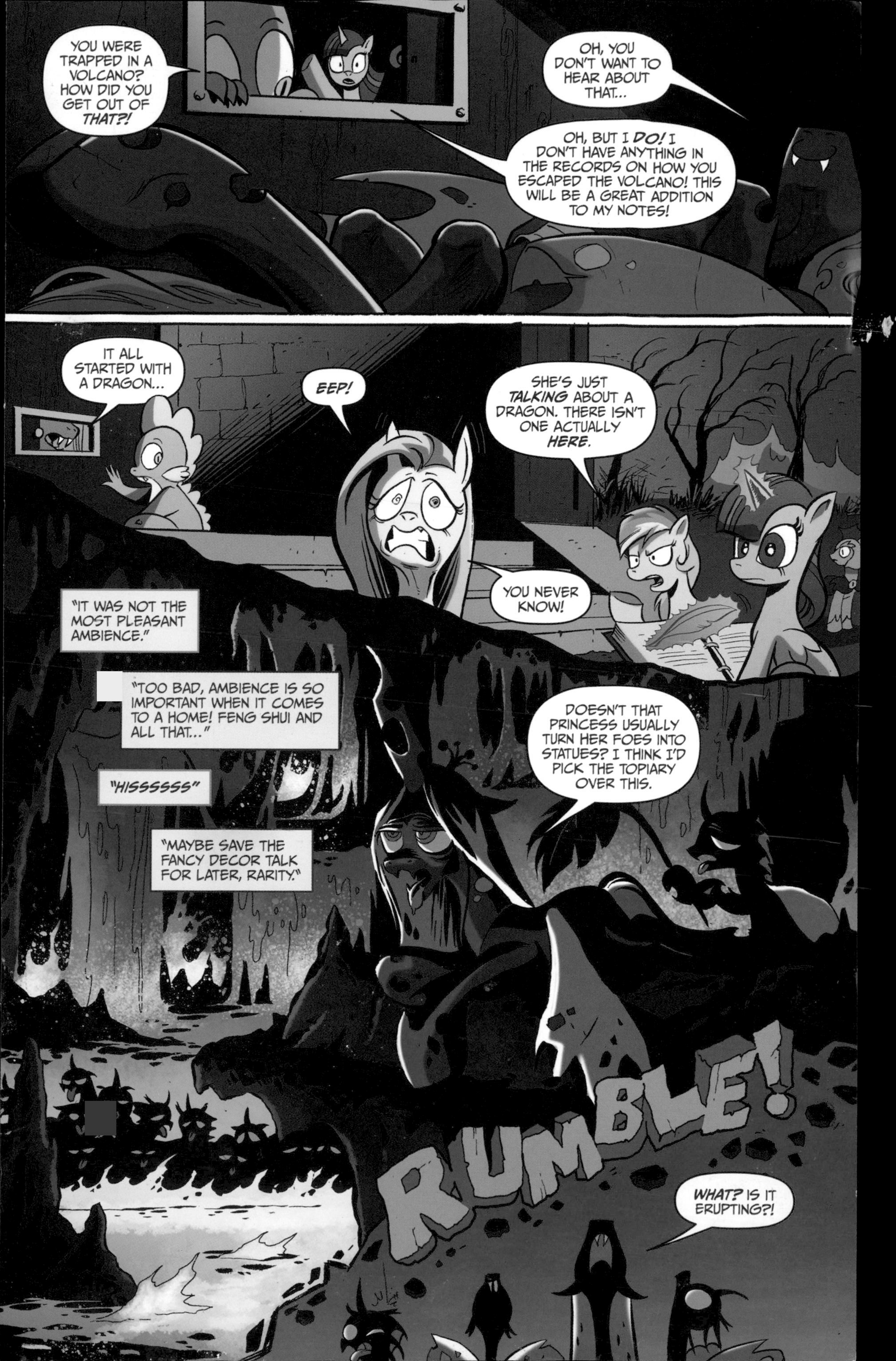
YOU WERE TRAPPED IN A VOLCANO? HOW DID YOU GET OUT OF THAT?!
OH, YOU DON'T WANT TO HEAR ABOUT THAT...
OH, BUT I DO! I DON'T HAVE ANYTHING IN THE RECORDS ON HOW YOU ESCAPED THE VOLCANO! THIS WILL BE A GREAT ADDITION TO MY NOTES!
IT ALL STARTED WITH A DRAGON...
EEP!
SHE'S JUST TALKING ABOUT A DRAGON. THERE ISN'T ONE ACTUALLY HERE.
YOU NEVER KNOW!
"IT WAS NOT THE MOST PLEASANT AMBIENCE."
"TOO BAD, AMBIENCE IS SO IMPORTANT WHEN IT COMES TO A HOME! FENG SHUI AND ALL THAT..."
"HISSSSSS"
"MAYBE SAVE THE FANCY DECOR TALK FOR LATER, RARITY."
DOESN'T THAT PRINCESS USUALLY TURN HER FOES INTO STATUES? I THINK I'D PICK THE TOPIARY OVER THIS.
RUMBLE!
WHAT? IS IT ERUPTING?!

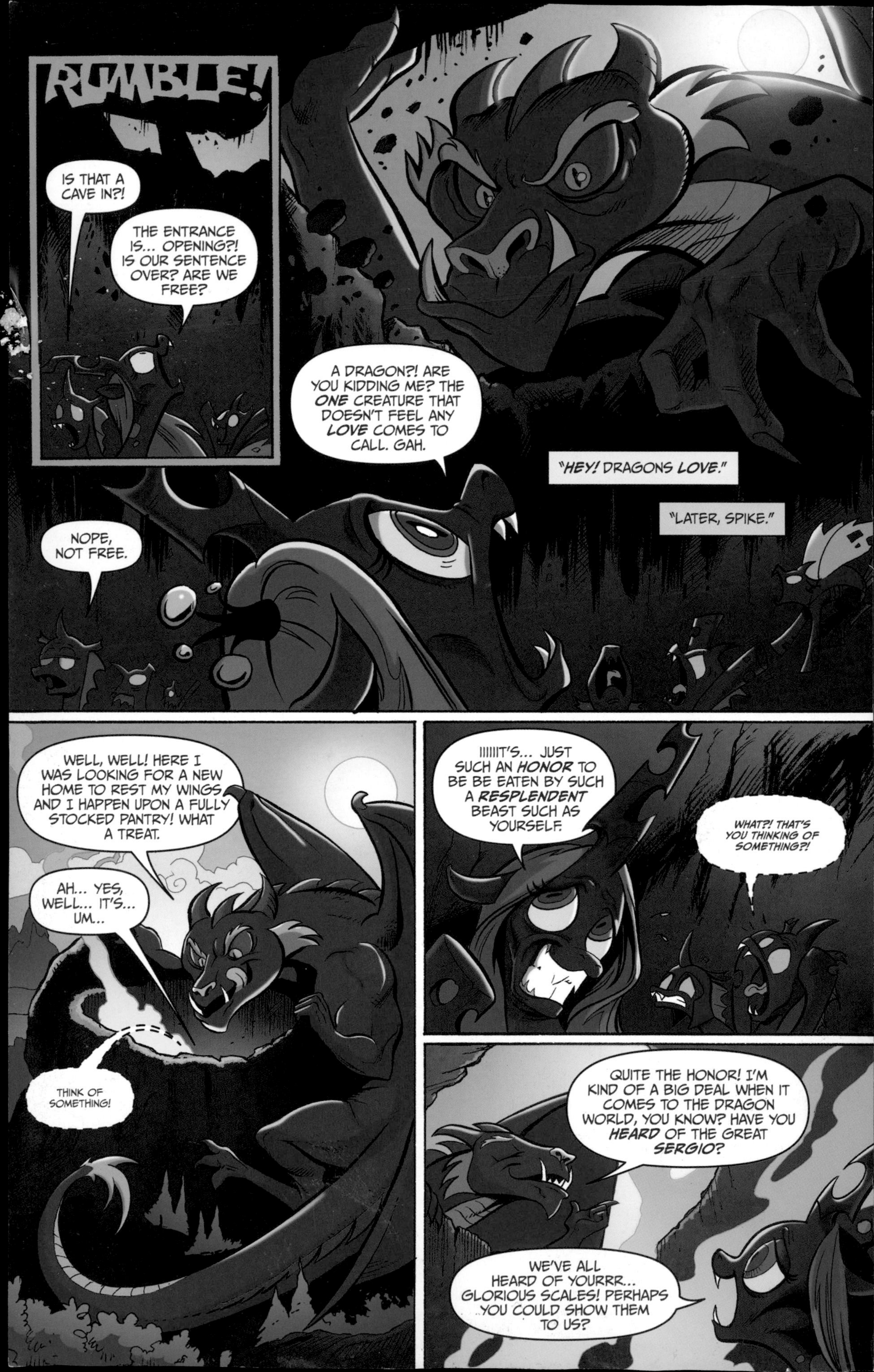
RUMBLE!
IS THAT A CAVE IN?!
THE ENTRANCE IS... OPENING?! IS OUR SENTENCE OVER? ARE WE FREE?
A DRAGON?! ARE YOU KIDDING ME? THE ONE CREATURE THAT DOESN'T FEEL ANY LOVE COMES TO CALL. GAH.
"HEY! DRAGONS LOVE."
"LATER, SPIKE."
NOPE, NOT FREE.
WELL, WELL! HERE I WAS LOOKING FOR A NEW HOME TO REST MY WINGS AND I HAPPEN UPON A FULLY STOCKED PANTRY! WHAT A TREAT.
AH... YES, WELL... IT'S... UM...
THINK OF SOMETHING!
IIIIIIT'S... JUST SUCH AN HONOR TO BE BE EATEN BY SUCH A RESPLENDENT BEAST SUCH AS YOURSELF.
WHAT?! THAT'S YOU THINKING OF SOMETHING?!
QUITE THE HONOR! I'M KIND OF A BIG DEAL WHEN IT COMES TO THE DRAGON WORLD, YOU KNOW? HAVE YOU HEARD OF THE GREAT SERGIO?
WE'VE ALL HEARD OF YOURRR... GLORIOUS SCALES! PERHAPS YOU COULD SHOW THEM TO US?

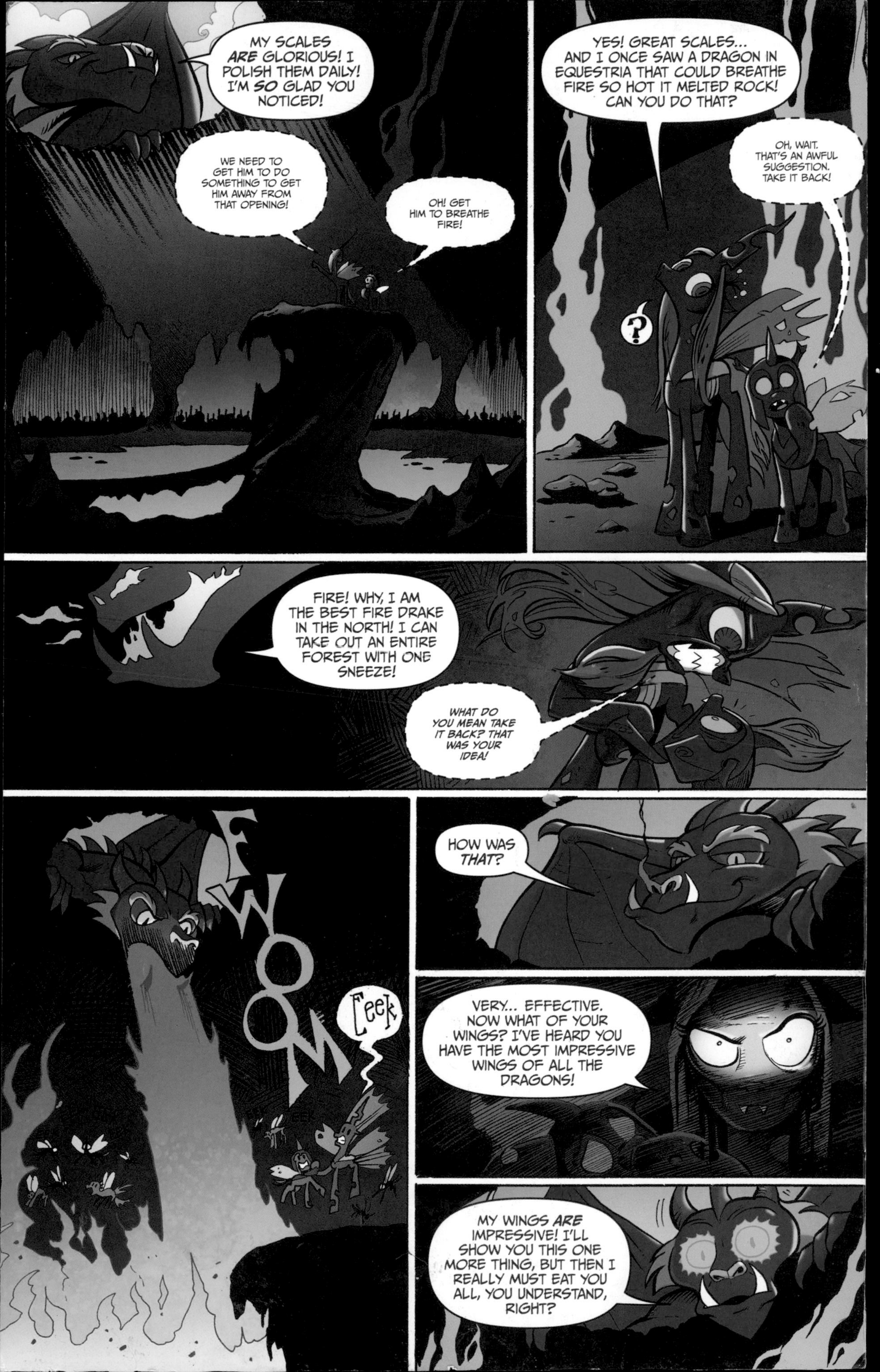
MY SCALES ARE GLORIOUS! I POLISH THEM DAILY! I'M SO GLAD YOU NOTICED!
WE NEED TO GET HIM TO DO SOMETHING TO GET HIM AWAY FROM THAT OPENING!
OH! GET HIM TO BREATHE FIRE!
YES! GREAT SCALES... AND I ONCE SAW A DRAGON IN EQUESTRIA THAT COULD BREATHE FIRE SO HOT IT MELTED ROCK! CAN YOU DO THAT?
?
OH, WAIT. THAT'S AN AWFUL SUGGESTION. TAKE IT BACK!
FIRE! WHY, I AM THE BEST FIRE DRAKE IN THE NORTH! I CAN TAKE OUT AN ENTIRE FOREST WITH ONE SNEEZE!
WHAT DO YOU MEAN TAKE IT BACK? THAT WAS YOUR IDEA!
FWOOM
Eeek
HOW WAS THAT?
VERY... EFFECTIVE. NOW WHAT OF YOUR WINGS? I'VE HEARD YOU HAVE THE MOST IMPRESSIVE WINGS OF ALL THE DRAGONS!
MY WINGS ARE IMPRESSIVE! I'LL SHOW YOU THIS ONE MORE THING, BUT THEN I REALLY MUST EAT YOU ALL, YOU UNDERSTAND, RIGHT?

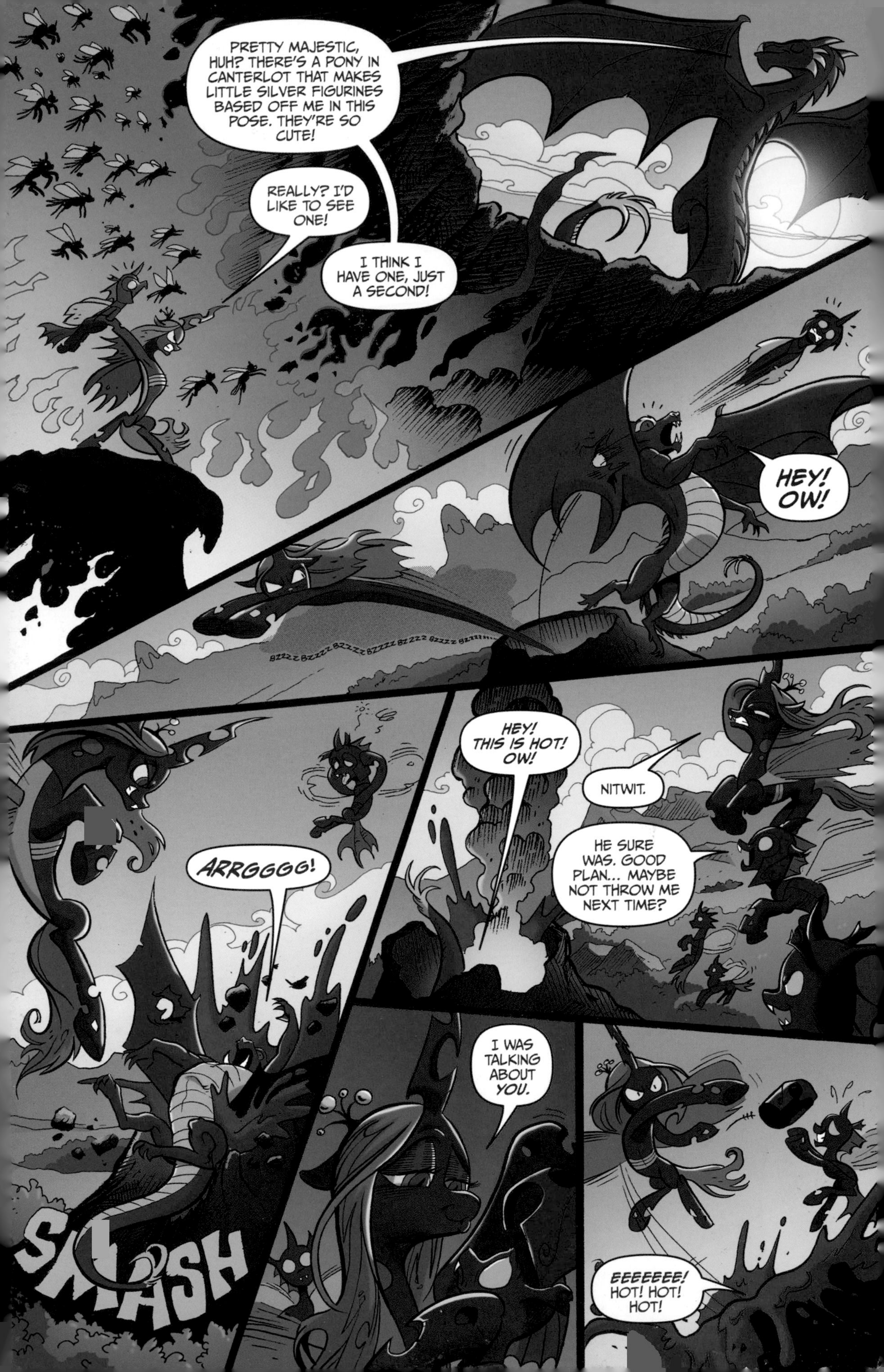
PRETTY MAJESTIC, HUH? THERE'S A PONY IN CANTERLOT THAT MAKES LITTLE SILVER FIGURINES BASED OFF ME IN THIS POSE. THEY'RE SO CUTE!
REALLY? I'D LIKE TO SEE ONE!
I THINK I HAVE ONE, JUST A SECOND!
HEY! OW!
BZZZZBZZZZBZZZZBZZZZBZZZZBZZZZBZZZZ
ARRGGGG!
SMASH
HEY! THIS IS HOT! OW!
NITWIT.
HE SURE WAS. GOOD PLAN... MAYBE NOT THROW ME NEXT TIME?
I WAS TALKING ABOUT YOU.
EEEEEEE! HOT! HOT! HOT!

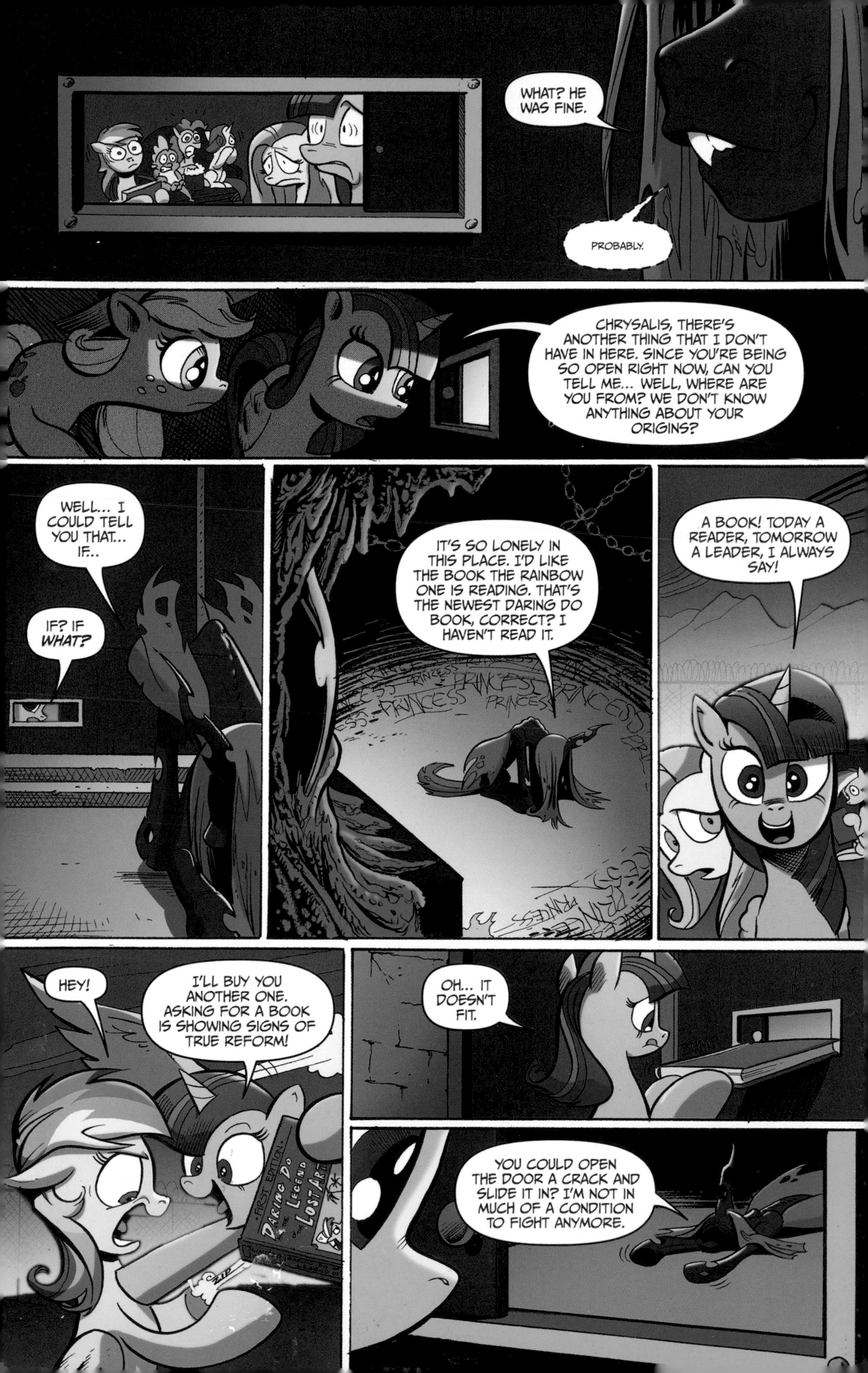
WHAT? HE WAS FINE.
PROBABLY.
CHRYSALIS, THERE'S ANOTHER THING THAT I DON'T HAVE IN HERE. SINCE YOU'RE BEING SO OPEN RIGHT NOW, CAN YOU TELL ME... WELL, WHERE ARE YOU FROM? WE DON'T KNOW ANYTHING ABOUT YOUR ORIGINS?
WELL... I COULD TELL YOU THAT... IF...
IF? IF *WHAT?*
IT'S SO LONELY IN THIS PLACE. I'D LIKE THE BOOK THE RAINBOW ONE IS READING. THAT'S THE NEWEST DARING DO BOOK, CORRECT? I HAVEN'T READ IT.
A BOOK! TODAY A READER, TOMORROW A LEADER, I ALWAYS SAY!
HEY!
I'LL BUY YOU ANOTHER ONE. ASKING FOR A BOOK IS SHOWING SIGNS OF TRUE REFORM!
OH... IT DOESN'T FIT.
YOU COULD OPEN THE DOOR A CRACK AND SLIDE IT IN? I'M NOT IN MUCH OF A CONDITION TO FIGHT ANYMORE.

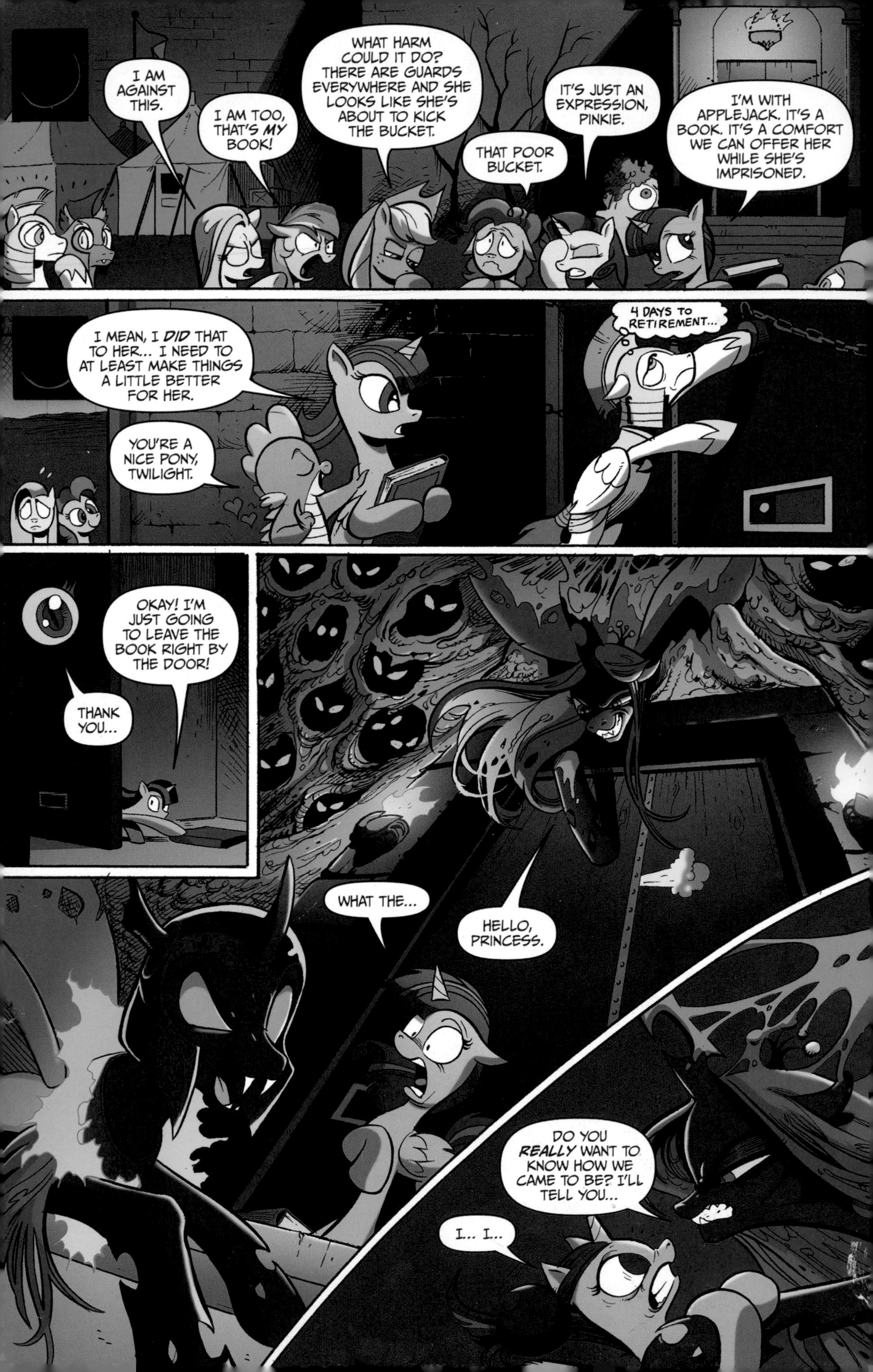
I AM AGAINST THIS.
I AM TOO, THAT'S *MY* BOOK!
WHAT HARM COULD IT DO? THERE ARE GUARDS EVERYWHERE AND SHE LOOKS LIKE SHE'S ABOUT TO KICK THE BUCKET.
THAT POOR BUCKET.
IT'S JUST AN EXPRESSION, PINKIE.
I'M WITH APPLEJACK. IT'S A BOOK. IT'S A COMFORT WE CAN OFFER HER WHILE SHE'S IMPRISONED.
I MEAN, I *DID* THAT TO HER... I NEED TO AT LEAST MAKE THINGS A LITTLE BETTER FOR HER.
YOU'RE A NICE PONY, TWILIGHT.
4 DAYS TO RETIREMENT...
OKAY! I'M JUST GOING TO LEAVE THE BOOK RIGHT BY THE DOOR!
THANK YOU...
WHAT THE...
HELLO, PRINCESS.
DO YOU *REALLY* WANT TO KNOW HOW WE CAME TO BE? I'LL TELL YOU...
I... I...

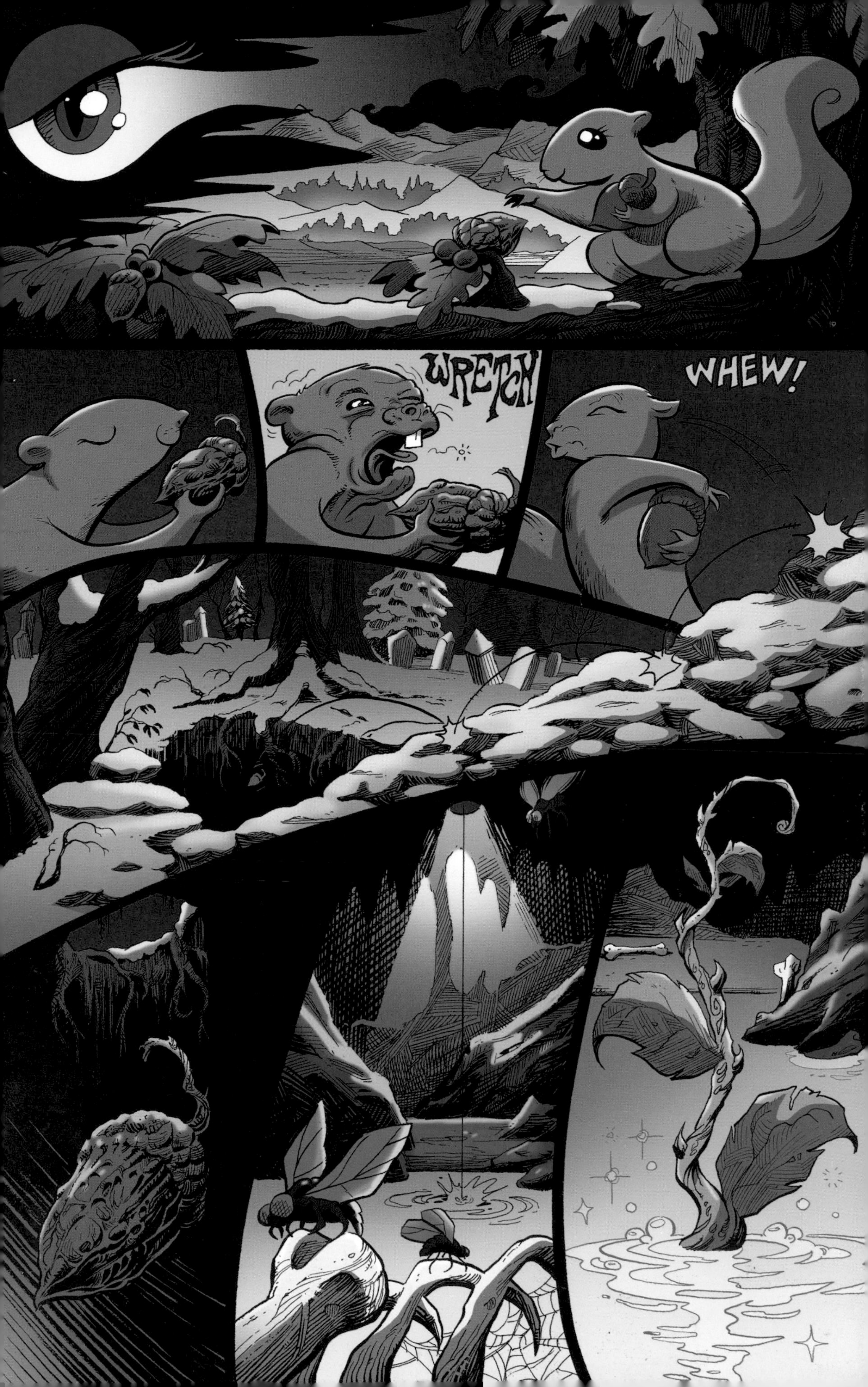
WRETCH
WHEW!

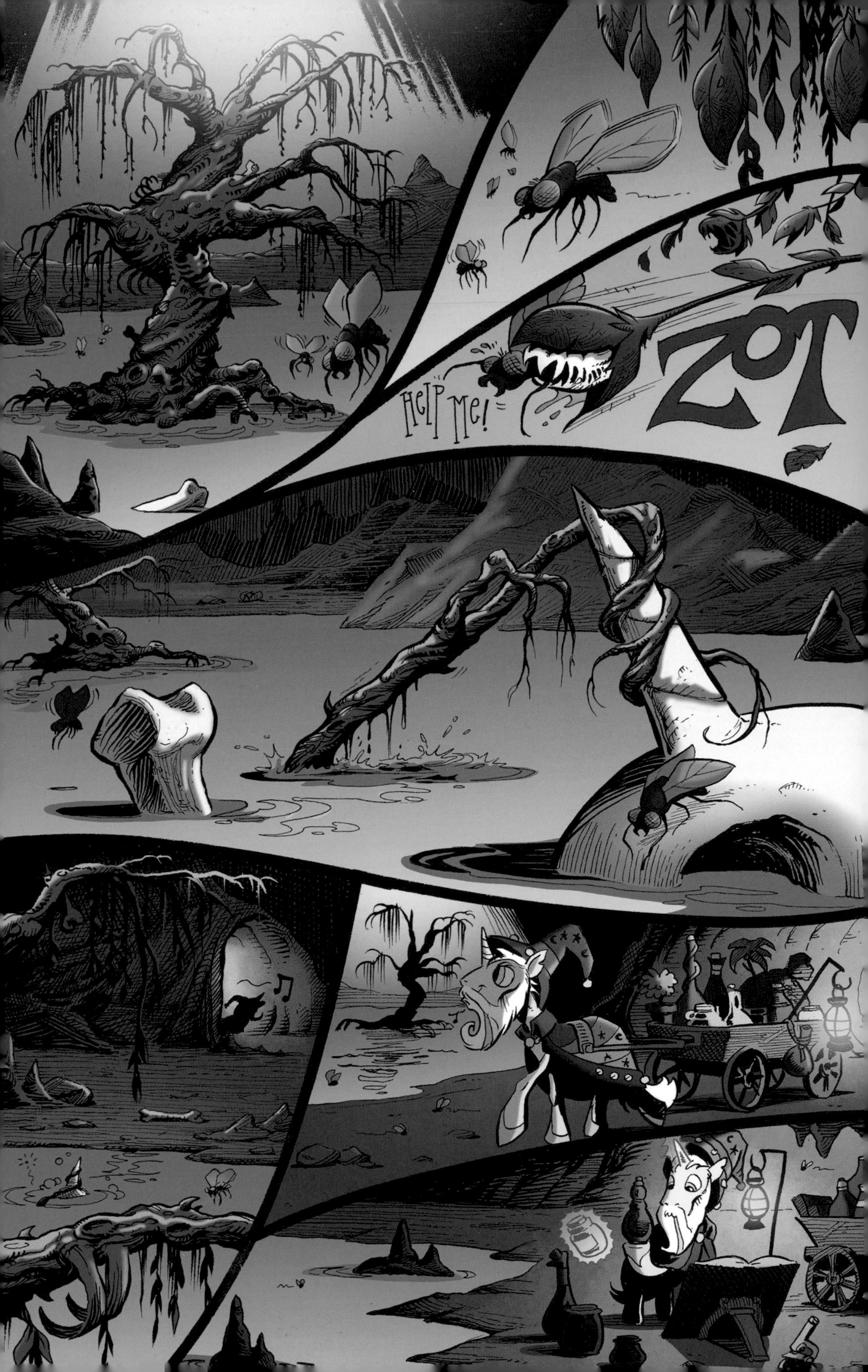
HELP ME!
ZOT

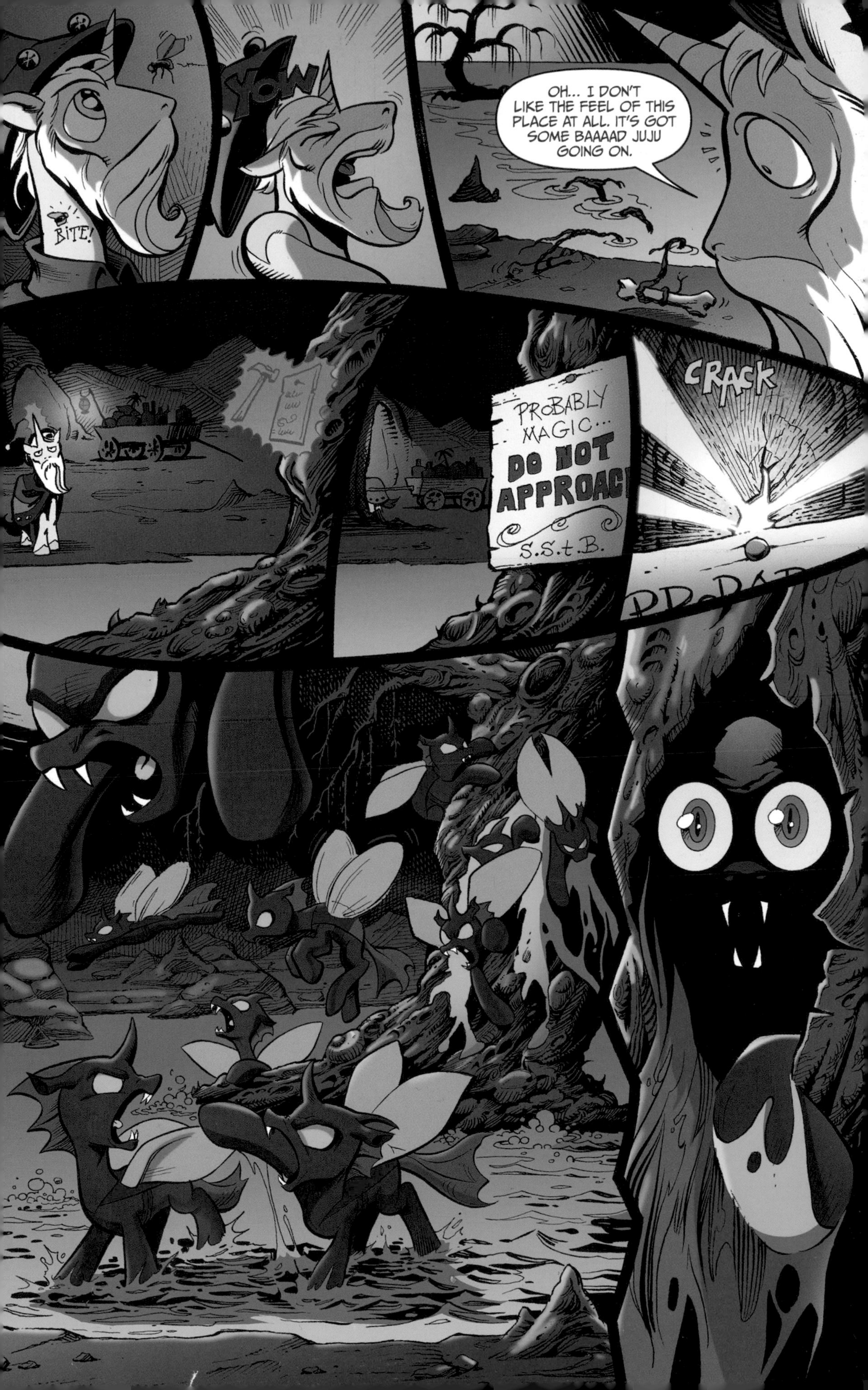
BITE!
YOW
OH... I DON'T LIKE THE FEEL OF THIS PLACE AT ALL. IT'S GOT SOME BAAAAD JUJU GOING ON.
PROBABLY MAGIC...
DO NOT APPROAC
S.S.t.B.
CRACK

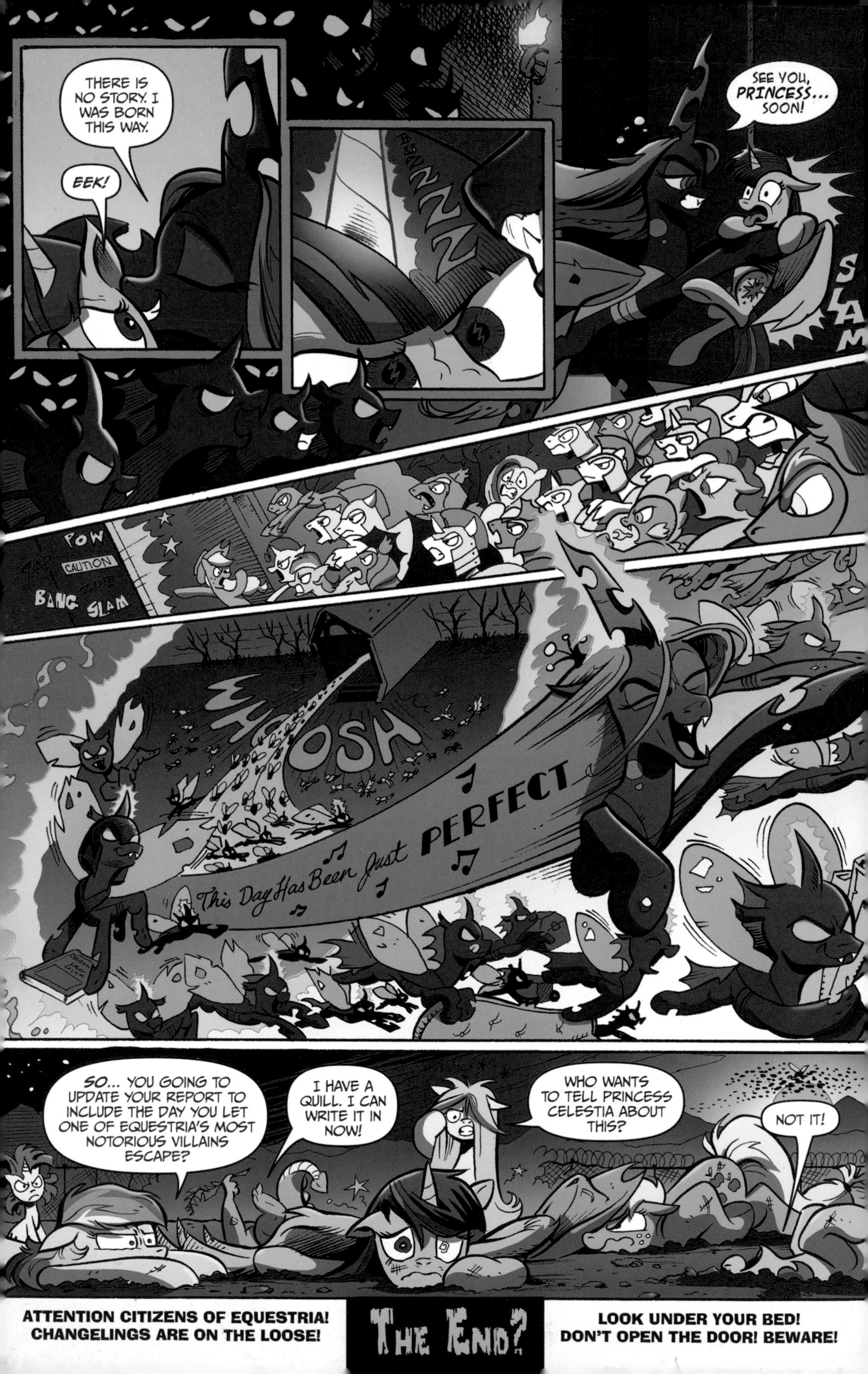
THERE IS NO STORY. I WAS BORN THIS WAY.
EEK!
BZZZNNN
SEE YOU, PRINCESS... SOON!
SLAM
POW
ZAP
CAUTION
ZOT
BANG
SLAM
WHOOSH
This Day Has Been Just PERFECT
SO... YOU GOING TO UPDATE YOUR REPORT TO INCLUDE THE DAY YOU LET ONE OF EQUESTRIA'S MOST NOTORIOUS VILLAINS ESCAPE?
I HAVE A QUILL. I CAN WRITE IT IN NOW!
WHO WANTS TO TELL PRINCESS CELESTIA ABOUT THIS?
NOT IT!
ATTENTION CITIZENS OF EQUESTRIA! CHANGELINGS ARE ON THE LOOSE!
THE END?
LOOK UNDER YOUR BED! DON'T OPEN THE DOOR! BEWARE!

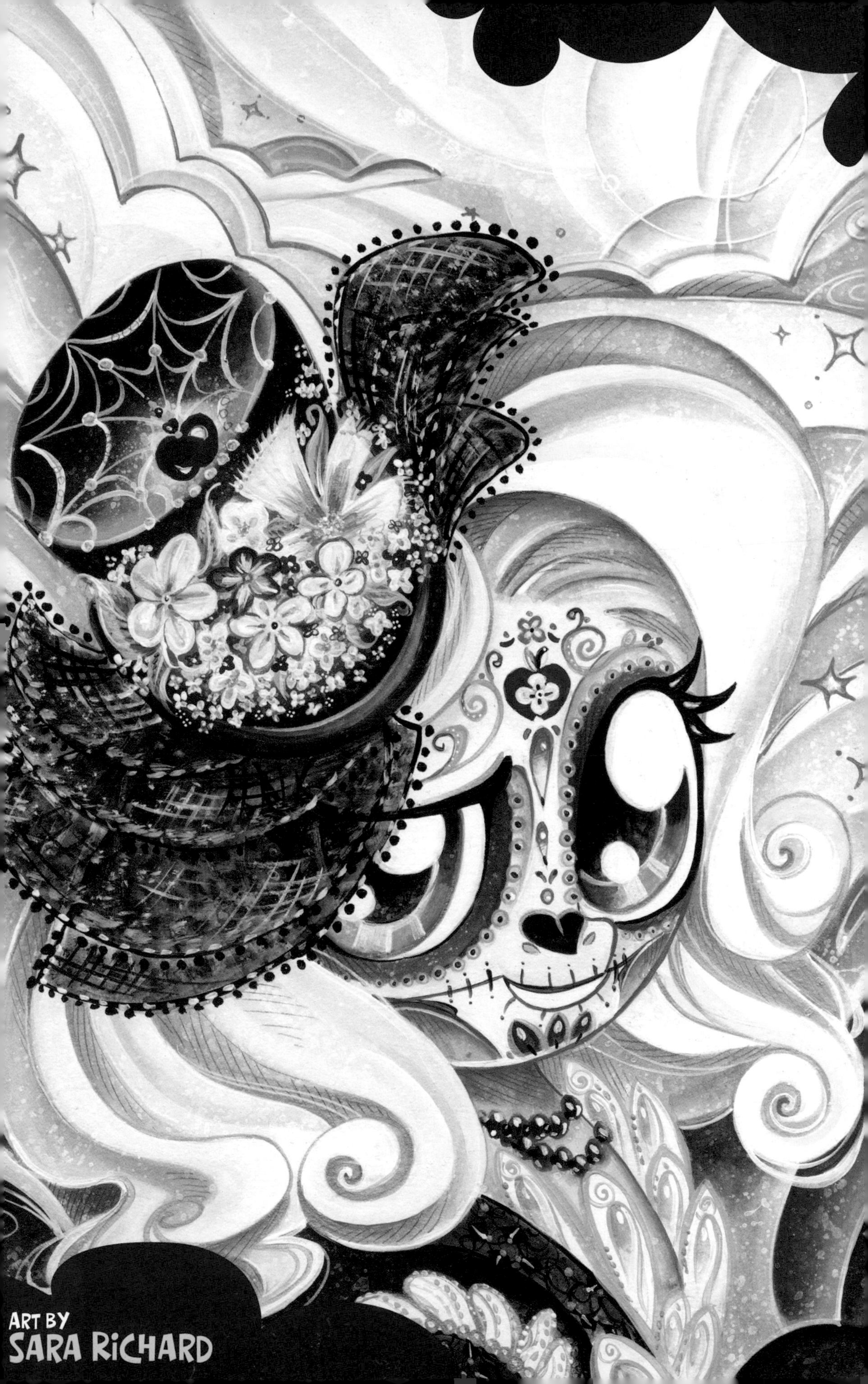

ART BY
SARA RICHARD

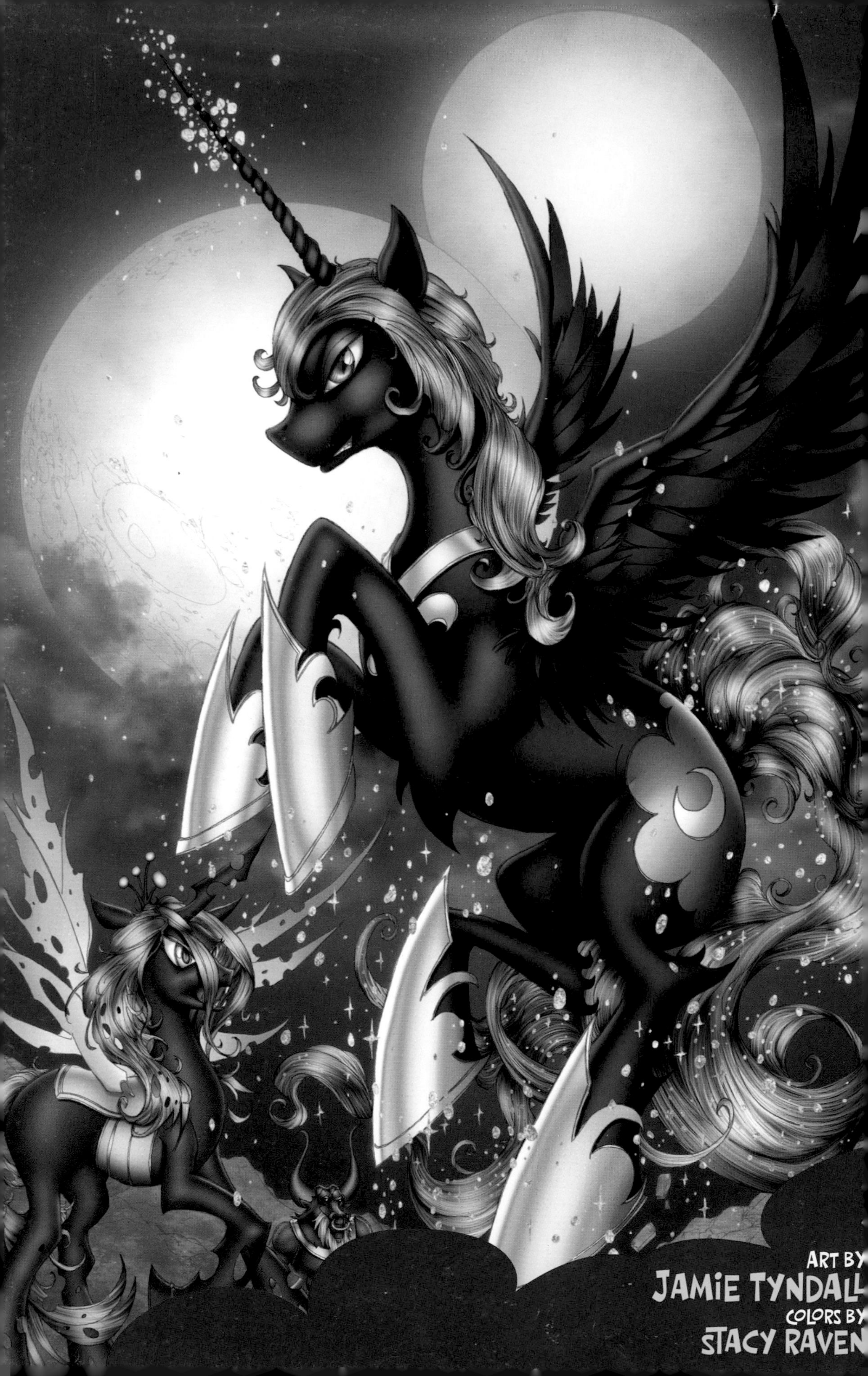
ART BY
JAMIE TYNDALL
COLORS BY
STACY RAVEN